GREEN LIGHT

THE IMPERIUM COAST SERIES
BOOK 3

ALACIA HALE

For my girlies with daddy issues.
And for everyone who's scared therapy will just dim their sparkle...you're made of glitter baby.
You're always gonna have that shine 🤍

TROPES & CONTENT WARNINGS

Tropes

Bully romance, TA/student dynamic, plus size FMC, best friend's brother, found family, college romance, university romance, dual POV, he falls first and figures it out last

Content Warnings

This book deals with themes that may be distressing to some readers including on page bullying, drug us, fatphobia, anger management issues, parental neglect, verbal abuse, sexual harassment, revenge porn, and mentions of pregnancy.

Green Light also contains open door sex scenes that include mentions of edging, begging, choking, light power exchange, and some kink.

If any of these elements are distressing to you, *please protect your mental health.*

1

AUTUMN

Three and a half years ago

I hate moving days. They're uncomfortable and unsettling and something unexpected always happens. Always.

Metal music pulses in my earbuds as I take one item at a time out of my only box, giving it a new home within my new four walls. They're beige and dull and nothing like the sapphire ones in my perfectly curated hiding place that we left behind this morning. I dispel the image of it and the hollow longing the thought opens in my chest, focusing on setting up my new space in another new house in another new town.

Avoiding the floor length mirror in the corner, I place another book on the built-in shelf.

I'll need to paint. Maybe a burnt orange? Would that be too on the nose?

Glancing down at the mess of red waves spilling over my shoulder and down to my waist, I frown.

Gold might work better. To be honest, green would be

best, but Mom would never allow it. She says it's kitschy to use green since it's our last name.

But it's one of the few colors I could wear in any shade. Plus, Green is only my name by proxy, so should that rule even apply to me?

"Autumn!" My mother's muffled shriek reaches me from the floor below, bunching the muscles in the back of my neck. My stomach sours and I close my eyes for a moment, still holding on to whichever book I just picked out of the cardboard box.

"Yes?" I call back measuredly, not bothering to open my eyes yet.

"Come down here!"

My shoulders sag and I drop the book back into the box, taking a second to glance at myself in the mirror again as I walk out.

My skin looks too pale. My hair is unkempt. My legs are too chubby to be showing this much. At least the cutoff overalls hide my stomach.

Finishing my preemptive assessment, I head out of the room, ready to face Mom.

Movers in black back bracing belts carry furniture and boxes throughout the house, two making me stop on the stairs to let them pass. They carry the massive, framed family portrait of Mom, Dad, and Sage past me, tilted at an angle. Our parents sit in matching highbacked chairs while my sister stands between them, a slender hand on each chair. Their three matching smiles and varied shades of chestnut hair mock me as my disheveled reflection slides across it, a ghost passing over them.

The irony makes me smirk as I descend the rest of the stairs, wandering through the mess of boxes and furniture in the foyer and turning toward the kitchen.

"You better!" Mom stands on the other side of the kitchen island, hands on her hips and face beet red as she screams at a mover. Her teeth are bared and I know the look well enough to assume this is why she called me down here. A large bald man in the mover's uniform stands before her, arms down by his side and seemingly relaxed in the face of Mom's fury. Meanwhile our new housekeeper Clara cowers in the corner, wringing her hands.

"Mom?" I walk up, keeping the island in between us. "What's going on?"

Mom's eyes move to me, releasing the mover who takes the opportunity to head back the way I came. "Can you believe this?" She pushes the box beside her, sneering at it. "They broke your sister's blender." Her hands start to fly as she works herself up. "Your father's bringing Sage home from practice in an hour. How is Clara supposed to make her nutri-shake now?"

Clara startles at the mention of her name and I wince.

Mom just continues ranting. "She needs the protein after ballet. I clearly can't just go get one since I need to be here to watch these BARBARIANS!" She flings the final word at the door.

"Do you want me to go get one?" I offer, knowing this routine by heart.

"Would you?" Like I could get away with not. "I think we passed a place on the way in that had a sign for smoothies. It shouldn't be too far of a walk." And here it comes. "Plus, you could use the exercise more than me."

I swallow down the familiar spike in the back of my throat. "Sure."

Her forced smile appears before she turns away to dig through her purse on the counter. "Perfect, take my card and get me one too. Make sure they have wheat grass in them and—

"And whey powder. I know." I walk around the island to where she holds out the card.

Before she releases it, she adds, "Maybe get one for yourself too."

I just nod, tamping down a grimace. Card now in hand, I head back out toward the front door, hearing a loud shatter behind me and then Mom's voice. "These IDIOTS broke Mimi's tea set too! Your father's going to be pissed when he finds out."

Doubt it.

The smile in her voice tells me she does too.

Aaron Green might love his mother, but he hates her gifts and her insistence on using them every time she visits. I'm sure he'll be happy to tell her about this incident the next time my grandmother comes to stay.

Making my way outside, I grab my shoulder bag and scramble to slide on my well-worn trainers. Stopping on the front lawn, I realize I have no idea where I'm going.

The early August sun beats down on me, making me instantly start to sweat. I pull the hair tie off my wrist, piling my waves into a knot atop my head and relieving the back of my neck. A few pieces still stick out I'm sure, but at least I don't feel like my skin is suffocating as much anymore.

The two huge moving trucks take up the entire view of the street, and I head toward them, passing through the wrought iron gate. A few men linger outside, downing water bottles from a torn open case on the sidewalk. Sweat drenches most of their faces and stains their grey shirts.

"Um, excuse me?" I squeak. Gripping the strap of my bag in front of my stomach, I feel my gut plummet when they turn toward me. "Do you know a place that sells smoothies around here?" My heart hammers against my ribcage.

"Lucy's diner has the best smoothies. Just up the road," the bald guy from the kitchen answers, leaning against the back of the truck. He has a clipboard in his hand and nods in the direction we drove past to get here.

"Thanks." I start to head that way, but stop, feeling the weight of Mom's card in my bag. Biting the inside of my cheek, I turn back. The men have already gone back to ignoring me, the bald one looking over something on his clipboard. "Do you guys want me to pick up lunch for everyone? Our treat."

The few sweating lingerers smile excitedly, but the bald man stands up, eyebrows furrowing. "You sure? These guys can eat a lot."

I nod, stomach twisting as adrenaline spikes my blood. Mom probably won't even notice. I doubt her or Aaron actually look at the credit card statements.

Turning toward the other guys, bald mover man writes down the orders and gets the last two from a pair who come out for the other half of our sectional.

"Add on some cheese fries for me!" someone shouts and the pen scratches against the paper.

"Alright, alright. That's enough." The bald guy tears off the paper and walks it over to me. "If it's too much, it's fine. You don't have to buy us all lunch, sweetheart."

"It's okay. I have my mom's card." I smile and the guy laughs.

"In that case, add on a milkshake for yourself. Her treat." He winks conspiratorially and I smile, taking the paper from him.

Turning back toward the others, the bald guy shouts, "Come on guys! Let's at least get the couch set up before she gets back." As I head off, the other guys all nod to me, grabbing stuff from the back of the truck while they go back to work.

I walk down the sidewalk, looking around at the new place I'll have to call home. For now.

Victorian houses line the street, all looking similar yet strikingly different with turrets and wrap around porches and even a stained-glass window or two. Mom's taste has always run eccentric so I'm sure the façade of the three-story mansion we're currently moving into will change drastically in the next few months. Our neighbors will probably hate that she's going to deviate from the traditional siding and restored features.

It happens every time.

We've moved six times since my mother put Sage in ballet.

We need to nurture her potential.

That is always the excuse she gives Aaron. Sage needs to learn under some new dance captain. Join some coach's class now that she is old enough. Start auditioning for companies. And he eats it up, knowing he can work from virtually anywhere and that Mom needs to live vicariously through Sage.

Since *I* ended her ballet career. And almost their marriage.

The residential area gives way to a sprawling commercial complex, designed to mimic the Victorian style of the well-off town. A cute bookstore calls my name, but I head toward the neon sign reading *Lucy's* in the heart of the promenade.

Stepping through the front door, my skin instantly protests against the blast of frigid air that pelts down on the entryway. A little bell announces my arrival, but none of the three girls running around behind the long counter seem to notice. A black sign sits in a silver frame reading *Seat Yourself* in plain white font. The black-and-white checkerboard floor shines clearly polished and well kept. Red and yellow booths surround maroon tabletops, everything adorned with shiny chrome accents. I almost feel like the waitresses should be gliding around on roller skates to complete the overdone fifty's theme.

Chatter seems to push in on me from all sides as I walk up to a clear area of stools at the counter. The red leather covering the seats is worn and cracked, but I climb atop and find them buttery soft beneath my thighs. My ass hangs off the sides a bit and I keep my spine straight, refusing to slouch and push my stomach against the front of my cutoff overalls.

Glancing up, I find a chalkboard menu hanging atop the open window looking in on the kitchen. I peruse their smoothie selection, making sure wheat grass and whey powder are add in options. The noise around me presses in against my skin, but I ignore the itchy sensation, letting my eyes focus on the artful curve of the letters as I slowly read through the menu again.

"Hi, welcome to Philly's. My name's Becca, what can I get started for you?" I look down, meeting the viridian eyes of a black-haired woman in a teal bowler's shirt with a pink collar. She holds a little pad of paper in her hand, pen poised at the ready while her red lips move around the gum she chews. The amount of color clashing makes my head spin.

"Hi, um, do you guys do take-out orders?" I stammer.

"Sure do," Becca answers, flashing me a smile before going back to chewing. She scribbles something on the pad quick before looking up at me again. "What can I get ya?"

"It's kind of a big order," I say, pulling the paper the mover gave me out of my bag and reading each thing off one by one while she writes it down. Once she has theirs, I add on Sage and Mom's smoothies, making sure to ask for no honey in either. Lastly, I hesitate for a second before adding a chocolate milkshake to the end. "No rush," I add quickly.

"That all, sugar?" Becca winks at me and I nod before she starts reading the order back in double time, making sure she got everything. I follow along on the paper before smiling at the end and she whistles. "Doug's going to love this one," she says, giggling. "Lemme put it in and then I'll get started on your drinks."

I grip the edge of the counter as she walks away, feeling the cacophony of the bustling restaurant filter back in and my heart rate pick up. I don't usually wear shorts out of the house, but Mom would have had a cow if I took the time to change and didn't just leave immediately. The prickly feeling of exposure zips over my visible skin, pressing in against me and making me aware of every inch.

Boisterous laughter ricochets against my eardrums and calls my attention to a booth in the back. It's raised up and curved, easily able to seat six to eight people, but ten seem to be crammed in, spilling out in all directions. My eyes go first to the white-haired giant taking up at least a quarter of the booth himself. He sits in the center, hair pulled up into a messy knot on top of his head, revealing a shaved undercut at the back of his neck. Scowling he watches the people around the table, not really entering the conversation, but his lips twitch when the girl beside him laughs. Another girl in all black leans over him to talk to the first, their faces slightly obscured by the side of a brown-haired guy's head. His hair is thick and lush, sloppily spilling over his forehead and around his ears, but looking like it would feel good to run your hands through. The owner, however, lounges in his seat, taking up a lot of the leg room under the table and cramming fries into his mouth as he talks and gestures wildly. He knocks into a third male, a leaner sandy blonde guy seated next to him. This one has a girl practically sitting on his lap, but his posture is more rigid than the first giant who caught my eye, almost as if he can't make himself relax. A scar through his lip catches my eye as a smirk lifts one side of his mouth and he says something to the animated guy beside him.

The lively one cackles, hitting the back of the booth and making me realize there is another sitting above them all, leaning back on his hands with his legs falling over the back of the red leather booth. He faces me but looks down at the table. Shoulder length brown hair sways around his face as he shakes his head, arms flexing as his shoulders shake too. A strawberry blonde sits at his feet, one arm posed on his thigh as she laughs with him, eyes darting from his face to the overly gesticulating guy as if she's checking for when to stop.

The final two occupants sit on the other side of the laughing girl. An icy, almost white, blonde girl with her hair up in a high ponytail at her crown bookends the booth beside a curly haired olive toned guy with his arms spread wide behind him. He sits back, completely at ease with his broad chest on display beneath a tight-fitting tee shirt as he surveys the booth, taking in each person around him. His lips stay flat, not engaging with whatever hilarity the rest are participating in, surveying the table like a hawk.

My blood beats like a pulsating baseline as his eyes slide slowly past the group around him and immediately find mine. Their warm maple syrup depths spark as he leans forward in the booth, arm falling away from behind the laughing blonde beside him, causing her to almost tumble out, but she rights herself and I notice in my periphery that her ponytail swishes around, but my eyes are locked onto his. I stay trapped in his gaze as his lips slowly roll into a wolfish grin, a row of straight white teeth gleaming at me. The look sends a shot of adrenaline down my spine, snapping me into an even straighter posture. I rip my eyes away, looking forward and trying to focus on the chaos of the kitchen beyond the little cutout window across from me. I ignore the prickly reaction racing through my body from one look alone, trying to calm my racing pulse.

People work around the stainless-steel interior through the little window, a couple of hot dishes being placed on the ledge. Becca walks by, grabbing both plates and walking off with them and out of my immediate view. My breathing stutters in my throat and I take a clearing deep breath.

I will not look over again.

A tap on my shoulder jolts me on the stool. My grip on the counter goes white as I snap my head to the side and annoyance surges through me.

Maple syrup eyes meet mine, only a few inches away now. His smirk deepens when I freeze, the two of us staring at each other for a moment. I glance back at the booth he emerged from, and nine pairs of eyes meet mine. Blonde ponytail stands next to the booth now; arms crossed over her chest and the daggers in her gaze aimed at me. The guy sitting atop the booth leans forward, eyebrows furrowed.

Hawk-eyes snaps his fingers in front of my face, and my annoyance multiplies tenfold, heating my gut.

"What?" I bite out, glaring at him now.

His teeth are on full display again as he laughs at me with his eyes. He leans sideways onto the counter and places his chin in his palm. "You're cute. And new. What's your name?"

His words don't register at first. Blood and fury pound in my ears and I glance back at his group. "What?" falls from my lips again in the same irritated tone.

Icy blonde looks livid. *Did he just call me cute?*

"Ignore them," hawk-eyes calls, waving the hand not currently propping him up lazily through the air. My eyes drift back to his. "What's your name?"

Something about his stillness and undivided attention sends a chill up the back of my neck. A zap of something zings through me, instinct telling me to be cautious right now. That this is a predator who sees me as prey. I square my shoulders, refusing to fear this pretty asshole. "Why do you want to know?"

He barks a laugh, standing up and taking a step closer to me. The move puts us within centimeters of touching, and I tamp down the urge to recoil. My chin tips back to hold his gaze as he stands over me.

"Stop playing with your food, Adams." The words ring through the diner, no one stopping to take notice. The noise around us presses back in, but the guy in front of me blocks everything so I can't tell which one of his friends said it. My face flames all the same.

Hawk-eyes ignores the gibe, still staring at me. *Has he blinked?* "You're feisty. The red suits." He nods his chin toward the top of my head.

My brain can't keep up with what's going on, wanting this to be over so I can get the movers' food and hide away in my boring new room again.

Hawk-eyes winks. "See you around," he throws out and turns away. "Love the haircut, Bex," he calls over his shoulder as he walks off.

"Thank you, Ramsey," Becca calls after him, placing my milkshake down on the counter in front of me. She smiles wide. "Cash or credit, sweetheart?"

I flounder, glancing back at the corner booth where hawk-eyes, Ramsey, now stands, speaking with blonde ponytail. She looks about ready to stamp her foot and throw a tantrum. Most of his group pay no attention to me, but the guy sitting above them all still leans forward and stares. I look away when our eyes meet, palms starting to itch.

"Um," I mutter, turning back to Becca. "Credit." I pull my bag up into my lap, pulling Mom's card out. Becca takes it, walking away.

I fidget on the stool, waiting for her to come back.

"Think she's got enough to drink?" The syrupy sweet voice comes from behind me, tinged with a familiar sharp edge.

"I don't know." The new voice is softer but comes closer than the last. "There's probably not much left in the dispenser though." I feel them both at my back, flanking me and trapping me against the counter. I press forward, squishing myself into the edge to try to create more distance.

Becca appears before me, smile dipping a little when she eyes the girls behind me. "Here you go, sweetheart." She places Mom's card down with a long receipt "I'll go grab your food. Just need you to sign." She hesitates but walks off when an older man down the counter calls her name.

I mechanically pick up the pen, signing Mom's name as the girls start to laugh. A buzzing starts in my ears.

"Jeez, she ordered half the menu." Becca reappears with

two big to-go bags. "Doug even have any food left, Bex?" I press my thighs together not daring to turn around and squelch my toes in my shoes as my overly exposed skin crawls.

Becca places the bags on the counter, putting a hand on her hip. "Do you need something, Paige?" She narrows her eyes, voice lower when addressing them.

The second voice mutters under her breath, "Probably not much left to order."

"No, we're good, Bex. Just wanted a change of scenery." The two girls sit down on the empty stools on either side of me. Blonde ponytail and the girl with strawberry blonde hair enter my periphery.

Becca takes the receipt, handing me my copy. "Oh shit, your smoothies! Give me one sec." She rushes off, pulling a blender out from against the wall on the opposite counter. I silently beg her to hurry.

The moment her back is turned, blonde ponytail, who I assume is Paige, sets in. "What do you think, Carly? See anything worth Ramsey's time?"

Strawberry blonde, Carly giggles. "Well, there's plenty to see, but not much appeal."

I fist my hand in my lap, letting my nails bite into my palm. My eyes are trained on Becca's back, muscles locked tight as I wait to escape.

"Mhmm, I agree." Paige leans in, and my eyes slide to the side to meet hers. "Ramsey Adams wouldn't waste his time on someone like you, piggy. Don't waste your time."

Her words ring around in my brain, but white-hot rage slides up from my chest and over my tongue. "He walked up to me," I spit out. Turning my head a bit more, I glance over her shoulder, noting that Ramsey seems to have disappeared from the group in the back.

The blender whirs and startles me. Paige laughs. The sound grates along my skin. "Don't be stupid, piggy. He came over for something, and you accosted him. I saw the whole thing."

I reel back slightly, eyebrows touching my hairline. "You're delusional."

All sickly sweetness drops from Paige's voice as she leans in even closer, hissing, "No you are if you think he'd ever willingly talk to you when he has me, his girlfriend, in the same room."

Ah, this is the real issue. I pause, feeling my body loosen as I turn to look at her head on. "If that's true, I'm sorry for you. He's a dick."

The girl pulls up short, balking at me. Becca walks back over and hands me the two green smoothies in a drink tray. I smile and thank her, getting off the stool.

Carly snorts on my other side. "Oh sweetie, that isn't going to help at this point."

I reach for the milkshake, squeezing it a little too hard so the plastic cup indents around my fingertips. "Fuck off," I mutter, starting to wedge the milkshake in the drink tray with the smoothies.

"Forget about Ramsey Adams, piggy," Paige sneers, even closer to my side. "He doesn't want anything to do with a fatass like you."

My hand acts before my brain can catch up to it. The milkshake spills from the wide opening at the top, covering Paige's blonde ponytail as I hold it upside down over her head. "You can keep Ramsey Adams for yourself," I hear myself say, fully having an out of body experience at this point.

My feet move as I start to process what I've just done, hands rushing to grab the to-go bags as I dash around the duo and out the diner's front door. The heat slams into me once again, more sweat forming on my lower back as I rush through the promenade and back toward the residential area.

"Hey!" I hear behind me but keep moving forward, not looking back. People gasp and jump out of my way. The sound of feet slapping against the pavement behind me starts beating through my ears. I already know I can't outrun them with my hands full.

Turning the corner out of the fancy outdoor mall, I find myself shrouded in a building's shadow when a hand clutches the back of my overalls, yanking me back into a hard chest. I yelp, carefully clutching everything as I'm jostled. If I come home without these smoothies, Mom is going to freak.

The group from the booth circle around me. The white-haired giant stands across from me at the edge of the shadows, hands in his pockets looking utterly bored. The wild one smiles, mania playing in his eyes while the scarred blonde openly stares, almost dissecting me as I start to shake in my trainers, chest heaving with my heavy breaths. The longer haired guy merely assesses me, glancing over my shoulder with a questioning look, but not as outwardly antagonistic as the other two.

A hand reaches forward into my view, ripping the order receipt off one of the to-go bags. "Autumn Green. Hmm." I can feel Ramsey's eyes on the back of my neck, hand still fisting the back of my clothes. "One of the Greenmart Dynasty Greens?" I dry swallow, my throat scratching against itself. The eyes of each person in front of me widen a bit. Even the white-haired giant looks me over with a bit more interest. Ramsey's breath slides across my skin as he speaks, closer than before. "You seem more like a Fall to me," he whispers and releases my shirt, pushing me forward a bit toward his friends. I stumble to a stop in the center of their group, spinning to face him, but very aware of the rest at my back.

Paige and Carly stand a foot behind Ramsey, Carly patting at Paige's shoulders with already ruined napkins as bits of milkshake still roll down from her hair to her already covered blouse. Ramsey crosses his arms, eyes travelling down from my face to my toes. The assessment makes bile rise in the back of my throat, Paige's words from earlier pressing against the front of my brain.

"What happened?"

I open my mouth, and his hand shoots up. "Not you, Fall." There is no trace of the playfulness from when we spoke before. The nickname stings.

"I was just sitting at the counter with Carly and decided to introduce myself and she spazzed and threw a milkshake at me, Ramsey." I bite the inside of my cheek so that I don't roll my eyes at the whine in Paige's voice.

"That's not what—

Ramsey's hand cuts me off again. His eyes have yet to leave mine, trapping me in place before him. I suddenly feel like I'm on trial, Ramsey acting as the judge, jury, and executioner.

"You ruined her outfit. And hair," he points out.

"She deserved it," I bite out.

Something lights in his maple syrup eyes, making them brighter, and he tsks. "That takes her a long time to put together." He reaches forward, sliding one of the muddy green smoothies out of the drink tray in my hand. I start to protest but he shakes his head. "Paige," he calls.

She steps forward, a saccharine smile painting her lips. I contemplate booking it, but we'd just end up in the same set up another block over. Ramsey hands her the smoothie, eyes still trapping mine. Paige steps forward and she unceremoniously dumps the contents over my head. Someone snickers behind me, but I stare Ramsey down as the icy drink soaks into my hair and slides down my face and over my shoulders. His lips twitch and with a final good shake, Paige steps back, laughing. I hear a deep sigh from behind me, but the other four boys just walk around, passing me and heading back toward the diner with Carly.

"Maybe you'll think before acting next time," Ramsey says, the condescension twisting my organs and bringing my fury back to a boil. He turns back toward the promenade, calling Paige along after him.

The heat licking through my veins has me place the drink tray and bags on the ground. I open a bag, grabbing the container of cheese fries sitting right on top. Taking the lid off, I wind up and toss the sticky contents through the air.

The fries fly, slamming into the back of Ramsey's head. Nacho cheese sticks to his hair and slides down his neck as he freezes. Paige shrieks as some stray fries pelt her as well. Whirling around, rage matching my own burns in Ramsey's eyes.

"Guess not," I say across the few feet separating us now. He stares at me, vibrating lethally with clenched fists. He steps toward me, and I remain in place, spine ramrod straight. We face off, while Paige tugs on his arm.

"Come on, babe. She's not worth it." She glares at me, but I don't back down, refusing to turn away first.

Ramsey's nostrils flare before his upper lip curls. He pulls his arm away from Paige's grasp and a jolt wracks through me.

Blindly grabbing the bags and sole surviving smoothie, I

take off toward the new house. Rage still simmers in my system, but the adrenaline come down starts to hit at the same time, making my breaths shallow and painful.

I don't know how I'll explain my smoothie-soaked appearance to Mom.

2

RAMSEY

The bitch is in my house.

My grip on the balcony railing tightens as I watch the red-headed little witch maneuver around the edge of the dance floor, capturing my attention once again with just her presence.

Fall.

She flits between people, her long dress swirling around her ankles. It's haltered, leaving her pale shoulders bare. The majority of the dress is black, but crimson bleeds into the top and bottom hems, making the material look burnt like dying embers nestled between coals.

Fitting, since her appearance stirs the roiling anger that filled me on the blacktop outside Lucy's last week. Something green and sparkly sits in her hair, pinning half of it up away from her face. I home in on the red strands, the first thing that caught my attention when she walked into my favorite diner with her head held high. They're decidedly clean of any traces of smoothie I last saw decorating them.

I watch her settle in to hug the shadows and sip from a glass of punch.

She looked cute and innocent when I first saw her enter the diner, all sweaty and shy. The baggy overalls and messy hair warded most off from taking a second look, but my eyes couldn't stop taking her in as she sidled up to the counter. Something held my attention, and I tried to place what exactly called me to watch her.

When our eyes met, I found it. The momentary spark, the flash of something deep in her eyes had instantly made me want to see more, want to see what she looked like when that ember crescendos into an inferno. My impulse control has never been stellar, but the moment our eyes met, I had no other option but to follow through with the idea.

Green light. The voice in my head started screaming.

I remember my therapist Diane's cool toned voice when she introduced me to the color system years ago. *Green light, aka no anger response. All systems go.*

Except the voice yesterday sounded nothing like Diane.

And Fall definitely triggers some sort of response. When our eyes met yesterday, I just knew I needed to see her squirm.

Her rebuff intrigued me. It didn't fan the flames the way a brush off usually would, but when I came out of the bathroom to a milkshake covered Paige crying about the new girl dousing her, they'd roared in my ears, blocking out every memory of control techniques Diane had taught me. I instantly wanted retribution.

How dare she give Paige her fire and not me.

And then to watch her, eyes blazing with indignation before me, like a righteous goddess doling out justice with the toss of her lunch. Even with green muck rolling down over her body, she'd stood tall and stared me down, not cowering like I thought she would. The rage in her sang to my own and I just know I would have reached out and snatched her if she didn't suddenly turn and run.

How the hell did she get an invite to my sister's birthday party?

Letting my eyes wander the crowd, I find Mira, standing with her best friend and surprise gift for the night, Bentley Marshall. I left her in his care after our obligatory first dance together and it seems the two have found the mini grilled cheese station. I watch Mira laugh, mushy grilled cheese and tomato soup showing in her mouth. The anger in my chest loosens along with my grip as I search her face for the usual signs of discomfort, relieved that they're minimal at the moment.

Letting my eyes wander the crowded room below, I again settle on the girl who shouldn't be here. I seriously need to talk to Mom about stopping these ridiculous parties.

"See something you like?" Paige's bubblegum sweet voice grates against my ear as she sidles up beside me, brushing my shoulder with her own. She's been extra clingy all summer, so I wasn't surprised when she glued herself to my side after Mira and I's big entrance, but I am in no mood for her overly attentive tendencies.

"Hardly." I continue to glare at Autumn. Paige's hand lands on my forearm, stroking against the sleeve of my dress shirt.

"Then why don't you come play with us?" She tilts her head toward the group behind me as she turns, facing me fully and basically leaning against me with her chest.

I glance at her before looking back at my best friends all crowded around the couch and coffee table. Tanner sits stoically in the center of the couch, taking up much more than the middle cushion with Ava and Ellie on either side. A flask is passed between them as they watch Smith deal out cards from his seat on the floor. A joint hangs from his lips as he speaks loud and rapidly, per usual, around it. Carly sits on his lap, sucking on the side of his neck. Royal leans against the wall, watching from afar with his arms crossed and a marred scowl. Harley leans back against the couch, taking the flask from the girl next to him and Tanner as he picks up his cards and frowns.

"No thanks," I murmur, turning back to watch the party from my bird's-eye view once more. "Smith cheats."

"You just suck, Rams," Smith calls around the blunt still hanging from his mouth. "He's more of a physical contact sports kind of guy, P. Only interested if there's bone breaking involve." He snickers and I grip the railing a bit tighter. I hear the couch creak and a muffled thump. Smith grumbles before they return to their game.

"The football team sucks this year." Paige's hand creeps up my arm. "Too bad you had to go and graduate. We're definitely not going to win much without you as quarterback."

I catch her hand before it can start moving over my shoulder and turn to face her, still gripping the railing as well so I don't put too much pressure on her hand. "I did personal training sessions with Erikson for six months last year. The team better be winning."

Paige's chest and neck redden, and I release her hand, turning back toward the over-the-top light and noise below. Football had been my outlet for the last four years. If Imperium Coast University had a team, I would have tried out. But of course, the only university my father would pay for couldn't partake in such a barbaric sport. I snort, thinking of his pinched face the first time I told him I made the Emerald Grove team. The spit of satisfaction turns faster over the flames in my chest.

As if thinking of him manifests his presence, I look over at the sound of footsteps on the stairs to see my father ascend toward the balcony. He has one hand in the pocket of his tux, the other gripping the railing as he stares down before taking the last step. His eyes meet mine before he glances at the guys behind me. Paige freezes between us, staring at my father as well.

"Shouldn't you all be at the party?" He looks back to me. "Downstairs?"

I see Harley sit up in my periphery, head turning between me and the man who donated some DNA.

I snort, turning away and looking back down at the guests. "That's rich since you're slinking off to your office already. Hypocritical, don't you think?" A blonde boy approaches Fall, making her stand up a little straighter before she blushes and takes his hand, following him toward the dance floor. I look back at my father, feeling the swirling flames blaze higher no matter where I look.

My therapist, Diane's words instantly flash in my head.

Yellow light. Think before you act.

My tightening grip on the railing bites into my skin.

Conrad Adams stares at me for a moment, placing both hands deep into his pockets as he assesses me. "Make sure your mother doesn't see the drugs." He heads down the darkened hall, not even glancing at the others or back at me as I watch his retreating form. I let my eyes lose focus as I stare at the shadows that engulf him.

"Geez, is he always so serious?" Paige shudders next to me, a playful smile on her lips as she waits for my reaction.

I look down at the crowd again, finding Mom mingling

amongst the people, all smiles and laughing at someone's joke as she works the event like she always does. The couples around her make her lone status a bit more glaring, but she holds her own, commanding the attention of those around her. I glance back toward the shadows, momentarily cursing her husband, though he hasn't made it past twenty minutes at a party in at least ten years. I'm surprised he even made it this long.

My eyes train in on the bright smiling boy whirling Autumn around in a waltz. Her face is frozen in a polite smile, but her eyes glance around every now and then and something in them makes me wonder if her hand is trembling in his grip. My eyes narrow as I watch them twirl, her skirt wrapping around her like a fiery swath and starkly standing out against the polished black and white checkerboard of the dance floor. The moving color reminds me of the blazing indignation in her face after she pelted me with those cheese fries, and I'm thrown back into the memory of our first meeting once again.

A delicate hand filters through my roiling thoughts as it enters my field of vision, coming down to close around one of my own. The moment slows as the flames roar and I hold my breath, counting in my head to tamp down the angry reaction crawling under my skin.

Red light, red light, red light.

At the last second, a masculine hand grabs the delicate one before it can touch my skin. I feel Harley wedge himself in between Paige and me, shouldering his huge frame into the miniscule space.

"That dress looks amazing on you, Paige," he murmurs into her ear, wrapping his arm around her waist to soothe the sting of rebuke.

She preens under his attention, simpering as she molds

herself against him. "Thank you, Harley." Her eyes flash to me momentarily. "I'm glad *someone* noticed."

Harley laughs, letting her settle in against him. I stare down at Fall, watching her nod along as the blonde kid prattles in her ear. My fist tightens once again around the iron railing.

"Staring pretty hard there, Rams." Harley bumps my shoulder, keeping his voice low but light. "Trying to burn a hole in the dance floor?"

I roll my eyes, the tension in my arms releasing a bit. "That annoying girl from the diner is here." Paige's head pops up off Harley's shoulder, and I feel her gaze try to turn me to stone.

"Where?" Harley scans the crowd before his eyes land on where Autumn is dancing. He smirks and my stomach coils. "Cleans up nice. Much prettier without all that smoothie on her." He chuckles but our eyes lock when he looks up and I can see him evaluating my reaction. His next words come in a whisper. "Careful Ramsey, you're locking in."

My best friend's words trigger Diane's voice in my head. *Breathe. Regroup. Control your reaction.*

I release the railing, taking a step back even as my eyes return to the back of Fall's head. "She tried to humiliate me."

"And letting Paige dump green sludge over her head didn't do the same?" Harley muses. Smith's roar echoes behind me and Paige's rancorous laugh grinds against it, raising the hair on my arms.

"That humiliation was well deserved. She ruined my favorite shirt." She pouts up at Harley who smirks and whispers something in her ear, making her laugh again, though this time the sound is much more harmonious. They turn, leaning back against the railing and no longer paying attention to the party as her hands come up against his chest.

I look away, rolling my eyes once again. I return to my fixation and the flames surge. Just as I find the pair, the boy decides to surprise dip Autumn low, causing her eyes to crash with mine as her head is flung back. Her cheeks flush and I gnash my teeth together when the dull roar fills my ears, drowning out the music and sounds of my friends laughing behind me. The moment seems to stretch impossibly long before she forces herself upright, breaking the connection and yanking herself out of the boy's grip.

The flames die out, but my eyes remain narrowed as I watch her flee the dance floor and run right out the back patio doors. They swing shut silently behind her and I continue to stare, hearing nothing once more.

My eyes pull to the left, finding Mira staring up at me. I startle, all rage dissipating and the sounds around me cascading back into focus. I've never wanted my little sister to see my anger. Not since that day.

She glances at the back doors before looking up at me and raising an eyebrow in question. I settle into a more austere look and shake my head, already knowing how much she likes to meddle when she's curious. We hold each other's stare for a few more seconds before I turn away, showing my back to the party and homing in on my friends.

Tanner sits forward now, a bleached white strand of hair falling over his forehead as he concentrates on the cards in his hand and takes a drag from the dying blunt. The girls on either side of him rub his back and shoulders, trying to get him to focus on them. Smith taunts him from the floor, waving his cards around haphazardly, but always keeping them at an angle so that only Harley, Paige, and I would be able to see the faces.

Carly laughs at his antics; arms wrapped around his neck tightly. Royal crosses his arms over his chest, casually watching in his intense way.

Tanner makes a move and Smith cackles, throwing his cards down and punching the air. Tanner throws his down with a sneer, sitting back quick and making Ava and Ellie scramble out of the way. He crosses his massive arms over his barrel chest, and they settle back in against him.

"Deal again," he bites out, jaw tense.

Smith laughs once more, gathering the cards in his hands. "New game. Anyone want in?" He tips his head back, looking at the three of us from upside down. Paige whispers to Harley and he nods, watching her attempt to saunter across the two feet of carpet as she joins their game.

Smith deals to the three of them and I force myself to breathe in through my nose and out through my mouth, feeling the fire inside me slowly recede to its normal simmer.

"You're only pissed because she stood up to you," Harley murmurs, still watching the game unfold before us. Tanner holds the end of the joint out while studying his cards and Harley leans forward to take it. I grumble, glancing over my shoulder at the glass doors the little witch disappeared through. Harley takes a drag, stepping away from the railing and waving away the smoke as he looks over the edge for my mom. "Okay, maybe pissed isn't the right sentiment? You are locking on though." He points at me, the blunt pinched between his fingers.

I glare at him, taking it and inhaling deep. The smoke curls inside me, a welcome distraction. "I am not locking on," I murmur, practicing my breathing techniques as the weed settles like a blanket over my flames.

Harley's eyebrows furrow. "She's not your usual type."

I take another hit, letting the tension eek out of me as the weed nestles in. "Fuck off," I say half-heartedly.

"Mmhmm." Harley laughs, clapping me on the shoulder. "Just forget about her, dude. We go back to the Coast tomorrow and then you never have to see her again."

The sound of heels on the stairs pulls both of our attention to the left and I find Mom ascending the stairs, looking back to scan the crowd with pinched brows.

"Grapefruit," I hiss, stubbing out the joint and waving my hands around to clear the smoke. Tanner reaches past Ava's thigh, pulling out the mini-Febreze bottle and spraying the air before handing it off so we can all spritz ourselves. Carly stands, smoothing down her dress while Smith pockets the empty flask off the table. Royal straightens, assessing to make sure everything is away before nodding to me. We all relax our postures as Mom makes it to the top of the stairs.

"Have you seen your sister?" She glances around as if Mira might be hiding behind the couch. It wouldn't be the first time she caught me helping to hide her away during one of these atrocious events.

I shake my head when her eyes meet mine. "Nope, not since we danced."

Mom frowns. "Do you boys mind looking around for her? It's almost time to cut the cake."

We all nod and Smith steps forward, taking my mom's arm and leading her back down the stairs. "Don't worry Mama A. We'll find mini-Adams for you."

Tanner bends down to pick up the abandoned cards while Paige and Carly link arms and head back down to the party.

Harley's hand lands on my shoulder. "Guest or game room?"

I shake my head, teeth clamping together for a moment. "No, she's probably outside. I wouldn't put it past her to follow that girl out there." I start toward the stairs, but Harley's hand squeezes my shoulder and stops me.

"Let me go look. You check inside. That way we can avoid you murdering anyone." I nod once, closing my eyes and taking a deep breath. Harley waits until my eyes open.

"I'm good," I say, nodding my head.

He nods too, taking his hand back. "Don't let her screw with your shit." I nod and he turns and leaves me at the top of the stairs.

He's right. *Control.* I can't allow her to get a rise from me and backslide into my impulsive tendencies. Neither of us could afford the repercussions. I stand up straighter, holding my chin high as I descend the stairs.

Red light.

From now on, my reaction will be the exact opposite. Autumn Green will get nothing but ice from me.

3

AUTUMN

I rush out the glass doors, balmy night air greeting me. Running across the patio, I lift my skirt, heart slamming against my chest.

He's here. The fucking prick from the diner.

Ramsey.

I practically trip down the steps, heels slipping and scraping against the stones. Grass greets me at the bottom, causing me to sink another inch.

His eyes were on fire. Absolutely blazing. The moment I saw him, it felt like stepping under the hottest spotlight, sweat and nerves instantly crawling over my skin.

I book it into the light cropping of trees, passing the first few layers before dropping my skirt and slamming into a hard trunk with both hands. The bite of the bark grounds me for a moment.

I just need to feel like no one is looking at me, no one can see me. The trees are good. They can hide me for a moment so I can break down and then put myself back together.

I press my hands into the trunk more, letting the scape

of the bark tear at my skin. My breath cuts in and out of my lungs in sharp jagged pulls and it feels like something barbed squeezes my chest, compressing my bones in against my fucking organs.

"I am not trudging through a dark muddy forest after some girl we don't know Mir."

The voice is close, just outside of the treeline, and definitely male.

"Ramsey seemed to know who she is," a softer, feminine voice answers, moving closer. I lug in a deep breath, sinking my nails into the tree trunk. "And what if she got lost?"

The care in her tone pulls me up short. I figure people saw me suddenly flee the dance floor mid-song but didn't anticipate anyone following me.

I don't know anyone here. I rarely left the new house the last few weeks after the fiasco that was my trip to the diner. School doesn't start for another two weeks.

And yet I got an invite to this party.

It seems like everyone in my year at Emerald Grove is here. The kid who asked me to dance wouldn't stop talking about how stuffy this party is every year, but everyone still goes just to save face with the birthday girl's parents.

Amiria Adams. That's who the invite said we were celebrating. And the second Mom investigated (called my grandmother and asked about the family) and found out how influential her father is, I "just had to attend."

"What if she got lost?" the girl's voice again breaks through the thick cropping of trees behind me, closer this time.

"Ramsey didn't seem too impressed with her, and it's like fifty feet of woods till you're out the other side and standing in Sander's backyard."

"She doesn't know that!" There's actual concern in the

girl's voice and it makes the muscles in my shoulders loosen. "What if she gets scared on her own in there? Or twists her ankle on a root or something?" The pitch of her voice increases, and I immediately start moving back toward the house.

"Call off the search parties," I call, holding my hands up as I cross back into the backyard. "I'm not injured."

Amiria Adams stands in her backyard, poofy powder blue dress making her look like a brunette Cinderella. I missed her grand entrance, but it was hard to miss the way everyone flocked to her, wishing her happy birthday throughout the night, and the way the guy I danced with followed her with his eyes.

The boy standing next to her towers over both of us, clearly already having hit a growth spurt that launched him into the stratosphere. He stands with his hands in his pockets, shoulders slouched and looking me over without much expression.

"Are you okay?" Amiria asks, stepping toward me.

I nod and wrap my arms around myself, not yet feeling back to okay. "Yeah, I'm fine."

"You ran out of there pretty quick for someone who's fine," the boy drawls, and I can't help but flinch.

Amiria smacks his chest.

My face and neck start to heat, probably matching the red of my hair. "Did everybody see me run out?" My eyes widen as I realize the kind of scene I probably just created.

"Nah," the boy replies. "They were all probably too busy trying to get a picture of the birthday girl unhinging her jaw for grilled cheese over here." He moves out of the way of her flying hand this time, chuckling to himself.

I smile and Amiria beams back. A couple moments pass,

the muffled noise of the music and people inside reaching us.

"It's a beautiful party," I say, glancing over their shoulders through the glass French doors.

"Thanks," Amiria replies, but her shoulders fall.

"You don't like it?" I ask.

She wraps her arms around herself, rubbing her own upper arms as she shrugs. "It's not really my style."

"Mira here doesn't like to be the center of attention." The boy nudges her shoulder with his own.

I snort. "I can't imagine why you wouldn't want two hundred people staring at you all night long." Sarcasm drips off my tone and I roll my eyes before I can stop myself.

"Exactly," Mira breathes, tension leaking out of her with the word.

"Birthdays are lame anyways. The only good parts are the gifts and cake."

Mira smiles at my statement while the boy groans.

"Another birthday hater, really?" He tips his head back to stare at the stars. "How are there two of you?"

"Bentley here loves to be the center of attention." Mira pats his chest as we share a smirk.

I cannot imagine anything worse than being the center of attention let alone wanting to be. I nod, and an awkward silence stretches out after a moment. I rub my arm. "I should probably go back inside."

"Wait." Mira reaches out, hand landing on my shoulder. "We didn't get your name." She smiles.

I return the grin, glancing at Bentley as well. "I'm Autumn. Autumn Green."

"Green," Bentley murmurs. "Oh shit. You're one of the Greenmart Dynasty Greens, aren't you?" His eyes grow wider. "Are you the new ballerina?"

I flinch before shaking my head. "No, Sage, my sister is."

Mira's brow furrows as her hand falls away but Bentley excitedly turns toward her.

"Her sister's the like ten-year-old ballet prodigy that everyone has been talking about coming to Emerald Grove. Remember Ella saying that she's apparently on track to become a prima ballerina before she's twenty-five, which I guess is a big deal or something?"

My nails dig into my arms as Bentley gushes.

"No, I didn't know everyone was talking about this?" Mira watches me and I break the eye contact to glance back at the party, biting my lip.

"Well, if you'd lifted your head out of your notebook at lunch last year, you'd have heard about her."

I dry swallow before squaring my shoulders and turning back to face them.

"It's a sketchbook," Mira mutters, still looking at me.

"I think I should get back inside," I say flatly. Turning to leave, I only get one step before Mira speaks.

"I don't like being compared to my brother either," she says, and I turn back around. "He was the varsity quarterback last year and still got straight A's, so a lot of the time, I feel like I'm crawling out from under his shadow at school."

An ache spreads through my limbs, and I scrunch my nose. "At least your brother is older." I give a weak chuckle, turning toward Bentley. "And she's twelve, not ten."

He has the brains to look contrite as he says, "Sorry, I speak without thinking most of the time."

"It's an only child trait," Mira adds and I smile.

"I resent what you are insinuating, Amira." Bentley tilts his nose up snootily at her and I laugh. We all end up smiling and start to amble leisurely toward the porch. The atmosphere feels lighter than anything I've experienced here so far.

"Thank you for coming after me," I say after a few steps.

"With the look Adams was giving you, be glad we're the ones that found you," Bentley mutters. Mira slaps his chest again and he rubs the spot after.

"Adams?" I pause, face scrunching at the use of Mira's last name.

Bentley and Mira stop too, turning back toward me on the porch steps.

"My brother," Mira says. "Ramsey Adams."

My spine snaps straight when she says his name. "Ramsey is your brother?" I whisper and my stomach bottoms out.

"Yeah." She bites her lip, eyes searching my face for a moment. "How do you know him?"

I chew the inside of my cheek. "We met at Lucy's diner a few weeks ago." I try to hold back, but memories of the last time I saw him invade my mind. "No offense, but your brother's a dick."

"He can be." She wrings her hands. "I love my brother but I'm also aware he's a teenage boy who used to rule our high school. How he treats my mother and me is not always how he treats other girls."

Bentley shakes out his shoulders, glancing back at the party. "What did he do?"

I glance away, reconsidering melting into the woods rather than walking back into the house or telling Mira about my run in with Ramsey and his friends.

She steps down so we're back on level ground, concerned eyebrows furrowing. "Did he hurt you?"

I rush to explain. "No, not physically." Mira lets out a relieved breath. "Him and his little wolf pack just made some stupid comments and then laughed about it." I leave out the milkshake/cheese fry exchange and the fact that it was Ramsey's girlfriend that made most of the comments.

"Want Mira to put Nair in his shampoo for you?" Bentley grins as he wiggles his eyebrows.

Mira smacks his chest again.

"Ow! What?! Like you haven't before?"

"I did not miss you," she says and he snickers.

"Liar," Bentley asserts.

I smile. "No, it's okay. I got him back already. I'm just going to avoid him from now on." I glance at the party. "Maybe I should just head home for the night."

Mira slings her arm through mine, pulling me to her side. "No, you should not. Come on, you can hang out with us. Avoiding Ramsey won't be hard. He'll spend most of the night on the balcony with his friends."

We start walking back, unlinking our arms to ascend the stairs.

"Besides, after tonight, should be easy enough since he's just home for the weekend. He's at university this year." I perk up at the news and Mira adds, "And he took his wolf pack with him."

Bentley snickers and I snort. Relief floods my veins making my arms feel lighter, shoulders less tense. After tonight, I hopefully won't ever have to see Ramsey Adams again.

4

AUTUMN

Present day

I am once again trying to ignore Ramsey Adams.

But it's a little difficult since I can feel him currently glaring at me as his mother wraps me in a bone crunching bear hug for the third time this morning. Despite my desire to avoid him forever, escaping Mira and Bentley's tractor beam of friendship proved impossible and so Ramsey and I spent the last few years spinning in parallel orbits around his sister.

And now we're about to spend three hours in a car together. Three hours with the bane of my existence, and Mira, who is still hiding the fact that she's heartbroken over Ramsey's best friend from Ramsey. What could possibly go wrong?

Ms. Adams pulls back and pats my frozen cheek. "I can't believe you're all leaving to go back to school already." She turns to Mira beside me, enveloping her once again. "And I have to rush off for a stupid meeting and miss our tradition!"

"Waving goodbye from the porch while we drive off is hardly a tradition," Ramsey grumbles from where he waits in the driveway beside his black Jeep.

Ms. Adams drops her arms and smile before turning to face her son. "Do we do it every time you leave for Imperium Coast?" She puts her gloved fists on her sides where I assume her puffy winter coat currently hides the location of her hips.

Ramsey sighs. "Yes."

"Then it's a tradition." Ms. Adams turns back to me and Mira. "You girls are going to have an amazing semester." She reaches out, once again touching both of our faces. "Call me if you need anything." She looks at Mira first, but then her eyes meet mine as well and she nods once to me.

"We will, Mom," Mira says, wrapping her in yet another hug.

Ramsey steams. "You've already hugged thirty times this morning! You'll see all of us in just a few weeks."

Ms. Adams pulls back, glancing down at her son once more. "And I better hear from *both* of you before then, mister." We all head down the porch steps into the shoveled driveway.

Ramsey nods as we approach, the tips of his ears and nose pink. "Of course, Mom. Someone's got to make sure you're eating every day."

Ms. Adams playfully swats him before capturing him in a hug as well. I try not to watch, but the way Ramsey tucks in and holds onto his mother with an extra squeeze grabs my attention. How nice it must be to have a mom who so freely gives out warm hugs.

Walking over to her idling car, Ms. Adams takes a second to turn back and wave at us from the few feet away and we all chuckle, waving back. She smiles before getting into her car and driving off.

"Finally," Ramsey sighs, turning back to his sister and me. "Where's her ride?" He nods toward me and my stomach dips toward my toes.

"About that..." Mira hedges. "She kinda doesn't have one and you have so much room in your car and I just figured—

"Mira, what the fuck? You said last night that she had a ride!" Ramsey's arms fold over his chest and the bottom of his circular glasses fog.

"I figured it'd be easier to ask for forgiveness in this case...you know since you two..." She waves her hand in some vague gesture between us as if some unnamable entity exists in the tension filled air separating our bodies.

"Us two, what?" He seems exacerbated and I know he's picked up on Mira's mood over break, trying to parse out what's been going on. As he stares down at her now, I can see the way he's assessing her, noticing her usual lack of drive. Mira stands a whole foot under her brother's height but would usually have no problem going toe to toe with him.

Now though, she pleads. "She just needs a ride back to school, Ramsey." Mira throws her arms open wide as she stands before him.

"Why can't Marshall take her?"

"Bentley's driving back from Maine with Janette and Axel, remember? You said you would drive me and Autumn back to the Coast with you!"

"I said I would drive *you*. I don't remember agreeing to bring *her*." His finger points in my direction, but his eyes stay fixed on his sister.

He hasn't looked at me once since we've walked down

here. I stand a few feet away from him and Mira and he hasn't looked at me. Not even one fucking time.

I should be used to this by now. Ramsey hasn't really looked at me in over three years. We've circled each other at least a thousand times since we first met. Adams' family dinners that Mira got me an invite to. Brief passings in the hallways of their childhood home. Random events like our high school graduation where he came to support his baby sister.

And in almost all that time though, Ramsey fucking Adams has never once looked directly at me. Around me. Over me. At a spot just over my shoulder, sure. But never directly at me.

There's only been one exception. The one time we ended up alone together for merely five minutes.

You look fuller.

The words still sting.

And for some reason, his otherwise lack of eye contact pisses me off. Something he has a particularly acute ability to do. At least to me.

"It's fine, Mir. I can uber to the train station. You guys get going." I pull my phone out, shuffling the bag on my shoulder. The cheapest option is going to be twenty bucks, but I still have the money Mimi gave me for Christmas. Fingers crossed the train ticket won't eat up the rest of my cash. I still need to get my textbooks when I get back to the Coast.

Mira says something low that I can't really hear, and Ramsey sighs, closing his eyes. "Get in the car, Fall."

"It's fine, really." I'm a hairsbreadth away from pressing the booking button on my phone screen when the weight of my bag disappears from my shoulder.

"Get in the damn Jeep," Ramsey grumbles, taking my

bag to the trunk and tossing it in without so much as a glance in my direction. He walks around to the front of the car and gets in, Mira smiling and giving me a thumbs up before she follows suit on the other side.

I sigh, watching my breath puff out in the chilly air. Here goes nothing.

Sliding into Ramsey's backseat, I purposely sit behind him so that I can see Mira's face more than him. Mira immediately turns around, asking me about classes and settling my nerves as we start an aimless conversation that allows me to tune out who's driving. Almost.

His presence feels huge, taking up more and more room in the car the longer we drive. His shoulders are tense, grip on the steering wheel tight and unyielding. Snow litters the sides of the highway Ramsey hurtles us down, probably trying to make the time we spend together as short as possible.

Mira chatters away, clearly trying to single-handedly fight off the tense atmosphere the two of us have created. "I hate the snow. Spring cannot come soon enough." Mira turns toward her brother. "I know you like the snow, Rams, but I seriously do not get the appeal." Ramsey grunts, not taking his eyes off the road. Mira bounces around in her seat, looking back at me. "What about you, A? You're team no snow, right?"

I love the winter.

Always have. Heat makes my hair frizzy, and my skin swelter. I hate the itch of humidity, the feeling of my thighs sticking together. Boob sweat.

I love sweaters and hot chocolate and having an excuse to dress cozy. I love foggy breath and that bite in the air, and I love love love snow.

But I also love Mira.

"Of course, Mir." I feel heat on the side of my face and glance toward the rearview mirror, but all I can see is Ramsey's forehead and dark curls. "Team no snow, all the way," I mumble.

Mira beams, turning back around and fidgeting as she proceeds to bug her brother.

They start arguing about the merits of seasons, something I'm sure they've done a thousand times before and I go back to tuning them out.

The deciding factor in picking Imperium Coast University for me was snow. The first time I walked across campus was on a tour in the dead of winter. The guide apologized for the sprinkling snowfall and chilly atmosphere, but I immediately fell in love with the sleepy school of intermingling old brick and new glass buildings covered in glittery white.

Mira and Bentley wanted to attend the Coast because they were legacies. It was practically in their blood. They begged me to come with them, always making room for me in their lives no matter what. It wasn't until that winter day though that following them once again felt like the right choice.

Of course, I almost immediately regretted it. Starting out the school year during a scorching New England summer made me question why I didn't just run away to Alaska. They have med schools, right?

Fortunately, the temp fell soon enough and by the first big snowstorm, I felt right at home at the Coast.

"Bentley should be back already by the time we get in. I've missed him." Mira's tone softens, losing some of the edge that's been present all of winter break.

I study the side of her face, noting that her forehead is pinched, eyes glassy, but a smile pushes her rosy cheeks up, probably stuck in that position at this point.

Mira had a lot going on over break. And she refused to let Bentley know about any of it. My best friends had very different starts to their college careers. Mira had her heart broken by the guy she's always been in love with. And Bentley fell in love with his roommate. And Mira's roommate. Who is now also dating them both.

Mira didn't want to ruin Bentley's happy love bubble. They've been best friends since childhood. He would drop just about anything to be there for her. But the same could be said in reverse so she made me promise not to tell him a thing until we got back.

Ramsey doesn't know either. Mostly due to the fact that the guy Mira was getting over happens to be his lifelong best friend. But I can tell he's getting suspicious. The two of us spending most of winter break holed up in her room watching horror movies and only coming out for meals might have tipped him off.

You look fuller.

I shake my head again, forcing myself to focus on the snow-covered rocks and trees whizzing by. My phone buzzes on the seat beside me.

ARIA

Just got in. You on campus?

I smile at my roommate's text, glad her train made it in on time.

Still thirty minutes out. Ramsey's driving like a maniac though so maybe closer to ten.

ARIA

See you soon!!

Another message comes in from my group chat with Mira and Bentley.

BENTLEY

dinner tonight? I miss you two.

Mira snorts from the front seat.

MIRA

yeah I'm sure we were top of mind while you were with J and Axel all break

I laugh and then feel Ramsey's stare through the mirror again. Refusing to look up I focus on my phone.

BENTLEY

I'm down for dinner. Need to hit the bookstore too. Cool if I invite Aria?

Bentley hearts the message and I smile. Mira's phone buzzes with the notification a second later.

"You two are hiding something," Ramsey singsongs.

My head snaps up at the accusation, but Mira simply rolls her eyes.

"You've been hiding something all of break. I don't know what it is, but I'm going to find out sooner or later." He taps his fingers against the leather on the wheel. "Might as well just tell me now."

Mira's face goes pale, and I feel her nerves jumping around the enclosed space.

Suddenly, my voice fills the space. "Leave it alone, Ramsey." His name tastes like ash coming off my tongue, but I simply swallow the feeling, sitting up straighter in the backseat.

Molten maple syrup eyes meet mine in the mirror and my skin prickles. A flare of heat pulses through my blood. Who knew the secret to getting him to look at me was just sitting in the backseat of his car?

"Stay out of it, Fall." His tone is deadly in comparison to the melodic one he used for Mira, and I know he expects people to follow his commands.

"No," I challenge, stomach warming as if I've downed a shot.

Ramsey's eyes narrow into slits. We face off for a moment before he's forced to look back at the road.

The loss of eye contact makes reason flood back into my bones. "We're making dinner plans," I tell him, knowing if he doesn't get some explanation he'll keep pulling this thread. Still, I can't help adding, "No one's plotting against you. Chill out."

Ramsey mutters something under his breath as we pull off the highway, and my phone buzzes again.

MIRA

thank you 🤍

I like the message, looking back up just as the spiral towers of the Coast's library begin looming in the distance.

Mira squirms to sit up in the passenger seat, excitement masking her momentary panic. The feeling thrums through my blood too as we make our way through the now familiar streets toward campus.

Turning onto Ring Road, West Tower dorms comes into view and I'm practically buzzing to get out of the car. The Jeep finally stops, and I fling myself out, both grateful to be standing and happy to be back.

Imperium Coast. The first steppingstone in my plan for freedom.

Ramsey gets out too, and Mira and I both meet him at the trunk, grabbing our bags when he holds them out.

"Make sure you call Mom this week!" Mira yells after him as he silently heads back toward the driver's side.

Waving over his head, he simply tosses out, "Have a good first week, bug." We wait on the sidewalk as he gets in, but he doesn't pull away at first. The passenger side window rolls down beside us. "And you're welcome for the ride, Fall."

The words lash me in condescension, and he stares straight ahead, not even looking at me as he says them. My blood boils and my mouth pops open to respond.

Before I can say anything, he's pulling away from the curb. For some reason, I can't stop myself from watching his car disappear down the road as he heads over to Ravens' mansion.

Now that the ride's over, at least I won't have to see him again this semester.

5

AUTUMN

I slip my key into the door to room 315, relief flooding me when I immediately see Aria's dyed black bob. "Hey, Bubbles." The image of the two of us dressed as Powerpuff girls last Halloween pops into my mind as it always does when I use her nickname.

Aria stands up and turns, a smile lighting her dark purple painted lips when I shuffle further into the room, stomping any leftover snow off my boots on the cheap welcome mat we bought together at the beginning of last semester.

"Blossom!" Aria rushes the few steps between us and wraps her arms around my waist. While Aria decided to go as her opposite in choosing Bubbles last Halloween, I stuck with what I know, choosing the type A redheaded character and spending the whole night explaining why we didn't have a Buttercup with us to complete the ensemble.

"I missed you." Aria mutters with an extra squeeze.

I toss my duffel onto my bed over her shoulder and sigh. "I missed you, too." I hug her back, able to rest my chin on top of her head.

She pulls away, walking over to the minifridge the Coast thankfully provides in each dorm room. Neither of us would have been able to get one with Aria's part time job and my zero dollars an hour income. The perks of attending an elitist school.

Grabbing a plastic container off the top, Aria turns back to me. "I've been waiting for you to get here. I brought back more of those pinwheel cookies you like." She opens the container, holding them out to me with another bright smile.

"Oh, Aria, you didn't have to spend money on me." I hesitate, reaching for one, eyes locked on the multicolored confections.

"Don't worry about it." She waves me off, pushing the container closer to my partially outstretched hand. "They're like five bucks. Consider it a late Christmas gift."

"Okay," I say, taking one and nibbling on it. "In that case, I brought you something too."

Aria frowns, placing the lid back on the cookies and walking over to the minifridge again. I unzip my bag and root around for the wrapped gift I hid among my clothes. Pulling it out, I pivot, holding the shoebox out to my roommate with an encouraging grin.

Aria sighs, stepping forward and taking the gift, but just holding it in her hands. "You didn't have to get me anything."

"Neither did you." I remind her with a raised brow before smiling. "But I wanted to." I nod toward the gift. "Open it."

She swallows, opening the gift slowly at first, then tearing the paper away when she sees the logo on the box underneath. "You got me Docs?" She squeals but her forehead pinches. "This is way too much, Autumn. I can't accept these." She keeps her hands around the Doc Martens box, knuckles white as she holds onto it.

I wave her off. "It's fine, Bubbles. They were on sale for Christmas, and I know you've always wanted a pair." Her fingers loosen a hair, but she bites her lip, staring down at the box. "If it makes you feel better, I didn't buy them." There was no way I'd be able to afford those boots on my own.

She furrows her brow. "You didn't steal them, right?"

I laugh. "No. I put them on my Christmas list when you mentioned wanting a pair. My grandmother got them for me." I smile, walking over to the fridge and pulling out a soda. "Had to act really excited about them and got the satisfaction of watching Mom grimace as she thanked Mimi for getting them for me. Might have to borrow them just to see what she does if I wear them in her house." Cracking the tab on my can, I take a sip, closing my eyes as the weight of the last six weeks slowly slides off my shoulders.

"Deal." Aria nods, staring down at the box in her hands as she carries it over toward her bed. "They still not letting you get a job?"

"Nope," I say, popping the p as I sit down on my own bed facing her. Mimicking my mother's incredulous voice, I recite, "*Greens don't work as kitchen staff, Autumn! What would your grandmother think?*" Taking another sip of soda, I roll my eyes and shake my head. Aria gives me a sympathetic frown, pulling out the Docs to try on.

The day I came home with smoothie in my hair and several bags of food from Lucy's diner, my mother had let me in on a new facet of our fun little family secret.

"Why the hell would you buy all the workers food? I gave you my card so you could get *us* food, not *them!*" Mom rifled through another bag in search of her own lunch, nostrils flaring and pale face turning purple with fury.

"I just thought..."

"Well, you thought wrong." She huffed, putting her hands on her hips and watching as the movers all happily grabbed food from the bags she already checked, the rest of our furniture forgotten. "You're just going to have to pay it back eventually."

My eyes had gone wide. "What?" I had no money and no way to pay for anything other than with the money Mom always gave me. Besides, she never mentioned owing them for any of the stuff I bought with her credit card before.

Mom nodded. "Mhmmm." Then she turned to me. "What? Did you think we would just fund your entire life? You know your role in all this, Autumn." She shook her head again, reminding me of the day she broke down and dumped all of the messy details on my shoulders. The day she disclosed "my role" and why Aaron couldn't stand to be in the same room as me. "It was hard enough getting your father to agree to pay for you to go to Emerald Grove with Sage. He already said he won't pay for anything past your first four years of college."

The second that ball dropped, my whole life changed. I might have been living in luxury, but it was on borrowed time. From that day on, I knew I would need to figure out how to make my way in the world. And I wasn't about to start by taking any more Green handouts.

So, I tried to work. After they showed us the student job center at orientation, I immediately applied for any available spot on campus. My meal plan covered food, but I wasn't sure how I was supposed to buy things like books or a cute rug for my dorm.

Plus, I'd never had a job and Mom always acted like I

didn't need one, but one day I would. One day soon. And I wanted some experience before that day came.

I lasted a whole three weeks. Barely had enough time to learn how to run the register and frost the donuts at the campus coffee shop. The moment Mom found out I was working, she demanded I quit. Loudly.

Aria was present the day I accidentally told Mom I had to go early on our monthly phone call because I was running late for work. The phone wasn't on speaker, but the screeching tone of Mom's voice still snagged my roommate's attention.

"If your grandmother found out you were working in the kitchen, she would berate me for a decade!"

I could hear Mom typing on her screen on the other end. Aria sat at her desk, watching my face as I chewed my bottom lip and held the phone to my ear, not really seeing the world around me.

"I don't understand why you don't just use your card, Autumn."

The credit card with my name on it that Mom gave me after the diner incident wasn't an option. That was part of Aaron's money. Which is just Mimi's money. And I've long since learned that Green money will never be *my* money.

I don't want to owe you anything more, I silently responded.

"You're quitting that job, Autumn. And I won't tell your father about this. He'd have a cow if he thought you were trying to humiliate the family again." She sighed. "God knows that man can throw a fit when he wants to." She started telling me about how amazing Sage's last recital was and I try to picture Aaron having a fit. I've hardly seen him raise his voice above a whisper around me. I've hardly seen him around me, full stop.

When Mom finally hung up, I broke down, spilling way too much to Aria as I tried to explain why a phone call with my mother would trigger a panic attack. Aria took it all in stride though, fully understanding and sharing some of her own mommy issues with me.It was the first time I was able to get through one of my panic attacks without needing to hide and just crash out on my own, the first time someone else sat there with me and went through it.

I shake my head, pulling out of my memories and cheering as Aria studies herself in the mirror. "Those look so good on you, Bubbles." Aria laughs and I take a deep breath. "I think I have a sort of plan for tricking my mom into letting me get a job," I admit in a rush. I haven't told anyone about this, having just come up with the plan over break and not wanting to make Mira deal with any of my crap on top of her own.

Aria smiles, loving mischief. "Do tell." She walks over and plops back down on her bed, facing me and bouncing a bit as she waits.

"Okay so, my advisor, Dr. Miller, he runs the clinic on campus where everyone goes when they're sick?"

Aria nods.

"He also runs an internship program for one pre-med student to get a chance to work alongside him at the clinic and get a little taste of field training before we go on to med school." I pause and my roommate leans in. "A *paid* internship program."

Aria's eyes light up. "And Tina can't say no to an internship. Not when it'll look so good on your med school applications."

I grin. "Exactly."

Aria smiles. "That's brilliant. A paid gig plus experience in a medical environment. It's an all-around win."

I nod, giddy at the idea of it. "Of course, he usually only gives it to a junior or senior and I'll only be a sophomore next fall." I shrug. "But I'm hoping since he's teaching my bio course this semester and seems to really like me when I go to my advisor meetings, he might make an exception?"

"Can't hurt to try," Aria reasons. "Worst case scenario, you don't get it this year and try again next year."

"Right." I sit back, feeling lighter now that I've told someone my plan and they didn't immediately tell me I'm crazy for even trying for an upper-level paid internship this early in my academic career.

"I finally quit the gas station," Aria drops, the new information pulling me out of my excitement.

I sit up. "You did?" She tried to get a job on campus with me, but the hours and pay had been too little for the amount she was trying to send home for Carter.

"Mhmm." She swings her legs. "You know that guy Harley, the one whose friends with Mira's brother?" My stomach twists as I remember glimpsing the tears in my best friend's eyes more than once over break. "His gym over on Fifth had an opening for a front desk girl. I had a phone interview with him yesterday and I got it!" She beams, her silver nose ring gleaming along with her white teeth. "The hours are so much better, and a lot of the trainers are students, so he has no problem working around my class schedule."

"That's great!" I wring my hands in my lap. She knows Mira, but I don't know how much I should share. "Thank God you won't have to walk back to campus in the dark at three AM anymore."

Aria laughs. "Yeah, I'll miss our safety chats though." After she was put on overnight shifts on Tuesdays, I insisted she call me, and we stay on the phone together while she walked home. Mira had been followed home to the dorms last semester and that was from her brother's house only a few minutes away. The gas station was twenty minutes downtown on foot.

I shrug, sipping my soda again. "You can still call me on your way home if you want."

She shakes her head, running a hand through her short hair before sitting up a little straighter. "So, how bad was it?" She brings one foot up onto the seat in front of her, hugging her knee with both arms.

I shrug, shaking some loose curls behind my shoulder. "Not terrible. Sage had her Christmas recital, so they were too busy taking her to practices and fawning over all that to bother with me. I mostly hung out with Mira since Bentley was on his trip with Janette and Axel till the sixth."

"That's good that they didn't bother you any." Aria searches my face. "How was it at your grandmother's?"

I shrug again. We only spent a couple days at Mimi's. I would have liked to stay longer. "It was fine. She got me some new headphones. Asked how school was. Mom freaked out about it later." I laugh, remembering Mom going on and on about it in the car. "She thinks everything my grandmother says to any of us is somehow a pointed question about her as a mother." I mimic Mom's voice again. "*She's always looking for a reason to criticize me.*"

Aria smiles, rolling her eyes. "Yeah, because everything is always about Tina."

I laugh. "Exactly. Honestly, I think she just asked out of obligation." I wipe some soda that spilled off my pants. I should just tell her why Mom's so paranoid. Why my family is this way. Instead, I chicken out for the millionth time. "What about you? How's Carter doing?"

Aria's smile hikes up ten more megawatts. "He's doing so

good! He still loves school, and I got to go and have lunch with him there last week. He introduced me to all his little friends, and his teacher loves him to bits. It was so cute, Autumn." She pulls out her phone, scrolling through before showing me a bunch of her brother smiling toothily up at the camera with a couple other kids and a middle-aged woman in a muted purple dress.

I lean forward and smile at the pictures, heart squelching at his cute little face. Aria looks at the last one for a moment before pocketing her phone again. "He's doing really good there."

I nod, finishing my soda and tossing the can in our recycling bin. "Your mom still doing good?" Aria's smile dims, but she doesn't frown.

"Yeah. She's doing good too," she says in an airy tone. With a snort, she adds, "Still working at the Dairy Barn which is a miracle. I don't think she's had a job this long since I was in middle school."

While I am forced to answer my mother's calls on a monthly basis, Aria calls home two to three times a week, checking in on her mom and little brother. Her mom hasn't always been the most reliable parent and leaving Carter with her was probably one of the hardest things she's ever had to do. She vented to me about it a couple weeks into living together. We ended up having a long heart to heart, staying up all night and just telling each other all the things we've never told anyone else. Well, almost all the things.

"That's good, though. It's good that she's keeping it up, for Carter's sake."

Aria nods, getting a little lost in space.

"I'm meeting Bentley and Mira for dinner in a bit then we're heading over to the bookstore after. Want to join?"

"Um, duh." She drops her leg and heads over to her bed,

starting to fold the laundry piled on top. "I need to get some textbook for my psych course. Cannot wait to be done with these gen eds and get to do some actual coding next year."

I lean back against the wall, staring down at my bag and debating unpacking it now or leaving it for tomorrow. "Yeah, I think the only one I actually need for Monday is my textbook for Gen Bio, but I should probably get the rest while I'm there." To be honest, Dr. Miller probably won't care if I even have that one Monday morning, but I already know my anxiety will be peaking if I try to go to the first class without it.

Aria tosses all of her unfolded laundry into the bin she likely dumped it out of. "Ten-minute break then we meet up with the crew for dinner?"

I nod. "Sounds like a plan."

Aria flops back down. "Don't let me fall asleep, Blossom," she mumbles, eyes already closing.

I smile, shaking off the last of the blanket of discomfort that covered me during my time back at home. "Wouldn't dream of it, Bubbles."

6

AUTUMN

I'm running late. For my first class. Again.

Stupid fucking first days.

Last semester, it had been an incorrectly set alarm clock that made me jog from West Tower all the way across campus to the new shiny science center, making it to the large lecture hall with only a few seconds to spare. This year, I really tried to start off better. I showered and did my hair the night before. Laid out my outfit on my desk and packed my bag. Set three alarms and triple checked them to make sure I woke up on time. And one shitty accident after another culminated in yet another jog across campus to the same building.

First my leggings ripped. The seams around my inner thighs had been getting worn down, but I figured they still had a couple more weeks left before they finally gave out. Then my oatmeal burned my fingers when I took it out of the microwave, causing me to spill it all over the olive sweater I picked out weeks ago for my first day. And of course, they had to forget to salt the steps leading out of the dorms so that I busted my ass on a patch of black ice rushing out of the building and had to take a second on the ground to consider my life choices.

Now, jogging in a completely different outfit than I envisioned for this day, through the throngs of students who don't seem to have a care in the world moseying between the tall brick academic buildings, I suddenly question if I've started my period. Checking my tracker app, I realize it's actually a few days late and let out a low groan as my stomach cramps and I reposition my messenger bag over my chest. Running with this thing always makes it slam against the side of my thigh and causes the wide strap to dig into the space between my breasts. The science center is just ahead. I just need to make it inside and there's a bathroom right inside the doors that I can go hide out in before I inevitably have to walk into Dr. Miller's class. Late.

If he wasn't my academic advisor, I'd be having a full-blown panic attack at this point. As it is, my hands are already shaking. People are staring at me as I pass, and I can feel their eyes on me as I rush through the shoveled sidewalks. Balling one fist around the strap of my bag and gripping my phone in the other, I ground myself in the feel of each biting into my palms.

Making it into the building, I beeline for the ladies' room, slamming the swinging door open with my palm and startling the girl washing her hands at the sinks.

"Sorry," I mutter, rushing past her and locking myself into a stall. Rummaging around in my bag, I check all the zipper pouches, sighing when I finally find a rumpled pad squished at the bottom of one of them. Sitting down, I check my phone. One minute till class starts. Maybe I can still make it.

I rush through my routine, glad that the bathroom is empty when I exit the stall and start washing my hands in a rush. Staring at myself in the mirror, I force my lungs to take a few deep breaths. My blood races as my thoughts fly around. I shift my weight from one foot to the other, trying to will the water to rinse the suds off my palms a little faster.

You're fine. Calm down.

Maybe I should just go back to my dorm and try again tomorrow. Hide out for the remainder of the day.

No. Today's the first day. I have to at least show up. Even if everyone stares at me as I walk in late. The idea makes a syrupy drip of panic sluice through my organs.

I turn the water off and grab my bag, not even bothering to try to dry my hands under the bulky grey dryer protruding from the wall. Slipping out the door, I speed walk to the stairwell, falling behind a group of guys leisurely walking up and blocking the whole of the stairwell so that I can't even pass. My hand taps against my thigh as I follow close behind them. I check my phone. Class started three minutes ago. Deep breath. Fingers crossed Dr. Miller doesn't start at eight on the dot.

Finally making it to the second floor, I veer toward the door the moment the group of guys gives me enough of an opening to do so. They continue to the third floor, and I silently hope to never see them ever again.

Room 275 is fortunately only a few feet away from the stairs. Slowing down my steps, I take a second outside the door to breathe out, hoping it's not obvious how desperate I was to be on time.

Pulling the door handle, the crack of the door's seal being broken seems to ring in my ears like a gunshot. Heads swivel toward me as I step into the room, dozens of eyes all burning past my clothes to sear the surface of my flesh. The sensation freezes me in place, hand still on the door, one foot extended in front of the other. I stare back at my classmates in terror as the moment I've been rushing to avoid slams into reality.

"Miss Green. Thank you for joining us," Dr. Miller calls, unknowingly breaking me out of my frozen stupor. I turn my head to the front of the class, eyes focusing in on my advisor as the world around him blurs. He crosses his arms over his chest. His eyes are less reprimanding than his tone. "Please take a seat." He gestures to one of the empty desks in the front row.

I swallow, taking my hand off the door and gripping the strap of my bag once more. With a nod, I duck my head down, letting my hair fall forward to shield my peripheral. I walk past Dr. Miller and the desk he pointed out, turning down a random row to get to an empty desk toward the back of the class.

Sitting down and dumping my bag at my feet, I take a second to flex my hands, trying to will away the slight tremor still present.

You made it. The worst part is over. Breathe.

Dr. Miller starts back into greeting the class and doing his opening speech about the semester. He gave the same one when I met him last year at our first advising meeting. I tune out a bit, getting the fresh seafoam colored notebook out of my bag and setting up the first page to take notes.

Lifting my head to start paying full attention, my eyes clash with maple syrup ones I know immediately. Indignation radiates toward me as I freeze in place for the second time in under an hour. Ramsey sits at the professor's desk just beyond Dr. Miller's shoulder, posture rigid and hand balled into a fist next to a stack of papers.

"Mr. Adams?" Dr. Miller's voice breaks the seething tension and unfreezes me yet again. Ramsey glances at the professor. "The syllabi."

Ramsey nods, standing up and grabbing the stack off the desk in front of him. He walks over to the first aisle, counting out the papers and passing them to the first student in the row. My breathing comes in sharp and staggered as Dr. Miller continues his speech and I watch Ramsey pass out the papers.

What the fuck is he doing here?

But I know what he's doing here. I've known since the moment our eyes met, and I realized he was sitting behind the professor's desk. And I only get further confirmation when the class syllabus lands haphazardly on my desk, unceremoniously dropped over the shoulder of the kid in front of me.

Ramsey Adam's is my favorite professor's TA. It says so in bold font at the top of the page.

I've promised myself over and over again that I won't have to see him, won't have to interact with him again. And now I'm going to have class with him every other day for five months. I'm going to *have* to interact with him at some point.

Possibly one on one. After the diner incident, we both made it a point to ignore the other's existence whenever we could. There had only been one time I'd been alone with Ramsey Adams, and it had only solidified my instinct to loathe him.

I spent the majority of the summer between junior and senior year of high school at my grandmother's. Sage booked a tour with some ballet company and Mom decided to accompany her. When she pitched the idea to Aaron, the immediate problem of my existence popped up. Aaron couldn't possibly be left alone with me for the entire summer. So, Mom pulled some strings and somehow got me a three month stay at casa de Mimi.

And it ended up being the best summer of my life. Sure, I was two hours away from both of my best friends and had no car or ability to get to them.

But I was alone. Utterly and completely alone. And it was amazing.

No Mom complaining about something or Aaron's silent presence reminding me how much I didn't belong at home. I wore shorts and tank tops, realizing on the second week that I'd stopped checking the mirror to find the faults before Mom could point them out. I let my hair grow wild and ate whatever I wanted, thanks to the live-in chef Fenley who was a baking wizard.

Mimi lived in a veritable castle, complete with a well-stocked library and beautiful gardens that I spent almost every day reading in for hours. Her pool was indoors, so when it rained, I went swimming. And on windy days, I read in her greenhouse, hidden away amongst potted plants and bags of soil.

Every night I had dinner with Mimi, and she'd ask me how my day was, accepting the same couple of sentences I swapped synonymous adjectives in and out of each day and then eating together in contented silence. She never asked anything more, never shared anything, and I found I quite liked the silence. Absolutely adored the freedom.

The day Mom came to pick me up, I felt whole in a way I never had before. Mimi saw me off, standing with her hands behind her back as one of her people loaded my single suitcase into the trunk of Mom's car. We didn't hug, but the single nod she gave me before I got into the car felt like the first time anyone in this family had seen me. And we weren't even actually related.

The second I got home, I texted Mira asking to come

over. The group chat immediately blew up with the two of them practically begging me to get over there instantly.

Walking up to the Adams' house, I remember smiling and feeling so freaking confident in my black shorts and a-line tank top.

Then Ramsey opened the door.

The scent of weed permeated my nostrils, choking out the warm summer breeze.

"Fall?" he said, squinting.

I froze, throat feeling suddenly closed as I wracked my brain for how to breathe. The nickname hit home, causing a twinge in my side. I scraped my nails against my palms, seeking the sting to stop myself from biting back.

"What did you do?" He stared at me intently. "You changed something." He stepped closer and my heart stopped.

We had never been alone together, never been near each other without someone we could put in between us. So, it never occurred to me that he might try to get closer if we were.

He inspected my face, trying to find something and the longer he took, the more my frazzled nerves sparked. But I was too trapped in the absurdity of the situation to leave, too struck by the impossibility of being alone with him that I had never thought to consider.

His eyes roamed my body.

Getting the jean shorts I wore on that morning had made me giddy for at least an hour. Even then in that moment, knowing they fit, that the zipper went all the way up and the button stayed closed, gave me a small rush of satisfaction. My summer of swimming and outdoor walks had paid off. I wasn't taking up as much space.

Ramsey's cloudy hooded eyes met mine again. He

studied them, leaning in even further. Only a few inches separated us now and the acrid smell of weed curled off him, seeming to soak into my nostrils.

"You look fuller." His eyes bounced between mine, still searching.

My chest burned at his comment, eating up the giddy excitement my morning accomplishment had created. "Fuck you," I managed to spit out just before Mira appeared over her brother's shoulder, ushering him away and pulling me into her radiant warmth.

That moment had been over a year ago, but the acidic burn of his fuller remark still lingers inside me. As I watch Ramsey sit back down behind Dr. Miller, the sting prickles to life and reality seems to crash into me yet again.

He's going to be grading papers. Teaching lessons. Holding office hours. I need to pass this class. I need to do well to get that internship. And Ramsey Adams might be in the perfect position to ensure I don't.

My hands start to tremble, and the room starts to blur.

No.

Clenching my fists, I turn my head down and count my breaths. I will not let this man affect me. Emotionally or academically. Getting a handle on my anxiety, I lift my head, focusing in on Dr. Miller. I still can't hear what he's saying but I refuse to look away from him for the rest of the class.

I will pass this course. I'll do well in this class. Ramsey Adams be damned.

7

RAMSEY

A couple of people walk by as I pace the hallway, but I can't register their faces. They pass in a blur, their movement the only thing registering against the shiny, overly lit walls surrounding me. My brain is wholly focused on one metal door, waiting for Miller's class to get out. I stare at it across from me as if that will speed time up and force it to spit out the one person who has once again invaded *my* space.

I have resolutely ignored Fall for three years now, speaking to her only a handful of times and never anything more than a few words. She was a blip on the radar, nothing to worry about. I had everything under control. And then I found out she was coming to the Coast.

"And Bentley and Autumn got in too!" Mira gushed, jumping up and down in the kitchen clutching her big manila envelope emblazoned with the Imperium Coast crest. My smile fell off my face, but I replaced it the second she stopped, beaming at me. I slid my foot up onto the bottom rung of the island bar stool I sat on.

"That's great, bug." Even as the words left my mouth,

images of dark coppery hair and blue rage-filled eyes invaded my mind. Tapping the side of my thigh, I did my breath work, forcing my heart rate to slow down while Mira started rapidly firing away about all the things she needed to do before the end of the year.

Campus is big enough. I won't have to see her more than a handful of times. Same as I do now.

The image of Fall seething in the parking lot had never left me, our white-hot anger coiling toward each other through the already stifling air of the mid-August heat. But I had resolutely forced an ice block around the need to engage with her. She didn't exist in my world. And when she did, I played ice, only engaging when absolutely necessary.

And then she walked into my TA class.

Her grand entrance had interrupted Miller's opening speech, drawing the attention of everyone in the room. Mine included. For a moment, I thought *maybe she's lost, maybe this is just a mistake and she's in the wrong room.* Then Miller called her name and my jaw nearly cracked from the pressure when I snapped it shut.

She didn't see me, but I watched her walk, head bowed to her seat. Her hair sat at the crown of her head in a tight high ponytail, the long strands swaying down to her lower back. She let it grow out all summer, and the length was getting a little ridiculous at this point. The oversized moss green sweater swallowed her and her grip on the strap of her black messenger bag remained tight as she pulled it over her head and sat down.

I got two more seconds to note that she didn't seem to have a winter jacket before bright blue irises pierced into mine. Her mouth popped open, and a fast blush spread over her fair skin, making my eyes narrow further.

Miller called my name. I broke the eye contact, glancing

up before standing and gabbing the stack of syllabi with a little bit more force than necessary. I passed them out quickly, refusing to look at the girl in the back whose eyes I could feel following me through the room. The burning of her gaze called to the embers I kept tamped down for three years, making my blood start to simmer.

Sitting back down at the desk, I tuned Miller out and glared at the source of my aggravation. This was supposed to be my easy semester. After the TA job from hell with Dr. Jenkins last year, Miller suddenly having an opening seemed like a miracle. Jenkins only communicated with me through email, asking for vague tasks at random hours and then getting mad when I asked for clarification. I ended up doing nothing at the end, wasting my time sitting through her class and having fully packed office hours with all her students wanting help understanding how to perform her labs. When I told her Miller had hired me, she just rolled her eyes.

But having Fall in this class would make an easy semester next to impossible. Out of the frying pan and into the fire.

I glared at her for the full ten minutes, noting the way her eyes refused to leave Miller's face. He prattled on about semester assignments and grading rubrics, and she stared at him like it was the most fascinating lecture she ever heard. To make things worse, I could see the way Miller's eyes floated around the room, coming back to her face more than any other student's.

The cracking noise alerted me before the ink soaking into my clothes set in. Looking down, I dropped the pieces of cheap broken ballpoint, holding my ink covered palm out away from my already ruined shirt. A few of the students noticed me fuck up, eyeing me as Miller continued to run through the final project for the course. I stood, holding my hand up to show him the ink as he nodded, not missing a beat in his speech.

Leaving the room, I took one last look at Fall. Her stare stayed fixed on Miller, never straying.

I shut the door a little too hard.

Staring at the closed metal now, I continue to pace outside Miller's class. Restless nerves itch under my skin, and I flex my fist. The still wet black ink covering my palm makes a squelching noise. My grip slips as my fingertips slide against my slick palm, and the usually soothing gesture only serves to aggravate me further.

The door opens and a blonde boy in a baggy coat rushes out, followed by more people slowly leaving the classroom in groups. I stop moving, watching for the redhead I need out of my life.

She walks out looking down at her phone, typing away frantically. I fall into step behind her, clenching my jaw as the burn in my chest increases. Her hair sways against her back, a few inches from my face. I fist my hands to stop myself from touching it. Fall walks with her head down, following the girl in front of her toward the stairwell. Just as she's about to turn, I reach out, wrapping my hand around her upper arm and pushing her into the alcove beside the stairs.

Autumn drops her phone, the clatter echoing sharply in the small space. "What the—

"Shut up," I grit out.

Her back hits the wall and I crowd her, keeping her arm in my grip, but leaving a few inches of space between us.

Her eyes flick up to mine and instantly narrow. "Fuck off, Ramsey," she spits out.

The air in the alcove seems to grow ten times thicker

and I try to breathe through my nose but just end up inhaling Autumn's scent. Something light and floral wafts over me but the calm effect creeping up my spine only irks me more.

Her narrowed eyes glare while her mouth curls as if poised to snarl. I glare right back, moving my gaze from her mouth to her eyes. Even in the shadows, the sapphire blue seems to glow.

I lean in closer. "You need to drop that class, Fall."

Her eyes flash at the name, chin tilting back further. My words seem to ignite her, the tension around us growing. "Not. Going. To. Happen." Her teeth grit after she spits the words in my face. She struggles in my grip for a second before huffing and nodding to my hand still holding her. "Let go of me, Ramsey." She shakes her shoulder for good measure.

I only tighten my grip on her arm, but she winces. The reaction unlocks my fingers immediately and I cross my arms over my chest to neutralize whatever threat she might see them as. "Drop the class, Fall. I'm not asking."

"Clearly," she bites out. Squaring her shoulders, she pushes back against the wall, trying to put more space between us. "I'm not dropping this class, asshole. I need it for my degree. Why don't *you* just drop the TA position if me being there is such a problem?" The fire in her eyes lights my own.

My lips curl back, and I lean away, letting another inch of tension fill in the space between us. "I'm not giving up this spot just for you." I watch her fists curl at her sides. "Just take the class next year."

"No! I'm not changing my whole schedule and graduation plan *just for you!*" She huffs, the air around us vibrating as we each bare our teeth at the other.

I finally see the girl in the parking lot all over again, a part of me reveling in her appearance, the demon only she seems to awaken who likes watching her try to defy me.

She breaks the mounting pressure though, looking down for a moment to collect herself. When her eyes meet mine, her fire is subdued. "Looks like we're going to have to tolerate each other's presence for the semester." She mimics my stance, crossing her arms over her chest. "Think you can handle that?"

The challenge bites into my pride. She thinks she's in charge here. Time to inform her that's not the case.

Leaning into her space, I uncross my arms, placing my palms against the brick on either side of her head. "*I* can make your semester miserable."

She shrinks back, a small gasp leaving her throat. Her shoulders drop and arms fall to her sides.

I lean in closer, shrinking the gap between us. "Grade every paper poorly, ruin your whole average. Fuck your GPA and set you back in your program."

Her cheeks and neck grow redder and redder with each word. The fire roars higher in her irises and I watch her swallow harshly. She opens her mouth, about to spew more vitriol I'm sure, but instead her bottom lip starts to tremble as her breathing comes in choppy bursts. We square off and for once, she has nothing to say.

That's right, little witch. I'm in control here.

Basking in the appearance of her concession, a smile paints my lips and my demon hums. "Drop. The. Class."

Her fists start to shake, and her harsh breathing makes her nostrils flare. She swallows twice before speaking, the sound airy and almost *soft*. "You even try to ruin me, and I'll report you to Dr. Miller or the dean or whoever I need to." The fire slowly dies in her eyes as something dull replaces it.

My gut twists and I lean back a bit to study her more.

Her teeth start to chatter as her bottom lip continues to tremble. Her breathing remains irregular, and the color quickly drains from her face. "I will not let you fuck up my life, Ramsey." Her voice rasps out low and shaky and the tremors in her hands travel up to her shoulders.

"Hey, what's happening?" My nails bite into the brick behind her head.

She doesn't respond. Her breaths come in deep then shallow, chest heaving to try to find a rhythm. She glances around frantically, searching for something around me.

I take a hand off the wall, sliding it to the side of her neck so my fingers can feel her racing pulse. "Breathe, Fall. Follow me." I drag in a slow deep breath, mentally counting to five and releasing for the same amount of time.

Her pulse continues to beat erratically under my fingertips. But then her eyes lock onto mine as she starts to mimic the movements, chest climbing in a hitched manner as we breathe in and out together. After a few breaths, her pulse starts to slow back to normal, coming back down and thrumming steadily against my skin. Without a thought, I let my fingers lightly caress the side of her neck.

That voice I haven't heard in years suddenly whispers through my mind.

Green light.

Autumn lets out a little gasp and pushes weakly against my chest. Stepping back, I drop my hand. Black ink smudges the side of her neck, leaving the smeared imprint of my fingers behind. The moment there's room, she rushes around me, scrambling to grab her phone off the ground and disappearing before I can register that she's gone. Looking back at the space she just occupied, I replay the last few moments in my head.

The need to follow her gnaws at my insides, but I keep myself rooted in place, unsure if the urge would result in concern or further intimidation. Something about her always seems to unnerve me, and it's the whole reason I *need* her not to be in the same room as me three days a week.

Remembering the color draining from her face, Harley's words from years ago float through my brain.

Don't let her screw with your shit.

I close my eyes, leaning back against the wall I shoved her against minutes ago. Breathe in. One. Two. Three. Breathe out. One. Two. Three.

On the third pass, I open my eyes, the ice firmly back in place around my fire. We're at a stalemate yet again. Looks like I'll need to find a way to freeze Fall out once more.

8

RAMSEY

I trace the faded ink-stained lines on my left hand with my right index finger, picturing the smear of my handprint on Autumn's neck. Miller sits across from me at his desk, typing slowly on a laptop with two fingers. His cluttered office presses in around us, open books and old coffee cups and random knickknacks interspersed on every shelf and flat surface. The single window behind him lets in a bare amount of light through the drawn blinds and I continue to wait for him to finish, glancing at the clock on the wall over his door. Seventeen minutes.

I wonder what Autumn's reaction to the ink on her skin was. Remembering her trembling with fear in her eyes, the pit in my stomach opens again, my organs all seeming to slide down into it as it sucks all the air from my lungs.

Shaking my head, I clench my fists, grit my teeth, and breathe through my nose. The dryness at the back of my throat eases.

At nineteen minutes, Miller finally sits back, removing his glasses and wiping a hand over his face. "Sorry," he muses. "The dean has been on my ass about the clinic's budget issue." He looks up at the ceiling, rolling his shoulders and neck. With a clap of his hands, he sits up. "First class seemed to go well. Minus the pen incident." He gestures to my hands.

I nod, pushing my glasses up the bridge of my nose. "Seems like a good group." I squeeze my fists in my lap, deciding to test the waters. "Even though that one girl was late."

"Autumn." He smiles when he says her name, a slight chuckle wrapped into his tone. My nails bite into the center of my palm. "Yeah, she can be a bit disordered, but she's very driven. Seems determined to leave here with a 4.0, but she's only in her second semester." He shrugs, sliding a finger over the trackpad of his laptop as he reads something on the screen.

I can make your semester miserable.

My hushed harsh words and the feral fear in Fall's eyes plague my brain as my eyes lose focus of the room around me. The idea of tanking her grades and ruining her GPA flits through my mind, feeding the fire demanding to see her squirm. But immediately my chest twinges, Fall's big blue eyes twisting a knife in my gut. I absentmindedly drag a hand through my curls, tugging a bit at the roots to ground myself.

Miller laughs again and it shocks me back into the room. My back teeth gnash together. His tone lowers as he adds, "Not too bad on the eyes either. First time she came to an advising meeting..." He shakes his head, a half smirk lifting only one side of his mouth. He looks up at me and winks. "If I were in my twenties again, am I right?"

My stomach rolls and I narrow my eyes. "And not married, right?" My tone drips with judgement and my eyes dart to a framed photo of him and his wife and son over his shoulder. Red creeps up his stubble covered neck and he clears his throat.

"Right, right. Of course." He looks down at his laptop again, clicking through things on the screen and avoiding my eyes.

I readjust in my seat, sitting up and setting my elbows on my knees. "About Autumn," I start. The knife in my gut seems to slide out a little as I say my next sentence. "It might not be a good idea for me to TA the class she's in. We have a...personal relationship."

His eyes narrow slightly.

I roll my eyes. "Not like that. She's my sister's best friend."

His eyes return to normal, but my fingers clench around each other.

I lean forward. "I probably shouldn't be involved in the class she's taking since it might be considered a conflict of interest." My stomach flips as Miller takes a second to regard me. If I lose this TA spot, I'm going to leave a lot more than an ink stain on Fall's neck.

The knife sinks back into my gut and I ignore it.

Miller waves his hand. "No big deal. We'll just make sure you don't grade anything she completes. I was going to have us split up the class for grading anyway so you can just take the second half of the list."

Air rushes back into my lungs and I sit back.

Miller starts to go over his plan for the semester again, pointing out the dates he'll need me to lead class discussions and noting the office hours he set for me on the syllabus. I nod along, looking over at the picture of his wife and son every so often.

If I were in my twenties again, am I right?

After he finishes his little speech, we get up and go over

to the little grey cubicle farm that is the TA pit in the middle of the prof office floor.

"You can take the one you had last semester." He gestures to the familiar blank white desk inside a three sided felt lined cube.

Poppy, the brunette in the cube next to me, sticks her head out and grins when she sees me.

"I won't be in when you host your office hours so feel free to use my office since most of the students will go there looking for you anyways." Miller nods, clapping me on the shoulder. "If you need anything, let me know." Nodding to Poppy, he walks away.

I slide into the rolling chair, dumping my bag on the ground and take my glasses off, pinching the bridge of my nose.

"Back so soon, Adams?" Poppy's giggle has me rolling my eyes behind their lids even as a smile paints my lips.

"Just couldn't stay away, Pops." I spin around, pushing my glasses back on and finding her leaning against the entrance to my cube. "TAing for Miller this time."

Poppy snorts. "Jenkins wasn't enough fun, you decided to up the ante?"

I raise an eyebrow. "Miller can't be worse than Jenkins."

Poppy smirks and looks me up and down. "To be honest, you're probably good. Don't really think you're his type." She pops the p on her last word and giggles again before heading back to her desk next door.

I pull my laptop out, mulling over her words. My phone buzzes and I glance at the text from Mira.

BUG

Hope you had a good first class, Professor Adams!

I chuckle, picking up my phone to text back.

> Not the worst. And that's Dr. Adams to freshman.

I check my other messages and emails, clearing all the red notification bubbles quickly. She's jibed back by the time I finish.

BUG
> you wish

I smile and toss my phone aside, logging into the Coast's student portal and going to my TA tab to add the office hours and discussion days to my school calendar. A niggling feeling in the back of my brain starts to push forward.

If I were in my twenties again, am I right?

Don't really think you're his type.

Something sharp slides down my throat and I grab my phone, opening my messages with Mira again.

> Can you give me Autumn's number? She was in my class this morning and I want to have it in case I need to reach out about anything.

The little grey typing bubble pops up and disappears a couple of times. I rub my forehead, feeling like an idiot. I think this is the first time I've ever directly mentioned Fall to my sister and no way in hell she doesn't ask a thousand questions.

BUG
> I'm not giving you her number just so you can harass her over the phone.

My fingers fly over the screen.

When have I ever harassed her??

As far as I know, the little witch never told Mira about the diner incident. Pretty sure she would have reamed me out and tried to make me apologize the second she found out about it.

My phone starts to vibrate in my hand, Bug written across the top and a picture of Mira flipping me off appearing on the screen.

"The cold shoulder counts as harassment, Ramsey." I can hear the thrum of people talking in the background and then a coffee order shouted above it all.

"Hello to you too, baby sister. Pretty sure ignoring someone is quite literally the legal antithesis to harassment." I hear Mira start to argue and cut in before she can. "And asking for someone's number is a pretty stupid tactic if you're planning to ignore them."

"So, you're done with the blood feud then?"

"So dramatic." I chuckle, staring at the black lines running over the palm of my hand. "She's in my class." I shrug, knowing Mira can't see me. "I just have a question about some wording in the syllabus." I cringe, waiting for Mira to pounce on my obvious lie.

The cacophony of the campus café plays in my ear as Mira hesitates. "Fine, I'll text it to you."

I exhale.

"But if I find out you've said anything even remotely mean to her, I'm coming over and kicking your ass. And Bentley will help." She murmurs, "Axel too probably."

"*Definitely*." Her roommate Janette's voice comes through in the background.

"Noted. I swear, I won't say anything mean." I cross my fingers as I say it, smirking at the stupid tradition.

"Yeah, okay, try that again without crossing your fingers."

I scowl. "You're a pest, bug."

"A great example of what you're not allowed to say to my best friend." Her voice goes sing-songey for a moment. "I'm serious, Ramsey. Don't you dare hurt her."

"I won't," I say, solemnly.

Mira hums in satisfaction and I hear her tapping on her screen.

My phone buzzes a moment later. "Thank you, bug. How's your week starting?"

She sighs and speaks a little quieter. "I submitted the change request form this morning. The woman at the registrar said it would take a couple weeks to change on the student portal, but I am officially a studio art major now."

I smile. Our father convinced her that chemistry was the best major for her financially and she spent all her time last semester miserable and failing. Its lucky dear old Dad seems to be avoiding the house like the plague ever since Mom told us they were getting a divorce at Thanksgiving, especially when I found Mira crying over winter break. I assume it was because of her final grades, both of us already knowing she wasn't going to have a stellar GPA for her first semester. I printed out the change in major form that night and made her fill it out.

"That's great! Why aren't you more excited?" I know telling our father that she's switched majors has been weighing on her, but I already told her I'll be there if she needs backup.

"I am," she insists. A long pause draws on, and I wait for her to get out what she needs to. "Just a little nervous about the semester. I dropped the chem lab and signed up for another gen ed filler, but it was too late to get into any of the requirement courses for studio, so I'm only in the one illustration class."

"Getting your gen eds out of the way is good though. You'll be covered in paint the next three years, no need to rush."

"You're right." Someone calls her name in the background. "Gotta go. Bentley and Axel just showed up. Play nice with Autumn!" She hangs up before I can say anything, and I shake my head at my phone. She spent most of break couped up in the house and miserable, so I'm glad to hear more than melancholy in her voice. I make a mental note to check in on her and Mom more this semester.

Closing my laptop, I pack it into my bag and head out of the building and toward my Jeep. Once inside, I open Mira's text and save Autumn's number under "Fall" in my phone. Waiting for the car to warm up, I type out my first text.

9

AUTUMN

I continue to stare at the text.

After fleeing from Ramsey, I booked it down the stairs before hiding in the very same bathroom I barged into on the way to class. Something about trying to walk all the way back across campus with shaky knees and a thundering pulse didn't seem possible, so I holed up in one of the stalls and tried to re-regulate after that clusterfuck of a morning.

What the fuck was that?

Why did Ramsey help me come down? Why did Ramsey *touch* me? Why the fuck is Ramsey my TA?!

I could feel the adrenaline leaking out of me from the panic attack upstairs. The minute Ramsey started threatening my grades I could see it all playing out, my first step toward freedom crumbling beneath me and my body instantly reacted.

But then he flipped. And I have no idea why.

Letting myself spiral for a good twenty to thirty minutes helped and after I finally felt like I could stand without having to lean on the stall door, I peeked out at the entirely empty front hall before booking it back to West Tower.

Seeing the remnants of his touch etched in ink across my neck scalded. I immediately tried washing it away, the rough towel considerably coarser than Ramsey's fingertips lightly smoothing over my skin. Shaking my head, I rubbed harder, leaving a giant red splotch across the side of my neck. Huffing back into my dorm, I collapsed on my bed face down with a viciously muffled scream.

My next class isn't for another three hours. My plan was to sit here, snuggled under my fluffy olive comforter and have a good cry before doomscrolling the time away. And then I got the text.

I type and delete a few draft texts before sending one.

> Ramsey? How did you even get my number?

The bubbles appear immediately.

UNKNOWN NUMBER

> Not important. Go request a new advisor. Now.

I sit up, wiping my face before replying.

> Go to hell. Now.

The bubbles pop up and disappear four times. I smirk, knowing he's probably trying to find a way to threaten me without incriminating himself over text.

UNKNOWN NUMBER

> I told Mira I would play nice, so I'll give you one more chance. Go request a new advisor. Now please.

I laugh mirthlessly.

> Playing nice? Reread that text. There's still a threat and a demand in there. Try again.

I drop my phone on the bed, suddenly feeling overheated. Getting out from under the comforter, I take off my fuzzy socks and cardigan before picking up my cell again.

UNKNOWN NUMBER

> Just fucking do it, Fall.

Sighing, I type.

> I'm blocking your number.

UNKNOWN NUMBER

> Fine, have it your way.

I stare at the text, suppressing the full body shiver wanting to break out. He's certifiable.

My phone starts to ring, making me jump and I drop it on the bed again. When the song finally registers, a shard of ice slides down my spine, touching each vertebra in its wake.

I sigh, do a full body shake out, sit down on the edge of the bed, and pick up the phone.

"Hi, Mom."

"Guess where your father is right now?"

I drop my head back to stare at the ceiling and hold in

the scream building at the back of my throat. *How would I have any idea?*

"Where?"

"The tennis club! It's the middle of January and he's at a fucking outdoor sports club. Can you believe that?"

I fall back completely, letting my torso lay across the bed while my feet still touch the floor. "No, I can't," I murmur.

Mom huffs on the other end. "Apparently, he's joined some boys club where they all meet up for lunches and smoke cigars like 1920s mobsters. It's ridiculous. I'm losing my mind here, Autumn."

Her voice comes in clear, but I can hear her moving. I picture her pacing the carpet in front of her huge white vanity, probably donning a full face of makeup and perfectly done hair wearing a square neck dress and the pearls Mimi gave her on her wedding day. The only gift from Mimi that Mom hasn't tried to get rid of.

"So, now I'll probably have to miss my massage with Julio, and you know how hard it is to reschedule those." The whine in her voice makes her sound on the verge of tears.

I bite my fist to stop a laugh from escaping.

Mom's tone flips back to the hard edge. "All because your father has decided to have a mid-life crisis and leave me here to take Sage to her rehearsal. Why couldn't he just buy more sports cars or another private jet or something?"

I wish she'd stop calling him that. But one thing Mom loves to do is verbally reinforce the reality she wants to exist. "I don't think going to lunch with friends constitutes a mid-life crisis, Mom."

"Sweetie, you're eighteen. What would you know about a mid-life crisis?"

I close my eyes.

"Oh! Did I tell you about Sage's new classmate yet?"

I grunt out a no and massage the bridge of my nose. Mom prattles on for another fifteen minutes, rarely even needing the minor hums I make to show I'm following along. I get up while she talks, actively losing brain cells as I start to walk around the small, shared dorm room to try to keep my energy from waning.

"Is that Autumn?"

I pause pacing, something sharp sliding through my chest at my little sister's muffled voice.

"Yes, but you can speak to her later."

I roll my eyes. *Or never* is what she really means.

"Hi Autumn!" Sage shouts anyway. "How's college going?"

I can tell Mom doesn't have me on speaker, so the question is moot, but the back of my throat starts to itch and I answer anyways. "It's going good. Classes aren't too bad so far." The lie slides out pathetically, heard by no one, as I listen to Mom's hushed tone telling Sage to go get ready. Sage tries to protest, getting closer at one point, but Mom wins in the end. Sage disappears with a frustrated exhale before Mom's voice returns.

"Sorry about that. She's been so nervous about this show. I think Delphine is putting a lot of pressure on her solo, making all these micro adjustments each time they practice." She continues to complain, and the sharpness slowly makes it to the pit of my stomach. Still, I stand frozen in the middle of the room.

Sage wanted to talk to me. Sage wanted to know how I was doing. Our lack of relationship has always burned, Mom holding the white-hot poker and wielding it whenever we're accidentally close enough to exchange a few words.

Has she always wanted to talk to me as much as I want to talk to her?

Probably not. I doubt she has any burning questions for me the way I have them for her. Well, I only really have one question I've always wanted to ask her.

What's it like when they love you?

Aaron's voice cuts through the background, muffled and low in tone.

"Okay, darling," Mom answers, voice farther away. "I've got to go Autumn. Your father is finally home, and we need to take Sage to ballet. I'll call again soon."

The line goes dead and the sudden silence echoes in the room around me. I stay completely still, just listening to nothing, not allowing myself to move, to process. Lingering in this liminal space where no part of today affects me yet because I haven't let the weight settle in, have yet to give it the space it will take up on my shoulders.

If I don't move, if I stay physically frozen, it hasn't touched me yet.

A key scratches in the door on my left and my breathing stutters and the moment is gone. The weight of that conversation, of Ramsey's invasion, of my crappy morning, drapes down over me and I quickly walk over to my bed before my knees buckle under it all.

"Hey Blossom," Aria says as she walks in, fighting with her key as it sticks in the doorknob like always.

I try to regulate my breathing, remembering Ramsey's hands on my skin, his deep breaths, his close proximity. *Why did he help me?*

Aria wrestles her key free, slamming the door closed and turning toward me. "Has today been the shittiest first day ever or is it just me?" She dumps her bag on the ground, walking over to her bed and flopping down face first.

A stammering laugh escapes me, and some strength

seems to return to my limbs. "Not just you, Bubbles. Literally the worst."

She turns her face to the side. "Right? And it's not even fucking over." She kicks her feet for a moment before pushing up and turning to face me. "I only have like twenty till I have to go to my next class anyways. What made yours suck?"

I lean back against the wall my bed is pushed up against, letting my spine press into my skull as my neck settles against the hard surface. "Where to even begin." I quickly tick off the ways this day has felt so abysmally long, skirting around the Ramsey of it all since I've never told Aria about my strained background with him and don't really want to get into all that right now.

"Oof, yeah, a call from Tina might trump me. I had my first shift at the gym after class this morning and of course spilled my coffee all over my jeans on the way there." She points out a faint dried stain on her upper thigh that trails down toward her calf. "Thank God they're black so I don't think anyone noticed. The shift went totally fine except in the last thirty minutes, this guy comes tearing through the front doors, doesn't even bother swiping his membership card and just storms over to the machines. I didn't know what to do since he didn't respond when I tried to call out to him, so I went to get Harley and turns out it was his best friend." My stomach drops. "Dude seems like a total asshole. Didn't even apologize once we cleared it all up, just sort of dismissed me and I felt like a total idiot, but Harley assured me it was fine and even apologized for him. I don't know what pissed him off so much, but guy needs to learn some manners. He freaked out a few of the people already working out too because like three girls just packed their stuff up and left after that. Why do you look paler than normal?"

I swallow, gut swirling. "I'm why he was so pissed off."

"What?" Aria's face scrunches up.

I sigh, tipping my head back so I'm staring at the ceiling rather than my roommate. "Ramsey is Mira's older brother. I've known him for a few years. We don't really..." I search for the right words to encompass what we don't do. "Get along." My chin tips forward, checking for Aria's reaction and she surprises me, looking scared.

"Autumn, he looked like he wanted to murder the treadmill when he was stabbing the speed button. What happened?"

I sigh, starting from the beginning as I recount how Ramsey and I met, the parking lot food fight, the hostile interactions over the years, all of it leading up to the giant fuck you message from the universe this morning.

"He was probably pissed because I didn't just follow orders and disappear the way he's always wanted me to." I roll my eyes; cheeks flushed from the second wave of anger retelling the whole thing gives me.

"Sounds like you set him off."

I sit up. "You're blaming me?" Guilt seeps in and starts to dissolve in the churning anger.

"No, of course not!" She gets off the bed, going over to her closet as she continues. "It's his issue how he reacts, not yours. Just sounds like he resorts to anger because he doesn't know how to handle you. Probably still attracted to you too which always muddies the waters for men." She starts shuffling through her clothes, looking for something.

"Attracted to me?" I screech. "Yeah, right."

"Blossom," she says, turning to look at me with an expression dripping in *come on*. "You said it yourself. He hit on you the first time you met. And you blew him off. That usually only makes them want you more." She goes back to the closet, pulling out a pair of fleece-lined leggings.

The memory of Ramsey's wolfish grin and laser focus rankles my nerves. "He thought I was cute. I wouldn't say that speaks to an unfulfilled well of attraction. Besides," I say, pulling a pillow into my lap and playing with a thread coming off one of the seams. "I doubt even if he was attracted to me then, he still is now." A blonde ponytail swishes in my memory. "He's got plenty of other attention."

Aria starts changing. "Exactly. You're probably the one that got away in his mind." Hopping on one foot, she laughs. "Or the one he can't have." She shimmies the leggings up and waggles her eyebrows at me.

There's no way Ramsey Adams has ever been interested in me longer than those brief few minutes at Lucy's counter. I've seen him with other girls over the years and it's always the same blueprint. Skinny, smiley, and mean. Three things I don't think I've ever been considered.

I wave the whole thing off deciding to close the lid on all things Ramsey for the day. "You're coming to the game on Friday, right?"

"Yep," Aria says, checking how the leggings fit in the mirror. "Mira said she got us all tickets since she needs us as a buffer in case we see Harley."

Well, that at least covers how I was going to be able to afford a ticket to the game.

Aria whirls around. "Thanks, by the way, for never mentioning that she had a thing with my new boss and it did not end well."

"Sorry." I wince. "I wasn't sure who I was allowed to tell. She told you?"

"Yeah," she walks back over to her bag, rummaging

around in one of the front pockets. "We had psych together this morning and she filled me in on some fuzzy details. Didn't realize he was her brother's best friend but makes sense why things didn't go to well."

"Yeah, I think it's all still too raw for her. She wants to go support Tanner at the Foxes first home game this semester but knows Harley and his little pack of friends will most likely be there too."

Aria nods, standing back up and looking at me. "He will be. He mentioned it to Ramsey when I was at work." She shrugs, shouldering the bag.

Great. So not only has the fucker ruined my favorite class for the semester, but he has all the potential to ruin my Friday night as well. Perfect.

I nod. "See you after class? We can get dinner later?"

"Sounds good!" She swipes her keys up, pocketing them as she walks out.

The door closes behind her, and I check my phone for the time. Hour and a half until class. Falling back with a full body exhale, I settle in again, wondering if I can just nap the rest of the day away.

10

RAMSEY

The arena is electric, half of campus turning up for the Arctic Foxes' first home game of the new year. The energy of the crowd pulses with anticipation as the guys warm up on the ice. My hands are buried in the pockets of my winter coat, face muscles aching as I smile and shuffle my legs to satisfy my nerves.

"How's he looking?" Smith asks, climbing past Harley and I without waiting for us to move our legs out of the way. He's carrying a large bucket of popcorn shaped like a white fox head and spilling handfuls all over our laps before plopping down in the plastic seat to my right.

"Good. He was zoned in all afternoon." Harley reaches across me to snag some popcorn and Smith swats at his hand. "Didn't even hear me when I wished him luck on his way to practice." Royal silently sits down on the other side of Harley, Lev making the poor kid behind him move so he can take up post at his boss's back.

I brush popcorn off my pants as I nod. "You know not to talk to him on game day."

Harley shrugs, fist of popcorn still pressed against his mouth.

"Gwenivere is covering the game," Royal says, and my head whips over to where the raven-haired menace stands, phone up as she shoots some video for the school's website. She's glued to the team, eyes flitting from player to player as she tries to capture the warmup action. A plastic press badge attached to a lanyard around her neck lets her stand in the Foxes' box behind the player's bench. Her icy blue eye stands out stark while the mostly brown one blends in, creating this ethereal effect that I've never been able to get over no matter how many times I've seen her over the last three years.

"Great. Tan's going to love that when he notices." I glance over at him just as he blocks another shot, dropping the puck to the side as he gets ready for the next one.

"Like he doesn't already know." Smith says, shoveling popcorn into his mouth. He grins maniacally at a couple giggling girls down the row from us, probably laughing at him for being the most underdressed one in the arena. He wears ripped black jeans and a tee shirt with only his leather jacket open over it. And yet, he sits wide legged, completely sprawled out and at ease as if the room isn't literally an ice box. The girls blush and he winks, chuckling when they all look away.

I check them out, all three dressed in warm gear, but cute with their rosy cheeks and pink noses.

"Which do you want?" Smith asks between mouthfuls of popcorn.

I shake my head, turning back toward the ice. "I'm good. I'll find someone at the party later."

Smith shrugs, smiling at them again. "More for me then."

"These for us?" Bentley Marshall suddenly blocks my view. A guy in a bright yellow and black Foxes hat with a giant pompom on top grins at his side looking around excitedly. His arm is slung around Mira's roommate Janette who shivers in her head-to-toe puffer jacket and fuzzy blue earmuffs. I piece together that he's Marshall's and Janette's shared boyfriend, Axel. My little sister stands behind her, watching the warmup and pointing Tanner out to a petite goth chick that I remember meeting last semester. She rooms with the redheaded witch, who just so happens to bring up the rear of this merry band of freshman, bright red curls piled on top of her head with some sort of clip. A few errant tendrils slide down over her neck, having escaped their confines and my eyes linger on her pale skin, flashes of my inky fingerprints playing from my memory of earlier this week.

"Yeah," Harley says, snapping me back to the moment. Fall hasn't turned her head this way yet to catch me staring so I start helping to gather the random hats and gloves we left in the row below us to save their seats.

All week I've been trying to come up with a plan to make Fall drop Miller's course, but all I've accomplished is glaring at her while she ignores my presence in each class. That and random flashes of what it felt like to touch her skin in the alcove.

Green fucking light the voice blares in my head and I clench my teeth.

"Thanks," Bentley says, and they all take their seat.

Mira turns around, a few people down and grins up at me. "Thanks for saving them for us, Rams." Her eyes stay locked on my face, not acknowledging the guys on either side of me who also put things down to make sure no one sat in their now occupied seats.

"Yeah, yeah." I pretend to roll my eyes. "You owe us, bug."

She seems to swallow, head nodding shakily as she goes to face forward again and I make a note to talk to her alone later. She's still acting off, and I want to figure out what's been bothering her.

Settling back in, I notice Harley seems stiffer than before, eyes completely focused on the ice.

I lean over. "You good?" I whisper-yell over the buzz of the crowd.

"Mmhmm," he replies, eyes flicking quickly down to the group in front of us.

I look over them again, noting Bentley's proximity. Last semester, Harley seemed to have some issue with the kid, and I never really got the whole story there. "You good with Marshall?"

My best friend looks over at me, eyes searching mine for a moment before he tries to smile. "Of course. Everything's fine, Rams."

Something's off and I know I won't get the answers while we're here. So, I settle in as the players skate off the ice, heading back to the locker room for a minute before the lights dim and they do their pumped up walk out.

The game starts out fierce, two players getting into it within the first five minutes. We're all yelling and standing more than once before the buzzer sounds, no one scoring on us thanks to Tanner's saves. He scuffs his skate against the ice around his crease, creating a little slush pile before gliding off the ice and waddling toward the locker room.

I notice Gwenivere watching him and smile when I see him take off his helmet in the tunnel, pointedly ignoring her existence and staying locked in as he passes her. She's never thrown him off at a game and I admire his ability to tune everything out on game days.

My head involuntarily turns to look at my own personal nuisance. Fall faces forward, hands in her jacket pockets as she listens to something her roommate says beside her. The tips of her ears are pink, and her breath fogs a little when she laughs, eyes crinkling closed.

Bentley and Axel interrupt her laughter, each carrying enough snacks to feed an entire row. She stands, leaning back to let them pass as they give away different things to each person on their way back to their seats in front of me. I lower my feet off the top of Axel's seat, watching as Autumn slides back into her own chair, leaning forward and switching sodas with Mira.

I'm really going to have to spend an entire semester near her.

The boys skate back out on the ice, circling around the half of the ice farther from us this time and I watch as Fall cups her hands around her mouth and screams, "Woooo, let's go 96!"

White hot rage blinds me momentarily and I have to force my eyes to focus on the game as it starts.

What the fuck was that? Get your shit together Adams.

I try to focus on the game, my ears suddenly tuned only to the sound of Fall's shouts and gasps as she reacts to the plays even while my eyes stay fixated on the ice.

We score twice before the period ends and I can't help noticing how Fall's hair bounces around her face when she jumps up and down, celebrating each time.

My jaw hurts from staying clenched so long. In the future, I'm saving one less seat than Mira says she needs and the little witch will just have to find somewhere else to fucking sit that's not anywhere within my fucking eyesight.

"You going to put a stop to this?" Harley hisses, tapping my chest with the back of his hand.

I blanch, thinking he noticed my fixation on the redhead down the row, but his eyes are glued to my sister who is now picking popcorn out of her hair.

The man sitting next to Royal helps fish pieces out with her, leaning forward and brushing it off her shoulders with his other hand. "I really am so sorry. The bag just slipped out of my hands." He chuckles uncomfortably and my sister blushes.

Harley's hand tightens on the arm of his seat.

"It's fine, really," Mira says, smiling to emphasize the point. "No big deal. At least it wasn't nachos."

"Let me make it up to you," the guy says. "I can get you a drink or something."

"Dude!" Harley says, a little too loud since Marshall glances back, eyeing my best friend with a smirk.

"It's fine, bro. He's not hurting her." I glance at the boards, noting that there's still a few minutes until the third period starts.

"He's hitting on her," Harley insists.

I look back, watching my sister take his hand and the two shake for a little longer than necessary.

"Good for her," I say, smiling when she nods and laughs a little at whatever he just said. "She's been down lately. And she can talk to whoever she wants," I remind myself.

Harley's eyes widen to saucers. "Who the hell are you and what have you done with my best friend? Ramsey Adams has never been this cool with anyone coming anywhere near his little sister."

He's not wrong. I've always been fairly overprotective of my sister. The incident from eighth grade speaks to that.

I shake my head, Diane's voice in my head, reminding me to let go of things I can't control, things I can't change.

I should book a session with her soon.

"We talked over the break." The team comes back out, skating around our side of the rink again and I watch Tanner mess with his goal posts, needing to get things just right. "She pointed out that I may have been a bit overbearing in the past and I don't ever want to be another person in her life telling her what to do. She dealt with enough of that with our parents." I look over at Harley, but his eyes are locked on Mira and her exchange with the guy sitting behind her. "I promised to tamp it down going forward. She's an adult. And it's not like she's meeting him at a sleezy bar." I shrug. "If she needs any help, she'll ask."

Harley doesn't look away from them, and I can see the veins in his neck. I glance between him and Mira, suddenly remembering a convo I had with her at the end of last semester.

Harley is not my brother.

I see your crush is still alive and well.

Maybe the crush wasn't as one sided as I originally thought.

I pat Harley on the shoulder, breaking his hard stare and getting to my feet. "I'm going to grab a soda. You want anything?"

"Nah," Harley says, slouching down in his seat and looking thoroughly pissed off.

I shake my head, pushing past him and Royal and cutting through my sister's little flirtation. She smiles at me as I pass and I return it, lowering and raising my eyebrows at her so that her eyes narrow after me.

The second I'm past Mira, I notice Fall's seat is empty. I must have missed when she got up and it looks like wherever she went, she's on her own. I slowly grin, deciding I can take a detour before hitting the concession stand.

Her hair is easy to spot, head bent as she stares at the floor while she walks, heading back toward our seats with a hot dog in her hand. It's almost too easy to walk up and push her into the shadows under the stands, cornering her against the metal beams once we're off the rubber mat path leading out to the concession area.

Her plush lips form an o as she lets out a little gasp, flushed skin already pinkened around her neck and cheeks from the cold.

I lean in, fire erupting in my veins at the sight of her caught off guard. "What are you doing here, Fall?"

Her momentary surprise morphs as the spark I always find in the blue of her eyes takes over and she registers her surroundings. My hands burn, wrapped around the arctic metal rafters on either side of her head, but I refuse to give an inch.

"I got a ticket. What are you doing here? First week of the semester and I've somehow seen you more than all of last term combined." The fire in her eyes lashes out with each word, meeting mine in the space between us.

"I could say the same, Fall. Drop the class and change advisors. Then we won't have to see each other at all for the rest of the year." My grip on the metal tightens.

"This again?" She rolls her eyes, leaning back to put further distance between us. "You know if you stopped cornering me, we'd see a whole hell of a lot less of each other." She studies my face, free hand fisted at her side. "Why are you so intent on the advisor thing?"

His comments about Autumn come rushing back, making me seethe for a moment.

If I were in my twenties again, am I right?

Bile rises in the back of my throat, and I swallow it down. "I'm hoping to intern with Miller again next year," I lie. "Maybe get a job at the clinic. Which means seeing more of *you* if you keep him as your advisor. Something I'm *trying* to avoid."

Her cheeks go from pink to deep scarlet, eyes narrowing to slits. "Well, you can suck it up, Ramsey," she hisses. "I'm not changing anything to suit *your* needs." She shoulders past me, and I drop my arm, letting her go.

"Hey," I yell out once she's a few steps away.

She freezes, looking back through already narrowed eyes.

"Quit cheering for Tanner." My teeth click together as I clamp my mouth shut.

Her forehead wrinkles as she shakes her head and looks at me like I've lost it. Pretty sure I have, but I'm blaming it completely on her presence fucking with me.

Autumn turns and darts away, heading toward our seats again.

I watch her go, counting to ten and then back down to one.

Why the fuck did I say that?

11

AUTUMN

I'm sitting in the Ravens' mansion. AKA Ramsey's house.

Ramsey's little gang of friends all live here too, but I'm only really watching out for him.

Their group has always been the Ravens in my mind ever since I heard the name whispered around the hallways of our high school. Apparently, the name followed them to college though since I've heard everyone on campus covets an invite to their parties, wanting to see inside the legendary Ravens' mansion.

Everyone except me.

The thought prickles against the back of my skull, alarm bells parading around in my brain ever since Mira accepted the afterparty invite Smith extended to celebrate the Foxes' win. Something tells me this party would have happened win or lose, but the 3-0 shutout Tanner pulled off makes things feel more intense, like the air is charged with everyone's collective excitement.

The only other time I've been inside this behemoth of a

Gothic Victorian was to celebrate Mira's birthday last semester. And I at least had Aria with me that time, so we got to hug the walls together.

This time, I've been coerced into not only entering Ramsey's domain, but donning a swimsuit in the middle of January by the pleas of my overly persuasive best friends. I'm in the only one-piece black bathing suit I own and shorts, sitting next to the indoor pool, sweating to death.

This room is essentially a giant sauna, the heated water creating a humid effect that makes the air feel like soup and my curls frizz out. Bentley sits beside me, Janette on his lap as they make out, their boyfriend in the water playing volleyball with some random jocks. Most of the hockey team is here and all the school puck bunnies, red solo cups and tiny bikinis everywhere. The house is also crawling with fully clothed people, music from the main part of the house trickling into the echoey space from the open door leading into the kitchen.

Glancing at my phone, I check to see if I've been here long enough to make an escape. I tried to bow out initially, but Mira begged me to come so she wouldn't be alone in Harley's house and Bentley promised they would both stay by my side.

That was before she ran into Cyrus when we got here though. The nerdy grad student apparently dumped his entire bag of popcorn over her head accidentally and then we got to watch him spend most of the third period awkwardly flirting with her next to Royal. I don't even know if he realized that her ex and her brother sat one seat over, but Harley seemed intently focused on the two of them, constantly fidgeting and glancing over while he pretended to watch the game.

Now, Mira sits on the other side of the pool, smiling up at Cyrus as he talks with his hands. Harley didn't stick around to watch when they showed up, grumbling some excuse and taking off in his truck when we first got here.

I watch her for a bit, smiling when she does and glad that she's starting to move on from last term.

Ramsey was oddly nonchalant about the whole Cyrus thing. He didn't try to interfere like he normally would and I don't think he noticed his best friend's discomfort or at least didn't acknowledge it.

Not that I was paying much attention to Ramsey after he accosted me *again* under the bleachers. The fucking nerve. I don't know what his obsession is with cornering me in dark places, but if he does it again, I'm going to seriously consider throttling him.

My fist tightens around the plastic cup containing whatever concoction Bentley mixed up for me and I force myself to take another sip, letting the burn smooth over some of my flared ire.

Quit cheering for Tanner.

Ramsey's last words to me randomly blare to life in the back of my mind. I have no idea what the fuck that was about. Who else would I cheer for? It's not like I know anyone else on the team. And all of us were cheering for Tanner.

Ramsey probably just said it as another weird command he expects me to blindly follow like dropping Dr. Miller's class or getting a new advisor. As if he suddenly gets to have a say in *my* life all the sudden.

Quit cheering for Tanner.

The words irk me for some reason. I'm sitting here seething, the pool and atmosphere around me utterly blurry as I work myself up thinking about the way he stared at me in class all week, attempting to bore holes in my skull with the intensity. Probably trying to mentally erase me as if my very presence threatens—

"Hey, you're in Dr. Miller's Gen Bio II class, right?"

The voice jerks me out of my tunneling thoughts and I glance up. A scrawny boy in salmon swim trunks with blue whales and a striped tank top stands next to the chair I'm perched on, fingers playing with the lip of his solo cup. His hair clearly used to be straightened and styled but the balmy out-of-season air messed it up and has caused some strands to curl.

I shake my head a little, willing my anger away as I answer him, "Yeah." I glance around for a moment. Everyone else seems absorbed with their own thing, no one paying any attention to the two of us.

"I'm Charlie," the boy says, sitting down on the edge of the unoccupied pool chair right beside mine. His knee presses against my thigh and I grip my drink a little tighter. "We were in Gen Bio I together last year." He laughs lightly when I nod too quickly, eyes widening slightly. "It's okay if you don't remember. I usually sat on my own in the back."

Gen Bio I was a filler class for most freshman looking to fill their science requirement. We were in a giant lecture hall last semester, and I sat near the front, off to the side, on my own. I would swear I've never seen this kid a day in my life. But if he's taking Gen Bio II, he's probably another bio major, might even be on the pre-med track with me as well.

His eyes skate over my face as he takes a swig from his drink, a small smile playing at the corner of his now wet lips. "You picked a lab partner yet?"

I shake my head, chest tightening a little. The air seems to get a little thinner, half of my attention still directed at the point of contact against my thigh.

Is this butterflies or bats? I can't fucking tell.

Charlie leans in, tongue darting out of the corner of his mouth for a moment. "Would you want to—

Ramsey's low tone cuts him off. "What the fuck are you doing here?"

12

RAMSEY

My chest is vibrating with rage. How dare she come here after refusing to get out of my life once again. How dare she talk to *him*. In my fucking house.

I have no idea who this kid is. Couldn't even tell you what he looks like, but the second I walked into the pool house trying to find Mira so we could talk, my eyes immediately found Fall and this random boy sitting a couple inches away, *fucking touching*. In my house.

She sputters as she looks up at me, eyes dim and unfocused. The warm air has created a dewy effect on her skin, and she looks flushed and fucking bitable. Her suit sits low on her chest and my eyes snag on the available skin for a moment.

I try to tamp down the rage roaring through my system, trying to see through the angry mist clouding my eyes, but then this random kid has the audacity to put his hand on her thigh and Diane's voice fades away, replaced by my inner demon's.

Greenlightgreenlightgreenlight.

Fall jumps at the contact and it's the only thing that turns the volume down in my head. She doesn't want him touching her.

"Get out," I order, not sure which of them I'm even issuing the command to.

Fall rises to the bait though, taken aback by my abruptness. "Excuse me?"

I need him to stop touching her. "I said, get out." I lean down, grabbing her arm and pulling her up to her feet. She comes easily enough, and my chest lightens ever so slightly when I note that she doesn't flinch at *my* touch, harsh as it may be.

The move, however, pulls the rando to his feet a second later and causes Marshall to disengage with Janette to our right. He takes one look at me touching Autumn and moves Janette off his lap, standing as well.

"Everything okay?"

"She's fine," I say at the same time as the kid decides to cut in.

"This guy just randomly came over trying to kick us out."

"Not us," I hiss. "Just her." I need her out of here.

Marshall's head whips back and forth, looking at each of us and I take a step back, dragging Fall with me to put some more space between her and this guy.

"Let go of me," she huffs, pushing at my hand. I release her arm and the volume in my head kicks up.

"Come on, man," Bentley says, walking toward us. "She's not bothering anybody. It's a party. Just let her stay."

My lip curls back about to respond, but Fall cuts in, voice dripping with fury. "Fuck off, Ramsey. I am not leaving just because you *demand* it." She fists her hands at her sides, and I see it, the fire that matches mine. She's fucking angry.

Good.

"Yes, you are. It's my house." My voice is rising, her anger calling to my own. I can tell other people are taking notice, probably openly staring but I can't look away, can't stop myself from pushing. "I'm starting a banned list and you're on it." I step closer. "In fact, you're all of it."

I should have seen it coming, should have known I was pushing too far. But one second, we're facing off, an electric current of ire creating a cloud around us and then next I'm tipping backwards, falling straight into the pool.

My head goes under last, but it isn't until I'm submerged that I realize what just happened.

She fucking pushed me.

The second the thought registers, my anger ratchets up another ten degrees, and I kick up, propelling myself to break the surface. Water rivulets rush down my face, clouding my vision as I whip my hair back and take stock.

Bentley and the boy both wear shocked expressions, the room decidedly quieter than when I entered the water. But it's Fall's face that I home in on.

Her eyes are wide, flush face far ruddier than I left it, and her plush mouth is open, jaw hinge cracked as if even she can't believe she just did that. I take one step toward her in the waist deep water, and she bolts, darting around people and toward the glass doors that lead into the backyard. I can feel people staring at me, but my eyes remain on her retreating form as I calmly place my palms on the side of the pool and hoist myself up out of the water.

A gallon of water slides down my body, slapping against the tile as I stand up, but the sound doesn't reach me. A buzzing has filled my ears, and I don't hear or see anyone as I stalk out toward the yard, teeth gnashed together and nostrils flaring.

This time, she pays.

13

AUTUMN

Holy shit, holy shit, holy shit.

I just pushed Ramsey Adams into a fucking pool. In his house. At his party. Into *his* fucking pool. I'm so fucking dead.

My legs carry me through the light layer of snow dusting the Ravens' backyard. Trees line the edges, and I start to head toward them, getting a sense of déjà vu from the first time I ran away from Ramsey's intense stare.

His eyes had been molten when he emerged from the water, their maple syrup depths trying to suck me in just so he could spit me back out. The weight of everyone else's eyes in the room looking at me felt suffocating on top of that, Ramsey's movement bringing that weight down on top of me and making me flee.

A black gazebo appears in a small clearing just beyond the cropping of trees, but the wrought iron structure feels too exposed. I dart to the left instead, needing somewhere to hide, somewhere no one can see me.

Bushes line the edge of the clearing, and I dart between two, sliding to the ground and hurrying to tuck my legs in after me so no part of me is exposed. Branches press into my skin, and my ass and legs freeze on contact to the frozen ground, but I don't care. My racing heart and pounding head demand I stay hidden, needing a moment to let everything crash down around me.

It feels like my lungs are in my throat, their walls trying to expand and getting caught on the edges, only letting in a pinhole of air and never really releasing it. I can hear myself gasping but can't move my limbs, my chest filling with fog.

"Breathe." Ramsey's face fills my vision, lines softer and face determined without any of the harsh rage pulsating around him. "Breathe, Fall."

His hands grip my upper arms, massaging and moving up and down as he acts out deep breaths before me again. My body seems to respond even though my mind hasn't caught up, still struggling to understand why Ramsey isn't murdering me right now.

"Good, just like that." His hands reach mine, gripping and squeezing them before placing them together and rubbing them in his own, creating friction. My eyes leave his face, chin tipping down to watch as he touches me, but he tsks, using one finger to tilt my chin back up. "Gotta keep breathing, Fall. Eyes on me."

My bottom lip drops open, stomach clenching at his words as he goes back to massaging his way back over my arms.

He glances down, hair getting caught on some of the bush and tugging. "Can you feel your legs?"

It takes me a second to register his words and even then, I still respond with, "What?"

"Your legs." He looks up, all wolfish charm replaced by genuine concern. "Do they feel numb anywhere?"

I take a second to assess, wiggling my toes in my

sneakers and registering how cold my thighs are. "Um, no. I don't think so." My voice is raw, coming out rough and unpolished.

Ramsey nods. The bottom of his glasses are fogged and my eyes catch on the detail. "That's good." His hands have stopped on my upper arms, eyes still taking me in. "Do you think you can stand?"

I don't trust my voice, nodding as his fingers press in against my skin a little more firmly. Why does he feel so warm?

He starts to pull me up, my legs unfolding beneath me as we slowly rise out of the bush. Branches and thorns scrape against me as we force our way past them and the second I'm upright I feel myself start to tip backwards.

"Whoa, I got you." Ramsey jolts forward, hands never leaving my skin, but supporting my weight as I find my footing. My knees are like jelly, but I force them to lock up beneath me as the icy temperature starts to penetrate my skin, my lack of clothing suddenly snapping me into the moment.

"I'm good," I whisper, tilting my head down and shuffling my shoulders so that Ramsey lets go. The lack of contact doesn't do anything for the wall of heat that is his presence in front of me, and I realize I can see puffs of steam coming off his wet clothes.

He takes a step back, out of the bush and then makes room for me to step out, hand hovering as if I might tip over at any moment.

"Thanks," I mutter, wrapping my arms around myself. "Where'd you learn how to do that?"

Ramsey shrugs, forcing his hands into the pockets of his soaked jeans and looking away. "Don't remember."

The words taste like a lie, but I don't really feel like

pushing him. Adrenaline is leaking out of my system, leaving me shaky and tired the longer we stand here. "Why did you help me?"

His eyes are back on mine, holding me captive as he stares. "You were hyperventilating when I found you. I couldn't just let you pass out."

"Oh," I whisper, feeling chastised. My eyes dart toward the ground and I start rubbing some warmth into my upper arms, shivering.

Ramsey sighs. "Come on. You're freezing. Let's get inside."

He moves to the side ushering me to go first and I start to follow our footprints past the gazebo and back toward the house. "What about you? You're the one who's going to freeze to death dripping wet out here."

"And who's fault is that?"

I scoff, pulling up short. "You're the one who chased me out here!"

"Yeah, after *you* pushed me into the pool!"

The anger from earlier starts to reemerge, but I stop, stepping back and taking a deep breath. "You're right. I'm sorry."

Ramsey stares at me. "What are you doing?"

I cross my arms, cocking my hip. "Apologizing."

His eyes narrow. "Why?"

I throw my hands up, looking at the starless sky through the trees. "You know what, I don't know. Maybe because this back and forth is fucking pointless and I've already had one panic attack tonight?"

Ramsey studies me, hands at his sides and broad shoulders tense. "You're right. We should probably back off for tonight."

I nod and we start to head toward the house again, breaking through the clearing of trees.

"But tomorrow is completely fair game, Fall."

I let out a frustrated scream, cutting it off short and feeling my face get hot. "I'm tired of fighting with you, Ramsey. Can't we just ignore each other and pretend the other doesn't exist?"

"I'd love to," he says, turning around, the party lights and muffled music stretching out around his shadowy silhouette. "Drop Miller's class and we can do just that."

My blood sings, pressing against every bone in my body as the live wire only Ramsey seems able to light ignites once again. "I am not dropping Miller's class," I hiss. "I am not jeopardizing my degree, and I will not risk graduating on time. I refuse to stay indebted—" I pull up short, spark going out instantly as I realize what I almost just admitted.

You're just going to have to pay it back eventually.

Mom's whispered threat filters through my ears and I can see Ramsey waiting for me to elaborate. When the pregnant moment becomes too much, however, he looks away, running a hand through his damp curls.

"Fine," he says, shoulders bobbing as he sighs. "A truce then." His eyes return to mine and that electric current lights up between us.

"A truce?" I mumble.

He nods. "We pretend the other doesn't exist. I already agreed with Miller that I wouldn't grade anything you hand in. You don't come to office hours when I'm there and we avoid each other like the plague outside of class time. Deal?"

My head spins as he lays out his plan. *Why would he talk to Miller if he planned to intimidate me out of the class?*

He holds out his hand, gesturing for me to shake on it. I

hesitate, waiting for him to say sike, but he merely waits, determination lining every ridge of his body.

With a huff, I latch onto his hand, finding his skin smooth and warm against my own. We shake twice, our hands stopping for a moment before we each let go.

"Raaaaaammmmmmmmssssssseeyyyyy. What arrrre you doin out here with Green?"

A tall figure stumbles into the backyard, slowly making their way into the light spilling outside from the party.

"Harley?" Ramsey calls out.

Harley Sanders laughs breathlessly, eyes glassy and body languid as he continues to walk toward us with a lopsided gait. A bottle hangs from his hand, liquid sloshing as he moves haphazardly.

Ramsey walks forward to meet him, catching his weight with an exhale and letting his best friend lean against him.

"Hi, buddy," he slurs. "I'm in love with your sister."

14

RAMSEY

arley is drunk. Like reeking of booze, giggling, babbling, stumbling drunk. I'm not even sure he knows what he's saying as I help him inside, Fall holding the door for us.

"Thanks," I say, nodding to her as I start to maneuver my best friend through the house. Glancing over, I sigh in relief that Mira and that guy are no longer in here, hoping he took her back to her dorm so she doesn't see or hear the shit Harley is spewing. Most of the people from earlier have cleared out, party obviously winding down. I watch as Autumn heads back over to Bentley, Axel, and Janette, satisfied that I'm not leaving her on her own with the stragglers.

"I fucked up, Ramsey," Harley whines, eyes drooping closed as he weighs heavier against my side, dry clothes starting to soak up the water still clinging to mine. The heat from the pool fogs my glasses and I push us forward on memory, really hoping I'm not walking us toward the water.

"Yeah, I can tell." I get us to the door, grunting a little from the effort. The fact that he owns a gym is obvious considering the two hundred and fifty pounds of muscle he's just laying against me at this point.

"I was seeing Mira last year," he whispers, red eyes tracking my face as the puzzle pieces of my sister's strangeness slowly click together.

"And lemme guess, now you're not?" My voice is deadly low, the kitchen and living room fortunately not too densely packed so he can still hear me even with music playing from somewhere.

"No," he whines, shaking his head against my shoulder. "I fucked it up."

We get to the bottom of the stairs, and I pause, glancing up and trying to figure out how the fuck I'm going to drag him up there. He takes the first step however, foot slamming down shakily before he places his weight on it and pulls himself forward on the banister.

"I lied and told her I slept with someone else."

My feet stop cold, Harley slipping out of my grasp as he continues to pull himself up the stairs, tilted back at a precarious angle.

"Made her feel like a dirty little secret," he mumbles.

I hurry to catch up, keeping my hands on his back and arm as he climbs the stairs in a swaying motion. "When you're sober, I owe you a punch in the face," I grit out.

Harley nods. "You owe me several." He swings his arm out and around my neck, leaning on me once again. "Surprised you're even waiting to be honest." The words run together, getting mushed in his mouth as he mumbles.

"Doesn't really seem like you'd feel it if I did it right now."

Harley nods, head bobbing all over the place. We reach the top of the stairs, and I silently curse the fact that that he took one of the rooms farthest from the stairs.

"I miss her, Rams." His voice shakes and he sniffles. "And she's just out there talking to some guy."

My heart squelches in my chest. I've never seen Harley this cut up over anything. But he definitely hurt Mira and the part of me that is solidly older brother takes some satisfaction in his misery.

I get him into his room, foisting him onto his bed where he sprawls out, eyes already closed. He must have dropped his bottle somewhere along the way, so I start fighting with his boots, not bothering to untie them as I wrestle them off his feet.

"I don't know how to stay away from her," he mutters, and I don't know if he even realizes he said it out loud.

The words trigger the memory of finding Autumn hiding in a bush. Her tracks had been easy enough to follow, my hindbrain seeming to take over and propelling me toward her without a second thought. But the minute I saw her sitting there, scratches on her cheek from the branches and chest stuttering to take in breath, everything inside me instantly melted away and it was like I couldn't help reaching for her, couldn't fight the need to ground her.

"I get it," I whisper, pulling his maroon comforter out from underneath him as he rolls onto his side, settling in against his pillow. "But you're going to have to." I don't know if the words are for him or me, but I tuck him in and start to head out, almost making it to the door.

"What were you doing outside with Autumn? Don't you hate her?"

The words are quiet and garbled but the feel like gunshots in my ears.

"I do hate her," I say, holding on to the frame as I picture her face while we shook hands and solidified our truce.

Harley laughs, eyes still closed and head laying at an

awkward angle. "Sure, that's why you're always baiting her to snap back."

I stare at him, hearing his breathing turn to light snores a minute later. Tapping the doorframe, I give up on going down that rabbit hole and walk out.

My room is diagonal from his, a little bit further down the hallway. I trudge toward it, the weight of this whole fucked up evening settling into my bones. The game, the party, the pool, the woods. My best friend confessing to hurting my little sister. I let it all spin around in my head, ignoring the pull of a dizzy spell and shucking off all my wet clothing. Hopping in the shower, I let my muscles relax as the hot water chases away the chill I've been ignoring.

Autumn in her pretty bathing suit, sitting by the pool with that guy touching her invades my mind. Anger swirls low in my gut as I close my eyes and press my hands against the tiles, letting the water rage against my face and erase the image. My head pounds and I get out, toweling off and grabbing some Advil out of the medicine cabinet. Staring at myself in the mirror, I note scratches and red marks from diving into a fucking bush for the girl I said I hate.

Wrapping the towel around my hips, I walk out, debating just falling straight into bed or getting some homework done before class tomorrow.

"There you are."

I jump a foot in the air, gripping my towel a little tighter. People have got to stop sneaking up on me today.

Poppy sits perched on my bed, hands on her bare thighs in only a string bikini.

"I saw you come up here, but you weren't here when I came in."

"Right," I walk over to my desk and lean back against it,

keeping one hand on my towel. "And you thought you'd just wait here until I showed up?"

She shrugs one shoulder, a sly smile slanting the bottom half of her face. "Figured you'd end up here eventually." She runs her hand over my comforter, leaning back and stretching out a bit.

The view does little for me and I chalk it up to being tired. I've had a shitty day, I might as well see where this goes. Getting off will probably help me sleep at the very least.

"Take your top off." I settle in against the desk, folding my hands against my chest and letting the towel hang off my hips.

Poppy beams, reaching back and pushing her tits out as she unties the back of her bikini string. They're viridian. The color would look amazing against Fall's skin.

I jolt, rearing back. *What the fuck?*

Poppy's uncovered chest lays before me and I can't banish the view of Autumn, flushed and confused, staring up at me from the pool chair an hour ago.

I take off my glasses, pinching the bridge of my nose. "Sorry," I mutter. "I think I'm getting a migraine." I put the glasses back on. "Can we raincheck?"

Poppy's eyes widen as she looks around, pulling her bikini top back up. "Sure, Ramsey." She rolls her eyes. Once everything's in place she stands up, sauntering over to the door. "Hit me up when you're *feeling better*." Another eye roll and I already know she's about to go rage on me to all of her friends. I walk over and shut my door, locking it for good measure.

The pain in my temples throbs and I drop the towel entirely, crawling into bed and shutting off my bedside light.

Today fucking sucked and the pièce de résistance seems

to be my muddled thoughts conjuring the little witch when I'm offered sex on a platter. I groan into my pillow, squeezing my eyes shut and remembering the view of Autumn's tits in her one piece.

She never really shows that much skin, usually wearing nondescript tees or baggy sweaters. I don't think I've ever even seen her in a bathing suit before.

My dick stirs and I sit up, shaking my head.

No fucking way I'm getting hard thinking about her. Absolutely not.

Pulling open my bedside drawer, I take out a pre-roll and my lighter, shuffling so that I'm propped up against the headboard and lighting the joint as I inhale. The vibrant ember glows as I toke and let the spiced smoke settle into my lungs.

I rarely *need* to use marijuana anymore. Diane helped me get over using it as a cope when I got to college, finally far enough away from dear old Dad to start unpacking why I needed to be high every time I got home.

But every now and then I like to shut my brain off. And this is definitely one of those nights.

That's why you're always baiting her to snap back.

Do I do that? I look back at all my interactions with Fall over the last week, analyzing why I felt the need to hunt her down and corner her. The joint slowly disappears as I come to the conclusion that I just need to. Something about her provokes me.

It's the same realization I had three years ago in Lucy's parking lot. She just makes me see flashing green lights, no matter how many times I tell myself *red light*.

She gets under my skin. Pisses me off. But there's nothing else there. Just boiling anger deep in my stomach.

I grit my teeth, holding the last remnants of my joint and

feeling the fuzzy tug of a dreamless sleep pulling me under. Stubbing out on the bedside table, I slide down, rolling onto my stomach and staring out the window on my left at the starless sky.

"There's nothing else there," I repeat aloud, willing it into existence.

15

RAMSEY

arley dodges my fist, ducking out of the way just in time to not get slammed in the nose yet again.

"We said no face," he grumbles for the fifth or sixth time.

I slam my other fist into his gut making him double over and groan. "You slept with my sister, Harls. Everything's fair game in this one." I shrug my shoulders and back away as he raises one hand up, warding me off.

"Okay, fair enough." Coughing a bit, he nods, still bent over and breathing deep. We've been at this for at least an hour, and it's definitely helped ease the simmering anger I woke up with. Remembering everything Harley confessed alongside everything that happened with the little witch last night, I couldn't help waking my best friend up for a little early morning sparring session. His gym is still closed, the early morning light just starting to peak through the wall of windows up front.

"Can we take a water break? I promise you can wail on me some more, I just need a minute." Harley stands back up, but his face is pale, shoulders hunched.

I wave him off, stomach curdling a bit. "We're good for today." I start unwrapping my hands, ignoring the itch in my arms to keep hitting something. Maybe I should call Diane for a session later.

"Just today?" Harley says, chewing on the inside of his cheek. "How many times do you plan to pummel me before I'm forgiven?"

I huff, tossing one hand wrap to the mat we pulled out onto the main floor. "We're good, man," I say, meaning it. "Besides I'm not the Adams you need to make things up to from what you told me."

Harley groans, rubbing the back of his neck.

I get the second hand wrap off, flexing my fingers and testing for any bad aches. I really want to go another few rounds on the punching bag in the back, this need for violence truly having nothing to do with my best friend and my little sister anymore. This leftover buzz belongs to a little witch who can't seem to stop invading my brain.

Harley walks over to grab a couple water bottles from the fridge behind his front desk and I follow, forcing my demon back into his cage. Tossing me one, Harley guzzles half of his, not even bothering with his hand wraps yet.

I play with the cap of mine, cracking the seal, but not fully twisting it off just yet. "You ever picture the wrong person in bed?"

Harley freezes, bottle still poised against his lips. Tipping it down, he looks at me with furrowed brows. "You mean like accidentally thinking about grandma or some shit?"

I roll my eyes. "No, not like that. Like have you ever thought of someone else when you're with a girl?"

"No," Harley says with a disbelieving chuckle. "If I'm

picturing someone else, then the girl who's there is the wrong person."

I open my bottle and hum, taking a sip and looking over the still gym floor. I can feel Harley studying me, but I keep my gaze locked away from him.

"I never pictured anyone else when I was with Mira, if that's what you're asking."

I choke on my water, head whipping back toward him. "Glad to hear it, but I so don't want to hear about you with Mira anymore dude."

Harley smirks before his eyes dull a little and he shakes his head. "Sorry. What's with the hypothetical then?"

I shrug, twisting the bottle cap again. "No reason. Just had a chance to get some last night and then had a weird thought that made me turn the whole thing down." I shrug again.

"A weird thought about someone else?" Harley hedges.

I nod, sipping the water to try to halt the conversation there.

But Harley never lets me get away with hiding anything. "A weird thought about Autumn?" he muses.

I swallow, eyes narrowing. "Why would you think it was about her?"

Harley just chuckles, shaking his head. "Maybe because she's the last person I saw you with last night?" His smile turns into a mocking smirk. "Or maybe because she's the only one you would consider the 'wrong person' while actively thinking about her during sex."

I stand up a little straighter. "It wasn't during sex." I roll my shoulders, the itchy buzz intensifying as Harley hits the nail on the fucking head. "We called a truce last night and I think it's messing with my head."

Harley flat out laughs, clutching his stomach as he does so. I consider punching him again.

"Yeah, good luck with that," he says, shoulders still shaking silently.

"Good luck with what?"

"A truce? Between you and Autumn Green?" He folds his arms over his chest. "Won't last a day."

I flex my hands, crushing the water bottle a bit in my fist. "We ignored each other for three whole years. I'm pretty sure we can handle a semester together." I don't know where all this bluster is coming from considering I've been the one gunning for the best way to make her disappear since Monday.

Harley crosses his arms over his chest. "You *avoided* each other for three whole years. Anytime she was in the vicinity, one of you either ran or you'd both get into it, but neither of you has ever ignored the other's existence."

My brain scrambles, pulling up every time I was forced to be around Fall and realizing we did always seem to trade blows no matter how much I tried to tune her out. Even the car ride back to the Coast, we couldn't avoid an argument.

"If you're already thinking about her when you're with another girl, I doubt this little truce is going to do much."

Fuck.

Harley's hand grips my shoulder, squeezing my trap to make me hone in. "Have you thought about her when you're with someone else before?"

"No. I've never thought of her that way full stop." Well, except for the first time. The way she caught my attention in the diner floods my system.

Harley squeezes my shoulder once more before releasing me. "You've never been this locked on to anyone for this long before." He shrugs. "Bound to mess with your head."

I scoff. "What about Lindsey? I dated her for almost two years." And regretted 75% of them.

Harley shakes his head. "You've never been locked on to any of the girls you've dated, Rams. Lindsey especially. All of your past relationships were always you trying to force a square peg into a round hole."

I rear back. "What's that supposed to mean?"

He shrugs, starting to unwrap his hands as he speaks. "You've always just filled time with the girls you've dated. Seemed more out of boredom than anything else. It's never really looked like you cared about any of them really, usually getting over your breakups in less than a day."

I consider his words, finishing the water bottle and tossing it in the recycling bin. "Autumn just pisses me off. That's why I lock in. You know anger is my go-to."

Harley laughs. "Yeah, I'm aware." He looks up, hand still unwinding the red tape from his skin. "But that's not all it is. You're attracted to her, dude. Probably because she never lets you get away with shit. Hasn't since the moment you met." He shrugs. "Just accept it."

I bark out a laugh, shaking my head. "Yeah, right. I *hate* her, remember?"

Harley shrugs. "Sure." He starts heading to his office, turning on some more of the overhead lights as he goes. "And do you always picture the girl you *hate* when you're fucking someone else?"

I gnash my teeth together, picturing the little witch again and cursing under my breath.

16

RAMSEY

It's been almost two weeks since our truce, since I promised to ignore Fall's existence. And yet I can't seem to stop looking at her, staring at her, watching her every time we're in the science center together. Harley's words play on a constant loop in my head.

You're attracted to her, dude. Probably because she never lets you get away with shit. Hasn't since the moment you met. Just accept it.

Only I can't. This can't actually be happening. I can't be attracted to her.

I always thought she just triggered my anger, triggered the part of me that wanted to give in to the chaos.

But now I'm not sure.

Was I *attracted* to her this whole time?

Sure, she provokes me. But that's the reason I always notice when she's nearby. That's the reason I feel the need to instigate shit with her. That's why she tends to cloud my vision when we get into it.

Not. Because. I. Want. Her.

Period.

Double fucking period.

My jaw hurts from how much I'm clenching it.

Miller asks the class a question and nearly every hand goes up, including Fall's. I watch her, eagerly tracking his movement as he looks over the class before calling on her.

"The rise of MRSA is an example of artificial selection. Humans synthesize methicillin and create environments in which bacteria frequently come into contact with methicillin."

"Correct, Ms. Green."

My lips twitch, pen still frozen over the lab I'm grading as I watch her blush and sit up a little straighter.

Shaking my head, I drop my smile and gaze back down.

Fuck.

Focusing fiercely on grading once again, I have to actively loosen my grip, not wanting a repeat of the ink incident from last week.

I can't see the paper in front of me.

I'm fucking attracted to her.

Just accept it.

Harley's voice floats in and I push it to the fucking side.

No. I thought she was cute one fucking time. That's it.

I slash a paragraph in the student's lab, writing a hasty "unnecessary" in the margins as my molars grind together. Anger boils up inside me, but this time the flames are directed *at* me. I dutifully ignore everything, willing myself to see the words on the page and ignoring the whole of class, including the two more times Fall gets called on.

We have a truce. We made a pact. Ignore each other till the end of the year. That's exactly what I am going to do.

Everyone is packing up, Miller having laid out what is going to be covered in class on Wednesday, when I finally allow myself to look up.

My eyes immediately find curly auburn hair in a mauve sweater.

Clenching my hand, I swiftly stand and start loading the barely graded labs into my bag, shoving them a little too forcefully.

"Autumn?" Miller calls out, making me stall and twisting my gut. "Can you stay for a minute?"

I look up, finding a handful of students still milling around, Autumn having just flipped the top of her messenger bag over as she smiles and nods.

"Sure." She shoulders the bag and walks up to the front, Miller standing beside the desk while I seemingly remain frozen in place.

"Excellent work today, Autumn. That MRSA example wasn't in the text."

Fall bounces on the balls of her feet. "Thank you, professor. I did some supplementary research after reading the chapter for this week. It was really fascinating."

I snort, and they both glance over at me. Fall's smile dims, but she turns it back up when Miller faces her again. He leans back on the desk and folds his arms over his chest.

I crush some of the papers as I shove them deep in my bag.

"I'm glad you're enjoying it so far. It's definitely showing in your participation in class."

"Got one wrong though," I mutter, looking down as I continue to slowly pack away my stuff and stall. The words leave my mouth unbidden, and I look up, finding both of them looking at me again, Miller with a muddled expression and Fall with a reddening face.

"Right, well." Miller turns back around, scooting over a little to block Fall from my view.

I bite my cheek to rein in the active volcano that rouses.

"You're still learning, of course. Have you put any thought into the internship at my clinic that we talked about last term?"

I pull my bag over my shoulder, drawing up to watch Fall answer over Miller's shoulder.

"Yes," she says, glancing back at me with irritation still before continuing. "I'm absolutely planning to apply."

She's planning to fucking *what*?

"Good! You'll definitely be in the final running. Helps when the one hiring for it is your advisor." He chuckles conspiratorially and leans toward her as she nods.

My eyes narrow. "Don't you have another class you need to get to, F—Autumn?"

Fall's steely blue eyes meet mine once again and her jaw flexes. "No, Ramsey. I don't." Disdain drips from every syllable as she stares me down, probably picturing my head on a spike.

The look makes my dick start to harden.

Fuck.

"That's alright," Miller says, standing up and adjusting his glasses. "We should probably all get going. There's another class here in ten minutes." He starts to pack up his stuff off the teaching podium he never uses, and Autumn and I continue our stare down, neither one backing off first.

"Sounds good," Autumn finally says, adjusting the strap of her bag while still glaring at me before turning another beaming smile toward Miller. "See you on Wednesday, Dr. Miller."

He nods as she walks out, turning toward me once she's gone. "What was that about? You and her get into a fight over the weekend?"

I sigh, removing my glasses and pinching my nose for a second. "No, just having an off day. I think I'm getting a headache." My temples throb as I try to will my semi away and just keep seeing Fall's narrowed eyes leveled at me. "Do you mind running office hours today so I can head home for a bit before my class later?"

Miller nods. "Sure, son."

The endearment pokes at my gut. He's used it a couple times, merely emphasizing the age difference between us, but also just tapping into my own personal shit.

"Take the day and get some rest." He smiles a second later. "Who knows? Maybe I'll get lucky, and Ms. Green will need some help today." He winks and my stomach plummets.

Before I can say anything, he's out the door, leaving me silently churning in the now vacant classroom. His words swirl around in my brain, mixing with the image of Fall smiling so goddam brightly at him.

Fuck this.

My legs carry me without much provocation, brain catching up once I'm already halfway across campus. Once I hone in on where I'm going though, I don't let up.

Just accept it.

Fine, I argue with the voice in my head. *Watch me fucking accept it.*

I walk up to West Tower dorms, finding the front door already propped open and saving me from having to stop and wait for someone with an access card to follow in.

Dorm 315.

I remember Mira mentioning it on their first move-in day five months ago.

I decide not to analyze why I memorized it.

Taking the stairs, I bound up toward Fall's suite, letting my boiling rage take over with each step.

Smiles. Internships. Eyes.

All of it jumbles together in my brain, culminating in the image of Miller's sickening wink. Harley was right. This truce is fucking over.

The numbers appear on an overly decorated door, and I knock without hesitating, tapping my foot while I wait.

The door opens and I push forward, making Fall step back so I don't crowd her.

"What are you doing here?"

I shut the door behind me without turning away from her. "You're switching advisors." Once we're alone, my rage seems to simmer, eyes roving around the...room. She has a dorm *room*. One side is covered in black, from duvet to posters to an open closet with clothes spilling out. The other is clearly Fall's, plush green covering her raised twin bed and minimal décor over the tiny space. Her closet is closed, and her desk is the only place that appears lived in, textbooks scattered around her open laptop.

She has a dorm room.

Why doesn't she have a suite? It's not like her family can't afford it.

My thoughts are cut off when Autumn steps into my space, arms crossed, and teeth bared. "What happened to 'we avoid each other like the plague,' huh? Thought we had a truce?"

I stare down at her, feeling that magnetic cloud of fury build up between us again.

It makes me pause for once.

Has this always been so *hot*?

I shut that thought down immediately.

"That was before Miller made one too many creepy comments about you. You're. Switching. Advisors. Now."

"What the fuck are you talking about?"

"Dr. Sleeze! The one who's more than twice your age.

The one who can't stop doting on you and making gross insinuations." I step forward, causing her to fall back. I pause. I think that might be the first time she's ever backed down so quickly. My muscles lock in place, stomach sinking as guilt trickles down my spine. Did I scare her?

Taking a deep breath and banishing the memory of Mira's fourteen-year-old face in the doorway, I continue, adopting a calmer tone. "He made a comment about you after the first class. I thought it was a one off, but he did it again today. And one of the other TA's made it seem like he's a little pervy with his female students. You need to distance yourself from him, now."

Autumn gawks at me, eyes wide and mouth propped open, before she tips her head back and laughs. My locked pattern breaks, shoulders falling as I watch her, my anger response returning in no time.

She reaches up to comically brush a tear from her eye. "Okay, now I know you're crazy. Dr. Miller has never given me a 'pervy' vibe." She holds up her fingers, air quoting in my face. With another laugh, she turns away, heading over toward her desk and dismissing me completely. "That is the lamest excuse to get me out yet. As if Dr. Miller, *married* Dr. Miller, would be interested in *me*."

I clench my teeth, biting back the sting of her dismissal. She's not taking this seriously. "So what? You think he offered you, a second semester freshman, an opportunity to work with him at his clinic because you're what? *Special*?"

I can hear her teeth click together as she balls her fists and whips her head around to glare. "He doesn't give me special attention, Ramsey. You're fucking delusional. I mean, come on. Look at me." She runs a hand down, gesturing the length of her body.

"I am," I snap, following her gesture with my eyes.

Something in my chest tightens and I smile, stepping toward her predatorily. "Do you think you're unattractive, Fall?" Past baggy sweatshirts and fidgety movements start to drop into place.

"What?" she squeaks, turning around fully and swallowing harshly. "No—I mean...well." She huffs, the air hitting my face as I stop directly in front of her. "I just meant, guys don't notice me that way." Her eyes trace up from my chest, meeting my gaze with a defiant stare of her own. "Especially not married guys."

I chuckle mirthlessly, palms itching as my dick twitches. Something about her getting flustered turns me on and I'm too far gone in this rage induced haze to consider any of the words spilling out of my mouth. "Oh, Fall," I mock. "You think guys don't notice you? That kid by *my* pool sure seemed to notice you."

Autumn pulls up short, bottom lip falling open. "What kind of tactic is this?" She backs up another inch, meeting the wall behind her.

I press in. "What do you mean?"

She pokes a finger into my chest, seeming determined to maintain some semblance of space between us. "You usually caution on the side of mean. But now you're coming off more *jealous*?" The word hisses out of her mouth, and I find I like the lash of it.

I laugh, the rancorous sound harsh in the space between us. I lean in a little further, letting my next words coast out cruelly. "You wish, Fall."

Her back jerks straight and her eyes narrow into slits. "Fuck off, Ramsey. We both know you've made comments about my weight before, so I don't see how—

That pulls me up short. "When?" I demand.

"W-what?"

My hands cage her in, pressing against the wall on either side of her head. "When have I *ever* made a comment about your weight?"

Her teeth set and she digs her finger a little further into my chest. An angry little furrow appears in her forehead as her eyebrows duck to shadow her lashes, the effect stirring my libido more than it should.

"*You look fuller,*" she hisses, lips puckering as the words slice out of her mouth. "That's what you said to me. After the summer I spent at my grandmother's."

I remember that summer. It was remarkably dull and hot, Mira and Bentley always underfoot at the house, wanting a ride to one place or another whenever Mom was out.

I remember those words too. The doorbell rang when I was fairly high, heading to the kitchen for a snack. Autumn stood there, sun radiating in behind her, shoulders relaxed and eyes shinier. I remember taking a full moment to look at her, something I rarely allowed myself since it usually resulted in a glaring match or some sort of argument. But she'd caught me off guard, appearing without warning and sneaking right past my defenses.

Something was different about her that day. I remember thinking maybe she got taller or did something new with her hair? She just seemed...more.

And with that thought, I remember words slipping out of my mouth. I can't even remember what they were. But Fall apparently does.

She's still talking in front of me. "Not to mention, the first time we met, and you let your girlfriend call me—

"That wasn't about your weight," I say cutting her off. Looks like I'll need to correct her on a few things.

"What?" She removes her finger from my chest, the spot branded beneath my shirt.

"The fuller comment. That wasn't about your weight. You looked…" I glance over her entire face, searching for the right way to explain that moment. "More you," I say lamely.

Autumn blanches, face flushing and eyes widening as she stares up at me, floored for the third time since I walked in here. "Yeah, right," she muses and I shrug.

"Believe whatever you want, Fall." My chest touches hers and our breath mingles in the space between us, air pulsating against my skin.

She studies me closely, voice coming out a little breathless. "You hate me, remember?"

An idea rings through my mind instantly. An idea where I get to hate her and have her all at once. I grin slowly, showing teeth. "I've heard hate fucking is one of the best releases. Ever tried it?"

17

AUTUMN

Ramsey Adams just asked me if I've ever *hate fucked* anyone.

Today is officially the weirdest day.

I'm backed into the wall of my dorm, completely surrounded by him and it feels like my body is on fire. Heat rushes everywhere, sliding around in my body and pressing against every inch of my skin. My nipples feel like they're being rubbed raw in my bra, achy and peaked. Ramsey just continues to loom over me, grinning as he presses even closer, the heat from his body meeting mine in the most delicious way.

What the fuck is happening?

His eyes light up a moment later, taking my panicked silence as an answer. "Wait, have you had sex, Fall?"

I swallow, taking a second to see if my sanity will return before I slowly nod my head up and down once.

His eyes narrow for a second before he leans in and whispers against my temple. "Have you had good sex, Fall?"

I close my eyes, mortification melting into my desire. I

shake my head, hands coming up to press against his chest so that he can't feel my heart trying to escape mine.

"Noted," is all he says. And then his lips leave my skin.

My eyes pop open and I tilt my head back to look him in the eye. Confusion swirls into the potent mixture coursing through my blood and I dig my fingers a little into his shirt.

He chuckles, reading me. "We'll have to go a little slower then." He quickly pecks me on the lips, heat zinging through me from the quick kiss. I unwillingly lean forward to chase after him when he pulls away too fast.

Ramsey fucking Adams just kissed me. My brain completely shuts down, rebooting as I try to recover from shock.

My mental reload allows him to capture both of my wrists, pulling them up over my head and pinning them there with one hand. I instantly try to tug them free, and he chuckles.

"Always fighting me." He tilts his head before leaning in and letting his lips trail over the side of my neck. At the same time, he steps forward, lining our bodies up completely. His warmth seeps into me first before I become aware of how hard he is against the side of my hip. Goosebumps erupt over every inch of skin he leaves in his wake and my eyes flutter shut, jaw dropping.

His free hand lands on my waist, bunching my shirt up in his grasp. "You've always been able to drive me to the brink." He rubs himself against me. "In more than one way, it turns out."

I gulp in air, sagging into the wall as much as I can in his grip. He's hard. Distractingly so.

Ramsey Adams is turned on by me. *Me.*

Something akin to power rushes through my veins, making me lightheaded. He may have me pinned against the wall but I'm the one driving him crazy, I'm the one he apparently notices, I'm the one who breaks his ironclad control.

Ramsey pulls his head back with a groan and my eyes pop open to watch him. He pants, forehead pressed against mine as his hand finally reaches the hem of my shirt. I can feel the open air on a sliver of my skin and that exposure makes my breath catch in my chest.

"Fuck, you're soft." His hand moves to my skin, scaldingly hot as he slides it over my waist and around my back. "So soft."

Every nerve in my body spasms at his touch, causing me to buck in his grasp once again.

Ramsey chuckles. "Easy, Fall. We're going slow, remember?"

A whine slithers out of my throat, unprovoked and uncontained. It makes him smile, eyes lighting up the same way they do when I verbally spar with him.

"Mmmmm," he hums. "I like you impatient." His hand on my back pulls me forward while his grip around my wrists keeps me pinned. The move causes my lower half to tangle with his, legs parting to allow for one of his to slide in between.

Holy shit.

He brings his leg up, grinding the seam of my pants against my clit in a very practiced move. The sensation ripples through me, eyes glued to his as he watches me react, twitching against his hold.

"Fuck, Ramsey."

He leans down, slowly closing the gap between us before his lips capture mine, teeth quickly following to nip my bottom lip and make me gasp. He immediately advances, tongue sweeping into my open mouth and lavishing against my own. I counter, our usually battle of wills playing out as he druggingly kisses me and I kiss him right back.

He groans into my mouth, knee pressing harder into my core as he rubs himself against me.

"Fuck," he says, pulling back. "Can I taste you?"

My brain is completely malfunctioning, synapses melting down after that kiss. "What?" I manage to respond, a little dazed.

His glasses are fogged, a little crooked and his mouth looks pinker, but I register what he just asked and freeze. No one's ever done that to me before. Of the two guys I've ever had sex with, neither seemed all that invested in my side of things, barely interested to begin with.

"Um," I stutter.

And of course, Ramsey catches on. "First time?" His tone is huskier, lower and coarse as the brown in his eyes seems to get swallowed by the black of his pupil. He leans in nipping at the edge of my jaw and forcing me to tilt my head back and give him more access.

What the fuck is happening?

"Has nobody ever gone down on you?" His hand flexes over my wrist at the words and I feel everything in my lower body contract.

"No," I mutter. I can't seem to lie to this man, even as telling him that causes poignant shame to wash over me.

He kisses the side of my neck, hand on my lower back sliding toward my waist once again.

"Want to see what it's like?" he whispers roughly in my ear, lips pressing against the shell.

I let my eyes fall closed, unable to look at this man I fucking hate as I slowly nod my head. He nips the shell of my ear and then he's gone, heat and presence disappearing from in front of me.

My arms stay frozen above my head as I rip my eyes open, finding him kneeling before me, his wolfish grin firmly in place. He pops the button on my jeans and slowly lowers the zipper.

"You're going to love this," Ramsey states, hands gliding up the outer sides of my thighs until they meet the banded edge of my pants. He pauses, eyes on me as I slowly lower my arms, pressing my palms against the wall on either side of me. I nod, biting my lip as I watch him slowly peel the denim down, tugging them from my ankles and tossing them behind him without looking back.

God this angle must be awful, and I don't even remember what underwear I put on this morning and—

Ramsey leans forward and kisses my skin, right above the elastic of my underwear, on the underside of my belly.

"God, you smell amazing." He inhales deep, and scatters my thoughts, hands caressing the backs of my thighs. His teeth snag the top of my underwear, pulling the elastic back and releasing so that it snaps against my skin and makes me jolt in place.

A small cry leaves my throat from the shock of it and the way the sting melts in past my skin, nestling against something pleasant inside me.

Ramsey grins, eyes alight as he gauges my reaction. "Oh, we're going to have fun with that." Another kiss, this time against my hip as he brings his hands to either side of my underwear, fingers curling in to start slowly pulling them down. "Next time. This time, we're going *slow*."

My lungs contract, walls touching each other as I exhale sharply. Next time. Implying there will be more times. My thoughts should be racing with the implications of that implication, but every single one of my cells is focused on

Ramsey's breath fanning across the exposed skin at the apex of my thighs.

I haven't shaved and Ramsey doesn't seem to care. He runs his nose across my skin, tracing it from hip to hip as his hands curl to palm both of my inner thighs and spread my legs a little wider.

"Perfect," he murmurs, and the word seems to embed itself into the fissure in my chest.

I'm breathless, panting above him, nails scraping against the concrete wall of my dorm room as his tongue drags a cool path along my flesh. He seems to be enraptured in it, eyes closing as he ducks down further, licking along my seam and making me gasp once more.

A guttural groan emits from his throat before he tips his chin forward and kisses me fully. He moans against my clit, and the vibration makes my knees buckle. His hands slide up, supporting me right underneath my ass as much as they're also helping to lock him in place, giving him leverage to hold me against him.

His tongue traces my entrance, making me squirm in his grip. His eyes open and he stares up at me, wedging it just a little inside. One of my hands comes off the wall, tangling in his curls and tugging so he can feel the same pull he's dragging out of me. His fingers press in against my flesh, and his lips move up, wrapping around my clit and sucking.

My eyes roll back in my head as I buck against his face, feeling the edge of my release right there. His lips let go, tongue massaging me as he backs off, the edge slipping away. My ass touches the cold wall, pressing his hands against it as well, and I feel more than hear him chuckle. His eyes narrow and he nips me, making me pull his hair a little more.

"Just make me come, Ramsey."

Something about my winded words or maybe the use of his name seems to spring him on, and he once again lavishes me with his tongue, sucking and nipping between long laps. The sound is absolutely obscene, my wetness coating my thighs as much as his mouth and chin. He brings me to the edge once more before backing off, making a curse rumble out as I glare down at him and grab another fistful of hair.

"This doesn't count as slow," I say between harsh breaths.

The challenge returns to his eyes, and I shake my head, silently begging him not to do it again.

He does though, quickly working me up so that I'm trembling and mostly leaning against the wall rather than holding myself up.

"*Please*, Ramsey," I whisper.

And that must be the magic word.

Ramsey doesn't hold back this time, tongue, teeth, and lips playing me to a T as he quickly sets me back up on the edge of my release. With a cocky wink, he uses his peaked tongue to flick over my clit, humming at the same time and I detonate. Words definitely fly out of my mouth, but I have no idea what they are as I close my eyes and experience the harshest orgasm I've ever had. It seems to rip from inside me, breaking like a tidal wave and washing everything else out.

When I come to a moment later, my ears are ringing, and my underwear is back on. Ramsey stands before me again, shoulders rising and falling with the crests of his breath. His hands rest against the wall on either side of me again, and he seems to be watching me, glasses smudged and lips puffy.

"It's been a few years since someone made me come in my pants."

The words filter in slowly at first, then all at once, meaning hitting a second later. I glance down, noticing a decidedly large wet spot on the front of his jeans.

My mouth gapes open as my eyes fly back up, and he chuckles.

"You taste good." He licks his lips, chin shining with the evidence of me. "Wanna try?"

Word formation seems to have left me as I nod, unable to do anything more.

Ramsey leans forward, tongue coated in me invading my mouth and something about the musky sweetness makes me groan, setting him off as his hand comes up to grip my jaw and deepen the kiss. I don't know how long it lasts but it feels like an hour before he finally pulls away, hand keeping me in place when I try to chase him again.

"So greedy," he chuckles, sharing my air. His eyes rove over my face and I try to imagine what he sees. "I have to go," he whispers. "But I'm curious, Fall." He leans in, lips finding my ear once more. "What do you think of hate fucking *now*?"

18

AUTUMN

*W*hat *do you think of hate fucking now?*
The words bang around in my brain as I wait impatiently in front of the elevator. My phone is clutched in my hand, anxiously waiting for a response to my panicked message from my best friend.

Where are you???

The second my door closed after Ramsey left; I started to panic.

I just sort of had sex with my best friend's brother.

I just definitely had sex with my best friend's brother. Who I *hate*. Who I *definitely* hate.

Not really thinking straight, I pulled my leggings back on and ran out of my dorm, taking the elevator up to the sixth floor and banging on Mira and Janette's door a little too loudly. After a minute of standing there, glancing up and down the vacant hall and gripping my phone so tight I thought it might break, I realized they must be out.

Fuck, does Mira have class right now?

I needed her not to have class right now. Sending that text, I waited another full minute before turning back around and deciding I need to walk around and get all these nerves out. Maybe the snow would help calm me down.

The elevator dings on its arrival and I step inside, jamming my finger into the G button as I waited for the doors to close. My phone vibrates just as the number on the screen hits two and I glance down, biting the inside of my cheek.

MIRA

getting coffee with Bent. You okay?

I exhale, feeling some of my panic start to recede. I know where she is. Now, I just have to get to her.

Stay there. I'm on my way.

Walking out of the dorm, I realize I've forgotten my coat, but the biting chill helps to clear the fog still invading my brain, so I push myself a little harder, practically power walking toward the campus café.

Mira and Harley kept everything secret. It is one of the many things I know Mira regrets about last semester. No matter what, I can't keep this from her.

And I'm kind of freaking out, because what the hell *was* that?

Reaching the café, I grab the handle and pull the heavy glass door open with too much force, the wind taking it and pushing me back as well. Pausing to take a deep breath, I step into the warm café, eyes darting around the room, in search of my friends.

Mira waves when we see each other, seated in a booth facing me, Bentley turning around to catch my eye as well. I swallow, marching over to them and hesitating at the head of the table.

Should I sit next to Mira? Or look her in the eye when I tell her?

"I slept with Ramsey," I blurt. My eyes are trained on the wood grain of the table between them, but I see both of them freeze in my periphery.

Taking a second to cower before I slowly raise my eyes up to glance between them, I find them both just staring up at me, mouths agape.

"Well, not really. Sort of? I don't know. But I didn't want to hide it from you," I say, looking at Mira. "You're just collateral damage," I mutter, looking at Bentley.

Mira bursts out laughing, scooching over on the seat and patting the space beside her. "Pay up," she says, making a grabby hand at Bentley.

"*Collateral damage?*" Bentley screeches. "Would you have even told me if I wasn't here?"

I look between them again, eyebrows I'm sure touching at the top of my forehead. "That's *it*? I just told you I slept with *Ramsey*, your brother," I say pointing to Mira. "And my arch nemesis," I say pointing to me. "And neither of you are going to act like that's a big deal?" I sit down in the booth next to Mira. "And what the fuck do you mean 'pay up?'"

"Bentley and I had a bet to see how long it would take for you to figure out you're into him." Mira shrugs, gripping the mug on the table in front of her.

"I thought it would take a millennia," Bentley says in a sing-songy voice then pouts. "I was truly rooting for you to never figure it out."

Mira scoffs. "You were not. You just didn't think they'd ever stop fighting long enough to figure it out." She takes a sip of her coffee, turning to sit cross legged in the booth and face me. "So, how did it finally happen?" She pauses before reaching out and placing a hand on my forearm. "Not *it*. That's still my brother. But like how did you guys end up together?"

"I can't believe this. You two have been thinking the two of us were secretly into each other and didn't think to bring it up to *me*? At all?" Bentley shrugs, drinking from his cup with a smirk. "And we didn't stop fighting. The fight just sort of...escalated."

"Interesting," Bentley murmurs as Mira's face freezes in shock.

"Oh," is all she says. "Yeah, turns out I don't want any details then." She looks down at her coffee, seeming to consider if she wants to continue drinking it. "I lied," she says a moment later. "I want to know one detail. You liked it right?"

I sputter, but Bentely's face goes serious, both of them looking at me pointedly.

"Yes!" I spit out, looking between them. "It was completely consensual."

"Good." Mira nods once, drinking her coffee again. "Then, other than that, I would like to know zero details."

"Okay, but what if I'm kind of freaking out?" I wring my hands together, pulling on my knuckles a little and biting my lip. "I didn't want it to be a secret from you, because, well you know." I wave my hand anecdotally and Mira nods, her eyes closing for a moment as she waits for me to form my thoughts. "But now that you know, I'm realizing I have to deal with the fact that that just happened. And I don't know what it means. Or how it even really happened. And—

"Okay," Bentley soothes, grabbing my hands from across the table and stopping me. "Breathe. It's okay."

I nod and realize Mira is also rubbing my arm, both of

my friends grounding me. I breathe, nodding and closing my eyes for a second.

"Okay. Everything is okay." I open my eyes, squeezing Bentley's hands before releasing him. Mira retreats as well.

"It means whatever you want it to mean," she says with a shrug. "If you want it to mean nothing, then let it mean nothing and move on. If you want it to mean something, then..." she trails off, eyes getting lost for a second before turning to look at me head on again. "Then make sure you nail down that you two are exclusive. That was definitely my first mistake."

I nod, looking over at Bentley.

"*Do* you want it to mean something?" he asks, watching me.

I slouch in my seat, exhaling all of the leftover nerves from the walk over here and settling back into the weight of my body. "I don't know."

"Okay, well do you want to be with Ramsey?" Mira asks.

I laugh, shaking my head. The notion doesn't even compute in my brain.

"But, do you want to sleep with him again?" Bentley asks.

I hesitate, remembering the giddiness I'd felt when he said *next time*. The idea of him moving on from this quickly doesn't surprise me. What does is the fact that I'm not sure I will. But I'm damn sure I have too much pride to go back to *him* and say that.

19

AUTUMN

Standing on the covered porch of the Ravens' mansion, I stare at the black painted brass knocker and try to swallow the bats attempting to fly out of my stomach right now.

It's been two days since Ramsey showed up at my dorm room, and he didn't show up to class today. Not a single text, phone call, nothing since he literally stormed in, made me come, and left. I thought I'd get to ream him out after class today, but he decided to play coward and not show up. Seething in the back of Dr. Miller's class, I hadn't been able to pay attention the entire time, thinking about all the ways Ramsey's head could explode. Heading back to my dorm afterward, I worked myself up to the point that when I reached the West gate on Ring Road, I stopped for a minute, before decidedly heading off campus without much second thought and straight to his doorstep to let him know what kind of inconsiderate ass he is.

But now that I'm standing here, I seem to have lost my fight. The snow was all slushy on the side of the road, car tires spitting ugly grey smudges against the slowly melting mounds of mush. My feet dragged the last few minutes toward his house, brain questioning why I thought confronting him would be a good idea.

I glance back at the Ravens' driveway. We need another good storm. Make everything look pretty again and not so dull and melty.

I raise my fist to knock, gripping the strap of my bag, but the door yanks open before I make contact.

Smith stands there, lazily leaning one arm against the edge of the door and raising an eyebrow. "Were you planning to take up residence out here?"

I swallow. "Huh?"

He points to my left. My eyes follow to find a doorbell camera screwed into the side of the Victorian doorframe. "You've been standing out here for five minutes," he says drolly. "I was worried you were planning to pitch a tent and stay."

"Oh, um, no," I answer, rolling my shoulders. "Is Ramsey here?"

Smith's brows furrow and he backs up, gesturing for me to come in. I step past the threshold, glancing around and surprised to find the space open and inviting in the daylight. They've modernized the Victorian interior, probably knocking down a couple walls to create an open plan between the living room and kitchen, while the stairs seem to be completely restored, matching the rich wood framing the walls and doorway to my right.

"Ramsey! Someone's here to see you," Smith calls up the stairs. He waits for a second, cupping a hand around his ear as if listening intently before shrugging and turning back to me. "Doesn't seem like he's here." My stomach somersaults, realizing I've just walked into a lion's den without the usual anonymity a crowded party affords. Smith leans back against the banister, one foot up on the bottom stair and smiles maniacally. "But if there's an itch you were looking for him to scratch...I could always—

The door swings open behind me and the cold air rushes back in, nipping at my heels. "Fuck off, Reznikov," Ramsey says with a glare. He closes the door behind him, dropping a duffel bag down beside the door. "Don't you have a class to pretend to attend?"

Smith chuckles, winking at me before straightening up and putting his hands out in front of him placatingly. He saunters off toward the kitchen, and I feel Ramsey step in behind me.

"This way, Fall." He walks around me, heading up the stairs without so much as a second glance.

I hesitate, grabbing the banister before following him, heading deeper into the house. We head down a hallway at the top of the stairs, Ramsey pushing into a room towards the end and holding the door open for me to enter before closing it again. He walks over to the giant bed pushed into the corner, plopping down on the edge and starting to pull his sneakers off.

"So, what are you doing here?" He doesn't even look up as he asks, concentrating on his shoes.

Some of my seething anger starts to return and I stand up straighter. "You weren't in class," I accuse.

He nods, removing his socks next. "Told Miller I was sick. Went to the gym for a bit." He shrugs.

"Yeah, well," I start, but he stands up, grabbing his tee shirt from the back of his collar and pulling it over his head. "What are you doing?" I sputter, eyes catching on the planes of skin and muscle now on display. A trail of dark hair leads down from his bellybutton, disappearing into his gym shorts.

"Getting undressed after the gym. What does it look like?" He smirks when I force my eyes back up to his face, dropping the shirt onto the floor. "Did you need something, Fall?" His words drip with harsh amusement, and I clench my teeth.

"Actually, no. I was going to tell you that I didn't *need* anything, but you didn't show up for class today." I cross my arms over my chest, feeling my face start to heat up.

"So, you decided to walk all the way off campus to my house and tell me—

"It's a five-minute walk."

He shrugs. "Seems awfully far just to tell me you don't need *anything*."

I huff. "Will you stop talking in circles! I just wanted—

He walks toward me, grabbing my jaw mid-sentence and slamming his mouth over mine. I'm so caught off guard I don't even close my eyes for a moment as he starts exploring my mouth with his tongue. His very talented tongue that seems to be doing an impression of a few days ago all over again.

Pulling back, he keeps his hand cupping my face, and sighs. "God, I needed that."

I rear back, pushing his chest away from me and dropping my bag to the floor. "What the fuck, Ramsey?" I start pacing the length of his room while he just stands there, head swiveling to follow me. "You can't just kiss me whenever you feel like it."

"Seemed like you were okay with it when you started kissing me back." He points at me before crossing his arms over his chest. His naked chest.

I shake my head, continuing to pace. "We need rules. Or a fucking treaty." I stop turning to face him again. "I need parameters for whatever the fuck is going on with us. I can't do vagueness."

Ramsey smiles at me, eyes the warmest I've ever seen them in my direction. Which is still just barely above a glare, but still.

"Okay," he shrugs, stepping back and sitting down on the edge of his bed again. "What are the rules?"

I sigh, throwing my hands up and stepping toward him. "I don't know what the fucking rules are, Ramsey. You just burst into my dorm and start demanding things of me and next thing I know we're fucking against a wall and then you just leave. No communication to follow. And then the next time I see you, you kiss me?" I shake my head. "I need something that makes all of *this* make sense." My hands fly around as I talk, ending with them splayed out on either side of me before I let them drop, smacking my thighs.

Ramsey leans forward, spreading his legs as he grips my hips and pulls me to stand between them. "Ah, you want *me* to make the rules?"

It rankles how much that sentence settles something inside me. "Please," I squeak.

His eyes light up behind the panes of his glasses. "Okay, rule number one, we fuck." He holds up his index finger. "Rule number two, we fight." His middle finger joins his index. "Rule number three, we probably do both at the same time." He drops his hand back to my hip and takes a second to think about it. "That seems hottest to be honest."

I slap his chest, feeling the heat from the sting radiate through my palm. "Unhelpful. I said I want this to make sense not be laid out more confusingly."

"I don't think there's anything confusing about it, Fall. I'll communicate more, if that's what you need, but you showing up here pretty much clues me in that you don't want this to end with just the other day?" His hands grip the backs of my thighs, holding me in place as I try to turn away. "I'm going to need to hear you say it."

"No," I sigh, looking up at the ceiling and away from his stupid smug face. "I don't want this to end with just the other day." Looking back down, I add, "But I don't know what the fuck *this* even is."

Ramsey shrugs. "It's fun." His hands slide up squeezing my ass. "Why dissect it any further?"

"Maybe because we've literally never gotten along a day in our lives?"

"I don't know. I think we got along pretty well on Monday." He pulls me closer, hands gliding up and under my shirt.

"Clearly you don't remember how that started as a fight."

Ramsey shrugs, leaning forward and pulling my shirt up to expose skin. The light in his eyes never changes as he places a kiss against my flesh. "So did this technically." He places another kiss, hands wandering back up and running along the edges of my bra. He tips his head back, chin still resting against my skin. "You staying, Fall?"

I release my fists, realizing they've been clenched this entire time and sigh. With a nod, I reach forward, running a hand through his dark curls. He closes his eyes, reveling in the tiny touch.

And then he's on his feet, my hand falling away and his height looming over me. "Shower with me." The statement isn't a request, but he waits, arms still at his sides.

I swallow, fear blooming in my gut and invading every limb. I've never been fully naked with a guy. And now the one I hate is demanding it.

His hand twitches, reaching for me for a second before he bites it back. He sighs, leaning down and aligning our faces without touching me. "I want you to shower with me, Fall. I'm tired and covered in dried sweat and I'd really like to fuck you against the tiles." He glances down, another smug smirk appearing on his lips. "And I really want to get my hands on your tits this time."

I roll my eyes, his words breaking my frozen state. "Nice," I sneer.

He winks.

I don't know what it is, but something about Ramsey's spikey heat up close helps calm my nerves. "Let's go, idiot."

He smiles triumphantly, standing back up and grabbing my hand to pull me toward an attached bathroom. I start walking with him, but stop, pulling on his arm before we enter. He looks back. "If we're doing this, I want us to be exclusive." I chew my lip, remembering Mira's advice in the coffee shop.

Ramsey nods once. "Deal," he says, and then pulls me forward again.

20

AUTUMN

His bathroom is green. The tiles, the countertop, the towels. All of it is accented with white and chrome, but the main motif is jade green. I smile, standing in the doorway and wrapping my arms around myself once he lets go. He walks over to the massive shower, leaning in past the glass door and turning the knobs to whatever temperature he likes.

Turning back to face me, he pauses, assessing me with a quirked brow. "You love it, don't you?"

I shift my weight from foot to foot. "Love what?"

He gestures around the room. "It's your favorite color."

I fold my arms, leaning against the doorframe and trying to tamp down my smile. "You think green is my favorite color?"

Ramsey rolls his eyes, putting his hands in his pockets. "You wear it in almost every outfit, decorated your dorm in it, and you once told Mira it was your favorite at our dinner table." He shrugs. "I know it's your favorite color."

"Someone's been paying attention," I mutter and he tilts his head.

"Maybe that's why I always see green lights around you," he says musingly, almost as if he forgot I can hear him.

"Green lights?"

He shakes his head. "Nothing. Take your clothes off."

I stand up, arms still crossed in front of me. "Just like that?"

He smirks. "Do you usually shower fully clothed?"

I sigh, forcing myself to slowly lower my arms. He takes one hand out, playing with his bottom lip.

I watch him, shifting on the balls of my feet. "Turn around," I say quietly.

He barks a laugh, shaking his head. "Uh-uh. I don't respond to commands. You want something from me, Fall, you know what to say." He rocks back and forth a bit, eyes sparkling.

I glare, fingers twitching as I consider leaving and just walking back home. Something in my stomach twinges at the idea though. "Turn around, *please*." The word leaves from between my teeth, but their burn doesn't necessarily sting coming out.

Ramsey's smile widens and he rocks so far forward, I think he's going to take a step closer. But he just whirls around, facing the shower and giving me his back. I smile, waiting a second to see if he peeks before grabbing the hem of my shirt.

"For the record, I'm going to see you naked in a minute anyways, so you're just robbing me of the floor show, and I will require repayment." His head turns to the side as he speaks but doesn't turn enough to see me. He takes his glasses off and places them on the counter beside him, hands running through his hair once they're free. I get the distinct impression he's fidgeting to stop himself from turning back around.

I roll my leggings down, tossing them onto the pile with my shirt before reaching back and uncinching my bra. The smile stays on my face as I study the planes of his back. There are too many muscles to count, my eyes roaming over the ridges in his smooth skin. He has a jaw that lends to his cruel beauty and as I'm removing my final layer, I have the invasive thought that I want to lick it.

Straightening and now completely naked, I consider what to do next. Having him turn around again feels anti-climactic but I can't just stand here, behind him, naked, forever.

He tuts, head shaking as he takes his hands out of his pockets and places both thumbs inside the waistband of his shorts. "I can hear you thinking, Fall." He starts dragging the material down, my eyes glued to every new inch he exposes, breath suddenly going shallow. He drops them altogether once they clear his mid-thigh, standing there just as naked as me. "Shut your brain off and get in the shower."

Fuck he has a great ass. I'm not even sure what the criteria is for a great ass, but I know he has one.

Swallowing the prickly nerves that dance across the back of my tongue, I square my shoulders and resolve myself to walk forward. I can see the corner of his mouth in profile, and it curls up as he hears me approach.

Fuck, here we go.

I walk past him, pushing the glass shower door open and stepping inside. Heading straight under the lukewarm spray, I don't even glance back, letting the feeling of being seen press in against me as I let the weight of my soaking hair tip my head back. Heat licks up every inch of my exposed skin, having nothing to do with the water sliding over me.

The door bangs closed behind me, and the noise jolts

me to look up, finding Ramsey still in the same spot, only now he faces me. His glasses are on the counter beside him, eyes freely roving over me through the clear glass. He's kept the water temp low enough that no steam fogs his image, but beads of water litter the pane between us. I lean back, cranking the hot water up, knowing it won't stop the shivers running down my spine.

He can see me. The thought coats down my throat and drips into my hollow stomach, filling it with sticky panic, but there's no going back now.

A moment passes of me watching him study me. Steam starts to billow around me, fog creeping in at the edges of my vision, but I can still see Ramsey's expression clear as day. His eyes are focused, explorative, darting everywhere beneath furrowed brows as if he's frustrated he can't take everything in at once. His hands are still at his sides, clenching and unclenching and another surge of power zaps through my blood, clearing the syrupy doubt from my throat.

Bravado feels like the only sensical way to play this. "You coming?"

"Mmmm, that's the question, isn't it?" He rocks back again, before reaching over and opening the shower door. Without a sliver of hesitation, he steps right inside and instantly crowds me back against the cold tiles. Grabbing my chin a little roughly, he pulls my face up to look at him, as if my eyes have ever really left him for long since we stepped into this room. "You are fucking beautiful, Fall," he whispers, eyes alight and burning into me, the predator I've always seen in him on full display in a completely new way.

I squirm despite the hot water, and he leans down purposefully slow, licking water off my bottom lip before tugging it in between his teeth.

The swat of his hand comes down lightly on my ass and I yelp. The water and angle lessen the blow, but my eyes widen all the same.

"Now, turn around."

He releases my face, stepping back and swiping his hands through his hair and over his face a few times as the water hits him and runs down over his head and chest. I trail my eyes over his pecs, watching the water sluice down his body. For as much as I've always avoided looking at him, it was never because of his looks. He's in shape, tall, and holds himself with all the over confidence of a man who knows he's hot. And at the moment, I'm not mad about it.

My gaze dips further and I grin, something sharp dropping low in my stomach. His cock is hard, water sliding down his cut thighs on either side. My head tilts, mouth dry, and I consider reaching out and touching him first.

"As much as I enjoy catching you ogling me, I believe I said *turn around*." His voice lowers on the command and my eyes snap back up to his face, now tilted out of the water. He smirks, twirling his finger in front of my face.

The movement jolts me back into our usual pattern, the need to push back at him surfacing. I cock my hip and cross my arms petulantly. "Why do you get to make demands, but I have to say *please*?" I snarl.

He leans down, placing his hands on my hips and pressing me into the wall. "Because I like being in control. And given your reactions, you like it too." He smiles and nips my cheek, hands massaging my hips. "Last time I'll say it. Turn around. Both hands on the wall." He taps my hip then leans back, a cocky grin in place.

I stew for a moment, mind racing with a reason to defy him, but the need growing inside me takes over before I find one. Keeping my eyes on him, I slowly turn around, placing my palms against the wall. The tiles are cold despite the warm water, and a shiver runs through me as I try to picture what Ramsey is doing behind me.

He steps closer, adjusting the shower head above us so that it sprays over our heads. The heat from the water radiates down, the overspray sticking to my lashes and peppering my skin.

Ramsey's hands suddenly land on my waist, making me squeak.

"Shhhh." His chest presses in against my back, his cock nestling against my ass. He leans down, hands venturing up over my ribs as he nestles his face in against mine, nose running along my cheekbone. "Feel that?" He rocks against me, hands fluttering back to my waist and adding more pressure before heading north again, the glide less smooth. "That's what would have happened if I went to Miller's class today."

My mouth falls open, wet air pulling into my lungs as I stare at my hands and blink. Fuck, he feels big. He looked decently sized when I was staring but feeling him behind me is a whole different thing. I keep comparing it to the only other times I've had sex, lights off, shirt on, facing away from them while they bumbled around behind me putting on a condom or asking if I liked the random movements they clumsily made with their fingers against my slit.

I start to tremble, thinking about how I've never done any of this.

"Hey, Fall? You with me?" He grabs my chin again, arm crossing the front of my body and tethering me against him. Twisting my face toward him, he searches my eyes. "I want you right here when I'm touching you, understand?"

I nod, squelching my toes as his intensity once again

dives right into the wide-open crack running through the center of my chest.

"Good." He takes my mouth, hand forcing my head to stay exactly where it is as he slants to get better access. My eyes fall closed as our lips move in sync, the taste of him, somehow mild and sharp, invading my senses.

He pulls back, eyes a little bleary and curls pasted to his forehead. My chest rises and falls at a harsh pace, breath puffing right into his face as we both regroup.

Ramsey shakes his head, chuckling. "You distracted me." His hand forces me to look back at the wall before dropping back down to cage me in again. He squeezes this time, kneading my sides as his fingers crawl up toward my chest.

"How angry were you when you realized I wasn't there?" His feet nudge mine wider apart, making me glance down then back up.

"W-what?" I stutter. My mind can't seem to follow his words and his hands at the same time.

"In class today." His hands start to slide against the side of my breasts, letting their weight slowly fill his palms. "How pissed were you that I didn't show up?"

His fingers find my nipples, teasing the already stiff peaks between his index and thumb. I tip my head back a little, the base of my skull nudging against his shoulder. I groan and he pinches harder.

"How pissed, Fall?" He keeps playing with my nipples, just holding my tits aloft. The words barely register as I squirm in his arms. "Scale of one to ten."

"Ten," I repeat, shifting on my feet. Every roll of his fingers feels like a lightning bolt running directly from my nipples to my clit, making every muscle below it clench.

"Mmmmm, were you wet?"

A sliver of shame slides through me. "What?" I pick my head up off his skin.

He pinches my nipples a little sharply before dropping my boobs entirely, hands running back down to my hips. "Were you wet? Were you sitting there, listening to Miller's lecture, seething with anger and squirming a little from how turned on it was making you?" His words are harsh, pressing in against me.

I don't get the chance to answer.

He pushes me forward, my chest touching the tiles as one of his hands slides through the curls between my thighs. Fast and rough, he parts me, immediately pressing against my clit and making me hiss. I'm wound tight, desire dripping down my parted thighs as he goes in for the kill.

His lips touch my ear, breath tickling against my damp skin. "Say it, Fall. Say it turns you on, how angry I can make you."

His fingers move fast, sliding lower and circling my entrance. The sensation makes my spine twitch, legs instinctually closing.

Ramsey tsks. "Uh-uh." His free hand grabs the side of my thigh and pulls my legs apart, freeing the hand I just trapped between them. But he doesn't stop there. He bends down slightly, wrapping a hand under my knee and lifting my leg as he stands back up and pins it against the wall. I balance unsteadily on one foot, unable to close my legs as his fingers start to dip into me.

I close my eyes as he enters me, one finger slowly pressing in and out a little further each time.

"Say it, Fall." His breath comes out harsh, the words strained.

He adds another finger.

"Yes!" I cry out. "It turns me on." His thumb slides up,

rubbing my clit in tight little circles as his other fingers glide in and out of me in smooth seamless slides.

My walls flutter and I swallow, feeling it coming. A few more circles and I explode, moaning and pressing my cheek in against the tiles. The cool sensation on my overheated skin soothes me as I start to come down, eyes still closed and hands getting pruney.

Ramsey kisses the side of my head, fingers still sliding in and out of me. "It turns me on too," he whispers.

Something akin to disappointment settles into my bones as my mind clears a bit more.

"Ramsey?" my voice comes out tentative, teeth tripping over my lip as I stutter.

"Hmm?"

His fingers keep moving in and out of me at the slowest, most decadent pace. "You said you wanted to fuck me," I pant, fingers sliding against the tiles as I try to find any purchase. My cheek presses against the fogged-up jade and I blink the buildup of water off my lashes.

"Always so greedy," he muses, continuing his slow torture.

"Ramsey," I groan, wanting to stamp my foot, but tired and still half pinned up.

He chuckles and then moves even closer, chest leaning into me, thigh lining up with the back of mine. "You want to participate, sweetness?" His lips brush my ear, and the fluttering sensation makes me clamp down around his fingers. He chuckles again. "Touch me," he whispers.

I blink again, lost at what he means for a moment before determination sets in. I slide my hand down the tiles, reaching back and wrapping my fist around his length behind my back. The angle is awkward, my elbow bent and unable to really move properly. But I squeeze him, clenching around his fingers again when I feel just how hard he is from making me come.

Ramsey sighs, hips thrusting into my hand as I grip him. His forehead presses against my temple as we work each other up, his thumb rubbing me lazily and fingers curling.

"Fuck, you feel good."

The praise makes me moan, my hand tightening more and Ramsey groans into my cheek, chest heaving against me.

"I need you to come." He picks up his pace, hips thrusting without rhythm behind me. "Fall. Come."

And I do. His fingers hit the right spot just as his thumb presses my clit down and I cry out.

Warm liquid hits the back of my thigh and Ramsey's cock twitches in my hand, his hips bucking as he groans and grips my leg harder. We stay locked together; my hamstring aching and fist still wrapped around his slowly softening cock.

He nuzzles my cheek before backing up, removing his fingers from my entrance and slowly letting my leg back down. His cock slips from my hand, and I push lightly off the wall, turning around and leaning my back to touch the tiles he just fingered me against.

The water is still warm, and I chuckle at the luxury he probably doesn't even notice, staring down at my feet.

His fingers tip my chin up, face an inch in front of me as he leans down. His eyes rove my face, narrowed and analytical. "Let's clean up," is all he says, pecking my lips before he pulls me under the spray and grabs some soap.

21

RAMSEY

I've gone insane.

And I don't think I really care.

The second the switch flipped in Fall's dorm, I lost all semblance of control. But instead of grasping for it, I reveled in the *release*. She pushed me over the edge and I immediately swan dove to the bottom, not even hesitating once I gave myself permission.

She admitted she'd never had good sex, and I felt determined to show her how easy it would be to make her come.

Her responsiveness surprised me though. I figured she'd fight me tooth and nail. Seems my little Fall loses all her fight when I'm touching her, her mind giving in to my demands without much delay.

Her whispered please made me come without any restraint.

I needed to talk to Diane about this turn of events. Maybe leave out some of the details. But definitely check in, make sure I'm not backsliding or about to spiral in every other facet of my life. So, I skipped class, got in a workout, texted my therapist to see if she had a session available today.

Fall completely derailed that plan.

When I heard Smith through the front door, I didn't know who he was talking to. The second I saw him that close to her, I lost it, needing him to back off and her to come upstairs with me. The second she followed, I knew we were venturing a little further down the rabbit hole.

She wants to fuck exclusively. And I don't mind it. The thought of anyone else touching her makes me homicidal so that's fine. And I also don't really see myself *wanting* to fuck anyone else if she's available. Something that I should definitely talk to Diane about because *what the fuck.*

Autumn stands naked, dripping on my bathmat while I run a towel over my hair. She has one draped around her shoulders but still seems a little dazed. I wrap mine around my hips, tucking the end in and sauntering up to her.

She stares at the center of my chest, eyes unfocused, even when I lightly pry the ends of the towel out of her hands and start pulling it back and forth over her back. "Fall? You in there?"

"You didn't fuck me," she says robotically.

"Yes, I did." I kiss the side of her head, getting a mouthful of wet curls. She smells like my shampoo, having to use it in the shower, and my chest rumbles with satisfaction.

"Don't pout," I admonish, flicking her lower lip with the pad of my finger. The move momentarily exposes her bottom teeth, and she finally looks up at me, eyes focusing and seeing me. "You're swaying on your feet and didn't open your eyes the whole time I washed you. Trust me, I fucked you." I rub the towel against her nipples and she jumps.

"You know what I mean." She pulls the towel out of my hands and focuses on drying herself off.

I lean back against the sink, watching her and trying to find any of the usual animosity I have when she's nearby. "Slow, Fall, remember? We're going slow." She's not a virgin, but I'm treating her like one. She seems a little skittish about her body and sex, and I don't want to spook her. I need her to know that I *want* to fuck her before I actually do.

And I have no idea why that's even registering as a concern for me.

She looks up at me, bent over and wiping at her extended left leg. God, she looks good when she glares. "What if I don't want slow? What if I just want to get it over with, flush you out of my system?"

I laugh, rolling my eyes. Yeah, there's no getting me *out* of her system. If anything, we're just going to keep sinking further into each other. I can feel it.

Quiet fear slithers around behind my ribs.

"Right," I bluster. "That's why you asked for this arrangement to be exclusive? So, we could get it over with quicker?" I tap my finger against the underside of the sink.

Fall straightens back up, cheeks and chest flaring red.

I lean in, biting her bottom lip before I whisper against them. "Stop worrying. I will fuck you properly, I promise. I'm just enjoying the buildup right now." She sucks in a breath, and I strike, hand curling around the back of her head as I hold her against me. I kiss her harshly until we're both breathless.

My cock stirs beneath the towel, waking up for round two and I pull back, keeping my grip on her head. "When's your next class?" I pant. Maybe slow is overrated.

"Oh shit." She shakes her head out of my grip. "What time is it?" She rushes over to the pile of her clothes, pulling her phone out of a pocket in her leggings. Breathing a sigh of relief, she looks up at me from her squatted position. "Still got another hour."

I grin, leaning back so both my hands grip the sink once more.

"Ramsey?" she asks tentatively as she slowly stands up, eyes on the ground.

I hum, watching her fish around for her underwear and feeling a little disappointed.

"I don't want this," she gestures between us without looking up, "to affect my grade." Her head peaks up, hands holding her bra. "In Dr. Miller's class. That part of our deal still holds up, okay?" She drops the towel, shimmying her chest into its confines.

I take a second to mourn the loss.

"It won't." I stand, turning to grab my glasses and pushing them up my nose. They're more than decorative, but I can see better up close than far away, making them mostly useful when I'm driving. I'm too used to having them on all the time though and with Fall all the way across the room, I want to make sure I'm catching all her little movements. "I don't grade your half of the class, remember? Can't touch any of your precious papers."

"Good," she says, pulling on her leggings and not looking over. A smile slides onto her face, and she muses, "Might help me get the internship if Dr. Miller is grading my stuff anyways."

Hot fury whips through me so fast I get whiplash. "You're *not* doing that internship."

Her eyes dart to mine. "What?" She grabs her shirt and stands up fully. "Yes, I am."

I take a step toward her. "No, you're not. Miller is a creep, and you shouldn't be anywhere near him, let alone working *under* him."

"What the fuck is that supposed to mean?" She pulls on her shirt furiously, covering herself completely and turning to face me head on. "I need that internship, Ramsey, and you're insane if you think you're going to stop me from applying for it."

I hold myself back from walking over to her, not trusting my shaking hands. "You are not doing that fucking internship, Autumn. Miller just wants to sleep with you, and you really need to wake up and switch advisors."

Her eyes widen and her fists clench at her sides. "Just because you fucked me, doesn't mean you get to control me, Ramsey. I'm going to do whatever the fuck I want outside of our arrangement. And when it's over, we're going to move on. So, you get no say in my choices outside of this."

The words lash against my chest, tightening the band I keep around everything and squeezing the breath out of me for a second.

When it's over.

The moment it loosens though, my anger seeps back in. She's already setting an end date. Fuck this.

"Fine, do whatever you want, Fall." I seethe, fists clenched and blood racing. Unfortunately, a lot of it races south, which is a little inconvenient when I'm pissed the fuck off and know I can't touch her like this. "Get out," I spit.

She reels back, watching me for a second before nodding, resolve in her eyes. "Fine. Text me when you've calmed down." She turns on her heel and walks out.

I stand there for a moment, listening to her grab her bag and head out of my room. The second the door closes, I let myself go, walking straight to my closet and dialing Diane as I pull on a pair of sweats.

22

AUTUMN

I 'm out with everyone when Ramsey texts me.

SATAN'S NEPHEW

Come over.

I stare at my phone in my lap, missing the joke Layla tells, but getting hit with the milkshake Mira manages to snort on half the table. Axel roars when some of it hits Bentley and Aria snickers beside me. Janette grabs a napkin off the pile in the middle of the table, passing one to me before using her own to wipe the side of Bentley's face.

"Thanks, Mir," he grumbles.

"Sorry," she says sheepishly, wiping some out of her own hair.

We're all squeezed into a round booth at Romero's, Aria and Layla bookending me, Mira, and the trio. Everyone decided to split the family style platter, four different pasta dishes littering the table in various states of availability.

I opted out with an excuse about wanting something healthier, already knowing the house salad is the cheapest item on the menu from the last time we came here. Aria agreed, squeezing my hand under the table as she said she wanted a salad too.

I pick at the leaves still left on my plate, hearing my mother's voice telling me I used too much dressing.

My phone buzzes again in my lap.

SATAN'S NEPHEW

That wasn't a request

I drop my fork, picking my phone up and typing back.

Can't. Out rn.

SATAN'S NEPHEW

Where?

Romeros. Bentley picked tonight.

SATAN'S NEPHEW

Ditch.

I sigh.

No. I'm not at your beck and call, Ramsey.

The grey dots appear quickly, somehow looking angry when I know who's on the other side.

SATAN'S NEPHEW

You're the one who wanted to be exclusive, Fall. It's been five days. Come. Over.

I roll my eyes. He's so dramatic. He literally kissed me yesterday.

Sure, it'd been in the alcove by the stairs that he pushed

me into on the first day. And it had a little more bite than any of our previous kisses. But it still counts. He'd spent the whole of the last two Gen Bio classes glaring at me and making me squirm in my seat. When I said he should text me when he calmed down, I didn't anticipate how long it would take. I was starting to crave our weird explosive interactions.

A couple of orgasms and apparently my body is hooked.

The kiss was hasty and a bit mean, but his words after stopped me from pushing for more.

"I'm still mad at you." He held my jaw as he said the words, fire roaring in his eyes.

He could be mad at me all he wanted. It seems to be his default setting. But I won't budge on this. He doesn't get to control anything about my life outside of his bed. Or walls I guess since we've yet to actually make it to anything else.

I sigh again.

> I don't have a ride. Bentley and Axel drove everyone. I'll come over after they bring us back to campus.

SATAN'S NEPHEW

> Fine. Text me when you're on your way over.

I smile. He's being curt, but he just gave in. The victory feels extra good knowing he's going to stew, probably coming up with some way to torture me for making him wait.

"Is that Ramsey?" Mira asks, playing with straw of her shake and waggling her eyebrows at me.

I open my mouth, but Bentley cuts me off.

"Oh, it totally is, look at her smile." He stuffs another piece of garlic bread into his mouth.

"Is he poetic?" Axel asks. "I picture him being a secret romantic in private."

I snort, unable to even conjure the image of Ramsey spouting poetry.

"Nah, poetry wouldn't make her smile like that," Bentley says, bread still in his mouth. "He probably sent her something dirty."

"Still my brother, guys," Mira interjects.

"Leave her alone, you two," Janette adds.

"Yes, it was," I say, looking at Mira. She smiles into her shake, and I wonder if I should let her know this thing with me and Ramsey is temporary. He'll get bored eventually once the fire goes out or we actually learn how to get along. She's had enough heartbreak the last couple months. Don't want her throwing her eggs into this bottomless basket.

"How's the front desk gig at the gym going?" Layla asks, looking at Aria and perfectly changing the subject.

"Great." Aria sits up, beaming, black lipstick really emphasizing how white her teeth are. "I get a fifty-dollar commission for every new member who signs up and puts my name down as their reference. You all should come get memberships sometime."

"Deal," Bentley says, Axel nodding beside him. Janette nods too and Layla smiles.

"I might bow out if that's okay?" Mira looks down as she says it, looking up at Aria to add, "Not sure I want to run into the owner there just yet."

"Of course. Don't sweat it." Aria nods.

"I have another date with Cyrus tomorrow," Mira announces, perking up as she looks around at all of us. I glance at Bentley over her head, and he raises an eyebrow at me.

"I can feel you both judging." We both quickly look away.

"Not judging, Mir," Bentley quickly soothes.

"What's wrong with him?" Layla asks, slurping the last of her soda through her straw.

"Nothing's wrong with him!" Mira insists.

Janette reaches around Bentley and puts a hand on her arm. "No, I don't think there's anything *wrong*." She looks over at Layla next to Axel. "He's just a little...persistent."

"I don't think there's anything wrong with that," Mira defends. She sits back, crossing her arms.

I twist my hands in my lap. Cyrus hasn't just been persistent, he's been *insistent*. After their first date, Mira got busy with classes and he called her nearly every night for a week, leaving a voicemail each time asking her to call back so they could set up their next date. She told us the date went fine, but they never setup a second and Bentley and I agreed it was weird that he wasn't asking, rather telling.

She said she was going to call him back last night and I guess one phone call changed her mind.

It's too early to tell if the flag is pink or red though so I plaster on a smile and ask, "Where are you guys going?"

Mira perks up a bit, telling us about the museum Cyrus wants to take her to. We all chime in, encouraging her, but I notice Bentley tapping the table and frowning when she isn't looking.

Thirty minutes later, we're still hanging out, taking up the waiter's biggest table, when my phone starts to buzz continuously. I glance at the screen.

Satan's Nephew.

I shake my head, Aria letting me out so I can take it. I walk toward the bathrooms, going past to a little area around the corner, leaning back against the wall beside the kitchen doors.

"You're so impatient," I hiss when the call picks up.

"I just want to see you, Fall," Ramsey breathes down the phone line. My eyes close and I soak in the double meaning for a moment. Ramsey Adams will surely be how I fall, dragged down by him kicking and screaming if he has his way.

I sigh in resignation. "We're still at Romero's."

"There's an uber out front."

I jerk upright. "What?"

"Black SUV. License plate MLU 7883. I'll be able to watch you on the app so I can see if they try to kidnap you."

"You're insane," I scoff. "I insist you can't control me, and you hire a car to come get me and drop me off at your door? Like a fucking doordash order?"

His tone drops, dripping with promise. "Pissed off, Fall? Why don't you come yell at me about it."

I let out a hushed scream of frustration. "You don't fucking listen, do you?"

"Other way around, Fall. I get it. You are woman, hear you roar."

I'm going to beat his fucking head in.

"Get in the car. Come over. I've calmed down from the other day, and I need to touch you. And you're right, I'm impatient."

I seethe. "Cancel the fucking uber, you caveman. I don't want your fucking charity."

"Charity?" His voice switches to confusion, hitching over the word. "How is this any different from me driving you back to school? You need a ride, I'm offering."

I look up at the ceiling, willing whatever forces of the

universe predetermine my moods to sprinkle in some patience. "This is so different, Ramsey."

Aria pokes her head around the corner. "The boys are paying for everyone. We're going to head back once they're done."

Fucking great. I give her a thumbs up. Glad I wasted my time eating a fucking salad just to owe Bentley for it.

"I have to go. Cancel the uber. Bentley's driving me back."

"Autumn, don't hang up! We're not done tal—

"Bye, Ramsey." I pull my phone away, hearing him shout something else as I tap the red disconnect button. It starts ringing again almost immediately and I silence it, sending him to voicemail and heading back toward the booth to grab my purse.

23

RAMSEY

She has this way of making me feel completely out of control. Even when she's turning me on at the same time.

I could feel her fury on the other end of the line, taste how much I was riling her up. But instead of giving in, she dumped a bucket of ice water all over my crotch and without any explanation, she ended the call, making me so pissed I couldn't see straight.

Jumping into my Jeep, I take a few deep breaths, needing a modicum of calm to drive over to the Coast. We are so not done with our conversation even if she thinks we are.

I pull out of the driveway and almost scream into the dash.

Charity? Why the fuck would she need charity from me? And why would she consider a ride to my house a handout?

I grip the steering wheel, reminding myself of my last session with Diane.

You care about her?

No, she just pisses me off. And turns me on. End of interactions.

Those things don't mean you can't care about her. Consider how you feel about her, underneath the rage.

I couldn't. There was too much boiling anger in the moment to see through. Diane's patient though. She said to work on it, and we'd come back to this next time I see her.

Which is her way of saying I couldn't get away with hiding behind the anger like I always do. Fucking Diane.

Parking a couple minutes later in the West Tower lot, I get out, leaving the car running and marching over to stand next to the front doors and wait for the little witch to appear. Fluffy tufts of snow drift down from the pitch-black sky and I tuck my hands in my coat pockets, eyeing the lot. The air clouds in front of my mouth while I wait, several groups of students passing and glancing my way each time.

How long does a drive back from Romero's take?

I hear Axel before I see him. "Why did we get ice cream when it was snowing again? My hands are freezing."

Glancing over, I find him, both hands holding ice cream cones, one pointed down for his girlfriend to taste while he licks the other. Bentley rolls his eyes behind them, carrying his own cone. My sister has her arm locked through Aria's as they rush toward the doors ahead of them. Another girl follows behind them and bringing up the rear is the little witch I'm freezing my balls off waiting for.

"Ramsey!" Mira calls, seeing me first.

Fall's head whips up, eyes clashing with mine, nose bright pink. Why the fuck doesn't she have a hat?

"Hey bug," I say, pushing off the wall and hugging my sister when she runs up to me.

"Did we have plans?" Her forehead wrinkles and she takes a lick of ice cream.

"Nope." The rest of the group catches up, Aria and the girl I don't know heading inside. Janette starts hopping from foot to foot when the other's stop and Axel ushers her in too. "I'm here for her." I nod to Fall, eyes locking with hers again.

"Awwwww," Bentley coos.

"Shut it, Marshall," I warn.

He clams up, looking a little sheepish. "Sorry, man." He scratches the back of his head. "You good if we go in, Autumn?"

Mira smiles at her, nodding while we all wait for her answer.

"Yeah, go on up." She gestures to the door with her elbow, keeping her hands in her pockets. "I'll be there in a sec."

Like hell she will.

Mira frowns, glancing over at me before squeezing my arm and walking past. Bentley follows, mouthing *text for help* to Autumn when he thinks I can't see.

She nods and I step forward. "That won't be necessary."

"We'll see if it that's true," she challenges.

I ball my fists in my pockets.

"What are you doing here, Ramsey?"

I step closer to her. "What did you mean on the phone earlier?"

She sighs, shoulders tight and glances around. "Which part?"

"When you called the ride I got you *charity*." I try to tamp down my anger response, knowing it'll only muddle this conversation.

She sighs. "Nothing, okay? Is that all?" She moves to walk past me, and I pull my hand out, lightly grabbing her arm.

"Hey, stop. What's going on? Why are you clamming up?" She remains silent, kicking some snow with the toe of her boot. "Come on, Fall. You're the most outspoken woman I've ever met. Don't give me the silent treatment."

Her head whips up, eyes sparking. "That cannot be true. You've met plenty of women, Ramsey."

I take the bait, leaning into her orbit. "Jealous?"

She laughs in my face, and I revel in it. "Hardly. Seems like I'm the one benefiting from all that *experience* now."

"Mmmm," I hum. "You would be. If you had just come over to mine."

She sighs, shaking her head. "Fine, Ramsey. You want me to come over? Let's go." She wrestles her arm out of my grip, turning around and marching down the sidewalk. I follow, a little trepidatious of this sudden change and expecting her to turn into the parking lot. When she heads past it, I pick up my pace, stopping her again.

"Where are you going?"

She huffs. "To yours!"

"My car's in the lot."

She folds her arms, forcing me to let her go again. "Thanks, but I think I'll walk. Meet you there." She turns and starts heading away again.

I stand frozen for a second, my anger swirling right under the surface. She's fucking crazy. Fuck this.

I jog past her, sliding in front of her and grabbing both of her upper arms when she almost bumps into me. "You are not walking to my house in the dark during a snowstorm! Especially without a hat or gloves." The words whip off my tongue, lava spewing over inside me.

"Well, you're not driving me! I don't want to owe you anything more than I already do!"

I look around, getting whiplash trying to understand her. "Owe me? What are you talking about? You don't owe me anything, Fall." Her eyes go wide as saucers and I step up to her, forcing my hands to stay by my sides so I don't grab her. "Do you think this arrangement is fucking transactional?"

"Isn't everything?"

I tilt my head, feeling another puzzle piece turn over yet unable to see how it fits into the picture. "No, Fall. Not everything is transactional. And especially not *this*." I let myself reach out, rubbing my hands over her arms to generate some heat. At least my anger can provide us warmth. "Jesus, is that why you got upset about the uber? Because you thought I was paying you for sex or something?"

Her neck flushes. "No, not directly. But you can't buy my time. Or throw money at me like that fixes every problem." She rolls her eyes. "I told you I was out at dinner, that I would meet up with you later. That's the answer, Ramsey. End of. You don't get to be in charge of this thing all the time."

I stare between her eyes.

You care about her?

"Okay." I chew on my tongue for a second then swallow fire. "I'm sorry."

Fall jolts in my hands. "What was that?"

"You heard me," I grumble.

"Not sure I did." She shivers, jumping up and down a little bit to keep warm. I start steering her back toward the lot. "I think I actually just had a stroke. Did *you* just apologize to *me*?"

"Yes, Fall. I did. I overreacted and I shouldn't have ordered the uber." I walk us up to my Jeep, currently running with the heat on inside. "I'm sorry. Now, please get in my car and let me take you back to mine so I can make it up to you."

Fall laughs, glancing back at West Tower. "Do you want to come up?" She looks up at me through her lashes, and my cock does a standing ovation.

"As much as I like the idea of sleeping wrapped around each other, I don't think a twin bed five feet from your roommate is the best place to do so." I open the passenger door.

Autumn shakes her head, smiling as she jumps into the car. I see her pull out her phone, probably texting to let my sister and her friends know she's not in fact coming up. I close the door, feeling something stir in my gut. Something beneath the anger.

I run a hand through my hair. I'll dissect that later.

Rounding the car, I get in and make sure the vents on Fall's side are pointed toward her before pulling out of the lot.

"Do gifts fall into your charity category?" I grip the steering wheel with both hands, keeping my eyes glued to the road as the wipers swipe the snow out of my way.

"What do you mean?"

"If I get you something, *as a gift*, will you consider it transactional? Or is that allowed in this arrangement?" I lean forward, driving ten miles under the speed limit.

"Um, depends on what it is. Why are you driving like a grandma?"

I glance over at her quickly, noting the mocking smile painting her lips and scowl at the snow. "I'm nearsighted. My glasses help, but I haven't gotten the prescription updated in a couple years. It's dark, and snowing, and I want to get home in one piece. So, no mocking my driving."

Autumn laughs at me. "You have a Jeep. And we're going two streets over. Pretty sure if you slid off the road and somehow tumbled us across someone's lawn, we'd be okay. It's a four second drive."

I purse my lips, deciding not to dignify that with a response. "Can I get you a fucking gift or not?"

Fall sighs. "Like I said, it depends on what it is. It needs to be within reason." Her tone dips lower. "I don't need anything lavish. And you don't *need* to get me anything, Ramsey. In fact, it'd be easier if you didn't get me anything." I can see her wringing her hands in her lap from my periphery.

I turn onto my driveway, pulling along the curved circle in front of the black Victorian. Parking and turning the car off, I turn toward her. "Okay." I push my glasses up. "I can work within those parameters."

She shakes her head. "Ramsey—

"And for the record, I'm not trying to control you."

She raises a brow, and I smile.

"Outside of our sex life, I'm not trying to control you. I just don't want you to freeze to death just to spite me." I grin. "There are much more fun ways you can spite me."

She crosses her arms, ignoring my shift. "And the Dr. Miller shit?"

My teeth gnash together, and I remember what Diane said about this.

All you can do is tell Autumn your fears, Ramsey. You can't control her actions, but you can try to get her to understand that you want to protect her. You're scared that she's going to get hurt.

It took me six days to accept that. That I was mad because I wanted to *protect* Fall. Apparently, I'm slow to see reason when it comes to this girl.

You care about her?

"I still don't like anything about it." She opens her mouth, and I reach over, clamping my hand around the lower half of her face. "*But*, it's your life. I just think you should be *cautious* around him." I can feel a vein in my neck popping out with the restraint it takes to get that out civilly. "And maybe check out some other internships? I did one at the bone and joint place back home. I can put in a good word for you if you want?"

Fall's eyes search my face while I continue to keep my hand over her mouth. Taking a deep breath, I release her face, steeling myself for her response.

She sighs. "I'll look at other ones. But only because you're being creepily mature about this."

"Blame Diane," I grumble.

"Who's Diane?"

I reach for my door handle. "It's getting pretty cold out here, let's head inside."

She rolls her eyes, and I can't help reaching across the center and grabbing her jaw. Pulling her in, I kiss her, softer than our last clash of mouths. When I pull back, her eyes are a little dazed.

"When we get up to my room, I'm going to fuck this whole shitty week out of you," I say before biting her lip and getting out.

24

AUTUMN

Ramsey does not uphold his promise to fuck me.

Instead, he feeds me.

While taking my coat off and hanging it up by the door, he hears my stomach grumble and immediately pounces on it.

"I thought you got dinner?" He accuses as I start up the stairs.

"I did." I shrug, slowing and looking over my shoulder at him.

"But you're still hungry?" He folds his arms over his chest, the black cable knit sweater he's wearing pushed up to show off his forearms. "Did you get that fucking salad again?"

I stop, turning around halfway up the stairs and leaning against the banister. "A salad is a meal, Ramsey."

"*That* salad is a side, Fall." He walks off toward the kitchen, and I rush down the stairs after him.

"Where are you going? I was promised fucking!"

Ramsey smirks. "Greedy as ever," he murmurs. "Keep your voice down. I don't want everyone in this house hearing you yell about us fucking in the kitchen." He heads to the fridge, opening the door and looking around.

I catch up, stepping around him so I'm in his line of sight next to the door. "I'm fine, Ramsey. Please take me upstairs and fuck me." I say everything in a hushed tone.

He gives me a wry expression. "Nice try." He reaches into the fridge and pulls out a leftover container. "Chicken?" he asks, holding it up.

I sigh. "You're going to insist I eat something, aren't you?"

"I don't want you passing out the first time my dick is inside you." He grabs another container, holding it up next to the chicken. "Mac and cheese?"

I sigh. "Fine. Chicken."

He nods. Taking both containers over to the counter and turning around to grab a plate.

"What are you doing? I said chicken." I walk over next to him, crossing my arms over my chest.

"I heard you. You can have some mac and cheese on the side." He starts dishing some of each container onto the plate.

"What if I'm lactose intolerant?" I cock my hip, throwing my hand there for emphasis.

He just rolls his eyes. "Unless you magically developed this intolerance in the last twenty-four hours, I know you're not. You had a yogurt in class yesterday."

I narrow my eyes at him. "And you were able to notice that while you were trying to bore holes through my skull with your laser vision?"

He smirks, picking up the plate and turning to put it in the microwave. "I have the ability to multitask, Fall." Once the machine starts whirring, he turns back around, arm sliding around my back and pulling me flush against him. "Why are you trying to provoke me? I want to feed you then fuck you and I don't see why you would be opposed to either of those things. Unless this falls under charity in that crazy brain of yours?"

"No." I pout. Ramsey leans forward, nipping at my cheek and then leaning down to lick up the side of my neck. "I just—

He bites my pulse point, pulling my skin a bit with his teeth. "You just what?" he says huskily against my skin.

"I j-just don't see why you're s-so concerned with w-what I eat." He keeps running his lips over my skin as I stutter my way through the sentence.

He pulls his head back, looking me in the eye. "I just want to make sure you're not hungry. Because I want all of your thoughts focused on my efforts to scatter them. And if you're hungry, some part of your brain will be focused on that. It's science. Trust me, I'm years ahead of you in bio courses."

I roll my eyes. "Be serious."

"Oh, I am." He pecks my lips again when the microwave bell goes off, releasing me to get a fork and water before retrieving the plate. I hesitate to follow him out of the kitchen, and he sighs, looking back at me. "Just chalk it up to my control issues, Fall. I need you fed first. You can be mad about it after you eat." He perks up. "In fact, I insist you take your anger out on me when you've finished eating."

I feel the last piece of my resolve crumble. "Fine. I'll eat the damn chicken, but I'm not touching the mac and cheese."

He shrugs. "I'll just tie you to the bed and feed it to you then."

I wrinkle my nose, following him up the stairs. "No thanks." The idea of that particular humiliation ritual feels like letting spiders crawl across the back of my neck. My shoulders shudder.

He turns around at the top step, forehead crinkling. "Not into bondage, or the force feeding?"

"Force feeding." I step up against him. "I've never tried bondage."

"Noted. I'll add it to the list." He turns, heading toward his room.

"The list?" I squeak, following behind him.

He sets the plate down on his desk, setting the fork and water bottle up before turning back around. "Of things that can constitute good sex that I want to show you." He throws his arm wide, sweeping his desk chair out with a stupid mock bow.

"How long is this list?" I ask, sitting down and picking up the water bottle.

He shrugs, heading over to a closet and taking off his watch. "Couple hundred pages."

I choke on my first sip of water, whirling around to face him. He shrugs.

"There's a whole world outside of vanilla that I've only dabbled in." Another shrug then he pulls his sweater off one handed. "We can explore together once you're up to my speed."

I shake my head, turning back around and picking up the fork. Stabbing into a piece of chicken, I consider his words and feel my chest heave. He certainly isn't talking as temporarily as I assumed this was. How long does hate fucking last?

25

AUTUMN

When I finish all the chicken *and* mac and cheese, Ramsey is lounging on his bed, hair tousled, and nose buried in a medical textbook.

"What's that for?" I ask, swiveling on his desk chair to face him on the bed.

"Org II." He glances up. "I have a quiz tomorrow."

"Oh." My stomach falls. "I can head back to campus. You should study. We can—

Ramsey closes the book, tossing it onto a stack next to his bedside table. "Nope. I'm not putting this off any longer." He stands, holding his hand out and waiting for me to place mine in his palm.

The second I do, he yanks me up. "I'm stripping you this time." His eyes stay on my face as he drops my hand and slowly brings both of his up to my hips. His grip pushes the edge of the denim into my skin.

I grab his wrists, stopping him from moving any further. My breathing is shallow, and he just waits, perfectly still in front of me. "If I let you strip me, we're done with this slow bullshit."

He smirks, fingers twitching against me. "More demands? What did I say about that?"

I grit my teeth, digging my nails into his wrists.

He just smirks, still simply waiting.

"We're done with this slow bullshit, *please*." My cheeks heat, the same feeling invading my gut and soaking my panties. Damn him.

"Better," he says, moving his hands up an inch and dragging the bottom of my sweater up with them. My grip does nothing to stop him, like he could break my hold in a second and was merely placating me by waiting. "But I set the pace. And I particularly like slow at the moment. Especially for our first time."

"Hardly our first time," I mumble, hands still wrapped around his wrists. I lose another inch, the top of my stomach now exposed.

His hands stop, eyes hardening. "You know what I mean." Then those maple syrup depths travel south, watching as more of my skin is exposed. "Plus, that was just fooling around. This time..." The edge of my bra is uncovered, my hands still circling his wrists. He sighs, grip moving from my skin to cup my breasts over the material. "I'm going to be inside you." He squeezes as he speaks, the veins in his wrists pressing into my palms. The feel of his hands is decadent, my nipples aching and breath getting stuck in my chest. He pushes them further together and I moan, his tongue coming out and wetting his bottom lip.

And then he moves his hands away, my boobs falling back down as he pulls the sweater up over my head. I have to break my grip on his wrists, holding my arms over my head so he can divest me of my first layer.

Once I can see him again, he smiles, the look somehow carnal and smug at the same time. "And that requires some patience so you can accommodate the stretch."

I roll my eyes, but he grabs my jaw, bringing my face closer so I can feel his words fan across my face. "Hush. After this, all bets are off, sweetness." His tongue darts out and licks my bottom lip. "So just humor me once more?"

Before I can answer his lips crash into mine and I swallow his intensity. His tongue dominates mine, stroking and sucking so I melt beneath him, both of us groaning.

After a minute, he lets go, keeping his face an inch above mine as he reaches down and pops the button on my jeans. The sound of my zipper opening invades the space around us, and I dig my nails into my palms to keep myself from squirming.

Shivers run up and down my back, and Ramsey's grin sharpens. "Anything else you'd like to say?"

I clamp my jaw shut, cheeks burning. "No," I press out. He'll only slow further down if I complain anymore.

"Good." He starts peeling my jeans down, kneeling as he goes so that when they're finally down around my ankles, he's on his knees in front of me. "Step," he orders and I place my hands on his shoulders, keeping my balance as I lift one foot and then the other. In just my bra and panties, I force my hands to stay at my sides, feeling his eyes moving across my exposed skin.

His lips touch the top of my right thigh, placing a kiss on the dimpled skin before moving to the left and repeating the action. I feel myself shudder, unable to hold it in and knowing the movement most likely made the parts of me I don't like shake.

"Open your eyes."

I blink, not realizing I closed them and glance down at

Ramsey. He stays on his knees, bare chested and looking up at me. Then he reaches down and unbuttons his pants, eyes locked with mine the entire time.

"W-what are you doing?" I murmur, watching his hand reach into his pants once his zipper is free.

He starts stroking underneath the material, hand moving rhythmically beneath the surface.

"Ramsey?" My chest rises and falls between us, breath moving rapidly through my lungs.

He shakes his head. "Sorry." His hand comes out of his pants, joining the other in gripping the tops of his thighs. "Needed a second."

And then he's standing again, cupping my jaw and devouring my mouth once more. I barely have time to think let alone kiss him back before I notice his one hand unhooking my bra. I try to pull back, murmuring, "There's a few extra hooks," into his mouth.

I feel the clasps free, the weight of my chest settling without support.

"I got it, Fall," he whispers against my lips, biting my top one sharply.

Letting go of my face, he slides my bra straps down my arms, leaning back so there's room to completely remove the garment. Once it has joined the rest of my clothes somewhere in his room, he steps back, putting a full foot between us.

"Fuck, I think I love your tits." He seems mesmerized by them, eyes locked on and roaming over my exposed skin and peaked nipples.

"Careful. Pretty sure this is a hate fucking arrangement, remember?" My teasing is cramped by the breathless way my voice comes out, unable to drag in enough oxygen to say it confidently.

He smirks though, still staring at my chest. "I've got plenty of emotions to go around." He frowns after saying it before shaking his head.

The front of his pants are still open and tented, his dark happy trail leading the way. He palms himself, getting a little lost for a second before looking back up at my face.

"Bed. Now." The words are rough and clearly rushed, all other semblance of sentence structure absent at the moment.

My feet move before I can think of anything witty to say. My thoughts are scattered, and my panties are drenched, everything in me aching for what's about to happen.

I climb onto his bed, not even bothering to reorient myself and just crawling on my hands and knees so that my ass is facing him from the side. I get into position, lowering my top half to the bed and using my arms to cushion my face. This is at least the part I'm familiar with.

"What are you doing?" I didn't hear him approach but I can tell he moved closer while I was crawling across his duvet.

I push myself up, looking back over my shoulder. "You said get on the bed."

He looks at me, head tilted and pants still precariously in place, only really held up by his tilted hips at this point. "Roll over. I want to see your face."

My brows furrow and I hesitate to follow the command.

He twirls his finger in the motion he wants me to make. "Now, Fall."

The nickname smarts and I twist, laying down on my back with my feet planted next to each other on the bed, knees pressed together. The position has me staring up at his ceiling while I contemplate how this will work.

He wants me on my back? Where he can see me? All of me?

My stomach contracts as I try to picture what I must look like from this angle.

And then Ramsey's face is filling my vision. His hand is pressing down on the mattress next to my head and he holds himself over me, not a single part touching my body. "What's going on in that head of yours?"

I bite my lip, pushing my jaw forward so I don't tuck my chin.

Ramsey's other hand grabs my face, pulling my lip free and then staying as a reminder not to do it again. "Talk to me, Fall."

"I've just..." I sigh. "I've never done it in this position."

He glances down my body, making me squirm. "Missionary?" he asks, a little incredulous.

I swallow and nod. "They didn't." I swallow again, looking up and away from his face. "They didn't want to see me."

The heat emanating from Ramsey seems to still. When I chance a look back at his face, every muscle in sight is locked tight. His jaw ticks once, twice, three times before he finally opens it and speaks in a deadly calm tone. "Well, I do. I want to see you, Fall. *All* of you." His eyes glint. "Especially when you're taking my fucking dick."

The harshness of his words and anger in his voice reorients me.

His hand on my face tenses, biting into my skin as if to emphasize everything before he releases me. He stands back up, and my eyes follow, locked on his while he pushes his pants down, but leaves his boxers. He reaches out, each hand cupping my knees so he can part them and then push them down to the mattress. The angle stretches the muscles in my thighs, but not beyond what I can handle, and the burn ramps up my desire.

"Fuck, that's pretty," he whispers, staring down at my saturated underwear. His hands stay on my knees a bit longer, eyes taking their fill and I feel a bit more of that power rock through me.

It doesn't feel like a lie. The more he says shit like that, the more it doesn't feel like a lie.

Trailing his fingertips across my inner thighs, he makes me fidget beneath him, the wispy feeling sending shocks and tingles up toward my spine. When his hands meet at my center, he dips his right index and middle finger under the seam of my underwear that lays over the junction of my thigh. I buck when his fingers brush against me, sliding all the way over to the other side before bunching the center of my panties and pulling them to the side. His eyes are locked on their movement the whole time and I watch his face, sharp expression honed in on everything he's doing.

Exposed completely for him, I fist my hands in the blanket, needing him to touch me, but knowing he'll only do it on his timeline.

His other hand smooths circles into my inner thigh, never moving closer or breaking pattern in a maddening way.

"I'm going to make you come three times before I fuck you. Think you can handle that?" He suddenly looks up at me, as if waiting for an answer. As if my protest would stop him completely.

But I don't want him to stop. I haven't since he pinned me against my dorm room wall.

"Yes," I breathe, thoughts completely consumed with him.

He waits, completely still.

"Yes, please." I intone.

His pupils dilate, the black chasing out the molten brown. "Good." He leans down and pecks my lips, the hand making circles on my thigh moving closer to my center at the same time.

Sinking down a little further, he licks the side of my jaw, following the path with his teeth afterward. His fingers however, run down my seam, parting my lips and immediately pinching my clit.

I cry out, fingers digging further into the blanket.

"Shhhhh," he soothes, finger dipping down to slowly coat my clit in my cum. He slowly circles it, using the lightest pressure and making my breathing become embarrassingly loud as I tip my head back and stare up at the ceiling.

His lips trail down my neck, teeth scraping against the side before he hits my collarbone and bites. I yelp, hips bucking into his hand and he laughs, adding a little more pressure.

Moving further still, he kisses the center of my chest in between my breasts, which have slid apart in this position. Using the tip of his nose to trail across my skin, he slowly makes his way to my right nipple. I try to control my breathing, losing focus as his fingers leave my clit, heading back down toward my entrance. When he reaches the edge, he circles me, once, twice, three times, tongue dipping out and mimicking the movement around my stiff nipple.

I gasp, driven straight to the edge a moment later when he plunges two fingers inside me while biting down on my nipple at the same time.

"Fuck," I cry as he sets a relentless pace in between my legs, the glide getting smoother with each pass. His tongue laps while his lips suck on the tip of my breast and I feel myself arching into him as I come the second his other hand presses into my clit. A guttural scream rips from my chest, and I feel Ramsey smile against my skin, eyes watching my face while his hands continue to move.

My throat is a little raw when I come back down, unable to catch my breath. Ramsey is kissing along my chest, moving toward my untouched breast and I already know what is coming but the second he bites down, I'm arching again, back bowed and suspended while he sucks my other nipple into his mouth and adds a third finger, creating a delicious stretch. The second orgasm rolls into the first, waves crashing over top of each other and I can't tell if I'm crying out again or if my mouth is just stuck in a wide-open expression, eyes screwing shut and body no longer under my control.

When my hips and spine fall back down, Ramsey's lips are trailing over the center of my torso, heading south while his three fingers continue to leisurely pump in and out of me. I can hear how wet I am, feel the cum seeping out around his fingers, but the groan he makes when he finally descends completely, mouth closing around my clit and lapping at the mess I'm making, erases any embarrassment trying to exist in the blanketed fog of my post orgasmic bliss.

Ramsey devours me, tongue running over his own fingers as he swipes up as much of my cum as he can. He zeroes in on my clit, stiffening his tongue and adding the perfect amount of pressure as he starts to curl his fingers inside me. I can feel another wave building in the background, this one rolling in with dark clouds and thunder as it continues to mount higher and higher with each pass of his fingers and tongue. He keeps the same pace, ever so confident and assured in his movements, merely waiting for me to fall apart again.

And I do, screaming his name and releasing the duvet with one of my hands so that I can latch onto the back of his head and hold him hostage between my thighs. He licks my clit through the whole thing, fingers pushed all the way in and fluttering against the perfect spot inside me.

When I finally release him, he pulls his fingers out first, my body clenching around air as he continues to circle my clit. Taking one last long lick, he sits back, staring at me from the edge of the bed. My eyes are barely open, the view hazy and moving.

"How was that for fast?" he grumbles, standing and leaning over me so that I can watch him suck his fingers into his mouth and groan at another taste of me. His weight presses me into the mattress, and I revel in the feeling of his skin covering mine.

When his fingers leave his mouth, he licks his lips. "Condom?" he says roughly.

My brain malfunctions, missing the word's meaning entirely. "Wh-what?"

He leans forward, looking at me sternly. "Do I need to use a condom?"

Oh. "Yes," I reply, my raw throat making the word hurt a little to say.

Ramsey raises a single brow, pressing his lips together while he waits.

"Yes, please?" I retry.

He rewards me with a satisfied smile, kissing my cheek before standing up. I reel from the loss, his weight and heat seeming to be the only thing that grounded me a second ago.

Without a word, he runs a hand over my thigh while rummaging around for a condom in his bedside table drawer. The feeling is soothing and my nerves settle, body completely boneless as I sink back into his comforter.

The next thing I'm aware of is his hands pulling my panties down my legs. I let my legs stretch out, helping him as best I can while the boneless limbs feel like cinderblocks to move. He chuckles, helping me more than I help him.

Once I'm naked, he wraps a hand under each of my knees, pulling me down the bed until my ass is almost hanging off the edge. I glance down my body in surprise, finding him already naked, condom on, and wholly in control.

He slides both of his arms forward, leveraging his strength and somehow balancing my useless legs so that he ends up standing, arms out at his sides and my knees bent over each of the pits of his elbows, spreading me obscenely before him.

The view makes him look like a god, chest pushed out and biceps on full display, while making it impossible for me to move anything below my waist. The light in the center of his ceiling sits directly behind his head from this view, shrouding him in shadows while also lining him in light.

"You ready for me, sweetness?" He tilts his head forward, creating a darker shadow over his eyes and highlighting the smirk painting his lips.

I swallow, feeling his tip brush against my wetness when he thrusts his hips. Nodding, I fist the blanket again and he tsks.

"I need words, Fall."

I steel myself. "Yes, I'm ready."

His smile grows. "Good. Put me inside you."

Everything goes blank. "What?"

"Reach down." He waits, eyes watching me as he stands there perfectly still.

I release the blanket, hand moving down between my legs where I can feel him hard and waiting.

Before I can touch him, he orders, "Take me in your hand."

I wrap my fingers around his cock, the condom creating a thin barrier between our skin.

"Line us up, and I'll do the rest."

I swallow again, feeling his tip touching my skin. Pulling him in a bit closer, I slide him down over my skin until he notches ever so slightly at my entrance. I clench around nothing, the movement brushing over his tip.

He groans, licking his lips and looking down at where I'm holding him against me. "Let go when you're ready," he whispers, holding himself back.

I take a second to breathe before slowly letting go. As my fingers uncurl, he pushes forward ever so slowly until his head is buried inside me. Even using three fingers before, I have to stretch to accommodate him, and he waits a beat before pushing in a little bit further.

Every inch makes me tremble, Ramsey moving slowly in and out with just the power of his hips. I go back to gripping the bed, mouth hanging open and eyes on the ceiling again. It takes him more than a full minute to sink entirely into me and when I feel his hips connect with the backs of my thighs, we're both panting, gasping like fish trying to find our breath.

The few times I've had sex, I wondered if they were even fully in by the time they came. With Ramsey settled fully inside me, I realize just how paltry my previous times really were. He's deeper than anything I've ever experienced and the longer he just holds himself there the higher the tension climbs.

"Ramsey?" I huff, attempting to get the two syllables out

on one breath. I tuck my chin, looking at where he's staring down at our joined bodies and holding my bent legs aloft.

"Hmmm?" he hums.

"Move." His head snaps up and I quickly add, "Please."

He pulls his hips back, eyes locked on mine as his cock slowly drags against my walls. The feeling pulls my jaw down further, but the second his tip is the only thing in me, he snaps his hips forward, thrusting into me hard and jolting me an inch up the bed. My eyes widen and he just smiles, repeating the slow retreat and hard entry once more.

Our chests rise and fall in the same rhythm, eyes never straying from one another as he slowly ups the pace, finding a more even beat. I claw at the bed, hips tilting as best they can to try to meet him thrust for thrust.

Unbelievably, I start to think that I might just come from this alone, my orgasm building toward the sweetest peak. But I get stuck at the top, unable to fall over the edge without something more and I snake one hand down to strum my clit.

Ramsey grunts when the move bushes the back of my hand against his skin, pace quickening and losing all rhythm, but I'm already falling, tears streaming down my face as I silently cry and lock up. My vision goes white and I hear Ramsey groan, feeling his weight crash down on top of me as his hips spasm with mine. My body grips him, the feeling causing his cock to twitch inside me and spurring both of our orgasms on.

When things start to settle, I realize Ramsey bit into my neck when he came down on top of me, my skin still locked between his teeth. The dull ache is pleasant, and I bring a hand up to run through the back of his curls. Exhaustion sets into my limbs, eyes drooping and head lolling a bit to the side.

Ramsey must release me because I can feel him wiping something soft against my inner thighs next and then the light turning off from behind my closed eyes. A blanket covers me and a pillow appears beneath my head, Ramsey's head tucking into the crook of my neck as he spoons me from behind, locking me in against his chest. One of his hands cups my chest and his thigh lays atop mine, leg bent so that his foot rests against my shin. I snuggle into his warmth, letting it carry me the rest of the way to sleep without another thought.

26

RAMSEY

Fall is still in my arms when I wake up. I'm hard and trapped against her ass, the feeling nice as I slowly come to. Readjusting a bit, I realize my arm is completely dead under the pillow we're sharing and a second later I realize I don't care. The air outside of our cocoon of blankets and limbs feels cold and I burrow a little further down, pressing my nose and lips against the back of her neck. She has this sweet scent, something floral in her lotion or shampoo I'm sure, but I can only really get a hit of it up close. Not that I'm complaining.

My eyes burst open.

I'm in bed, cuddling, holding, *sniffing* Fall.

And I like it. I'm warm and comfy and absolutely content sharing my space with her.

Something I've hated doing with literally anyone else. Even my exes that were more than just a one-time fuck.

Red warning lights flash everywhere, a dull alarm ringing in my ears.

I slowly ease my arm out, wiggling it as little as

necessary to free my top half from around her. The movement causes Fall to roll, still dead asleep, but now lying on her back instead of away from me.

She's beautiful asleep. Her lips are parted but she makes no sound, the only evidence that she's breathing the rise and fall of her chest. Her hair is wild and everywhere, strands still clinging to my chest with static. And I realize she has no worry lines. When she's awake there seems to always be a little wrinkle in between her eyebrows. But right now, there's nothing, her face clear and peaceful.

Without realizing it, I find myself stroking the spot with the tips of my fingers, running them back and forth over her skin before pulling away.

Last night was mind blowing, soul consuming, earth shattering. Every time with Fall has been transformative, something inside me getting rewritten over and over again. But last night felt solidifying. Like whatever it was that was changing is now wholly new and in place somewhere in the center of my chest.

I've had plenty of sex, good sex. But it never felt like anything about me changed before. This is *something* different and I can't tell what it is.

Except I know it's her, the fact that she was the one with me. That is the only difference. That is the *key* difference.

You care about her?

Diane's words haunt me, turning in the back of my brain and burrowing into the twisty feeling filling my gut.

Do I care about her? Is that the difference?

I want to protect her. I want to provoke her, fight with her. And now I know I *need* to fuck her. As many times as she'll let me.

Does that equal caring?

I stare at her, finding the easy anger seeing her always provokes. Even sleeping, my blood simmers looking at her. It's not necessarily anything she does. It's the reminder she stands for. The image of those fiery eyes glaring at me across the parking lot of Lucy's diner. The fact that I know if I give something, she'll give it right back with all the vehemence of a viper. The fact that her existence invades my concentration, capturing it and making it impossible to look anywhere else. I hate that I can't stop noticing her, can't stop myself from poking at her, can't help myself from seeing what I'll get with each push. I hate that she invades and takes up so much of my brain by simply being near.

But there's that solidified something underneath the anger. Some feeling niggling in my gut and swirling around in my chest. I felt it swell last night when I came, her cunt gripping me so tight I think I saw stars.

You care about her?

I dig, watching her eyelids flutter. A smile slowly sweeps over me, my lips moving before I make the conscious connection why.

Fuck. I do. I care about Autumn Green.

I'm a little worried I always have.

And I'm suddenly very worried she doesn't care about me. Not the same way.

Fuck, she hates me and I'm only now realizing I don't want her to.

Great timing, idiot.

She starts to stir, face turning and nuzzling a little deeper into my pillow. Our legs are still tangled together, and she rubs her foot against mine, stretching out a bit before her eyes open.

She smiles first and that solid thing glows. Then it drops

off her face and she sits up, holding my comforter against her chest.

"What time is it?"

I grapple with the revelation I've just had, realizing I have no idea how to act around her now, always relying on intimidation to try to piss her off before and then turn her on more recently.

"Um," I sit up, letting the blanket fall away from me. I glance over at the digital clock on my bedside table. "Almost ten." I wrack my brain for something else to say.

"Fuck." She rolls away, untangling her legs from mine and taking the duvet with her. "I never texted Aria telling her I was staying the night. She probably thinks you murdered me or something." She gets off the bed, walking over to grab her phone still sat on my desk next to her plate from last night.

I slide over to the edge, letting my feet touch the ground and watching her frantically text, blanket shoved into her armpits to keep herself covered from me. Instead of frustrating me, I find it cute. I rub my hands over my thighs.

She pays me no attention.

How do I get her to like me?

"I should get going," she says, not even looking up from her phone screen. She takes a step, stumbling a bit and I jump up, grabbing her elbow.

"You okay?"

"Yeah." She laughs, a pretty pink blush blooming in her cheeks. "Just a little sore."

The solid thing inside me glows a little hotter but I blank, feeling a little out of my depth in new waters.

She rights herself, pulling her arm out of my grasp. "Where did my underwear end up?"

She starts hunting for it and I watch for a moment

before shaking myself out of this weird in between space. "You can stay if you want. Let me make you breakfast or something." I run a hand through my hair, feeling so fucking lame.

"That's okay." She picks her underwear up and starts awkwardly pulling them on under the blanket. "I need to get back and shower and change before class."

"Skip it," I blurt, grabbing my boxers and pulling them on just to have something to do.

She moves back to her pile of clothes, dropping the blanket and dressing quickly. "Can't. Only get one for this class and I don't want to waste it if I'm not sick." She's buttoning her pants as she speaks, and I realize she hasn't looked at me since she woke up.

I pick up my pants, holding them as I say, "Okay, I can drive you." I start to walk toward her, but she tosses a hand out, placing it firmly against my stomach.

"No, that's okay. It's daylight out and not snowing." She nods over to the window where it looks sunny and clear outside. "I'll be fine."

The solid thing in my chest cools about thirty degrees. "I'd rather take you," I try.

Her hand presses more firmly against me, holding me back. "I don't see why." She finally looks up at me, eyes looking back and forth between mine. "We're not friends, Ramsey. This is just fucking. Right?" Her eyes turn pleading, begging for me to uphold our rules and answer completely differently from how I want to.

"Right," I spit out. "Just fucking." The solid thing dies a little.

She nods her head once, eyes falling away from mine.

Did I just say the wrong thing?

"I'll see you in class then." Her hand stays on my

stomach for an extra beat, and I wrack my brain for some reason to make her stay. But before I can come up with anything she's grabbing her stuff and heading out the door, looking at the floor as she quietly closes it behind her.

What the fuck was that?

27

RAMSEY

My mood is fucking sour. Has been for a couple days. The guys have all noticed, even Tanner who rarely notices anything outside of hockey and hockey. Harley finally broke the wide berth they've all been giving me, telling me to come to the gym after class, no exceptions. I already know he's going to make me work out until the anger waves rolling off me calm down. I probably need it.

After Fall left the other day, I got pissed. I fucking like her. And I've spent years pushing her away again and again and reveling in the sting of it. But she indirectly asked me if we were more than just fucking and I thought I was saying what she wanted to hear. She wanted rules, boundaries, clear lines separating us from the more complicated stuff. I was the one trying to cross them.

So why did she look disappointed when I said yes?

And why was I so fucking slow to put together my own feelings for her?

I don't want to just be fucking her. I want Fall to be *mine*.

As all of this swirled around in my brain, I just got angry.

It's been my go-to emotion for so long and I tried using Diane's techniques to stay in control, but it was way too easy to just give in and become a black fucking cloud of rage the last few days.

Better than being a mopey stupid fuck.

Walking into Miller's class forty minutes ago, I had been practically vibrating with it. As students came in, I didn't even look up, fully focused on the work I've been putting off. The second Fall walked into the room though, I knew. Like I have some sixth sense radar for the little witch. It made me grind my teeth and keep working, pen pushing a little harder than necessary into the papers I was grading.

Great back to square fucking one.

Feeling too much anger to deal with her at the moment, I avoided looking up through the whole class, blatantly pulling out my phone and scrolling once I was caught up on their last lab grades. Miller didn't give a shit, never calling me out for it through his whole lecture.

Packing my shit up now, I feel her approach.

"Hey," she says and I glance toward her, noting how tightly her hands are wrapped around the strap of her bag.

"Hey," I repeat, tone more clipped than hers. She's wearing her hair up and my first instinct is to grab her neck. Pretty sure I'd just end up pulling her closer if I did so I refrain.

"Haven't heard from you the last few days." She rocks on her feet, and I adjust my glasses, still looking down at my bag and stuffing random things off the desk into it. "Thought you said you'd be more communicative." She chuckles to lighten her words, but I can hear the hesitation beneath them too.

I close my bag, grabbing the strap before I look up at her. "Thought we weren't friends." I shrug the strap over my shoulder. "Didn't have any pressing need for pussy the last few days."

She jolts before her eyes narrow, feet firmly planted now. "You're being a jerk, Ramsey."

I know. I can hear it, feel that part of me that isn't blinded by all this fucking fury screaming behind a locked door. But I don't have the fucking key right now. "Isn't that what you like about me?" I lean back, feigning boredom as I wait to see how she responds.

She stares at me, eyes hard and fingers trembling. I can feel her fire reaching out to meet mine.

She's pissed.

Good.

Her tone comes out calm though. "Don't reach out to me again until you've gotten rid of all this." She waves a hand over me, shaking her head before stomping away.

I watch her walk out, part of me wanting to follow, pin her to a wall somewhere and fuck some of this anger away. That part has been in charge around her too much lately though. I take off my glasses, pinching the bridge of my nose. Miller's already gone, not even bothering to debrief the class with me since I clearly wasn't paying attention.

Maybe I'll walk to the gym. Spend the time cooling off in the snow a bit.

I throw another punch at the bag, Harley moving back a little with it as he holds it in place. My jaw aches from how hard I've been gritting my teeth, and my arms are basically useless after the last hour of weights and machines I've been circulating through. Sweat covers me, my shirt long gone and glasses smudged from where I've pushed them up hastily with my fingers on a lens. Curls are plastered to my forehead and I'm sure if I slowed down and tried to take notice, I would smell disgusting.

But I feel better.

The exhaustion helps chase away the anger, my body not having the energy to hold onto it so tight. And that freed up space has allowed my thoughts to flow a little easier.

"I fucking like her, dude." I punch the bag two more times, hands wrapped and covered in the pair of boxing gloves I keep in my locker here at Harley's gym.

"I told you that weeks ago." He grunts when I throw a knee in with my next combo.

"I know. But I thought it was in a 'like to fuck her' way not a flowers and chocolate kind of way!" I hold my gloves up again, shifting my weight into my next punch and trying to correct the angle I messed up on the combo.

Harley raises an eyebrow, pursing his lips to stop himself from laughing. "You want to get Autumn flowers and chocolate?"

I punch the bag again. "No. But I want to be around her. For more than just a quick fuck." I glance over at him before focusing on the bag again. "I made her dinner the other night." Punch. "Heated up leftovers, but still." Punch. "I did it because I knew she was hungry and I needed her to not be." I punch the bag again, forcing my aching muscles through the motion. "I think I want more with her. And I don't even know how to begin telling her that."

Harley crosses his arms, studying me like he doesn't know how to respond. "You're already exclusive. She's already yours." He shrugs.

I stand up. "No," I pant. "She's not. This is still just sex to her." I start unstrapping my right glove. "Plus, she fucking hates me."

"Can you blame her?"

I whip my head up and Harley holds his hands up. I grab my water bottle with my freed hand and spray it into the back of my throat.

"I just mean you've always had it out for her. She's never really experienced a nice version of you. Maybe you should start there?" He leans lightly against the bag, letting the weight counter his angle without toppling over.

I take a smaller sip of water, thinking over his words. "I tried that the other night. Didn't really realize I was doing it, but we got into a fight, and I drove all the way over there to fix it." I shrug.

Harley laughs. "Yeah, I mean maybe don't start with a fight. Try being nice to her right off the bat. See how she responds."

I roll the idea around a bit. "She's skittish. Thinks men don't notice her."

He furrows his brow and I nod.

"I know. I don't know if she'll think I'm messing with her. She hasn't responded great to me being nice unless I thread in a little mean or tell her it's for me not her."

Harley stands up. "Find a balance then. And just keep reinforcing it. Once she's used to you not constantly jumping down her throat, tell her you want more. Worst she can do is say no."

I laugh. Something tells me that's not the worst thing Fall could do. I have more faith in her than that. She could definitely destroy me if she wanted.

"And looks like now is your first chance." He nods over my shoulder to the front desk and I turn, finding Fall first. She's standing with Marshall and her little group of friends, sans my sister. They're all smiling and chatting with her roommate who Harley hired to work the front desk at the beginning of the semester. Aria's not overly cheerful, but she gets the job done and personally I prefer her to Cheryl's saccharine greetings any day.

I turn back to my best friend. "How bad do I smell?"

"What?"

"How bad do I smell? Quick smell me." I step closer and he shoves me away.

"I'm not smelling you. Just go talk to her, weirdo."

I nod, running my hand through my damp curls and then cursing when that just covers me in more sweat. Jeez, why was this easier when I thought I hated her?

Adjusting my shorts, I head over. I lied earlier. I've gotten hard thinking about her almost every other hour. I just angrily took care of it myself since I didn't know how to be around her without screaming. Diane's going to get another call soon and I wouldn't be surprised if she didn't already know it's coming.

Weaving through the gym, I reposition myself so that I'm behind her when I approach.

"Sign right here." Aria holds a clipboard out while Axel signs using a pen attached to a chain. She smiles, adding, "You guys didn't actually have to do this."

"Yes, we did. You're making $250 right here," Axel says, handing the pen back and beaming. "That's worth a quick signature and who knows? Maybe I'll actually start working out here." He glances out at the floor, looking overly excited as usual.

"Abusing the bonus system?" I whisper, standing directly behind Autumn at the back of the group.

She jumps, whirling around and looking up at me with a shocked expression.

"I might have to report you to the owner," I tease, folding my arms over my chest and smirking down at her. Her eyes wander over my skin at the movement before abruptly pulling back up to my face. I preen under the attention, everything inside me rioting.

"What are you doing here?" Her eyes narrow and she takes a similar stance to mine.

The move pushes her tits up in her sweater and I lick my bottom lip before answering. "It's a gym, Fall. I was working out."

She nods, breaking eye contact to shuffle her feet. "What happened to the asshole who dismissed me earlier?"

I reach out, tipping her chin up and catching her off guard. "He's gone for now." My eyes pinch and I sigh before adding, "Can't promise he won't come back though."

She just looks up at me, studying my face. The wrinkle in between her brows is present and I fight down the urge to smooth it out for her. She sighs, tilting her head so my hand falls away.

"Don't tell Harley." Her eyes rush back up to mine. "Please," she adds.

I smile. God, I love when she says that. "He probably already knows." I lean back rolling my shoulders a bit. "Doubt he cares though. She only gets the bonus if you guys keep your memberships for the full month, so he gets something out of it too."

Autumn nods, biting her lip and looking out at the fairly clear floor. Two women walk on the treadmills, an empty machine separating them. A couple guys lift weights by the mirrored wall. One girl wears headphones and sets up to deadlift, her spotter helping.

I step closer to Fall, getting an idea. "Would you want to work out together?"

She turns toward me, eyes wide and mouth pressed closed. "Um, no. That's okay." Her neck splotches red and I frown. "I'm just getting the membership for Aria's bonus. I doubt I'll come back other than to cancel it in a month or two."

I shrug. "It could be fun. Getting you all hot and sweaty." I let my eyes trail over her from head to toe. "I can definitely see benefits." My eyes return to hers and I instantly recognize my error. "I didn't—

"Bye, Ramsey." She turns back around, stepping up to where her group has moved forward, each one already signed up waiting to the side for her to give them the first timer's tour.

"Fall, I didn't mean anything by it." I step to the side trying to catch her eye. "I wasn't saying you need to change *anything*."

She huffs. "Yeah, sure."

I step in front of her, forcing her to glare at me, though she decides to direct it at my chest rather than my face. Some anger sparks back up inside me. "Have I not made it clear enough how attracted I am to you?"

"For hate fucking. Yeah, I got it." Her fingers are pressing into her upper arm, and I fist my hand, so I don't yank her face up to look at me.

"Fall, you're fucking beautiful. I've told you I think so before. I didn't mean to imply anything other than it'd be hot to watch you get sweaty." Her eyes blink up at me before staring ahead again.

Some of the tension in her shoulders eases a little.

I reach out, twisting an errant strand of copper hair near the side of her neck in my fingers. "There's plenty of other, more private venues I can do that in though."

Fall rolls her eyes, the rest of the tension in her shoulders loosening. "Knock it off." She swats my hand away, swallowing and pulling her sweater away from her a bit.

I frown and wait, watching her face. With the solid thing lodged in my throat, I ask, "Come over tonight?"

She tips her head back, looking up at me, something sparking in her eyes. "Have a pressing need for pussy all of a sudden?"

I smirk, stepping forward and pulling her against me by the waist. "With you? Definitely." I push my dick against her stomach and her mouth pops open, a small sound coming out.

She glances around, but I keep my eyes on her. She bites her lip before looking back up at me. "I kind of need to study tonight."

"We can do both." I massage her lower back with my hands as I continue. "I've already taken all your classes so I can help." I lean down, running my nose over hers. I'll spend time quizzing her if that's all she wants. "Take advantage of my brain, sweetness."

She pushes me back, but I can tell she's breathing a little unsteadily. "How do you manage to make everything sound dirty?"

I shrug. "It's a gift." I put my hands in the pockets of my shorts. "Come over tonight."

"Autumn? You're up!" Aria calls. I glance back and all her friends are off to the side, staring at us.

Autumn leans around me to look too. "Fine," she says, going to step around me, each of us turning to stay facing each other as she does. "But I'm walking this time."

"I'll let you walk if you stay for breakfast in the morning." I waggle my eyebrows to make the suggestion seem dirty and who am I kidding? I'll probably press my luck in the morning if I know she'll stick around this time.

She rolls her eyes, finally wearing a smile. "Deal." She turns around, walking up to the desk and leaving me to watch her from behind. I stay there for a second, smiling at her back before I glance at her friends again. They're all watching me, Marshall grinning like a loon with his arm around his girl.

"Shut up," I say to him, and he just laughs while I walk away.

Heading to the locker room, I quickly throw my shirt back on and change into a pair of sweats. Pulling on my coat, I go to grab the winter hat Mom got me in the Coast colors. I stare at it for a second before grabbing my bag and heading out.

Spotting her bright red hair still in the group over near the individual training rooms, I walk over. Aria is giving her practiced spiel, skipping some of it and adding in little quips about how none of this probably matters if they're planning to just cancel in a month. Axel parries with her and they're all laughing by the time I'm next to Fall.

She glances over, sensing me next to her. Her eyebrows furrow, that little worry wrinkle deepening as she stares up at me.

"For the walk later." I press my hat into her hand, using my other hand to close her fingers around it. Once she has it, I release her, smiling and then looking her in the eye again. "Wear it," I say before heading out.

28

AUTUMN

Ramsey lit a candle. One single candle.

It was the first thing I noticed when I walked into his room. Royal let me in, taking my coat and telling me Ramsey was upstairs even though Smith and Tanner sat on the couch in the living room, waiting for Royal to come back to keep playing whatever video game they had paused. I just headed up without saying much of anything.

The first thing Ramsey notices is me still wearing his hat.

"Good girl," he says, standing and kissing my forehead. It makes me squelch my toes in my socks, stirring an ache in my stomach that I decide not to investigate further.

"What's with the candle?" I blurt, pulling the hat off and attempting to comb my hands through my hair.

Ramsey glances over at it, the tips of his ears flaring bright red. "Oh, nothing, just wanted to light one."

That's the end of it for the next twenty minutes, but something about the candle keeps pulling my focus. I'm pretty sure he didn't have it the last two times I was here.

Did he go out and buy one? And why did he pick one called Gardenia Falls? I can't figure out how he would know that's my favorite scent. Fortunately, the dollar store shampoo I like has one scented like gardenias or I'd rarely get to smell it.

"You're concentrating really hard over there."

I glance back over at him. We're spread out on his massive bed. He sits up against his headboard; a couple textbooks open around him and his laptop perched in his lap. My back rests against the wall, legs perpendicular to him. My laptop is beside me, a model of the female endocrine system pulled up while I use a notebook to sketch out and label my own diagram.

"You were staring into space pretty intensely for a minute," Ramsey adds, still watching me. "Need help with something?"

"No," I murmur. "Just thinking. I'm trying to get this system memorized for the quiz tomorrow." I hold up my half-labelled diagram.

Ramsey nods, his phone buzzing on the bed between us. He picks it up, setting his laptop aside and getting off the bed when he sees the notification. "You have the thyroid and thymus mixed up," he says before heading out of the room.

I glance down then look over to the model I pulled up and curse. He's right. I shake my head, erasing my labels and switching them before he comes walking back in, two bags of Chinese food in his hands.

"What's all this?" I sit up, putting my notebook to the side.

"Dinner." He puts the bags on his desk, opening one and starting to pull out the takeout containers. "Can't study without brain food."

"Lo mein is brain food?" I chuckle.

He smiles. "Yes. Not so sure crab rangoons are though." He pulls a bag of them out, pretending to weigh them against the lo mein.

I scooch down the bed, grabbing the bag once I'm kneeling on the edge and making him laugh. He passes me the bright red sweet and sour sauce, and I get off the bed, settling down on the floor.

"What are you doing?"

I look up at him, midway through pulling the top off the sauce. "Taking a break to devour these?"

"Why are you on the floor?"

I get the top off and pull out a rangoon. "So, I don't get sauce all over your bed. If I'm expected to sleep in it, I would prefer it not be sticky."

He smirks and I already know what he's going to say before the words leave his mouth. "It'll be plenty sticky if you're sleeping in it."

"Gross," I deadpan, biting into my sauced up rangoon.

He just shrugs, grabbing a few more containers before joining me on the floor. He spreads the food out between us, sitting crisscross and starting to open his container of Mongolian beef.

A few minutes pass with just the sounds of us eating settling in. "How'd you know what to order?" I ask, chewing my fourth rangoon. I grab the container of chicken lo mein and start to pop the top.

Ramsey reaches up and grabs a set of paper wrapped chopsticks from the bag still sitting on top. "I've put your order in with mine, Mira, and Bentley's plenty of times back home." He shrugs, passing the chopsticks over to me. "Not hard to figure out what was yours versus theirs with some simple deduction."

I stare at him, that squirmy feeling invading right at my

waist again. I reach up, grabbing one of my textbooks off the bed behind me and opening it on my lap as I start to eat my noodles. "You paid quite a bit of attention for someone who hates me," I whisper. It feels like stepping over some unspoken line, one I'm not sure who drew anymore.

"I don't hate you." He says it so easily, but I force myself to keep staring at the textbook, too scared to look up.

If he doesn't hate me, what does that make our arrangement?

I push that question aside, not even daring to touch it or the can of worms lying underneath it.

He sighs, and I hear him adjust his glasses, nails tapping against the frames. "I think I just hated how we met. Hated how easily you got to me every time after that." He trails off a bit, and the air feels pregnant, like he's waiting for me to say something.

But I chicken out, chewing my food and pretending to read about the circulatory system.

Ramsey goes back to eating and I can feel his eyes on me as I reach back and grab one of my highlighters off the bed, uncapping it and highlighting a line I know will be on the quiz tomorrow.

"Why are you trying so hard?" Ramsey asks around a mouth of food. "You're a Greenmart Green. You'll be fine even if you fail a whole semester."

"Sage is a Green." I highlight another section. "I'm technically a Kenton," I add without thought.

Ramsey freezes, and the words I just spoke slowly register to me.

Glancing at his face, my stomach twists into a double knot.

You can't tell anyone, Autumn.

"What do you mean?" His eyes narrow as he speaks,

demeanor slipping into the foreboding one I know will pick at this until he gets an answer.

I chew my lip, realizing I've just callously thrown my family's biggest secret out into the universe. To a man I've always hated, nonetheless.

Ramsey leans in, taking the highlighter out of my hand. "Explain, Fall."

I wilt slightly, feeling the dig of the callous nickname a little deeper this time. Leaning back, I cross my arms over my chest, looking out the window at the tops of trees and darkening sky.

I've never spoken these words out loud to anyone outside my family. Never even tried. Mira and Bentley know I don't have a great relationship with my parents, but they never asked questions. They just accepted it and helped me get out of the house as much as they could. Or covered me when I pretended to forget my wallet. Or swallowed the lie I told about wanting to live in a dorm to get the authentic college experience. Aria knows pretty much the same thing, aware that my financial situation is a little weird but doesn't really know who my parents are.

Mom made it clear not to tell people. And I always thought if I was good and kept their secret, maybe Aaron would look at me.

But I can feel Ramsey staring at me.

And I want to tell.

More specifically, I want to tell him. This way if it blows everything up, at least we already don't like each other much beyond fucking. It won't be a great loss.

My stomach knots itself a little tighter at the thought.

"Aaron Green is currently the sole heir to the Greenmart fortune. When he married my mom, his parents set up a trust so that he could access more of his inheritance with the sole stipulation being that he produced his own heir first. My mom couldn't get pregnant. She was a prima ballerina when they met, an elite athlete that had put her body through the works to get there. They assumed it was her and were exploring other options. IVF, surrogacy." I wave my hand through the air rather than say et cetera. "In the Green world, it had to be a biological heir. But before they got to needing those options, she got pregnant with me. Problem solved." I push out a laugh, feeling my throat start to close. "She quit being a ballerina and they celebrated their little miracle. Except Grandpa Green thought her sudden happy news was a little convenient after years of trying. And after I came out with red hair and blue eyes."

I look back at Ramsey. His jaw locks and rage simmers in his eyes. I fall into their maple syrup depths, letting everything else wash away as I confess.

"He had me tested and whoopsie, I'm not a Green. Turns out Aaron was the one with the fertility issues. And Mom's ballet captain? No such issues. IVF and surrogacy? They were expensive. Especially when she could have her own pseudo-Green and everyone would none the wiser." I swallow, wetting my dried throat and testing to make sure it's not completely collapsed like it feels.

"From what I've been told disownment was on the table. Aaron refused to leave Mom. I don't know why because from the insider view of their marriage, I don't think it was love." I snort and realize my cheeks are wet. "Well, family money would not be passed down to some nobody interloper. So, Sage was created to solve the problem. Their little petri-dish miracle. And once they had her, all could be forgiven." I shrug, breaking eye contact and wiping my face. The highlighted words still blur beneath me. "Aaron wanted to put me up for adoption. He might have forgiven Mom, but I'm not his kid." My eyes meet his again. "Mom was all for it, but Grandpa Green stepped in yet again. Imagine the scandal? The great Green prince putting his supposed heir apparent up for adoption? The whole empire would fall to ruin." I roll my eyes, straightening my spine. "So, they kept me. Sage got ballet classes, and I got shoved in the background. Grandpa died with the secret as far as I know because my grandmother is the only Green who has ever treated me like part of the family. Which to be honest isn't the highest ranking for her so she's only slightly above tepid with all of us."

Ramsey stares at me, fist clenched around my highlighter. His jaw ticks and the air around him seems to radiate prickly energy. "Fall," he says through tight lips, voice raw. The sound of it pierces my chest and all the air in my lungs freezes. I've just shown him my bleeding heart, and his only response is that stupid nickname?

Refusing to cry anymore, I gnash my teeth together, swallowing past my body's reaction. My words come out like acid while I look down at my textbook again. "Right, well, now you know. Why I buy everything myself and *work hard*. I'm not really a Green and I'm not going to see a dollar of that money once I graduate. Aaron has made it plenty clear that he's only paying for my college for the image of it all, but this is where the gravy train stops." I laugh bitterly. "As if I've been sucking them dry and not avoiding adding a penny more to the amount I'm already indebted to them."

"*Charity*," Ramsey whispers and I look up. "That's why you think every relationship is transactional." His grip on my highlighter is so tight, I'm scared he's going to repeat the pen incident from the first day of school.

Instead, he throws it across the room, pushing his food to the side and crawling toward me. He grabs my jaw roughly and forces me to look at his face an inch away. "You don't owe me anything. Do you understand me? With me, nothing is ever transactional. *Ever.*" His fingers tighten for a second. "I want to kill your parents for making you feel like this."

I gasp at his words, the sound a little garbled with my mouth only able to move so much in his grip. He leans forward, kissing me harshly and pouring his anger into me. Except it seems to wrap around me like a blanket, joining his words in helping to fill the crack in my chest just a little bit more.

He leans back, still holding me in place. "You're staying with us for the break. You're not going back there."

I chuckle and his fingers loosen. "Mira already invited me. I have to go home though or I'll never hear the end of it from Mom." He opens his mouth, but I press on. "At least for the first few nights. But I'll be over at your house the majority of the time."

He scowls. "I can't believe my sister, or her little blabber mouth best friend, never said anything about this." He lets go of my face, scooting back to his position from earlier, but spreading his legs out so that my foot rests against his thigh.

I remember Mira constantly wiping her tears before Ramsey came into the room over winter break. "They don't know." I go back to my textbook, pretending I have an iota of interest in studying still. "And you'd be surprised how well they can keep a secret."

Ramsey smirks, picking his food back up. "You mean about her and Harley?"

My head whips up from my book. "You knew?"

"At the time? No." He laughs. "Harley got drunk last month and spilled the beans. Absolutely blubbered about it to be honest." His expression dims as his eyes lose focus.

"I've never really seen him that way about someone." The silence stretches a beat too long before he comes back, sitting up and shuffling his shoulders. "But he fucked up and he knows it so until he gets his head out of his ass and figures out how to fix it, I'm not interfering."

I set down my textbook, looking down at the words before me and seeing only bleeding ink. "Does Mira know you know?"

Ramsey shrugs, eyes on his food as he moves it around. "Probably not. I haven't had a chance to tell her." He looks up at me. "But she knows how I feel. We talked when I first thought something was going on last year and I told her to be careful."

I nod. "I told Mira about us hooking up."

Ramsey smiles, eyes darkening. "I know. I got a text from her the day after saying I better not break your heart." He chuckles, looking down again. "As if you'd ever trust me with it to begin with," he murmurs. His grip on the container tightens and I stare at the corded veins popping out against the back of his hand.

Do I trust Ramsey? A month ago, the answer would have been a definitive no. But now?

My thoughts fly around too fast to grab on to as I pretend to be inordinately interested in my cold lo mein. I pick at a mushroom, the squirmy feeling from earlier filling in the lightness my confession created.

Shit. Am I falling for Ramsey fucking Adams?

My stomach swoops down the slope of a rollercoaster, but before I can fully spiral out, he starts talking.

29

RAMSEY

I 'm still boiling mad from Fall's revelation, the puzzle pieces I've gathered clicking into place to reveal a jagged fucking picture. One that makes me want to drive all the way home and knock on Aaron and Tina Green's fucking door. But I stop myself by opening my mouth.

I told her our relationship wasn't transactional, but it feels like I owe her something after she handed over so much information. Like I want to return the favor and let her a little further in.

"I go to therapy," I blurt.

She looks up at me quizzically. "What?"

"I go to therapy. You shared all of that just now, so I wanted to tell you something I don't really advertise to most people."

She squints at me. "That's your big secret?"

I wring my hands in my lap, abandoning the cold food around us. "It's for anger management."

She laughs. "Does your therapist know they suck?"

I frown. "Diane does not suck."

"Ramsey I can make you angry in two seconds. Your therapist sucks."

My jaw clenches and I count to five in my head. "Yes well, you're an anomaly in my system so that doesn't really count. Besides Diane helps me cope, helps me work through the anger instead of being consumed by it. There's no cure."

She nods practically. "Of course there's no cure for anger. It's an emotion, not an illness." She assesses me for a second. "I never thought there was anything wrong with you."

I tilt my head and give her an *I smell bullshit* expression. "Sure, you didn't."

"You're psychotic, don't get me wrong. But in your patented control-freak, predator way. Not in a 'whoa there's something clinically wrong with him' way." She shrugs and that solid thing in my chest thumps.

Fuck, she's so effortlessly forward. It's fucking hot.

I shake my head. "You're distracting me. I was trying to tell you something."

She sets her food aside, folding her hands in her lap. "I just meant, you seem to have your anger pretty well managed."

"I didn't always." I swallow, feeling everything in my chest contract. And then I say the words that I know will scare her off. "I put someone in the hospital once."

Her indifferent expression falls away, but the remaining look almost feels like sympathy. "When?"

"Years before we met." I tap my index finger against my thigh, wanting to reach out and touch her, but scared she'll pull away. "My dad used to build rockets with me."

Her eyebrow quirks and I narrow my eyes.

"Stay with me, Fall. I promise it all ties together."

She mimes settling in, waving her hand afterward to indicate that I have the floor.

"When we were little, we were well off, but nowhere near the level Dad has built it out to now. Mira and I didn't go to private school and Dad came home after work and helped with dinner and homework and all the normal shit parents do. I was seven when my mom got her first book deal. I think that was when things first started to change. He wasn't happy where he was in the company he worked for, and Mom's success started to grow. She never outshone or outearned him or anything, but looking back, I think he got jealous of her. She was doing something she loved, excelling at it and he wasn't moving up as quickly as he thought he would. He decided to go back to school, get some degree through his company and stopped making dinner. Then he got a promotion and started travelling more. Then it was a move to a new company and suddenly we had to move."

Autumn sits still, rapt attention on me the whole time as I disappear into my memories.

"When we started at Emerald Grove, I hated it. I wanted to go back to our old, smaller house. Dad was made an SVP and that meant more money and responsibility or whatever, but it felt like that meant a completely new life all the sudden. And we never built rockets anymore. So, I got pissed. And I stayed pissed." I swallow, running my hands over the tops of my thighs.

"Mom noticed and she tried to get Dad to, but he was too wrapped up in chasing corporate success. That's when they started fighting more." Mira thought our parents' divorce was her fault when they told us last Thanksgiving break. She thought their happiness was resting on her shoulders for a while, but I was the first blow to their foundation. And I'm too much of a coward to tell her.

Autumn nods for me to continue when I pause, not realizing the next part gets worse.

"This kid was messing with Mira that first year after we moved and I was already carrying around so much pent-up aggression. I went to find him, bringing Harley with me since we bonded over our shitty home lives. We were just planning to scare him a little, make sure he left Mira alone. But I lost control. He didn't back down, and I just blacked out." I remember the light clicking out. One second, I was standing there, fist balled in this kid's shirt while he sneered at me and the next, I was shaking while Mira's terrified face filled my vision.

"Mira found us. I was standing over the kid while he clutched his broken leg, and she looked so fucking scared." I pinch my thigh to keep myself from getting lost in the agony of that moment.

Autumn sits forward, placing her hand over mine and gently pulling my fingers away from my thigh. Her touch startles me and I look up, trying to read the fear that should be in her expression. But she just keeps my hand in hers, squeezing and waiting for me to continue.

"When we got home that night, I heard Mom and Dad fighting about 'the right way to deal with me.' Mira was crying in her room and I just kind of lost it. Diane says I was in survival mode, susceptible to overwhelming emotions, but all I remember is just screaming at my dad about how I hated who he was here and how he was never around anymore and how he abandoned Mom. He slapped me."

Fall gasps, hand tightening around mine. I move to better grip hers, squeezing back to assure her I'm okay.

"Mom started crying and Dad looked shocked. After that, I started seeing Diane. She helped me channel a lot of my anger into football and find better ways to cope. And she gave me tools to stay in control even when everything feels like it's spiraling around me."

"Wait," she says, eyes looking back and forth at the floor below us.

I hold my breath as I follow her command.

She looks up, face wrinkled with confusion. "So, the Ramsey I first met, that was post-therapy Ramsey?" She stares at me in shock for a minute before a grin peaks out and I sag with an exhale.

"Anomaly," I grit out and she laughs.

I just told her one of the most traumatic things in my past and she's laughing. And making me laugh. It's light but it comes out involuntarily as the tension around me dissipates.

She leans forward, hand cupping my jaw lightly and meeting my gaze with her now more serious blues. "I'm sorry you went through that. I'm sorry that it took things going that far for them to help you."

My breath catches in my chest, and I lean a little farther into her touch.

"And for the record, I've never been scared of you Ramsey."

Fuck. She cuts right through to the crux of it as if those words don't crack through my carefully constructed armor with a perfectly aimed tap.

"Even when I've run or left right after an argument it wasn't out of fear of you. More fear at how far you push me."

I turn my head in her hand, kissing her palm. This fucking girl.

"Get on my bed."

She startles. "W-what?"

I lean forward, biting her lip in admonishment. "Get on my bed, Fall. And take off your pants." I go to pick up some containers of food, putting their lids back on and cleaning up.

Fall just stares at me. "But...we were studying."

I nod, giving her time to catch up. "We can continue after. Right now, I need to be inside you." I meet her eyes, pausing my clean up and deciding to concede one more thing. "Please," I whisper.

She shudders, eyes closing slowly before opening back up with blown pupils. I file that information away for future use.

She hastily works to stand up, popping the button on her jeans and shimmying them down her hips. I stare, food cleanup completely forgotten.

"No underwear?" I say a little breathlessly when her bare skin is revealed.

She smirks down, placing a hand on her hip after she tosses her jeans away. "I knew what I was coming over here for."

Her cockiness slams into me, nearly knocking me over as she climbs onto the center of my bed, pushing our laptops and books to the side.

Fuck. Confident Autumn will wreck me.

I scramble to finish putting our dinner away enough that none is on the floor and all of it is closed. Once that task is done, I pull my shirt over my head, finding Fall staring at me from where she kneels in just a tee shirt and cardigan in the center of my bed. Her eyes are devouring my bared skin, and I chuckle, flexing a little under her perusal.

"Lose the sweater," I command and she goes to take off the cardigan without hesitation. "But stay there. Just like that." Her position and newfound comfort level give me an idea and I'm curious if she'll go for it.

I walk over to my closet, opening one of the built in

the drawers. "Do you trust me, sweetness?" I start thumbing through the ties I have laid out in here. Finding a black silk one Smith gifted me a few years ago, I start pulling out the material before realizing she hasn't answered me.

Looking back at her over my shoulder, I find her worrying her bottom lip, eyes a little lost as she watches me. My fingers freeze.

"It's okay if you don't," I whisper, the words making that solid thing inside me crack at the edges. "I want to try something, but you need to be comfortable first." I pull the tie out and hold it up so she can see it. "For your eyes."

She stares at the material, eyes flicking back to mine after a minute. She takes a deep breath. "I trust you, Ramsey," she says, with a nod.

I slam the drawer closed. "You sure? You can say no to anything; you know that right?"

She nods again, shoulders pushing back a bit. "Yes, I know. I trust you. I know you'll listen to me if I need you to stop."

The solid thing in my chest heats up. I walk over to the edge of the bed, leaning over the footboard and kissing her chastely. "Always, sweetness," I breathe against her.

Leaning back, I hold up the tie. She turns around, letting me place it over her head and holding it against her eyes while I tie it behind her head.

When it's secure, I kiss her shoulder, letting my lips travel over the cotton of her tee shirt and then biting into the junction of her shoulder and neck. She squeaks, making me chuckle and my rock-hard dick twitch in my pants.

"Can you see?" I ask against the side of her neck.

She shakes her head.

"Words, Fall."

Her shoulders move and I know she's rolling her eyes. "No, Ramsey. I can't see."

I grab one side of her ass roughly, making her yelp. "Good." Releasing her entirely, I step back, listening to her breathe unevenly as I step away. She faces my headboard, ass out and knees spread apart as she kneels on my comforter.

So fucking pretty.

I squeeze the head of my dick through my clothes, staving off some of my lust so I can at least set up my idea before I come in my pants again. I turn back to my closet, sliding the pocket door closed and smiling to myself. This is going to be so good.

Heading back toward the bed, I remove the rest of my clothes and walk around to the side. Placing once knee on the edge, Fall's head turns in my direction. I pause, taking a second to stare at her some more.

I trust you, Ramsey.

Those words make me reach down and stroke myself a few times, reveling in the new level we've sunk down together. She's got my fucking tie over her eyes. If this goes well, I might start investing in some toys we can play with together.

Reaching over, I grab another condom out of my bedside table, quickly ripping it open and rolling it on. Then I climb the rest of the way onto the bed, maneuvering so that I'm kneeling in front of her, our knees the only thing touching.

"How you doing, sweetness?" I can just barely see her nipples, the outline of her bra stark against the form fitting tee shirt.

"Impatient." She growls. "Thought all bets were off and we were done with slow?"

I smile. "Always so fucking greedy."

Grabbing her by the back of her neck, I haul her in against me, her hands coming up to catch herself on my pecs. Kissing her, I lick against the seam of her lips, and she parts them without pause. My hand grips her a little bit harder, her nails scraping against my skin as she digs in as well. My other hand wanders, sliding over her side and around to grip her ass before venturing back and testing to see how wet she already is. Coming away soaked, I pull my mouth from hers, sliding my fingers into her mouth and pressing them against her tongue. She laps at them eagerly, tasting herself and moaning.

When I remove them, I lean in, whispering, "You okay with me taking you from behind?" in her ear.

She shudders, nodding her head.

"Words, Fall," I say harshly, reaching around and swatting the side of her ass. It jiggles perfectly and I watch, mesmerized. That's going to be fun to play with later.

Fall jolts from the sting but her panting gives away how much she enjoyed it. "Yes, I'm okay with it."

I grab her shoulders and start turning her around to face the footboard. I make sure her legs are spread on either side of mine, slotting in behind her and rubbing myself on her ass. "I promise, I still want to see you." I kiss her neck again.

Staring over her shoulder, I reach for the hem of her shirt, slowly pulling it up and being careful not to dislodge the blindfold just yet. Her body comes into view, and I press my hips against her a little more. Unsnapping her bra and removing it, I toss it aside, quickly bringing my hands up and watching myself palm her breasts.

Fuck I love her tits. They spill over in my hands, and I splay my fingers wide, making her squirm as I continue to play with them and avoid her nipples.

She whines and I shush her, biting a little against her

flesh and leaving another hickey on her neck. She melts into it, shoulders leaning back against my chest to keep herself upright.

"You're fucking gorgeous," I whisper, feeling her tense up against me. I pinch her nipples in admonishment, and she yelps before settling back in with a relaxed sigh.

I frown and the solid thing tremors. Seems I'll have to work on her ability to take a compliment without mixing in any pain.

I let go of one of her breasts, reaching down and circling her clit, her ass bucking against my cock. Groaning, I venture further, testing her entrance to make sure she's ready. Two of my fingers slide into her with very little resistance and this time I suck them off, savoring the taste of her and making a mental note to eat her out for breakfast in the morning.

"You're ready for me, sweetness."

She groans and I smile, reaching down and parting her legs a little further so I can line myself up and push the head of my dick against her. She feels so fucking warm and soft, even through the barrier of the condom. I meet some initial resistance and rock through it, placing my hand on her hip to steady her. When I push a little further, she moans but tips forward and I growl.

Reaching around, I snake my arm across her torso, banding her against me and gripping the front of her throat. She drips onto my dick when I collar her, and I bite her earlobe.

"You like wearing my hand as a necklace, Fall?" The words are husky and rough, most of my limited brain power focused on not coming too quick and ending this before she gets to see the grand finale.

"Yes," she pants, rocking her hips with me as I press the rest of the way in.

I test my grip, squeezing ever so slightly on the sides of her neck and her cunt clenches like a fist around me. My eyes close as I hold perfectly still, needing another second.

When I'm able to move again, I start fucking her at a hurried pace, eating up the gasps and sounds she makes while I watch the two of us together. One of her hands is gripping my arm, holding on for dear life, while the other wraps around my head, tangling in my hair and gripping perfectly.

The blindfold stays in place as I start whispering against the side of her head. "You look so fucking perfect taking my cock." She moans, lips staying open in a wide O as her head lolls back against my chest. "So pretty and perfect." She clenches around me, whispering my name and I nearly end it all there.

Biting the inside of my cheek, I stave off my release, tightening my grip on her hip. We're bent forward just enough that the angle feels impeccable, all of me sliding in and out of her over and over again.

"Do you want to see, sweetness?" I squeeze her neck slightly again, her body bucking against me when I do.

She nods, head moving jerkily but fervently.

"You want to watch me fuck you?" I need her to say it before I pull the blindfold off.

"Yes," she whispers hoarsely. "Ramsey, *please*." Her cry is guttural, emitting from the back of her throat.

I release her hip, keeping her throat in my grasp, body pressed against mine. Tearing the blindfold off her head, I watch as her eyes adjust and she stares forward, meeting the sight of the two of us together in the full-length mirror covering the door of my closet.

Our eyes meet and I continue fucking her, watching as she peruses the sight. Every line of her body is on display, every curve and dip that I want to one day spend hours just tracing with my lips. I thrust into her from behind, my cock appearing and disappearing between the apex of her thighs. My breath stutters in my chest, waiting to gauge her reaction before allowing me the vital oxygen I need to keep this up.

And then she squeezes me, pulling my hair at the same time and I watch as that light I saw in her eyes on the porch years ago burns like an inferno, encompassing her whole reflection in the mirror.

I exhale, picking up my pace and driving into her like a madman. She's loving this just as much as I am. Thank fuck.

"Look at you," I whisper. I reach down with my free hand, sliding it across her skin and watching her eyes follow it with interest in the mirror. Dipping in between her thighs, I quickly find her clit, circling and pressing at regular intervals. Her hips buck with no rhythm, mouth gaping open and closed as she tries to make a sound.

Swiveling my hips, I continue fucking her fast and hard, feasting on the exquisite site of her falling apart in my arms. Her body locks up and then starts to spasm against me, cunt clenching me harder than each time before. I bury myself to the hilt, my own orgasm racing down my spine and making my hips stutter as I come. I force my eyes to stay open, watching hers screw shut as she groans out my name.

We stay taunt for another moment or so before things finally subside and I slow my fingers on her clit down to a leisurely touch. She twitches against me, eyes opening and meeting mine in the mirror.

"So fucking perfect," I whisper, kissing the side of her head. She blushes, shuddering again but doesn't tense.

Seems like she can only accept a compliment when I'm either fucking her or right after. Noted.

I use my fingers on her neck to maneuver her jaw to the side and kiss her. She gives as much as she gets in this kiss and I revel in it for a moment.

Pulling out of her and sliding back, I start to remove the condom. Autumn sits down, stretching out her legs and then sliding under the covers.

"Did you still want to study?" I ask but her eyelids droop as she glances over at her laptop and notes.

"We'll make time in the morning?" she asks, voice low and hoarse.

I chuckle, leaning forward and kissing her forehead. "Yeah, sweetness, we'll make time in the morning." I get up, disposing of the condom and then turning out the lights. The last thing I do before getting into bed, with the full intention of cuddling Fall until morning, is blow out the candle. I don't need it tonight since I'll have the real thing in bed with me.

30

AUTUMN

My heart is in my fucking throat as I climb the stairs in the science center to the fifth floor. This is such a bad idea.

I've been sleeping at Ramsey's more often than I've been in my dorm the last two weeks. And the nights that I don't spend with him, he finds me at some point in the day and punishes me, usually by edging me until I apologize and then explode on his face or cock, sobbing through my orgasm. One time he trapped me in the alcove from that first day of classes and covered my mouth with his hand while his other just pushed into my pants and played with my clit till I was squirming against him. He just stared into my eyes the whole time, that wolfish grin in place as he asked me if I would be coming over tonight or if I wanted to deny him again. We ended up fucking in the Jeep since I couldn't really wait to get back to his place after his torture.

This idea though is definitely going to get me in trouble. I'm not sure how he'll respond, but he's been pretty open with location, even telling me he wants to take me to the gym sometime and try to sneak me into the showers so that every other guy there can be jealous when every noise I make echoes off the tiles.

Showing up to his office hours in my winter coat with absolutely nothing else on underneath though feels riskier. Well not absolutely nothing. The temp outside is warming up but not nearly enough to walk across campus with my legs bare. So, I have a functional pair of leggings hastily thrown on.

I've never shown up to his office hours, but when he texted me a little while ago saying he was bored and asking what I was wearing, the idea popped into my head to just show up and show him. I'd left him on read long enough though that he was getting whiny, my phone buzzing in my pocket the second I step out of the stairwell on the fifth floor.

SATAN'S NEPHEW

I know you don't have class right now, Fall.
Where'd you go?

I decide to tease him a bit, heading toward the bio department's little cubicle farm.

Chill I was taking a shower

SATAN'S NEPHEW

Send pics

Better yet, facetime me.

My phone starts ringing in my hand, the camera turning on for a FaceTime call. I roll my eyes. Well, at least I know he's not with a student right now.

Walking over to his TA cube, I find it empty. Good. This would be way too out in the open for me. Looking up, I see him sitting at Dr. Miller's desk through the open office door, phone held up as he stares at the outgoing call waiting for me to pick up.

I decline it, watching as he grits his teeth and the vein in his forehead pops out. He immediately starts typing, completely oblivious to my approach.

"You are so impatient," I say, once I'm standing in the doorway.

His head whips up, face slightly confused before his wolfish grin takes over and he slowly peruses my bundled-up state.

"You do not look freshly showered," he muses.

I roll my eyes. Leave it to Ramsey to say something stupid before his brain catches up to him. Shaking my head, I walk in, closing the door behind me and locking us in.

He's at my back in an instant, both hands coming forward to press against the door on either side of me. "What are you doing here Fall?"

I swallow, feeling the temperature in the room spike my blood. "You said you were bored." My voice always gets this breathy quality when he invades my space and I used to hate myself for it, but ever since the night we trauma traded and he made me watch him fuck me in the mirror, I've found I don't really care *how* I am with him anymore. I just am.

His nose nudges against the shell of my ear. "So, you just thought you'd pop over and get some help on the homework?"

I sigh, just letting all the jittery squirminess Ramsey elicits inside me exist. "Nope." I turn around, leaning my back against the door and grabbing onto the sides of his sweater.

He leans forward, grin still on his lips as he slowly gets closer. "No?"

I smile, our lips touching as I whisper, "I don't need help with the homework."

Ramsey chuckles before biting my bottom lip and pulling it a little with his teeth. "Well then what will we do, all alone, in this office right now?"

I sigh dramatically, rolling my eyes to the side and starting to unzip my coat between us. "I could think of a couple of things." Once I get the zipper free, I slide the coat off my shoulders, letting it fall and leaving me in nothing but my leggings and sneakers.

"Fuck, Fall," Ramsey groans, fingers scraping against the door behind me. He stares down at me, mouth slightly open and glasses slipping down the bridge of his nose. Without pushing them up, his eyes move to mine and his mouth curls up on one side. "I'm going to fuck you on his desk right now."

My eyes widen, but before I can say a word, Ramsey strikes. Grabbing me by my waist, he picks me up, pivoting with me in his arms. I squeal, stomach rioting at being moved this way. Ramsey slams me down on the edge of Dr. Miller's desk, keeping his hands on my skin as he pushes me down so that I'm laying flat. Papers and a couple books end up underneath me, but Ramsey is already stripping off my leggings, unconcerned with anything other than getting me naked as soon as possible. My sneakers are long gone, already ripped off in his haste.

I laugh, hands on his shoulders when he kisses my hip, hands on my inner thighs and spreading me so he can take a long lick up my center.

"Shit," he says, popping up between my legs.

I sit up on my forearms, half crunching to look him in the eye. "What?"

"I don't have any condoms." He runs a hand through his hair, looking around genuinely concerned as he kneels on the floor of Dr. Miller's office. His glasses are askew and he rights them, still looking off to the side, one hand still running up and down my thigh.

"Ramsey?"

He hums, looking back up at me.

"In my coat pocket."

He stands, rushing over to my puddled coat and fishing around in the pockets before he uncovers the condoms I stashed there on my way out the door. His eyebrow quirks as he looks over at me, holding them up.

I kick my feet, letting my legs swing a little as I half shrug in this position. "I came here half naked, remember?"

"What if I'd been with a student?" He meanders the few steps between us, lazily returning to stand between my still spread legs and tossing the condoms on the desk next to me.

"You were texting me bored." I shrug again, following his path back to me. "I took an educated guess that you'd be alone."

He shakes his head, smiling as he leans down, hands touching the desk on either side of me. His nose touches the tip of mine.

"And if you weren't?" I add.

He nods.

Another half shrug and a lazy smile from me. "I'd wait."

He laughs, the sound sharp and quick, but forcing my heart to start galloping in my chest.

Without another word he kisses me. I press up to meet him, our lips fighting for dominance. I've been less quick to succumb to him lately and found that he very much likes the little bit of fight I can muster before I sigh and give in, needing him to take control as much as he needs to have it.

He nips my lip before things go as far as I'd like and chuckles again, palming my chest and making me moan when he goes right to pinching and rolling my nipples. My thighs shake as I let my top half fall back against the desk. Ramsey looms over me, long fingers relentless in their torture before he leans down and sucks on my skin. He bites a few times, and I know my chest will be covered in hickeys when I leave.

I lay back, letting my hands roam over the collar of his dress shirt, peaking out at the neck of his sweater. My fingers tangle in his curls as I writhe, panting and impatient, pulling on his hair as if that will have any effect on how Ramsey wants things to go.

"Greedy, greedy, greedy," he hums against my skin, punctuating each word with a kiss or bite.

"Someone could show up." I roll my hips against him, hoping it will spur him on at least a little. "Just fuck me. Please, Ramsey."

He reels back, satisfaction dripping off him the way it does every time I use that word without prompting. Add in his name and I can sometimes actually get what I want when I want it.

He quickly unzips and takes himself out, one hand holding my thigh down and to the side on the edge of the desk. Stroking himself a few times he just stares down at me, completely naked, while he stands fully clothed.

"You're so goddamn perfect."

He's been saying that lately. At least once right before we fuck. Usually, he pauses to gauge my reaction, pinching me if he doesn't like it.

It's working though because I don't shudder. The words

leap right into my chest, tucking themselves into the ever-growing pile of validation he's heaped into the crack I've been harboring almost all my life. I glow under his praise, feeling warm and tingly all over as he grabs one of the condoms and rips it open with his teeth. Rolling it on quickly, he grabs both of my legs and steps closer, wrapping them around his hips and squeezing to silently command me to hold on before he lets go.

I can feel him hot and hard against my center, sliding through my lips as he takes his time lining himself up. I'm soaked and ready, but Ramsey loves to tease, rubbing his tip against my clit a little before dragging himself down over every sensitive nerve he can find. He finally lines up and presses in, gliding all the way in one slow smooth slide. The feeling of him filling me like this, no rocking, just one long press forces a long moan from my chest. I lean back, bringing my arms up to grab the edge of the desk behind my head as my eyes roll back and my spine arches.

"Fuck, sweetness. You're gripping me so fucking tight." His voice is rough, gravelly from the restraint he's holding onto for no fucking reason.

"R-ramsey," I breathe, voice hitching as he just holds himself there, buried inside me and seeming content to let the anticipation climb.

"Hush," he admonishes, hands settling on either side of my waist as he leans forward, somehow pressing even further inside me. I cry out and he laughs.

And then he's fucking pounding into me. His hips snap at the fastest speed I've experienced yet and the drag of it all pulls even more garbled words from my mouth. I hold on to his waist with my thighs, hands white knuckling the desk as I don't even try to keep a coherent thought alive. Every time I breathe in, it stutters, air rushing from my lungs before I can contain it. The feeling is almost too much, sitting right on the brink and creating a heart pounding build up.

"So." *Thrust.* "Fucking." *Thrust.* "Perfect."

Ramsey's lips close around one of my nipples and I release a hand to fist his hair and try to pull him up. His tongue and teeth are relentless, completely ignoring my need to kiss him right now and simply continuing his torture from earlier as he continues to piston his hips in and out of me.

My climax hits in one sweeping crash, a scream echoing in my ears that I distantly understand is mine, but all I can see is rolling shapes as I arch completely off the desk and come.

Ramsey roars in my ear a few thrusts later and then lazily keeps pumping into me for a few more beats.

My brain is completely offline, allowing my body to simply float back down onto Dr. Miller's desk and settle amongst the random objects beneath me. I can feel Ramsey's head against my chest, hear his harsh breathing mixing with mine in my ears but everything is distant and out of reach for a long enough time that my eyelids droop and close, though all my other senses stay online.

"You should come to all of my office hours, Fall." Ramsey kisses my collarbone, his weight lifting off me as he slowly pulls out.

I whine a little from the loss, feeling my core flutter around nothing. I stay lying there for another moment, eyes closed and body sated while I listen to him right himself, zipper ascending after a moment. One more moment and then I finally decide to get up.

Sitting up fully, my head rushes and I tip to the side for a second, righting myself with one arm on the desktop while Ramsey flinches to catch me. Once I'm stable, he grabs my jaw, pulling my face up so that he can lean down and devour my lips, tongue fully invading as I simply let him kiss me, unable to muster the strength to kiss him back.

"I'm taking you to lunch," he announces, pulling away and grabbing my leggings.

"What?"

He gets on his knees again, starting to pull them up my legs and I lean forward, hands on his shoulders.

"You still have another hour of availability."

He looks up at me, continuing to help me get dressed. "I know. I'll just send an email about an emergency and cancel the rest of the day." He leans back, grabbing my hips and pulling me off the desk so I'm standing before him.

"Ramsey!"

"Fall!" he mocks. He pulls my pants up for me, standing as he does and then leaning down to kiss me quick. "No one's going to show up anyways. The midterm isn't for another week and that'll be when everyone starts coming in to ask all the questions they should have asked two weeks ago." He taps my ass firmly. "I'm taking you to lunch. And then probably back to mine to fuck you a few more times." He leans past me to grab the extra condoms and tucks them into his pocket. "Where's your shirt?"

"I didn't come with one, remember?" I cross my arms over my naked chest, head still a little foggy as I try to keep up.

"You didn't bring something to change into after?"

"I kind of figured you'd send me on my way after." I cock my hip. "Didn't expect you to clear your whole day for me."

He smiles, leaning down and biting my lip again. "Should have anticipated I wouldn't just let you leave after. Gotta make sure you hydrate and replenish."

I roll my eyes. He has an obsession with making sure I

eat full meals and drink water every day. "Control freak," I mumble.

He smiles wider, hand snaking around to pull me flush against him. "Mmm, love it when you talk dirty to me." He grabs my ass with both hands, squeezing me between his arms.

I'll never tell him, but I love when he holds me like this, with a lot of pressure on all sides. Feels like I'm being squeezed in the most delicious way.

"You can wear my gym shirt." He lets me go, walking over to the other side of the desk and pulling his duffel out from underneath. "I was going to go after this, but you showed up to fulfill my cardio needs instead." He winks and I shake my head, still holding my arms over my chest for some reason.

Ramsey pulls out a tee shirt and starts walking toward me.

I swallow, tongue seemingly stuck to the roof of my mouth. There's no way that fits me. His chest and shoulders are broad, and I try to do the mental gymnastics to figure out what to say.

But before I can think of anything, he's back in front of me, grabbing my wrists and pulling my arms up, dropping the tee shirt over them without a care at all. I bite my lip, and he yanks the shirt down.

It's snug, but not uncomfortable. The fabric is soft, clearly worn and washed often and it smells like the skin at the base of his throat that I often snuggle my face into when we're falling asleep together.

An adrenaline come down washes through me, shoulders sagging in relief as I pull the shirt down a little and adjust to being in something a little tighter than I would usually let myself wear.

Then I look up and freeze. Ramsey is staring down at me with the most predatory look I've seen on him yet. His eyes are narrowed, lips parted to show just a little bit of his teeth and most of his canines as he just stares, burning me with his gaze.

"Maybe we'll get takeout instead. I don't know if I can sit across from you in a public place for long like this."

"Does it look bad?" I squeak, pulling the shirt away from my stomach a little.

"Bad?" he growls, grabbing my hand and pulling me against him before pinning my arm to my lower back. "Sweetness, you look fucking decadent in my clothes. I don't want to share you with others right now."

I startle and he squeezes my wrist a little tighter. Breathing him in, I feel his words rush through my lungs and fill my chest. The look in his eyes is a little bit feral, and I smile, feigning the most saccharine innocence I can muster.

"What if I want to go out though?" I bat my eyelashes, testing a theory I've had.

He snorts, backing me up against the desk again. "Too bad," he hisses, diving in to claim my mouth once more.

Looks like my power only goes so far.

Another condom gets used before we finally make it out of the office, his tee shirt never leaving my skin.

31

AUTUMN

The back of Ramsey's Jeep is a lot more comfortable than last time, as he races down the same highway he drove six weeks ago. There's no tension in the car this time as we make the trip in reverse, heading home for spring break.

"I still think you should have sat up here," Mira says, half turned around to face me in the back as we talk over the radio Ramsey has been blaring for the last hour or so.

"Nah, I'm good back here."

Ramsey's eyes flick to mine in the mirror, checking in with a quick head tilt. I nod and he's back to looking at the road.

"You two are so cute," Mira gushes and Ramsey reaches forward to turn the music dial up another notch. He warned her each time she makes a comment about us he would tune her out, but she doesn't seem to care that he's melting all our eardrums, rolling her eyes at me and slapping his shoulder.

"Cut it out," she yells, switching the dial back down to a semi-decent volume.

"Why didn't you ride with Marshall again?" Ramsey grumbles.

She shakes her head, facing forward and leaning down to grab something out of the bag at her feet. "Because he's taking Janette and Axel home to stay at his grandfather's and the tension around the three of them in a confined space is dizzying." She sits back up, pulling down the visor and sliding open the mirror so she can put on her chapstick. "You two are much easier to deal with for a few hours."

I snort, remembering how a few weeks ago everyone would work hard to make sure we weren't ever together, ready to tear each other's throats out.

Oh, how a few orgasms can change things.

"How are things with Cyrus these days?" Ramsey asks, clearly done discussing our arrangement with his little sister.

Mira's hand pauses for a second before she finishes her lips, pushing the mirror away a little forcefully. "Fine. He's going back to the city for break."

"Didn't want to introduce him to Mom?" Ramsey teases.

"Knock it off," I murmur, his eyes sliding to mine in the mirror again. He's being playful but I can see the tension in Mira's shoulders.

Mira smiles over her shoulder at me. "It's okay. I think it's a little early to be introducing him to Mom since we've only been on a couple dates." She shrugs, looking out the window before turning back around to face me. "What are we doing for your birthday tomorrow?" Her face lights up as she beams at me and my stomach squirms.

Mira might not like being the center of attention and absolutely abhorred the giant ball her mom used to put on for her birthday, but she always wants to do something for everyone else's. She's never pushy though. If I said I just wanted to eat pizza and play games at her house, she'd make it happen.

"I don't know, Mir. I'm fine with doing nothing." I glance at the mirror, but Ramsey seems particularly focused on the road in front of him.

"We can't do nothing! What about a little get together? Something small? Just me, you, and Bent?" She glances over her shoulder at her brother. "Ramsey can come too if you want?" She grins at me, eyes pleading.

I sigh. "Nothing over the top," I insist.

She runs her finger over her heart. "Cross my heart. Small and simple I swear. But there will be cake." She nods once, uncompromising in this stipulation.

I laugh. "Okay. I doubt my parents will remember so I can be over at yours in the morning. Help you set up whatever you're already planning in that head of yours."

"No way! You can't help set up your own party!" She shakes her head. "Stay home and we'll come get you when it's time." She smiles and sits back in her seat, facing the windshield once again.

I frown. "Okay," I say, looking out the window and avoiding the mirror even though I can feel that Ramsey isn't looking at me.

My friends might not know the extent of why I don't get along with Mom and Aaron, but they've never questioned that our relationship is rocky. Still, I feel a little disappointed that I'll have to stay home all day tomorrow. Maybe I'll go for a walk, see if I can find something at the bookstore that's good on clearance.

An hour later, we're pulling up in front of Mom's

mangled modernized Victorian, Ramsey parking against the curb and getting out to get my bags from the trunk. Mira leans back through the seat and hugs me.

"Promise we'll come get you the second everything is all set." She squeezes me again and I nod against her shoulder.

Getting out, I head to the back of the Jeep, finding Ramsey still holding on to my rolling carry on and tote bag.

"I don't want to let you walk in there." He stares at me a little desperately.

I walk up to him, grabbing the sides of his jacket and using it as leverage to get on my tippy toes and kiss him. He makes me work for it, barely leaning down with his neck to meet me in the height difference.

"It's just one day. I've survived much longer, trust me." I put my hands on top of his on my bags, waiting for him to let go.

He grits his teeth, still holding on.

"They're probably not even going to talk to me. I'll spend most of it reading, not even bothering to unpack before I'm heading over to yours tomorrow anyway. I'll be fine."

He sighs, closing his eyes for a second before slowly relaxing his hands. "You'll call me if you need anything?" he asks, lingering a little longer.

"Sure, Ramsey." I take the bags from him, shouldering the tote and rolling the bag so that it's in front of me. Making sure I have everything I start to walk away, but Ramsey steps forward, both hands coming up to grab my face.

His lips meet mine and I open to him on instinct, taking the deep gratifying kiss he pours into me. Leaning back but keeping his hands on my face he just stares at me for a second.

"Tomorrow," is all he says before releasing me and placing his hands in his pants pocket.

I nod stupidly, mouth still hanging open and limbs clumsily pulling my bag behind me on the cobblestone as I walk away, feeling him watch me all the way to the door.

Once I'm inside, I glance out the window through the sheer curtains, watching him stare up at the house for a second with a scowl before getting back in the car and driving away.

"Autumn!" Brown hair races toward me as I turn around, slender arms enveloping me a second later and squeezing with an impressive amount of strength. "Happyalmostbirthday! How was school? Did it snow there as much as it did here?" my sister spits out, words mashed together like my organs.

She's dressed for ballet, soft lavender leotard on with black tights and beige leg warmers. Her head is pressed against my shoulder, tight circular bun touching the bottom of my chin. Shock freezes me for a second before I slowly hug her back, arms coming around her shoulders.

My sister is hugging me.

"Sage!" Our mother yells and we both jump apart. Sage looks back, jaw locking the second she sees Mom at the bottom of the stairs. "Get in the car. We're going to be late." Her tone is clipped, eyes narrowed.

I stand as still as I can, holding my breath as Sage looks back at me for a second with apologetic eyes. Grabbing a jacket off the rack, she heads around me toward the garage door, head bowed.

Once she's gone, Mom sighs, sagging and shaking her head. "I don't know what's gotten into that child. Must be all the audition stress lately." She plasters a fake smile onto her face, walking toward me.

I stay still, waiting for her next move before I make mine.

"We're meeting your father at a charity dinner after practice, so you're on your own tonight." She pats my cheek like she used to when I was little. "Don't order anything too dense."

And with that barbed sting, she walks out after Sage, garage door shutting behind her.

I stand in the same spot for another couple minutes, feeling my limbs slowly unlock as the fissure in my chest widens a little farther, parts of me crumbling and falling in at the edges.

I lied to Ramsey earlier. I've never really survived any amount of time here. Not without leaving a piece of myself behind in the process.

32

AUTUMN

11:59pm

One more minute until my birthday.

I lay tucked under my blanket, snuggled away in the dark of my room, staring at the ominous glow of my phone, watching the numbers move. It's the same tradition I've done for every other birthday under this roof, counting down the years until I don't have to return. Only three more after this and I'll be free.

I'll have to go into debt for medical school and figure out how to live on my own. But I'll be free. My heart leaps at the idea of living on my own, having a place to go to where my mother and Aaron are decidedly not.

Maybe I could invite Sage over some time.

12:00am

My cheeks hurt from the beaming smile that takes over my face. Alone in my room, I revel at another year down.

And then my phone starts buzzing in my hand.

Satan's Nephew.

A picture of Ramsey that I did not take appears on the

screen. He's shirtless in bed and I'm cuddled up asleep under his chin. Rolling my eyes, I swipe the arrow, picking up the phone and pressing it against my ear.

"What are you doing awake right now?" I whisper.

He chuckles. "Happy birthday, Fall."

My beaming smile is back, something warm and sweet sweeping through me. "Thank you, Ramsey."

"I thought you'd be asleep. Planned to leave you a long voicemail singing the whole song. Wanted you to wake up to something fun."

I can hear him messing with his glasses on the other end and laugh. "You could always sing it now?" I suggest.

He chuckles. "I don't think so. Looks like you'll just have to wait till next year."

My stomach drops off another rollercoaster peak, and I stutter to catch up.

"Mira's going all out for this party, just so you know. Planning to surprise you with a few more people than just her and Marshall. I nixed the dj idea she had, but I think she spent a whole hour curating a playlist instead."

I laugh then sigh. "Yeah, I kind of figured when she brought it up in the car that she was already planning something. I trust her though. We're birthday haters for life so I know she won't go too overboard."

"You don't like your birthday?"

I hum. "I don't hate the day in particular. More the idea of everyone staring at me. I don't mind the gifts and cake, I just don't think it requires everyone staring at me singing or blowing out candles to enjoy it."

Ramsey tsks. "Well, I should warn you, whatever Mira's planning will involve candles and singing."

I smile. "Thanks for the warning. Now I can pre-stress about it all day."

"Won't have time."

I furrow my brows. "Why not?"

"I'm coming to get you at eight so we can go on your birthday adventure." He says it so matter-of-factly that it takes me a second for the words to sink in.

"Why would you do that?" I whisper.

"Why would I come get you from that house of horrors you insisted on staying the night in and make sure you have a good time on your birthday before I take you to the party my sister is throwing you? Gee I don't know."

I feel like there's some giant reason staring me in the face and I can't freaking see it, but the feeling is too raw when I try to sink in, so I just ignore it and change the subject.

"Why'd you tell me about the party?"

"Because I know you hate surprises."

I squeeze the phone a little tighter. "How do you know that?"

"We've already established I pay attention, Fall. Mira knows you hate them too, by the way. She's just categorizing this as a 'good surprise.'" He chuckles. "I don't think she understands how much of an oxymoron that is to you."

I laugh breathlessly.

"Can I pick out a dress for you?"

"What?"

"If I pick out a dress that I want to see you wear, will you wear it?"

I swallow and force out a laugh. "You're asking?" I tease. "This feels like something *you* would demand."

"I only demand things in the bedroom. And even there, I check in." The crack in my chest trembles. "I know you have issues with your body. And how you dress accommodates them. But I've rarely seen you in dresses. Actually, I think the only ones I've seen you in are at Mira's birthday balls. So, I want to check that this isn't something that will make you uncomfortable."

The fracture fills up another couple inches. He notices I don't usually wear dresses. And figured out why. "You can pick out a dress. I'll decide if I want to wear it."

I can hear him grin in the way he says, "I can live with that."

Silence stretches out on the line between us, but I feel so comfortable in it, like he's lying next to me and I'm not alone.

"What are we doing tomorrow?" I ask sleepily.

He tsks again. "If you go to sleep, you'll find out faster."

I laugh, the sound a little rushed as my hand on the phone starts to get heavy. "Okay, goodnight, Ramsey."

"Happy birthday, sweetness. I l—I'll see you soon."

The line goes dead, and I toss my phone to the other side of the bed. I start to drift off to sleep, my last thought being that I'm actually excited to celebrate my birthday for once.

33

RAMSEY

I stand on the porch of the Green's house bright and early at 7:52am. Ringing the bell, I grip the gift bag in my hand extra tight.

You can't punch anyone, Ramsey. Breathe and smile. You cannot scare Fall.

A woman opens the door, and I immediately know it's not Tina Green.

"Hello," she greets cheerfully, wiping a hand on an apron around her waist. "How can I help you?"

"I got it, Clara. He's here for me." Fall comes rushing down the stairs, already dressed with sneakers on and bags in her hands as she descends the stairs.

I smile, watching her rush toward me and feeling that solid thing inside me get bigger.

"Where are you going?" a new voice calls from down the hall and I turn, finding Tina Green herself standing next to the stairs. Clara rushes past her, heading back to the kitchen I presume.

I take a step forward but Fall places herself between us. "I'm going to hang out at the Adams' today, remember?"

She mumbles a response, waving her hand at us. "And why is *he* picking you up? Where's the other one?"

"Bentley, Mom. He's at his grandfather's for the week. Ramsey is Mira's brother. He's just—" She glances back at me, and I place my free hand on her lower back. "J-just taking me over there since Mira doesn't drive."

Her mother's eyes narrow and I narrow mine right back, counting down in my head and clamping my mouth shut. If I let myself say anything, Fall will kill me for what comes out.

"Your grandmother will probably call. Try not to miss it. I don't want to hear about how terrible of a mother I am lapsing at teaching you girls good manners."

Fall nods and my fist tightens around the little paper strings of the bag I asked Mira for this morning.

"Okay, Mom. See you in a few weeks."

Tina waves her hand, not even bothering to say anything else as she turns away.

Fall pivots to face me, pushing me out the door and hastily closing it behind her. I chuckle, backing up, but stopping once we're outside.

"I was hoping I'd get to see you put this on," I say holding out the bag to her.

Fall rolls her eyes, taking it from me and trying to push me back further. "Ramsey, come on. I want to get out of here."

I grab her bags, taking the totes out of her hands and leaving her with just my gift.

We head over to the Jeep, and I glance back at the house, feeling all my dark energy spark. *She didn't even say happy birthday to her own fucking daughter.*

"I hate your mom," I say after putting her stuff in my trunk and getting into the driver's side.

Fall ignores me, head bent over her gift and hands sifting through the tissue paper to find the material underneath. "You already bought me a dress?" Her head whips up to look at me. "How long have you had this?"

I shrug, starting the car and pulling out of the Green's curved driveway. Reaching over, I grab her thigh, squeezing and already knowing her mind is rioting at the idea of accepting this.

"I saw it online and thought it would look pretty on you. I got it around the time I started asking about gifts, when I didn't know why you were upset about ordering you the uber." I turn down the road, passing the promenade and the giant Lucy's sign before having an idea and doubling back.

I can feel Fall staring at me, the silence pregnant with her racing thoughts.

Parking in the lot we had our first fight, I turn toward Fall, grabbing the sides of her face similarly to how I did yesterday when I dropped her off. "It's a gift. Today is your birthday and therefore gifts are expected. We talked about this last night. If you don't want to wear it, that's fine, but I want you to go try it on at least."

Fall stares up at me, hands crumpling the tissue paper as she fidgets. "Okay," she finally concedes.

I smile, leaning over the center console to kiss her quickly. "C'mon then." I get out of the car, head over to her side, and open the door for her before she can get it herself. She steps out, bag clutched in her hand.

"Where am I changing exactly?"

I'm surprised she hasn't caught on yet, but maybe I've put more significance into this moment than she has. "They have bathrooms up here." I point to Lucy's as we walk, wrapping an arm around her waist when I feel her start to slow down.

"Ramsey, is today going to be some sort of humiliation ritual?"

I stop looking down at her. "What? No, why would you think that?"

"Maybe because you're taking me to the place where you first chased me down and let your girlfriend pour a milkshake over my head? Are we reminiscing at all the sites you tortured me in?"

"Paige was not my girlfriend," I mutter, suddenly feeling like this was a really stupid idea. I step in front of her, anger swelling in my chest, but it poignantly spreads from the solid thing, seeming to infect me rather than push out toward her. Grabbing the tops of her arms, I lean down so that I'm in her face. "We don't have to go in there, but I saw it as we passed and thought it would be a good place for you to change. I don't consider this place tainted, but I can see why you might so we can turn around and find a completely different restaurant for breakfast. But I am feeding you before we head out for the day." I smirk, still feeling like this might be a bad idea all the sudden, but adding, "Besides, I owe you a milkshake."

Fall snorts, rolling her eyes and shaking her head. "Let's go then." She nods toward Lucy's, and we continue walking past the stores on the way to the diner.

The inside is warm and pretty deserted. Two girls I don't know lounge behind the counter, one wiping the same spot over and over again while looking at her phone in her other hand.

"What do you want?" I ask as we walk up to the counter, the other girl coming over with a friendly smile and asking if we want to order and then pick a booth. I nod to her, looking up at the menu and seeing if they still have the breakfast sandwich I used to love.

Fall shrugs, moving the gift bag from on hand to another. "Whatever. I don't usually eat breakfast, so whatever you think is good will be fine. Nothing spicy, please."

I stop, looking down at her. "You don't eat breakfast?"

She glances up at me. "Not usually. I try to sleep in as much as I can and then have to run to classes. I'll make microwave oatmeal or grab a yogurt sometimes, but usually I'm running too late to stop."

I clench my fists. "I'm going to start bringing you something to Miller's classes at least."

Fall raises an eyebrow. "Pretty sure everyone else in the class will find it weird that the TA is bringing me breakfast, Ramsey." She glances at the girl at the register, still smiling and waiting as we talk.

"I don't give a fuck what everyone in class thinks." I look back at the menu. "We'll get two egg and cheese sandwiches on bagels. Bacon on the side. And two chocolate shakes, please."

Fall's lips twitch when I say the last word and I squeeze her side, my own smile breaking out. The girl rings us up and I take out my wallet, handing over my card.

"Go get changed, witch," I whisper and tap her ass as we walk over to one of the vacant booths. I squeeze her waist again before releasing her, sliding into the side that will let me see her emerge and watch as she walks away shaking her head and sliding her hands over the paper handles on the green gift bag.

Ten minutes go by, and I start to worry that I should go check on her. What if she's freaking out and this triggered her in some way? She hasn't had a panic attack in weeks as far as I know, but I'm also not with her twenty-four seven.

She never really wears dresses, always opting for a baggy

top and leggings or jeans. The ones she's worn to my sister's parties tend to be floor length tailored ball gowns. That black and red one from the first time I saw her at one still turns up in my dreams.

The dress I picked out is shorter. It wraps around the front, a little tie on the side keeping it all in place. It creates this draped effect that I instantly wanted to see Fall's tits in the second I saw the ad online. It should fall to her mid-thigh, exposing her legs which I also can't wait to see out and about. She has the softest fucking skin and if she wears this dress all day, I'm going to have a hard time not rubbing myself all over her.

My palms start to sweat, and I rub them against my jeans, checking my sandwich to make sure hers will still be warm if she comes out now.

Looking up, red hair emerges, head bent down and blue eyes glancing around from beneath it.

She's wearing it. And fuuuuuck, it looks good.

The bottom hits her right where I pictured and even with her hands crossed in front of her, holding the gift bag as if it will protect her, I can tell I'm going to be staring at the top all fucking day. The sleeves are long and flowy, and I hoped exposing one set of limbs while covering another would be enough of a compromise for my shy little witch.

Fuck, I remember almost blurting that I love her last night and shake myself out completely, standing when she gets closer to the table.

There's no way that's what this is.

Fall looks up at me, hair falling away from her face while her shoulders still stay tensed up. "The sneakers don't really go with it."

"Couldn't care less, Fall. You look amazing." I lean down,

kissing her to stop myself from saying anything else. "How do you feel?"

She giggles, shoulders falling as she slides into the booth and sets the bag aside. "I've worn dresses before, Ramsey." Her false bravado would be believable if I didn't see the way her hand shakes a little as she pushes some of her curls behind her shoulder.

"I've never seen you in one like this. So, humor me, Fall." I lean forward, watching her settle in and pick up her breakfast sandwich after taking a sip of the milkshake. "How do you feel?"

She bites into the bagel, avoiding answering and my eyes for a moment. I wait.

"I like it, Ramsey. I'm just not super used to the skirt." She shrugs, still talking to her breakfast sandwich. "Gimme ten minutes and I'm sure I'll be fine." Her eyes flick up, a small smile creasing her cheeks as she chews. "I really like the color."

I sit back, feeling the pinched tension in my chest lessen. The dress is a mint green that looks so pretty against her skin and makes her hair look even more vibrant and shocking than usual. She has a little bit of makeup on today too and her eyes look fucking ethereal with glitter on her lids and cheeks.

I drink my fill, absolutely forgetting about the food in front of me as I watch her happily eat and consider what I almost told her in the early hours of this morning.

Do I love Fall?

I love provoking her. And I love fucking her. I know I care about her, but has that gone completely off the rails?

The solid thing in my chest burns and I realize it's not off the rails at all. This was always where this speeding train was heading and I just never looked down the tracks to see it coming.

Fuck, I need to convince this stubborn girl to fall in love with me. I know she likes spending time with me. At least, when there's orgasms mixed in at some point. Have we ever just hung out without fucking? Maybe I should try to see if we can.

The idea of not touching her though sounds abhorrent.

"You're not going to eat? After all that nonsense about making sure I have breakfast when we get back to the Coast?" There's a teasing tone in her voice, and she shakes her head in faux disappointment.

I roll my eyes, pushing my side of bacon over to her and picking up my breakfast sandwich.

Okay, Ramsey. Just have to get the girl that thinks she hates you to realize she can't live without you. No big deal.

Biting into the cold bagel, I go over my plan for the day, thinking about anything extra I can add in that might help.

$$34$$

AUTUMN

Ramsey has dragged me all over town, and I'm starting to think he's trying to tire me out before the party tonight. I'm not sure why but the fact that he took me to a really fancy shoe store and bought me a new pair of boots to wear with his dress, then over to the local farmers market to check out all the stands of locally made jewelry and crafts, before driving all the way back to the promenade to stop at the bookstore and get me whatever I could grab in twenty minutes (an endeavor that ended up costing him way too much money, but he insisted on buying all of the books for me), makes me think his plan involves exhausting and overwhelming me.

Each time we've gone somewhere new, it's been because of something I said one time or something he noticed about me all that time I thought he absolutely hated me. And I don't know how to process that, feeling so overwhelmed with how much he pays attention but also how much he's willing to spoil me. He has yet to show an ounce of boredom, even when Mimi called and we sat in his car with the engine running so I could tell her about how school was going and thank her for the birthday money she sent in a card directly to my dorm last week.

I keep catching him watching me, but I'm not sure if that's because of me or the dress he picked out.

It really is a great dress. Definitely something I would have seen and liked but talked myself out of buying. An indulgence. That's what this whole day has been. One indulgence after another and I'm not sure if he realizes how high he's setting my bar for when this *arrangement* eventually ends, and I have to go back to before.

I don't know if I'll ever be able to undo the change Ramsey has caused in me. I feel freer with him, paying less attention to the people around us or spending time thinking about what they're thinking about me. The incessant voice in the back of my head that speaks in my mother's voice has been quiet around him too, replaced by one that sounds suspiciously like Ramsey, telling me I'm beautiful or perfect while he squeezes me tight.

I really hope I don't lose that voice when this inevitably ends.

"Last stop before we head to the house." Ramsey parks the car, making me sit up and look around, having zoned out staring out the window. We're at the park, Breezy Cone ice cream stand in front of us.

"They're open already?" I rush to unclip my seatbelt, bouncing a little in my seat as I disregard the egregiously long line of people braving the barely tolerable temperatures for fresh cones.

Ramsey opens my door, holding out his hand to me with a big grin. "Opening day," he mutters, pointing over at a big sign strung over the park entrance a few feet away.

I smile, dropping his hand once the door is closed and racing over to get in line. I can hear him chuckle over my shoulder before he joins me at my side, hands in his pockets and angling himself against the wind a bit.

My skirt blows against my legs, and I grab a little bit of the material on the sides keeping it in place as it billows and moves against me.

"Do you remember when you said we're not friends?" Ramsey randomly blurts.

I glance over at him, moving up with the couple in front of us and trying to figure out what he's on about. "Yeah?"

"I think you were wrong." The tips of his ears have gone red, and he glances away before looking back at me. "I think we are friends. Only a friend would know you intimately enough to set up this whole day." He chews his bottom lip, staring at me once he's done with his proclamation.

"Eh," I bluster, shrugging one shoulder and trying not to smile at how pissed I know this will make him. "I'd argue you only did all this to get in my pants later. Which is not a very friendly motive."

He bristles and I bite the inside of my cheek to stop myself from laughing. "So, you think my motive makes me less of your friend? What if I did all this just to make you smile?"

This time I do laugh. "Yeah, because you're so famous for your magnanimous intentions. Come on Ramsey, just admit it. You know what all of this will lead to. Why do we have to pretend otherwise?" I ignore the ache that blooms in my chest thinking about him spoiling me just for sex.

You know what you want him to have done all this for.

I shove the stupid little Ramsey voice away.

"Why do you do that? Why are you assuming everything I do for you has some sinister motive?" He folds his arms over his chest, eyes catching in the sunlight and burning crystalline as he stares down at me.

"Because that's what our arrangement is." I hush my voice as I start to get a little loud, looking around to make sure no one else is listening. "We fight, we fuck, usually at the same time, remember? So, all this just fits into that, right?"

We move up in line, Ramsey staying quiet for a moment and facing forward.

"Why can't it be both?" he whispers before glancing down at me. "Why can't it be that we fight and we fuck and we're friends?"

"Because usually friends hang out without fucking, Ramsey." I sigh, twisting the fabric of my dress in between my fingers. Why is he pressing this so hard?

"Okay, maybe we're not friends then," he concedes. "But," he says, pointing at me. "You have to admit I know you intimately. In *and out* of the bedroom."

"You got a lot of things right today," I concede, feeling that warmth from earlier press into me. "Thank you for a really great birthday. Probably one of the best I've ever had."

Ramsey beams, his whole face lighting up as I praise him. My head spins for a second with the unfamiliarity in our role reversal.

We move up in the line again and I can finally see the menu over the three windows people are ordering from. I start reading over the new specials and sundaes they've added since last year.

"I want to know you more, you know?" Ramsey whispers.

"Hmmm?" I look over at him, not connecting his words.

"I wouldn't mind getting to know you more. Not just what you like sexually, but *you*." He stares down at me, face so serious that my stomach swoops and I turn back to continue reading the menu, unable to withstand whatever onslaught of nerves his face and words are creating inside me.

"Wanting to know someone sexually and wanting to know them intimately are two very different things, Ramsey." I warn, pretending to continue reading the menu.

Ramsey grabs my chin, turning my gaze back on him.

"I want to know you every way, Fall."

My stomach plummets down another rollercoaster slope, air seeming to go still in my lungs.

Ramsey stares at me for another moment before leaning back to his full height, slowly releasing my chin. A satisfied smile plays at the corners of his mouth, and my eyes get stuck on his lips, brain still restarting.

"Why do you still call me Fall?" is what I manage to blurt when it comes back online. Moving my eyes back up to meet his, I find them swimming in confusion.

"Why would I stop?" he asks.

The line moves forward in front of us, and I face forward, stepping closer to the window with him.

"I don't know," I say eventually, right hand tangling with the skirt of my dress and rubbing the fabric back and forth. "Maybe because it's an insult?"

Ramsey falters. "It is not."

I can feel his eyes on the side of my face again and refuse to look at him. "Right. You want me to believe that the nickname you gave me when you first learned my name is not meant to be some stupid deprecating version of Autumn?"

And then he laughs. Ramsey Adams fucking laughs at me.

I turn my entire body to face him this time, folding my arms over my chest and waiting for him to compose himself.

Once he's only lightly chuckling, he wraps an arm

around my waist, tilting his head so that he blocks the sun, wrapping me in shadows. "You really think I'm a monster, don't you?"

I huff. "You were a monster to me then."

His responding grin is goofy, and he leans in closer, taking up more of my space. "Your monster."

The words drape over me, making my stomach clench. I lightly push him away, unable to stop myself grinning a bit. "Stop," I say with absolutely no heat.

His grin grows, body swinging back and then closer again. "It's short for downfall."

"What?"

"The nickname." He faces forward, keeping his arm around me still. "When we met, I had the idle thought that you looked like my downfall. That's what I meant when I said, 'you seem more like a Fall to me.' I liked that the shortened version paired with your actual name once I knew it." He looks down at me a little sheepishly. "It was meant to be a reminder to stay away. Kind of a 'warning danger ahead' signal in my head. I think I got too used to it though because I only see green lights flashing *go* whenever I say it now."

I stare up at him as he chews on the inside of his cheek. When we go to move forward, up next in line, I admit, "I will never understand the way your mind works."

He shrugs. "Good. Then you'll never get bored of me." A giant smile takes over the lower half of his face, and his hand squeezes my waist.

"Not possible." I murmur and his grin unbelievably widens.

"Next!" the girl at the third window yells. Ramsey leads us over and lets me order first.

35

AUTUMN

Mira may have gone overboard. It's not her mother's over-the-top fanfare, but it's definitely bigger than the little get together we talked about in the car yesterday. There's about fifty people in her house right now and I'm pretty sure I only know half by name, even less beyond just that.

They've all slowly shown up and I'm sure more will come as people spread the word that there's a party at the Adams' mansion. Most of the Ravens are here and a good amount of the people are from their high school class not just mine.

I'm standing against a wall, Bentley, Mira, Aria, Janette, and Axel all around me. Mira surprised me by secretly flying Aria in last night to be here for the party and Bentley immediately enveloped me in a bone crushing hug when he showed up, much to Ramsey's chagrin. He hadn't left my side until they showed up, leaning down to let me know he was going to go find Smith and make sure he wasn't breaking anything before disappearing into the living room. People tend to flock him and his friends so I don't mind him not sticking to me tonight, wanting to avoid as much attention as I can at a party specifically thrown in my honor.

"I swear I told people small," Mira says, fingers fidgeting around the glass in her hands.

"It's okay, Mir. It's nice." I smile to try to sell it and Bentley nods over her head in a way that tells me I very much did not.

"I can get Ramsey and the guys to start kicking people out if you want? I just thought inviting a few people from high school might be fun."

I take a sip of the drink Bentley made me, some concoction heavy on the lemonade and light on the alcohol that feels nice as it settles in my stomach. I'm still wearing the dress and boots Ramsey bought me, but I freshened up my makeup and pulled some of my hair back for the party, and for once, I don't feel completely out of place.

"No, it's okay." I take another sip. "I'm having a good time I swear. Just spare me the group sing along, and this might actually be a good birthday this year."

Mira smiles, taking a deep breath and nodding. "Deal."

"I'm just going to go to the bathroom quick." I push off the wall, passing between them and heading through the house toward the first-floor bathroom near the living room area. The house is huge, but mostly open concept, a few rooms cut off on the ground floor like the one we've been hanging out in to avoid the people I don't really know.

As I head toward the bathroom door, I glance over toward the couch and see Ramsey sitting there, Tanner on his other side and Smith sat on the back of the couch somewhat between them. He's scowling as Smith entertains per usual and like I predicted, a small crowd has formed around them. Royal stands off to the side, typing furiously into his phone.

I pause at the door, watching Ramsey across the room. He's tense but no more than usual and even though his mouth is set, his eyes are clear of tension, so I know he's not absolutely hating this evening entirely.

His eyes suddenly sweep through everyone, finding mine and locking on in a matter of seconds. The tension eases out of his mouth completely and he smiles, predatory as ever. I swallow against the sudden attention, my body almost vibrating with it.

Blaming the alcohol, I shake my head and wave a little, his eyes glinting as I disappear into the bathroom.

I'm not drunk but the second the door closes behind me and muffles the noise, I stare at myself in the mirror. "Get yourself together," I whisper. "You're *hate* fucking him. Once the semester's over, there's no way this continues. So. Lock. It. Up."

Taking a deep breath, I go about my business, ignoring my rioting heart thrumming against my ribs the whole time.

Heading out, I try to force myself not to look again. I can feel that he's not looking, if he's even sitting there anymore so why should I look?

Making it almost to the door of the sitting room all my friends are in, I turn at the last minute and look back.

And my stomach falls through my ass.

Perched on Ramsey's lap with one arm thrown over his shoulders and tits pushed up into his face, is Paige whateverthefuck. I never bothered to learn her last name, passing her in the halls after the incident at Lucy's and pretending to not even see her the same way she did to me.

I definitely blame the tiny amount of alcohol for my immediate response, feet changing direction and cutting through the crowd to walk directly up to the two of them.

Alarm bells blare in my head but I can barely hear them over the hornet's nest buzzing in my ears.

As I get closer, I can see that Ramsey's hands are on her, trying to move her without being too forceful. It calms some of the rioting in my head but can't seem to stop my feet.

"Get off him," I hear myself say the second I'm close enough for them to hear.

Ramsey looks up at me first, eyes wide for a moment before he grins.

"Who the fuck invited you?" Paige hiccups. "This isn't a piggy party." She giggles, leaning a little too far back.

I can feel my face go beet red, the words hitting me physically and prying the crevice in my chest a little bit wider. People nearby turn to stare, some smiling in a way that sets my teeth on edge.

Ramsey stands, dropping Paige to the floor in one swift move. "What the fuck did you just say?" A swathe of heat hits me as his anger pulses through the room, everyone now turning to stare.

But all I can feel is them looking, every inch of exposed skin being sized up by the same people who barely moved out of the way in the halls when I walked by, the same people who snorted and oinked behind my back, the same who made high school miserable.

"Get the fuck out of my house and don't ever fucking speak to her again, you pathetic fucking bitch."

Paige goes to stand, face screwed up as she starts to say something, but Smith swoops in, grabbing her shoulders and turning her around a little too quickly. "Out you go, princess," he mocks, walking her through the crowd and toward the front door.

No one moves and I can feel myself start to hyperventilate. The second Ramsey turns toward me, eyes finding mine and crinkling with fucking concern, I bolt. Pushing past people with my head ducked down, I run upstairs and straight for Mira's room.

I can hear him on my heels, more than one person following me up the stairs, but I don't care. I just need to be somewhere else where I can put a door between me and this whole awful moment and just spiral for a minute in private.

Wrapping my hands around my waist, I let myself gulp in air, pacing the carpet next to Mira's bed.

Warm hands pull my face up, Ramsey swimming into view as he stops me. "Hey, sweetness, look at me. Don't let her ruin today, she's nothi—

"Stop, Ramsey!" I push his hands away, feeling tears brim over in my eyes and hearing the shrill hysterical tone in my voice. It's all too fucking much. "Just stop! I need a second, just give me a second."

The room comes into sharp focus, Mira, Bentley and the rest of our group at the door behind Ramsey's shoulder, all looking in with more concern. I laugh wetly.

Great. More witnesses to my fucking humiliation.

"Get out, Ramsey." I whisper, turning back to start pacing again.

Ramsey's brow narrows. "No, I'm not leaving you here to let her words settle in that stubborn head of yours." He steps forward, grabbing my face again and swiping at my tears. "She's a jealous bitch who's never been able to take a hint. And I'm not letting her ruin your fucking birthday."

I laugh again, shaking my head as more tears pour out of me. "You can't control freak your way through this, Ramsey."

"Watch me," he says, tipping his face closer to mine.

"No!" I pull back. "You don't just get to distract me away from this, Ramsey. You don't get to hold me together right now! Not when it'll make it that much worse when I have to do it myself again."

Ramsey drops his hands to his sides, voice coming out deadly calm. "What does that mean, Fall?"

"This," I say, pointing between the two of us. "This is going to end soon. And I can't keep relying on you or it'll ruin me when it does."

His face gets darker somehow, a thunderstorm brewing in his eyes. "This is not fucking ending."

I snort, rolling my eyes and throwing my hands out. "We're fucking awful together, Ramsey. One of us says something and sets the other one off and half the time it's not even intentional. All we do is fight and snipe at each other. We're doing it right fucking now!" I can feel the hysterics rising too far, my words completely out of my own control, but I need him to get out right now and I'm willing to say anything to get him to give up on this. "We don't work long-term."

He takes a step forward, coming toe to toe with me and leaning down so his face is right in front of mine, blotting everything else out. "Yes, we fucking do. You're mine, Fall." Then he leans down and grabs my legs, tossing me over his shoulder and hoisting me up.

I grab onto his waist as my panic immediately morphs into fear and mortification. He turns and carries me toward the door, where all my friends and some of his are still standing, witnessing everything.

Out in the hallway, Ramsey shouts, "Party's over. Everyone get out," down the stairs while I just stare helplessly at my friends. Mira is smiling and Bentley's mouth is open, but everyone else just looks confused.

Continuing the caveman routine, Ramsey walks me down the hall to his bedroom, opening the door and walking in before slamming it closed behind him. It rattles in the frame and before it settles, he's already sliding me down the front of his body, returning my feet to the ground.

Once I can stand, he releases me, heading further into the room and starting to undo the buttons of his dress shirt.

"What are you doing?" I ask, brushing the cold tears off my cheeks while one arm wraps around myself.

"Getting ready for bed." He pulls the shirt off once the last button is undone, throwing it to the floor. Every muscle in his body seems tense, air still pulsating with his anger. He seems to be holding onto his control as hard as he can and I sigh, knowing there will be no fighting him now.

And alone in his room I'm not sure I want to. The moment that door closed behind us all the fight seemed to go out of me, Ramsey's words rattling around in my head.

You're mine.

"You should too," he pushes out, continuing to strip before he pulls back his duvet and then looks up at me. "You're sleeping here."

I sigh, sagging a little. "Do I get any say in this? Maybe we should cool off for the night and—

He marches back over to me, grabbing my jaw and kissing me. The suddenness of it sparks my reaction, lips parting for him and hands immediately pressing into his hot skin. He pulls back a moment later, eyes still blazing as he holds me hostage before him. "Either get in my bed, or I will put you there, Autumn."

Him using my name jolts through me and I nod, resigned to the fact that there's no arguing with him right now.

Stripping off my dress and shoes, I leave my underwear on, pulling the clip out of my hair and too exhausted to do anything about my probably ruined makeup.

I climb into the nearest side of his bed, Ramsey climbing in behind me from the other side and immediately pressing himself against me. Silence presses in, both of us laying together but neither saying a word.

As I just start to get comfortable in the quiet, heart rate finally back to normal and the emotions of the last hour lowering a bit, Ramsey speaks.

"You don't end things with me. Not when you're upset like that, okay?" His tone is soft and a little scared, making me look over my shoulder at him. He's staring at me, arms wrapped tightly around my body, holding me against him as if I might run away.

I sigh. "I won't, Ramsey."

But you will, I think to myself as I slowly drift off to sleep.

36

RAMSEY

Autumn is still asleep when I wake up. At first, I just cuddle closer, used to waking tangled up with her, but then last night's catastrophe filters in and my eyes snap open.

She tried to end things. Because she thinks we don't work together.

The solid thing in my chest trembles. I fucking love her and she thinks we don't work together.

Breathing her scent in through my nose, I take a second to let her nearness calm me down a little. I panicked last night when she said that, grabbing her and running away like that would stop her from ending things indefinitely.

But I know she works in patterns. And something in the back of my brain tells me this won't be the last time she panics and tries to burn everything down around her.

I'll gladly burn if it means she knows I'm not going anywhere.

Leaning up to kiss the side of her head, I untangle myself from her and get out of bed. She stays asleep which doesn't surprise me. I've found she's a very deep sleeper a lot of the time, barely making a noise and scaring the shit out of me sometimes when I have to check if she's still breathing.

I grab my glasses, throw on a pair of sweats, and ruffle my hair.

Mission "calm Fall down" starts with breakfast. As much as she wants to pretend she doesn't eat it, she always eats whatever I cook her at the Coast house, usually in the morning before I take her back to campus.

Padding down to the kitchen, I find Mom already up and cooking, her usual routine whenever we come home from school. I head toward the fridge, debating if I should cook something myself or just take some of Mom's up to Autumn.

"Good morning, sweetie." She reaches up and pats my cheek, making me stop so she can kiss the side of my face.

"Morning, Mom." I glance around at the living room, finding it pretty spotless. The guys and Mira must have cleaned up last night after I holed myself and Autumn up in my room. "How was your show last night?"

"Good," she answers, returning to whatever she was whisking before I walked in. "How was Autumn's party?" She looks over at me with knowing eyes and I groan.

"Mira already told you everything didn't she?" I grab the jug of orange juice out of the fridge and lean against the counter, sipping directly from it.

"Well, she was still awake when I got home," Mom muses, putting her bowl down and grabbing the juice out of my hand. She walks over to the cabinet and gets a glass, pouring me some before re-capping the jug. "And I had a few questions when I found *her* best friend in *your* bed." She stops moving, looking up at me. "Please tell me this isn't retaliation for her and Harley falling for each other?"

"What? No! I wouldn't do that to Autumn." I sip my juice shaking my head. "Or Mira for that matter."

Mom sighs, placing a hand over her heart before returning the OJ to the fridge. "Sorry, sweetie. But you sometimes overreact to things." She walks back to her bowl, picking up the whisk and testing the batter's thickness. "I know you wouldn't do that though. I shouldn't have said that." She shakes her head frowning.

I tap my finger against my glass, not looking up as I say, "You're not wrong. I do overreact at times." Like last night. I shouldn't have pushed. I should have just given her space. But the idea of leaving her alone to cry over that stupid cunt's words wasn't an option.

"Hey, Ramsey." Mom drops the whisk again, grabbing a hand towel and wiping off her fingers. "What's wrong?" She leans against the island and faces me fully.

I sigh. "I think I love her, Mom."

April Adams fucking beams. She holds her clasped hands up to her mouth and practically coos at me. And it unfortunately makes me smile.

"That's amazing, sweetie. Why are you upset about it?"

My smile falls and I tap my orange juice glass again. "I don't think she loves me."

Mom's hands fall. "Oh, Ramsey."

"No, Mom." I put the glass down and stand up. "I really don't think she does. She might like me, but even that seems kind of iffy." I run my hands through my hair, turning toward and then away from the fridge. "We got into a fight last night and I panicked and...Mom I spent three years being mean to her. Why would she fall in love with me? I don't even know how to go about getting her to."

Mom sighs, straightening up and walking toward me. "Ramsey, sweetie, breathe." She takes a deep breath, making me mimic the movement.

I let my hands fall to my sides, releasing my hair, and sag back against the counter.

"You can't orchestrate something like this, baby. You've always been so quick to assume the worst, but you can't try to control how Autumn feels. And trying to is the only guaranteed way to lose her." She pats my cheek, making me look her in the eye again. "All you can do is show her how you feel. And give her time to come to terms with her own feelings. I know you want to push this right now, but slow down and breathe. Just be with her. That girl can be headstrong, but she wouldn't let you anywhere near her if she didn't have feelings for you, sweetie." Mom leans in and I instinctively lean down to return her hug.

I take another deep breath, feeling more centered with her advice. She's right. Autumn wouldn't have given up the fight and gotten into bed with me last night if she truly wanted to end things between us. She just got scared. So, I'm just going to keep showing her I'm not going anywhere. I can practice patience. At least, I hope I can.

Mom pulls back, arms still wrapped around me as she adds, "And don't fuck this up. If you make it harder for that girl to come over here, I will never forgive you." She releases me with a nod, turning back and tending to her food again.

"No pressure though, right?" I hedge, wiping a hand over the back of my neck.

"Oh no, all the pressure." Mom ladles some batter onto a warmed skillet, the crackle of contact echoing in the kitchen.

"Gee, thanks," I grumble, grabbing my abandoned OJ and taking a sip.

"You've always thrived under pressure, Ramsey." She looks up smiling. "Don't forget that."

I stare at my mom, watching her hum and cook for a little bit before I ask, "How have you been, Mom? With us gone and you being alone in the house? You okay?" I check in on the phone every week or so, but I know my mother would never tell me if she was upset or lonely. She just wouldn't want that to weigh on us.

Mom laughs, flipping the mini pancakes without looking up. "I've been fine, Ramsey. Your father was never really around much before anyways so the transition hasn't been all that unfamiliar." She bites her lip, poking one of the pancakes. "Would you be upset if I were seeing someone?"

My eyebrows rise. "Are you?" The idea doesn't evoke any anger in me, which is interesting, but I'm not sure I'm settled with it either.

She looks up, frowning. "No. I've just been talking to someone. Someone I think I might want to see. Romantically. But I wanted to check with you and Mira first. This might seem sudden considering your father and I just filed a few months ago, and nothing is finalized yet, but I've been on my own for a while so for me it doesn't feel sudden. But I can see how it might bother you guys and—

"Mom," I cut off her rambling, smiling a little. "It's okay. It wouldn't bother me. I doubt it'll bother Mira either. She's always been the first in line to advocate for your happiness."

Mom smiles. "True. But I'm a little worried it might sting if that happiness isn't with your father."

I consider this, knowing my sister has always taken our parents happiness on her shoulders. While I got angry about everything slowly falling apart, she always tried to hold everything together, feeling like things fell on her shoulders more than they should have. I walk up to my mom and place my hands on her shoulders. "Mira loves you and just wants to see you happy. If you tell her this is something you want for your happiness, I doubt she'll be against it. If anything, she'll probably want to help in some way."

Mom nods, considering my theory. "I don't know if she'll go that far when she finds out who it is."

I release her shoulders, crossing my arms over my chest. "Who is it?"

Mom looks sheepish as she answers. "Jack Clifford."

The name sounds familiar and it takes me a second to place it. "Clifford. Like Axel Clifford. You're talking to Marshall's boyfriend's dad?"

Mom nods. "We met at their first move in day and were talking about how strange it is to suddenly be empty nesters, and I offered my phone number in case he ever wanted to lament. He lost his wife a long time ago so he's all alone in his house now too and we just sort of clicked. Do you think Mira will be wigged out?"

I laugh, shaking my head. "No, Mom. I don't think Mira will be 'wigged' out." I consider it again. "If anything, Marshall will probably be the one with the biggest reaction. Probably throw you guys a party after she tells him."

Mom smiles, turning back to the food and plating the pancakes. She adds some eggs and fruit to two plates and then turns and hands them to me. "Thank you, sweetie. Now go take some breakfast up to your girlfriend and then bring her down here so I can give her the birthday gift I got her."

I take the plates and don't bother correcting her, letting the word girlfriend swirl around in my chest and settle into the solid thing as I head back up to my room. I definitely want Fall to be my girlfriend, but I need to breathe and take things slow like Mom said. Give her some time to settle after the shock of last night and then poke around to see how she's feeling. Hopefully I won't have to be too patient, because I'm not sure how long I can hold out before the part of me that just wants to throw her over my shoulder and hide away with her until she loves me makes a reappearance.

37

AUTUMN

The snow has completely melted when we get back to campus and it's late enough in the year now that I doubt we'll get anymore. Part of me is sad but the bigger part of me that has been in the forefront lately kind of couldn't care less.

After my big birthday, with its explosive ending, Ramsey woke me up with breakfast in bed, followed by shower sex that rivaled our first time in his jade bathroom. We didn't want his family to overhear so he spent the whole time with his hand over my mouth and something about him having to keep me quiet always makes me come that much harder. After that, I spent the rest of the week pretty much wrapped up in all things Ramsey. He refused to let me go home for longer than to change and grab some toiletries, insisting that I stay with Mira at least if not him. But I ended up spending every night in his bed, with my days filled with activities similar to my birthday.

We did a beach day with some of the Ravens, Mira, Aria, Bentley, Janette, and Axel at the lake a few towns over. I spent most of it reading and attempting to tan without freezing. I probably would have just burned if it weren't for Ramsey's insistence on lotioning me up every hour on the dot. When I finally tried to fight him on it, he countered, arguing that he wouldn't be able to touch me for a day or two if I burned. I tried to make it seem like that would be fine with me and that ended in him picking me up and walking me into the freezing cold water while all of our friends cheered him on.

We also spent a day in the park, Ramsey doing some midterm grading while I read more from my birthday haul. It was gorgeous out and he convinced me to wear another skirt, finding it in my closet one of the times we stopped at my parent's house.

"So, you do own some of these," he mocked, holding up one of the frillier pieces clamped to a hanger.

I rolled my eyes, continuing to scrunch my curls in front of the mirror. "My grandmother gets me one every year. Some are better than others." I pointedly shook my head at the one he held and he replaced it, going through the small section of skirts in my closet.

"You should wear these more."

I rolled my eyes, turning to face him in my towel. "You just want to be able to stick your hands up them in public."

He shrugged. "Sue me." His eyes crinkled when he looked back at me over his shoulder. "You look good in skirts, though, Fall. You're gorgeous and should feel fucking beautiful in them."

I sighed. "I'll think about it."

He left it at that, but I couldn't stop thinking about his words, eventually picking one out to put on much to his elation.

Something about the way Ramsey unabashedly says shit

like that, as if it's a fact I should already know, makes me feel like he's not just saying it so I'll fuck him. He doesn't really have a problem in that department, easily figuring out new ways to make me tongue tied and delirious without needing much help.

I stare at the homework I've been trying to do for the last forty minutes and realize I've been laying here daydreaming about him without even realizing it.

Fuck, I can't get too attached. This will all end eventually and I can't be the embarrassing girl who tries to cling to our non-relationship just because I went and fell in love with him.

Holy shit.

I sit up.

Do I...love Ramsey?

My heart starts pounding, sweat instantly forming on my palms as I try to parse through the rush of emotions swelling in my chest.

No, no, no. This cannot be happening. We're hate fucking. Exclusively, but still, that's all this arrangement is. No strings, no feelings, just sex.

And birthday adventures.

And study time.

And eating meals together and sleeping wrapped around each other and flirty texts and.

Fucking fuck.

You're mine.

Those words have floated in and out of my head on occasion since the night Ramsey said them. In the midst of all that was going on, my mind seems to have latched onto those angry words and buried them in my chest where they think they're safe and protected.

But there's no way Ramsey meant them, right? He was

just freaking out because he wasn't in control. This arrangement has been fully on his terms, and I've been okay with that, liking the fact that I can hand over the reins and let go.

But maybe I should have held on to them a little bit since my heart seems a little confused as to what the deal is all of the sudden.

My phone buzzes next to my homework.

SATAN'S NEPHEW

what are you up to?

I bite the inside of my cheek, picking up the phone and swiping to open our messages. Before I can respond he's already typing again.

SATAN'S NEPHEW

I just got back from the gym. You should come over.

I tap my fingers against the edge of my phone.

I'm not feeling great. Gonna just take it easy in the dorm tonight

Fucking coward.

My phone instantly starts ringing.

"What's wrong?" he asks the second the call connects.

"I'm fine, Ramsey." I roll my eyes, picking up my pen and starting to chew on the cap. "I just have a stomach thing. Nothing to freak out about."

"Do you want me to get you some meds? Or bring you some food?"

Fuck, why is he making this so hard? "No, it's okay. Aria is here in case I need anything, but I'll probably just sleep it off."

"Okay." He hesitates. "Text me anyways if you need anything."

I roll my eyes. "Okay, I will."

"Night, Fall." He hangs up and I swallow, staring at my phone.

"Any reason in particular that you're lying to him?" Aria asks

I scoff, sitting up fully and facing her on her bed. "I am not. My stomach does feel queasy."

Aria rolls her eyes. "Because?"

I sigh. "Because I think I might be falling for him."

"Blossom, you've been with him nonstop for almost two months. I'd be concerned if you weren't falling for him." She continues typing on her laptop, blue light glasses reflecting back at me so I can't see her eyes well.

"Yeah, but what if this has been his plan all along? Like what if he's just being nice to get me to fall for him so that he can pull the rug out from under me at the last minute and get the last laugh? Or what if I'm imagining everything and we really are just compatible sexually and I'm being one of those clingy girls who suddenly thinks she's in love with a guy just because we fucked and he thinks I'm too much? Or what if—

"Okay, stop." Aria holds her hand up, looking at me over the top of her laptop. She removes her glasses, sitting up a bit and closing her laptop. "You're spiraling a bit. Ramsey can be a dick, but he doesn't really seem like someone with the temperament for a long con. So, I don't think he'd be able to do all this just to string you along and drop you at the last minute."

I nod, picking up my pen and chewing on the cap while staring into space a bit. "True."

"And I don't think you're making anything up. I saw him

with you all last week and he seems pretty intensely into you. Like borderline obsessed. He spent half our beach day just watching you read. I'd say he's pretty head over heels about you too."

I swallow, heart galloping at the idea.

"And Autumn?"

I hum and look up at her.

"It's okay if you're falling for him, you know? If he's what makes you happy, you can just let him make you happy. You don't have to look for a reason why it's not real. You deserve good things." She pauses, gripping her laptop. "Do you love him?"

I swallow, taking the pen out of my mouth and playing with it in my lap. "I don't know," I lie. I can feel my face heat up as my blood races with the truth.

Aria smirks. "Try again."

I sigh, running my fingers through a few of my curls. "Fine, yes, I think I do." I throw the pen down. "But I don't think I should."

"Why?"

"Aria," I sigh, looking down at my hands while my stomach bottoms out. "Look at me." I shrug my shoulders. "He's going to wake up one day and..."

"And what?" Aria scooches to the end of her bed, sitting forward and placing her laptop aside. "Autumn, I am looking at you. You're gorgeous. Like men-stop-and-look-at-you-when-you-walk-into-a-room gorgeous. You might not notice but trust me they do. You are not ugly by any means. And you can tell your bitch of a mother I said that."

I chuckle and she folds her arms over her chest.

"Besides, you're also smart and one of the nicest people I've ever met. Do you know how glad I am we got randomly paired up as roommates? You literally took me under your wing and are pretty much the only reason I stuck around last semester."

I frown. "What?"

She nods, swinging her legs. "Yeah, I kind of considered not even coming at first. And then most of the way here, I considered dropping out after the first week if I was miserable. It's really hard being away from Carter and trusting my mom and grandfather with everything. When I first got here, I knew I would probably be all on my own since most people tend to avoid the weird goth girl with her face glued to her computer screen. But you didn't. You pulled me into your life and your friend group as if it was nothing. As if it wasn't something I've literally never had before. Autumn, you're magnetic without even trying. Ramsey is fucking lucky you've fallen in love with him."

I sit back, shoulders hitting the wall as I stare at my roommate. I had no idea she felt that way. Bringing her in on things with Mira and Bentley just felt so natural. And I never thought twice about her style. She pulls it off so effortlessly.

"Autumn, you're so much more than whatever any idiot who takes one look at you and writes you off for your size is ever going to think. And Ramsey isn't an idiot. Trust me, he sees you. And given the whole *grunt grunt 'you're mine' grunt* barbarian act he pulled at your birthday, I don't think he's going to be letting you go anytime soon."

She pulls her laptop back out and puts her glasses back on, leaving me to consider everything she's just said. I can feel her words settling in that rational part of my brain that I don't listen to all that often.

Aria knows me. Aria doesn't lie.

I sigh, going back to my homework, but mostly just staring at the page and turning everything over in my head. I allow myself to consider the alternate possibility.

What if I fall in love with Ramsey and everything turns out okay?

38

AUTUMN

I'm chewing on my pen again, staring at Ramsey as he sits at the front of the class, staring back at me. We haven't broken eye contact in at least twenty minutes and I'm sure the whole class and Dr. Miller have noticed by now. But it feels like a challenge.

Everything with him does.

But I refuse to look away first.

Ramsey is grinning, sitting back in his chair and ignoring all of the papers and work he's supposed to be doing. It's been two days since the last time we were together and somehow as things go on, the window of time we seem to be able to go without touching gets smaller and smaller. I don't even care that I'm fully not paying attention and probably missing all of the answers to the next quiz, I need to be the one to win this. Even as I know I won't be.

People start moving around me, but I hold my position, biting into the pen cap as we still stare at each other. Ramsey winks, reaching back and placing his hands behind his head. And I know he's willing to sit like this all day if we need to, end of class or nuclear disaster be damned.

"Make sure you submit your final lab make ups by Thursday," Dr. Miller yells above the sound of the class packing up. He crosses through our path of eye contact, going to his podium and starting to pack up as well.

The break causes me to glance around, immediately losing the little battle of wills Ramsey and I were having and I curse under my breath. Looking back, his grin is impossibly wide, victory shining in his eyes.

Son of a bitch.

I don't even know what I just lost, but it feels like I've handed him another inch toward completely having the upper hand.

Packing up my bag, I grip the strap as I head over to him, stopping just short of touching him when he stands and looks down at me.

"Fall." He smirks. "Feeling better?"

I nod, swallowing against the onslaught of bats that take flight in my gut. "Yes, much better." And I'm wet and wanting thanks to whatever the fuck the last thirty minutes were. "Are you free right now?"

He chuckles. "Always so fucking greedy," he whispers. "Unfortunately, I have to go to a meeting with my advisor. She wants to narrow down my med school prospects."

"Oh." I deflate a little, and his hand starts to reach forward before he glances around at the dwindling class.

Running it through his hair, he looks back at me. "Come over tonight?"

I nod, probably a little too emphatically. But Ramsey just smiles, grabbing his bag and gesturing for me to walk ahead.

I start to turn, but at the same time, Dr. Miller calls out, "Autumn? Could you stay a minute? I wanted to discuss something with you."

Ramsey goes completely still behind me. He hasn't brought up Dr. Miller since the beginning of the semester, dropping the whole "he's interested in me" thing since we haven't really interacted much besides class time. He cancelled our advisor meeting right before break and hasn't rescheduled and I was fine with that since I don't have to pick classes for next semester yet.

I look to Dr. Miller. "Sure!" Taking one step forward, Ramsey's hand on my arm stops me.

"You're free to go, Mr. Adams," Dr. Miller says, continuing to pack his leather bag without looking up and waving his hand.

Ramsey's jaw is tense when I turn back toward him. "Do you want me to stay?" he whispers.

I bite my lip. "I'll be okay. I promise." When he doesn't let me go, I add, "Do you want to stay?"

"Kind of." He sighs, closing his eyes for a second.

"I'll be okay, Ramsey. You can wait right outside if you want. I'll tell you everything that happens."

He opens his eyes, staring at me before shaking his head. "I have to get to that meeting." He lets go of my arm, still staring between my eyes. "Call me if you need me."

I nod, and he hesitates again before heading out.

Turning back around, I find Dr. Miller watching after Ramsey's departure and realize all the other students have filtered out as well. Some of Ramsey's paranoia leaks into me and I push it away.

"You wanted to discuss something, Dr. Miller?" I step forward so that we're not standing so far apart.

"Yes," he says, looking down at me and smiling. "Your labs have been amazing this semester, Autumn. You should be proud of yourself."

"Thank you. I really enjoyed the one we did on genotype changes."

Dr. Miller nods, smiling and not saying anything for a beat too long. I knit my fingers together, feeling the hairs on the back of my neck rise.

"So, I read over your application for my internship next year and I was very impressed."

"Oh, thank you, sir." I fake a smile, surprised by that. My resume is lacking since I've had one job for less than three weeks and I'm only a freshman, so my academic background doesn't exactly make up the difference. Plus I kind of phoned it in for the cover letter, not really sure if I spun "I need experience and money" into a good enough selling point to beat out all the other applicants who are probably applying for the same reasons.

"I wanted to see if we should reschedule our advisory meeting and tack on some time for an interview?"

My mind blanks for a minute before my smile turns real. "Seriously? Yeah, I would love that!" I know several people in our class applied for the spot and getting Dr. Miller's clinic internship as a sophomore would be practically unheard of. Usually, he offers interviews to prospective junior and senior applicants first.

"Great!" He turns and grabs his organizer, flipping through and finding this month in the calendar pages. "How does the eleventh sound? I have an hour block open at noon."

I pull up my calendar on my phone and pretend to check that I don't have anything. "That should work." I block out the hour, titling the event CLINIC INTERVIEW!!!

He pencils it into his schedule before turning back and reaching out to place his hand on my shoulder. "Awesome."

He squeezes me for a second and something drips down my spine.

Keeping my smile in place, I nod and subtly shake his hand off, pretending to shuffle the weight of my bag. "Thank you so much. I look forward to it, Dr. Miller."

He nods and there's another long, pregnant silence before he turns to finish packing up. "Alright, well I need to head off. Keep up the good work!" He walks past me, walking out in a rush and I stand in the empty classroom for a second.

Shaking my head, I decide Ramsey's bias must be infecting me, squealing a little when I realize I actually just set up an interview for my dream internship. Heading out, I immediately go to call Ramsey, but stop, finger hovering over his name in my recently dialed list. He's in a meeting. And if I call him, he'll pick up and panic immediately.

Scrolling down, I press on Aria's name, waiting for the call to connect and deciding I'll tell Ramsey later when I go over to his.

"Hey, Blossom."

I walk out into the cool spring day, beaming as I say, "I got an interview for the clinic spot!"

Aria screams on the other end, making me bounce on the sidewalk a bit. "We have to do something to celebrate!"

"Wanna get lunch? My treat." I consider dipping into the Green funds, figuring Aaron can front one celebratory meal off campus.

"No, my treat! I just got my commission bonuses from everyone's first month gym sign-ups. I'm taking you to Warrick's."

I laugh, heading in no direction with the flow of traffic on the way across campus. "Oooo splurging are we? A whole lunch at the sandwich shop?"

"Hells yeah, baby. My roommate got an interview for the campus clinic internship!"

We laugh together, my whole body feeling light and floaty. It may seem small but if I get this internship, I'll be taking my next step toward making my own money, the next big step in my grand getaway plan. I'll be building up my resume for med school and Mom won't be able to argue that it'll embarrass the family. It feels like the precipice, like if I get this, I'll be pushing the boulder over the cliff and everything after should be smooth sailing.

Breathing in the smell of impending rain, I shake my head in disbelief, telling Aria where to meet me as I change directions and head toward Warrick's.

39

RAMSEY

The house is weirdly quiet when I get home, later than I intended. My meeting with Dr. Phillips ended up making me spiral more than anything, needing to go to the library and research med schools with rolling admission since I didn't apply to enough in his opinion. Burying my head in research, I kind of forgot to watch the time as I googled average acceptance rates and differences in programs and specialties and all the shit I thought I already had a handle on.

Harley sits on the couch, hands in his lap and head down as he stares at the ground.

"You good?" I call out, dropping my bag and toeing off my shoes.

Harley looks up, startled by my voice. "Oh, yeah." He spins something in his hands and as I head over I realize it's a folded piece of paper. Pencil markings seem to cover it, but I can't tell what they are.

"I saw Mira today," he says, looking up at me over the back of the couch. "She was with that guy again." He hesitates and I put my hands in my pockets, feeling weirdly sorry for him. "She's moving on, isn't she?"

I sigh. I specifically told Mira last semester that I didn't want to be in the middle of anything if these two ever got together. But now that the reality is in front of me, I can't help it. "Yeah, buddy." I shift on the balls of my feet. "I think she is."

Harley nods, not really seeing me as he sighs. He looks back down at the paper, swallowing. "I think I'm about to play a longer long-game than I first anticipated."

I take one of my hands out, patting him on the shoulder. "If it makes you feel any better, I think I'm rooting for you."

He chuckles mirthlessly. "Yeah, I think it does. Thanks, Rams."

I head toward the kitchen, adding, "You're not going to go out and get wasted again, right?"

"Nah," he calls out. "Probably going to replace that with some long runs instead." He gets up off the couch, heading over to the door and pocketing the paper. "Autumn's upstairs by the way."

I smile, grabbing a second water bottle from the fridge. "Thanks," I throw over my shoulder but he's already heading out the door. Jogging up the stairs, I remember the stare off the little witch and I had in class today and my dick wakes up.

Fall has been weirdly challenging lately, playing a little longer for dominance before going pliant against me. And surprisingly, I really like it. Usually, her immediate surrender is a huge turn on, but the two of us wrestling a bit for control seems to ramp things up to an eleven. Like with the staring contest today. It doesn't even have to be something sexual, just getting a tiny win in over her makes all my blood run south.

I open the door to my room, ready to pounce on her immediately, but pull up short.

She's asleep. Passed out across my bed with her laptop precariously balanced on the edge and some notes spread out around her. Her hair is splayed out and she's so breathtakingly beautiful, I just stop and stare at her.

God, I fucking love her.

Shaking my head, I step in and shut the door behind me, placing the water bottles on my desk before I head over and rescue her laptop.

I haven't been able to gauge how Fall feels about me. She seems easy to read, but every time I think I see evidence that she might like me beyond just fooling around, we start down that path, and I dash that thought process, chalking it up yet again to the orgasms I can give her.

"Sweetness," I whisper, kissing her eyelids and lightly shaking her shoulder. I've found that it usually takes some time to wake Autumn up from a dead sleep so when she immediately opens her eyes and sits up, nearly headbutting me, I startle backwards.

"Shit, sorry!" She looks around, checking my clock for the time. "I didn't mean to fall asleep. I was just going to study until you got here and then I planned to surprise you, but now you're here and—

"Hey," I reach forward, grabbing her jaw the way that always makes her shudder and her eyelids flutter a bit. "You're okay, Fall. Harley told me you were here. And you can sleep in my bed whenever you want." I wink, leaning down and thoroughly kissing her.

She sighs when I stand back up, eyes opening as a lazy smile slides across her face. "I got an interview."

I let go of her, stepping back and furrowing my brow. "An interview? For what?"

She sits up a bit. "The clinic internship. With Dr. Miller." Fall's smile turns up in wattage, and I can see how proud of herself she is, but my blood starts to boil and the solid part of me seems to rattle in warning.

"What the fuck, Fall?" I take another step back, away from her.

Her smile drops and I shake my head, trying to stop the slow creep of anger rolling over me. "Ramsey?"

"You said you were going to look for other internships. I gave you the email for the one I did. Why the fuck would you apply for Miller's?" My hands start to shake, and I run them through my hair, adjusting my glasses when that does nothing to settle my nerves.

Fall sits up fully, brows furrowing. "I did look at other ones. I applied to four of them. The clinic's is just the first one I've heard back from. Dr. Miller offered me the interview after class today."

I scoff. "Oh, I'm sure he did." I turn away, starting to pace as my hands continue to shake. "An opportunity to be alone with you probably seems like a lottery win to him."

"Ramsey, it's a job interview not a casting couch. Calm down."

"Calm down?" I can hear my voice getting too loud, and the solid thing bangs against my chest, begging me to listen to her. But it's not in charge right now. "You can't go. He's just trying to get close to you because he's a fucking perv."

Fall stands up, eyes flashing with the familiar spark I tend to ignite in her. "You think he offered me an interview to his highly sought after, paid internship, at the on-campus clinic, *regulated by the freaking school*, because he wants to risk his job and his reputation on *me*? Be so fucking for real, Ramsey."

I step up to her, getting in her space and hearing a buzz

in my ears. "You can't seriously think he offered you, a freshman, an interview for his 'highly sought after, paid internship' because he's just so fucking impressed by your base knowledge of organ systems and genome types? You be so fucking for real, Fall."

Autumn's face blanches and something punches me on the inside. "You're being an asshole, Ramsey." She shakes her head, anger pouring out of her and meeting mine. "You're looking at this from some jealous possessive angle and it's making you act like the jerk you were before this year. I don't like him."

I laugh, the sound echoing in my ears. "I don't need to look at this from a possessive angle, Fall. You're mine, remember?"

She wraps her arms around herself, looking away from my face as she says, "Not if you're going to act like this." Her eyes are back on mine a moment later, voice deadly calm. "Not if you're going to try to tell me what I can and cannot do like this."

I ball my hands at my sides and grit my teeth, feeling the solid thing sink right through my organs. Potent anger and panic slide into the empty space and I practically growl, taking a step forward.

Fall flinches.

And everything freezes. My whole body locks up, rebelling against the idea of scaring her. My fire instantly cools, replaced by a gnawing ache as I stumble back, putting more distance between us in an instant. My eyes widen and air catches in my throat.

"I'm going to go." She turns and starts packing her stuff up, shoving her laptop and notes haphazardly into her bag.

My thoughts liquefy, seeming to race around in my brain

without containment as I try to think of something to say or some way to go back in time.

"I was really excited to tell you about this, *to celebrate.* But I think I need some space right now." Fall looks at me, eyes glassy before she walks out.

I watch her go, keeping myself perfectly still as I replay her flinching over and over again.

She turns back at the door, mouth downturned. "I was hoping you'd be proud of me."

Fall disappears as everything explodes inside me.

I scared her.

Of course, I'm proud of her.

I scared her.

I still don't want her to go to that fucking interview.

I fucking scared her.

Standing in the same spot for an eternity, I slowly resign myself to the fact that I need to listen to her and stay away from Fall right now.

40

RAMSEY

"I scared Autumn." My knee bounces as I sit at my desk and run my hands over my thighs, staring at Diane on my laptop screen. "She flinched because I...I scared her." The narrow band around my chest constricts further.

"Breathe, Ramsey."

I inhale slowly. The band stays tight.

"Good. Now go back. What happened?"

Taking another breath, I start. Recounting the fight with Fall feels like emptying myself out then slowly filling the empty space with dread. "She got an interview. For the internship. The one with Miller. When I came back from the library, Harley said she was here and I went up to find her asleep. She told me when she woke up."

Diane scrawls something on her notepad before she asks, "And how did you react?"

"Poorly," I concede, remembering the immediate flash of anger her excitement created in me. I grip my jeans under the desk. "I got angry."

Diane just nods, waiting for more.

I sigh. "I told her it was a bad idea. Taking the interview." I wince remembering some of the words I used while I was out of control. "Well, I more or less insulted her. I told her the only reason she got an interview was because Miller's into her." I sit back, a blend of shame and guilt permeating the layer of anger I'm able to set down in these sessions. The feeling starts to choke me, rushing up the back of my throat as I remember my harsh words hurled at Fall not an hour ago.

Diane tilts her head on screen. "And what did she say?"

I close my eyes. "She said I was acting like the old me. The one from the start of the semester."

Diane's pen scratches against her paper. "Explain."

My throat constricts further and I have to swallow before answering. "Before..." I open my eyes. "Before Autumn and I became anything, I tended to be mean to her. Ignored her or poked at her, saying things I knew would piss her off, just to see her fight back." My mind whirls through old memories of her heated glares and hissed comebacks. "We didn't get along much until a couple months ago."

"You told me once you hated her."

I laugh. "Yes. I thought I did." I pause and slide my hands over my thighs again. "I'm not sure I ever actually did though. I think I just hated how much she got to me. How much just seeing her set me off."

"She made you angry?"

"Yes."

"And does she still?"

I stare down at my keyboard as I answer, unable to look at myself or Diane. "No. She's..." The solid thing thrums in the pit of my stomach. "For as much as she still riles me up, she's one of the few people I can feel utterly calm around as well." I glance up, finally looking at the image of myself and Diane onscreen. Renewed panic and desperation rushes through my veins. "That's why she can't do this internship. It's not safe for her and I *need* her safe. I didn't say stuff tonight because I was trying to get a rise out of her. I was trying to get her to see what Miller's doing." I lean in closer, gripping the edge of my desk. "I already hate that he's her advisor, her professor. If she gets the clinic spot, they'll be together, alone, more often." I shake my head, dizzy from all the unsettled emotion, and look over at my bed. "She deserves an internship, but not with *him*."

"Did you tell her that?"

My head whips back toward the camera. "Tell her what?"

"That she deserves an internship."

I roll through our argument again, the angle of my words suddenly hitting me. I sit up. "No, but I gave her the info for the one I did. And I told her I would reach out to them as a reference if she needed one. She has to know I think she deserves an internship." My thoughts race as my blood cools. "Fuck. Autumn needs direct reassurance." I run a hand through my hair, tugging on the short hairs at my nape. "I'll tell her," I resolve.

Diane nods, shuffling her posture a bit. "After she flinched, how did you react?"

I shrug. "I locked up. I just stopped and held my breath while she walked away."

"That's new for you."

My eyes bounce around the room again. "I guess."

"Ramsey, where were you on the light scale before Autumn flinched?"

"Red," I answer without thinking.

Diane nods. "But you stopped. You kept yourself in

check in the middle of a highly emotional moment. That's not nothing, Ramsey."

My palms start to sweat. "Does it matter? Sure, I stopped, but she's still scared of me!" My breath races out of me sharp as ice and the room looks like it's swimming.

"Did you hurt her?"

I sit up, looking Diane square in the virtual eye as I say, "No, I would never."

Diane nods. Another note scribbled in her notebook. "So, you still trust yourself around her?"

"Of course! I would never do anything to harm her."

"Then why do you think she would write you off after one incident?"

My spine thumps against the back of my desk chair as my posture falls. "Why wouldn't she?"

"Ramsey you tend to think the worst of yourself. And from what you've told me about her, Autumn doesn't. She sees you and tends to rise to the occasion."

I adjust my glasses, avoiding looking at the laptop screen again. I know Fall rises to my baits. Does she rise to meet more than just my anger?

"Give her the benefit of the doubt."

I sigh, tipping my head back and feeling all my energy wane. Give her the benefit of the doubt. I'm not even sure what that means.

Sitting back up, I glance at the time and realize we don't have much left in this session. "I don't know where to go from here."

"Start by taking some time. Autumn asked for space. Maybe you should give her some. You said you regretted not listening to her the last time she asked." Diane shrugs, closing her notebook and setting it and her pen primly on her lap.

I nod, feeling all my organs sink at the idea. Part of me is screaming to get up and rush over to her dorm. To barge in and demand we finish our conversation, make her see what I was trying to tell her. What I need her to know.

The other part of me keeps replaying the image of her flinching as I stepped toward her.

"And when the time comes, hear her out. You stopped, Ramsey. Autumn reacted and you stopped. That is not nothing and it matters."

Diane waits for me to acknowledge her words. With another sigh, I nod.

"Hear her out. When she's ready, give her the space to explain and listen to what she has to say."

I nod again, sliding my palms over my thighs one more time. "Okay."

"And if you need to talk, you know where to find me."

I grin. "Don't I always."

Diane smiles before she signs off and the call ends. I stare at myself in the reflection of the laptop screen feeling somehow better and worse all at once.

Give her the benefit of the doubt.

I sigh, standing up and take off my glasses, rubbing the corners of my eyes. Both parts of me war some more, pushing and pulling my thoughts in every direction. Giving up on deciding anything more tonight, I walk over to my nightstand and grab my lighter and stash of pre-rolls. Lighting a joint, I climb into bed, wishing I'd just done that earlier when I found Autumn asleep here.

Instead, I think I fucked everything up.

41

AUTUMN

"You have a copy of your resume?" Aria looks me over, dusting invisible lint off my shoulders for the fiftieth time.

"I made three just in case." I bite my lip, gripping the strap of my bag and feeling like my stomach is going to eat itself.

"Three?" Aria's eyes bug out of her head.

I gulp. "You think that's too many?"

Aria laughs, squeezing my shoulders. "I think that'll be plenty. One to give him, one for backup, and one in case the backup somehow spontaneously combusts."

"Exactly," I murmur with a definitive nod.

It's interview day and I've spent the last week and a half pulling Ramsey's contact up and then chickening out. His words have rattled around in my head, making me question if I got this interview on my own merit or not. If I'm just wasting my time going right now.

I told Aria about it, right after the third class Ramsey skipped, avoiding me just as much as I'm avoiding him. I laid out everything Ramsey's brought up and the weird vibe of the way Dr. Miller gave me the interview, and we spent way too long dissecting all my interactions with him last semester in our advisory meetings. Aria even did some sleuthing online and couldn't find anything official on Dr. Miller that sided with Ramsey's point. When I told her how he reacted to me getting the interview, she immediately chalked it up to his jealousy.

"Fuck him. You are an amazing student, Blossom. You got this interview because Dr. Miller thinks so too. There's no way he gave you this interview solely based on attraction. He'd never be able to justify it to the school if they approve his hires. This is an amazing opportunity and you're going to kick ass in that interview."

I tried to keep that in the forefront as I continued to prep for the interview, but Ramsey's reaction to me flinching kept popping up too. I knew when I did it, I'd fucked up. He was so immediately appalled and the whole temperature of the room changed.

I've been wanting to reach out and check in on him because I know he's beating himself up about it, but everything he said before that just keeps enraging me every time I start to type out a text or stare at his number without pressing it.

"Alright," I say, tugging on my blouse one more time before turning toward the door. "I better get going or I'll be late."

"You got this! Call me after if you need a debrief."

"Thanks, Bubbles." I hug her quick before heading out, gripping the strap of my bag and going over the practice answers I've been memorizing.

What if he asks me questions I didn't think of? Or what if I can't remember anything? Did I bring my resume?

I start to breathe shallowly, feet slowing down and the science center feeling that much farther away.

Swallowing, I realize my heart is racing and my palms are sweating and I can't seem to catch onto one thought as they all zip around in my mind.

Oh, fuck.

My phone is against my ear and ringing before my brain catches up to what I'm doing.

"Fall?" Ramsey's voice picks up on the third ring.

My words come out in a rush. "Ramsey, I'm heading to the interview, and I think I'm having a panic attack."

"Breathe, sweetness." He starts talking me through deep breathing, having me mimic him over the phone. "Good. Can you sit down?"

I look around, finding a vacant bench a few steps away and crossing in front of a couple students to beeline toward it. "I am now. Oh, God, Ramsey."

"Shhhh, you're okay. Put your hand over your heart. Feel your pulse slow down as you breathe."

I follow his instructions, closing my eyes and just listening to him continue to breathe with me.

Opening my eyes, I whisper, "I'm sorry."

"Hey, no," he says sharply. "*I'm* sorry. I shouldn't have reacted that way. You got this interview because you're smart and you work hard and I shouldn't have said what I did." He swallows and I wait. "You know I'm proud of you, right Fall? I didn't mean to make it seem like I'm not." He sighs and I can hear him shuffle around on the other end of the call. "And about Miller. I *know* you can handle anything. Just sometimes, I feel this need to handle things for you. But I'm going to work on that."

I sigh. "I like you handling certain things."

Ramsey chuckles in my ear. "You deserve this, Fall.

You're smart and capable and you're going to ace this interview."

I breathe a little deeper.

"I'm sorry for implying you didn't earn this. I'm so fucking proud of you, Fall."

I close my eyes, feeling my lashes stick together with some errant tears. "Thank you," I whisper. "I needed to hear that." We sit together for a moment before I open my eyes. "You weren't in class all week. I thought you were still mad at me."

"I know." He sounds guilty and I consider changing the call to FaceTime so I can see his reactions, and he can see mine. "You said you needed some space, and I didn't want to barge in too early. I was..." He sighs. "I was nervous you would be mad at me for scaring you." I can hear him messing with his glasses as they hit the phone on his end. "I was mad at me."

"Ramsey, no," I breathe.

"I had a session with Diane after you left." He hesitates and I wait. "I never want you to be scared of me, Fall." His voice cracks a little, and my heart does the same.

"I never have been. I have never been scared of you a day in my life, Ramsey, and I'm sorry I made you think that I was. I..." I swallow, shame coating my insides. "I knew it was the only way you'd stop, but I shouldn't have done that."

I hear him exhale through his nose and picture him relaxing, wishing he was here so I could hold him.

"You did the right thing, Fall. You wanted me to stop and I wasn't listening." He breathes a little more before adding, "Maybe we should add safe words into our arrangement."

I laugh, feeling the tightness in my chest start to slowly dissolve. "Maybe."

"I need you to know that if you are ever scared of me, it's

okay to tell me. I *need* you to tell me because I don't ever want to take things too far, do you understand me?"

I nod, even though he can't see me. "Yes, I promise I'll tell you."

He sighs in relief. "Good."

We sit in silence together and I glance down the path, biting my lip. "I have to go to the interview now."

"Okay. Come over after?" His tone is hopeful and I smile, feeling like something slides back into place.

"Okay."

"I missed you. You're going to do great." He sounds like he's smiling and I can hear him shuffling around on the other end.

I bite my lip. "I'll see you in a bit."

"Alright. Go kick ass. I lov—I'll see you after."

I nod again stupidly, heart skipping a beat as I consider what he almost just said.

Fuck, I can't think about that right now.

"Bye, Ramsey." I hang up, checking the time and rushing toward the science center, Ramsey's half confession ringing in my ears.

42

AUTUMN

The TA cubes are practically full when I stop outside Dr. Miller's office. I try to tamp down my labored breathing from jogging the rest of the way here to make up for my convo with Ramsey. His cube sits starkly empty and I smile at the lone coffee mug sitting in the otherwise undecorated space, remembering his reassurances.

I lov—

I shake my head to clear *that* thought, then end up shaking out my whole body, forcing my nerves to reset before I go in.

Dr. Miller is squinting at something on his computer when I knock on his open office door. "Ah, Autumn!" he says standing and gesturing for me to come in.

I walk in, half closing the door behind me and glancing at the desk Ramsey and I fucked on top of less than a month ago. Memories of him pressing me against the door, on top of the desk, fucking me while fully clothed, attack me as I walk over to the chairs we pushed out of the way last time I was in here.

I lov—

"Excited that the weather is finally warming up?" Dr. Miller asks, walking over and fully closing the door.

"What? Oh, yes." I smile, taking my bag off my shoulder and placing it by my feet. I'm reaching into it to pull out a copy of my resume when I feel him sit down in the chair next to me rather than return to his spot on the other side of the desk. I sit up, resume forgotten and blink at him.

Dr. Miller just smiles. "I like to do interviews face to face. More personal than me sitting behind this awful monstrosity." He pats the wooden surface, and I try not to blush remembering again what Ramsey and I did in here.

"Right. Well, I brought a copy of my resume if you need it." I go to lean down again but Dr. Miller waves his hand.

"No need, I have a copy somewhere and I've already looked over it. Plus, I think we can skip the formal questions. I've been with you the whole of your academic career." He chuckles and something sloshes around in my stomach. "At the clinic, we're going to be working together much more closely than we do in a classroom setting and I like to make sure my interns are the right fit, personality wise. I want to use this time to get to know you better, Autumn." He steeples his hand against his mouth, looking me over and I shuffle in my seat.

This is not what I prepared for.

I subtly lean back in my chair, pasting a smile on my face. My heart races as I try to remember anything I memorized that was geared more toward the get-to-know-you variety of interview questions. I didn't fucking plan for this scenario. My thighs rub together and I can feel the press of the chairs arms on my hips, making the room suddenly feel like it's squeezing in on me.

"What would you l-like to know?" My voice shakes a

little and I cringe internally, trying to call up all my bravado and practiced answers as I readjust in my seat again.

He chuckles. "No need to be nervous." His hand comes down on my knee, and the touch is innocent enough, but my skin seems to itch beneath the soft material of my dress pants. "I know you're a good student Autumn. Right now, I want to hear more about what you like to do outside of the classroom?"

I stare at his hand as I answer robotically, muscles seeming to freeze up as my brain goes on autopilot. "I like to read. Fiction mostly. My best friend's mom is an author, and I've read all her books."

"Oh?" He removes his hand, and my eyes track the movement, air feeling less stifling when it crosses back into his territory. "Have I heard of her?" He crosses his leg, one foot resting against the other knee. The movement turns him toward me more, his bent knee now resting against the arm of my chair.

I lean back a bit, fingers hooking together in my lap. "Maybe. April Adams?"

He smiles, shaking his head. "Afraid not. I'll have to check her out sometime." The silence stretches a moment too long and I swallow, feeling the hairs on the back of my neck rise. One thought starts to get louder in the back of my head.

Ramsey was right.

"So, other than reading, what else do you do in your free time?"

"Um." I shift again, glancing at the door over his shoulder. "Study mostly. I really like what we're learning in class and—

"Autumn," Dr. Miller says in a low tone. He leans forward, crossed leg dropping away and removing the barrier between us as his hand comes down again on my knee.

This time it snaps my spine straight, a shard of ice sliding in between each vertebrae. The movement does nothing to dislodge his touch though as he continues speaking.

"There's no need to be nervous." His hand starts to move, rubbing over my knee in a slow, deliberate motion and the air around me seems to press in. "I don't want to talk about school."

I swallow, looking up at him and moving my leg so that his hand falls away. "I don't feel comfortable with you touching me, Dr. Miller."

He smiles, the edges a little too wide and eyes suddenly seeming sickeningly intense. "Come on, Autumn. Relax. We both know why I offered you this interview today. You're a very pretty girl and this internship can help you get into some of the top medical schools in the country." His hand comes back up to touch me, but I stand before it does.

He seems startled by my movement, looking up at me in confusion.

"I have to go." I grab my bag, rushing to get past him and toward the door, but he turns and grabs my arm just as I reach the knob.

"You're throwing away an amazing opportunity, Miss Green." His eyes are narrowed, voice low as he issues the words.

I yank my arm free, heart racing as I rip open the door and rush out of his office. One of the TAs in the cubicle farm stands up at my abrupt appearance, watching me rush out to the stairwell with a bewildered expression.

I run from the building, tearing down the sidewalk and veering toward the west gate. I know he's not following me, but the cloying feeling from inside Miller's office still clings to my skin. I can't seem to get away fast enough.

Running past the residential houses and manicured lawns, I only slow down when the Ravens' mansion comes into view, jogging up their steps and ringing the doorbell more than once.

Royal opens the door, scarred brow furrowed and lip curled. He takes one look at me, panting and panicking on his front step and moves aside. "He's in his room."

I rush up the stairs, not even bothering to take my shoes off. I barge into his room, Ramsey ripping a pair of headphones off as he turns toward me in his desk chair.

"Fall? What are you doing here?" He glances at the clock before getting up and starting to walk toward me.

Tears blur my vision as I finally drop my bag and start shaking. "You were right."

He engulfs me in his arms, and I crush myself against him. "You were right, he was trying to..." A sob steals my voice when I think of even saying the words. My skin crawls and my stomach rolls, the spot on my knee that he rubbed burning as if infected.

Ramsey pulls back enough to see my face, cupping my jaw and swiping tears off my cheeks. "What did he do?" he says between bared teeth.

"He blocked the door, and touched my knee, and he was saying how he wanted the interview to be *personal* and asking what I do for fun." I start hyperventilating and Ramsey curses, pulling me back against his chest. I can feel him shaking, arms wrapped around me and giving me the perfect pressure to ground me as I break down. "I ran out before anything happened, but he made it clear why he offered me the interview. You were right." I sob into his shirt, feeling stupid and defeated. All my fears from before the interview turn sour in my gut.

"Fuck, Fall." He rubs my back. "I didn't want to be right." He places his chin on top of my head, tucking me even more in against him. His hands ball into fists as he continues rubbing them over my back. "I'm going to fucking kill him."

I shake my head, gripping the back of his shirt tighter. "No. You'll get expelled. Or arrested." I hiccup.

"I have friends in high places, sweetness. I can get away with it."

I pull back, looking up at him. "No, Ramsey. I don't want you doing something like that."

He swipes more tears off my cheeks, sighing. "He can't just get away with this."

I take a deep breath, nodding in his hands. "I want to report him for sexual harassment. Bring it to the school board."

Ramsey raises one eyebrow, looking a little skeptical. "You sure? I feel like making him disappear would be a lot easier."

I shake my head, pulling on his shirt again. "No, I don't want you getting in trouble. And I don't want him pressuring any other girls like this."

Ramsey stares down at me, eyes searching before he nods. "Okay. I'll go with you."

I nod, tucking myself in against him and squeezing before releasing him and taking just his hand as we head out together.

43

RAMSEY

y teeth feel like they're about to crack under the pressure I'm putting on them, wrapped hands flying at the punching bag in front of me without finesse. I've been here for thirty minutes, and my anger has yet to subside, crawling over me like fire ants and invading every part of my body. I didn't even bother with gloves today, needing to feel the sting of my hits.

We went through the proper channels, Fall putting an official report in with the school and they didn't immediately remove him. They're *investigating* it. Royal immediately promised to get involved, but I told him to hold off. For now.

Fall wants to do this all officially. She wants justice and while I want to honor her wishes, this route is slow and messy and pissing me off every second of everyday.

"You're bleeding." Harley steps into view, holding the bag steadier as he stares at my hands.

"The student hearing is tomorrow," is all I say.

"Ah." Harley nods. "Royal isn't getting involved?"

I shake my head, grunting with another punch. "I told

him to hold off right now. Autumn wants to do this by the book."

Harley nods again. "Have you talked to Diane?"

I stand up, breathing deep and shaking out my sweaty curls. "Every other day. She recommended finding a physical outlet for my aggression. Hence," I gesture to the bag. Grabbing my water bottle, I chug from it, feeling my abs scream with the lack of oxygen.

"How have you been doing with Autumn? With your 'aggression?'" He finger-quotes around the last word and I give a short laugh.

"There was an incident. I thought I scared her. I talked with Diane about it and then with Autumn, but it really fucked with my head for a bit. Since all of this started though, I think she's well aware why I'm angry all the time. And none of it is toward her, so." I take another swig from my water, brows furrowing as I try to parse through my emotions.

"She's good for you, dude. She tests your control, but she's strong too."

My phone buzzes on the ground and I see a text from Fall light up the screen.

"I've seen her go toe to toe with you," Harley continues as I bend down. "She's your match."

FALL

Where are you?

I type back, nodding to Harley.

At the gym. What do you need?

FALL

I don't know. What if tomorrow is a
disaster?

The grey bubbles immediately appear again, and I look up at my best friend.

"I gotta go." I grab my bag, not even bothering to put my shirt back on or unwrap my hands.

"What's wrong?" Harley leans forward, concern etching his face.

"She's spiraling. I need to go find her." I pause. "And thank you. I'm in love with her, so I'm glad someone else sees it too."

Harley chuckles, clapping me on the shoulder. "I'm happy for you, man. Go get her."

I head out, dialing Fall's number and holding the phone to my ear.

"Ramsey," she breathes when the call connects.

I throw my bag in the back of the Jeep, climbing in as I respond. "Where are you?"

"In your room."

The solid thing thumps at the idea of my bedroom being one of her safe spaces. "I'll be there in five. Talk me through the spiral."

She starts to pour out her fears, hiccupping and taking a deep breath every now and then when she speeds up too much. I drive to my house the whole time, connecting her to the speakers and talking her down.

"He won't get off scot-free, Fall. I promise." I park in the driveway, jumping out immediately after hitting the button to turn off the car. "I'm coming up now. Do you want anything to eat?"

"No. My stomach's in knots. I haven't been able to eat."

I sigh, heading up the stairs and directly into my room. Hanging up, I toss the phone on my bed before crashing down next to her and pulling her against my sweaty body.

"Ew, you're wet." She presses against my chest, laughing breathlessly.

I rub my hair against her, making her laugh and screech. "I prefer you wet," I murmur.

She rolls her eyes when I look back up at her, face splotchy and eyes red rimmed. "That was lame."

"But true." I palm her jaw, pulling her in for a quick kiss. "They're going to believe you." Her bottom lip starts to tremble, and I nip it quickly before pulling back. "He's said shit before that bullshit interview, and he's made other people uncomfortable. Poppy mentioned it at the beginning of the year. If you need me to testify or whatever, I will and I'm sure she would too."

She swallows, nodding, but still worrying her lip. Her hair is messily piled on top of her head, my tee shirt adorning her chest, and she doesn't have a speck of makeup on. And she's so fucking beautiful I can't breathe.

"You should eat something, sweetness."

She shakes her head. "I'm too nervous to eat."

I sigh, rubbing my thumb over her cheek. "Fine. A compromise?"

She eyes me skeptically. "What is it?"

"I make you come three times, and then you eat something." I lick the side of her neck, and she squirms beneath me.

"Ramsey!" She laughs and the solid thing glows inside me.

"What?" I pull back, looking down at her. "We both get what we want."

"Pretty sure that's just you getting what you want twice," she grumbles.

I slide my hands to the hem of her shorts under my

duvet. "You're telling me you don't want to come before I feed you?" I slide them down slightly and she shudders.

Her eyes close and her breathing thins. "This is manipulation."

I scoff. "Hardly. This is a trade, Fall." I continue removing her loose shorts, sliding down the bed with them and peeling back the duvet once they're at her ankles. "You get something and so do I."

One of her hands tangles with my sweaty hair. "And what exactly do you get?"

I smirk up at her, pushing her legs up and out and settling down on my stomach between them. "Well, we both get a meal out this."

I lean forward, separating her lower lips with my tongue. She's already a little wet and I savor her taste, fingers digging into the flesh of her inner thighs as I hum and close my eyes.

"Fuck, Ramsey." She opens her hips further, half propped up against the headboard.

I lean in and swirl my tongue over her needy clit, watching as her chest rises and falls in deep stuttering pulls. "Clear that head of yours, Fall," I say against her skin and she shudders. The hand not currently tangled in my hair comes up and grips the edge of my headboard behind her.

I dive in, feasting on her and watching every little reaction. The way her cheeks flush and mouth opens when I run the tip of my tongue around her entrance. How her legs stiffen under my hands when I press in, eating her out slow and steady. The hitch in her throat when I slide one of my hands up over her stomach and squeeze her chest under *my* shirt that she's still wearing.

She starts riding my face as I up the pace of things, switching between teasing her clit and thrusting my tongue in and out of her. I can feel her getting closer, legs trying to close around my head and eyes hazy as she tries to keep them open and watching me. Her lids droop, hooding her dark blue eyes and I smile, sucking her clit into my mouth and pushing her over the edge with a long pull. Fall gushes all over my face, crying out as her back bows and I watch, continuing to lick her through it.

When she's panting and sated, I lean up, capturing her mouth and slipping my tongue inside so that she can taste herself on me. She moans, reciprocating lazily and I rub my covered hardness over her drenched center.

"One," I say, pulling back. Autumn laughs, the sound throaty and a little languid and a part of me feels so satisfied, I just hover over her smiling for a moment, feeling the solid thing expand into every corner of my being.

Reaching down, I start to play with her clit, rolling it between my fingers and making her jerk on the bed beneath me. Both her hands stretch up and run over my shoulders, gripping the hairs at the nape of my neck as she stares at me with her mouth hanging open.

I slide my fingers through her wetness, trailing them down until they're circling her clenching hole. I can feel the muscles contracting as I skate my touch lightly over her before thrusting two fingers in at once. She moans, calling out my name and starts to ride my fingers, hips rolling against me. I use the heel of my hand to rub against her clit at the same time, and she shatters again a moment later, staring into my eyes the whole time.

I lean down, fingers still inside her as I take her mouth, stealing the breath she's trying to catch. "Two," I say against her cheek as I pepper her face in more small kisses. I pull my fingers out, popping them in my mouth and making her watch me clean them off. She smirks, pupils dilated and fingers sliding out of my hair to ghost over my skin. Goosebumps erupt in her wake, spreading down my back and making my cock twitch.

I reach down, pushing my shorts off before I reach over and grab one of the condoms I regularly stock up on. Rolling it on while she continues to stare up at me and touch my shoulder blades and neck feels damn near impossible, but I get it on and quickly line myself up. Fall's legs spread, ready for me to settle in against the cradle of her hips. I sink forward, pressing in on one go, and we both groan together, her muscles contracting around me and making the breath in my chest stutter.

I keep my weight on my hands and off her, using my hips to set us a mixed pace of slow drags and sharp thrusts. She gasps a little each time I enter, maintaining that eye contact that makes every synapse in my body tingle. She moves her hands back into my hair, pulling slightly each time I start to drag myself out of her and then letting up when I thrust forward. Our breath mixes between us, the air humid, yet somehow electric, with little sparks skating over my skin every now and then.

This one builds slowly, the wave creeping up over her, but I can see the moment before she's about to fall, her body like a coil being wound tighter and tighter before it finally pops. She throws her head back, my hand coming up to catch her at the last minute before she can bang it against the headboard, letting out one long breathy moan while her muscles contract around me and make my hips falter. I start pumping faster, chasing my own release and spurring hers on. It only takes a few more thrusts and then I'm filling the condom and burying myself deep inside her. She pulls me down, making me lose my balance and taking all my dead weight on top of her with a contented sigh. I kiss her, long and slow, taking my time to taste every inch while our hips continue to writhe against each other, riding things out.

When we both stop moving, the kiss ending and our noses touching as I fall to the side, pulling her with me, I whisper, "Three," in a satisfied tone.

"Mmmmm," she hums, eyes closing as she snuggles in against me. "Ten minutes, then you can force feed me."

I pull the duvet up around us, laying my cheek over the top of her head. "Thought you weren't into that kink, Fall."

"I just came three times in under thirty minutes. You can do whatever you want if you let me rest for a sec."

I laugh, running my hands over her back and tangling them in her disheveled hair. She can have her ten minutes. To be honest, we'll probably be here for longer since I can't seem to find it in me to disturb her right now. I'll feed her when we do eventually get up. For now, I'll let her settle in her cleared mind. Tomorrow's going to be enough to fill it back up.

44

AUTUMN

The student hearing consists of a panel of three students and three faculty. I idly wonder how they're picked as we sit in the random classroom that was available for today. The panel sit at the head of the class, two tables pushed together so that they have a makeshift imposing authority over the room. One of the school secretaries is here to record and take notes like a pseudo stenographer and there's even a gallery, aka the rest of the classroom behind the front row where I currently sit, alone, tapping my foot and trying to stop my stomach from eating itself.

Ramsey sits directly behind me with Royal next to him for some reason. A buff silent dude sits next to Royal, back ramrod straight and eyes moving around the room at regular intervals. I swear I've seen him before, but I can't really put my finger on where.

My friends sit in a group just behind them, Bentley's arms crossed and jaw locked as we wait. A couple other students are attending as well, probably either law students wanting to see how things are conducted or nosey journalism students.

I hear the back classroom door open and glance over my shoulder, double taking when my mother, Aaron, and Sage walk in. Mom looks at me with a pursed expression while Aaron doesn't even look my way and Sage waves, mouth downturned. They take seats in the absolute back row and my stomach plummets.

"Sorry," Dr. Miller says, walking at the front of the room. "Had to wait for someone to show up at the clinic and relieve me."

My stomach rolls at the sight of him. He crosses in front of me to get to his seat on my right and I stare at the panel once he's out of eyesight but feel him right there like a beeping radar blip a few feet away.

The faculty member in the middle, a brown middle-aged woman, nods. "Now that everyone is here, we can begin. This hearing is for the allegations brought up by," she checks her paper. "Miss Green against Dr. Miller. She purports that during an interview for an internship position at Dr. Miller's on-campus clinic, Dr. Miller behaved inappropriately and inferred that the position was only being offered in exchange for sexual favors."

"Objection," Dr. Miller interjects.

The faculty member looks up at him with a raised brow. "That's not really how this works."

He chuckles. "Sorry, I've never had to attend one of these before."

I can hear Ramsey shift in his seat behind me and I tighten my grip on the arm of my chair.

"As I was saying, Dr. Miller is refuting these claims outright and claims to have evidence to the contrary, hence the assembly of an impartial panel to determine claim legitimacy and whether disciplinary action is required." The other members of the panel nod their heads, and I hear Royal scoff behind me.

"We will be interviewing each of you and allowing you time to present any evidence today as well as any witnesses who might be able to corroborate your stories."

I glance back and Poppy gives me a tight-lipped smile. Ramsey convinced her to come and when he introduced us, I realized she was the TA who saw me run out of Dr. Miller's office the day of the interview.

When I look forward again, Dr. Miller has his hand raised.

The woman sighs. "Yes, Dr. Miller."

"Will I be able to play a video as part of my evidence?"

The woman looks over at a student on her left and he nods. "Yes, if you can email me whatever it is, I can play it on the projector."

My stomach knots for the quadrillionth time, sweaty palms slipping on the edge of the desk. *What the fuck does he have on video?* If he taped the interview, that would only be in my favor, so it has to be something else.

Ramsey sits forward behind me.

"I'd rather not send it over email to a student. I brought it on a flashdrive."

My confusion grows. *What the fuck is this?*

The student nods again, looking bored. "Yeah, that's fine I can plug it in."

Dr. Miller nods and the faculty member seems to hold in a sigh.

"Very well," she says before turning toward me. "We will start with you, however, since you are the accuser."

I take a deep breath, drawing on the feeling of Ramsey right behind me and trying to ignore the fact that my family is sitting in the back of the classroom. I start with the beginning of the semester, explaining that Dr. Miller encouraged me to apply for the internship and at first, I thought it was because of my academic performance, but then when he invited me for the interview, I started to feel something was off, mentioning how he squeezed my shoulder.

"Did anyone witness this?" one of the female students asks.

My stomach swoops as I answer. "No, we were alone after class. His TA Ramsey Adams had just left, on Dr. Miller's request."

"So, no one can corroborate this?"

I swallow, forcing myself not to sink lower in my seat. "No."

The girl nods, writing something down on a notepad in front of her.

"Please continue, Miss Green," the faculty member in the center says with a small smile.

I start explaining what happened when I came for the interview, voice shaking a little no matter how much I dig my nails into the arm of the chair. When I finish, it feels like my throat is raw and the backs of my eyes sting, but I hold everything back, looking each of the panel members in the eye.

"You said you ran out, and someone saw you. Are they here today?"

"Yes." I turn and Poppy stands up, holding her hand up a little awkwardly.

"Please state your name."

"Poppy Wilson. I'm a junior and one of the biology department TA's for Dr. Mackenzie."

"And you saw Miss Green flee Dr. Miller's office on April eleventh?"

"Yes," Poppy says, nodding. "She seemed distressed and ran out of the building immediately. I stood up in my cube and watched her, then looked over at Dr. Miller's office."

"And what did he do?"

"He came to the door and seemed to look around, but then just went back to his desk without much issue. It was really weird."

"Right," the faculty member nods. "Did you hear anything while Miss Green was in his office?"

"No, but I will say, they closed the door completely which is one of the floor rules. Professors are only allowed to close the doors fully if they are conducting an adverse advisory meeting, otherwise they have to remain partially open."

"We are aware of the rule, thank you Miss Wilson. Anything else of note you would like to add?"

"Um, the TA's talk." Poppy slouches a little, avoiding Dr. Miller's eyes as he stares back at her. "Some of Dr. Miller's previous TA's have mentioned getting weird vibes from him. And his last TA quit before the end of the year, which is why Ramsey joined him halfway through. Just something to note."

"Thank you, Miss Wilson. Are any of his previous TA's here today?"

Poppy bites her lip and shakes her head.

"Okay, well we will take that under verbal advisement then. Thank you for coming today."

Poppy nods, looking over at me as she sits down. I smile, mouthing *thank you* and then facing forward again.

"Miss Green, is there anymore evidence or any other witnesses you would like us to question?"

"Yes, Dr. Miller's current TA Ramsey Adams would like to testify on my behalf."

"Very well, Mr. Adams can you stand."

I feel Ramsey stand up behind me, leaning forward and placing a hand on my shoulder and squeezing. He lets go a moment later and I can feel Dr. Miller's eyes on me, the feeling cold and unpleasant.

"What evidence do you have to help Miss Green's case, Mr. Adams?"

"As Dr. Miller's TA, I have spent a lot of this semester with him, in class and in private meetings working together on grading and my notes on his class time. On more than one occasion in these one-on-one settings, Dr. Miller has made inappropriate comments about Miss Green specifically, things like 'if I were twenty years younger' and telling me I was lucky to have a personal relationship with her as the brother of her best friend." Ramsey's voice takes on a darker tone. "Both times, I reminded Dr. Miller of his wife and child, feeling it was inappropriate for him to make those comments, as benign as he might make them seem."

The girl who questioned me earlier nods, writing something down on her notepad again. The main faculty woman nods her head. "Thank you, Mr. Adams. Is that all?"

I close my eyes for a second, willing Ramsey not to go on a tirade about that being enough, but he merely replies with a curt yes and they thank him for participating. He sits back down, and I can feel the waves of anger rolling off him pressing into me.

"Alright, Dr. Miller, you now have the floor."

Miller nods. "With pleasure, Maisie." The woman narrows her eyes, but Miller just continues on. "While I agree that Miss Green did come to my office on April eleventh for an interview for my clinic internship, I was not the one making inappropriate comments of the two of us."

My jaw immediately drops and stays there as he continues.

"Miss Green started the interview off by closing my door completely which I didn't see anything wrong with at the time since this was going to be an interview for a job and salaries and past experiences were going to be discussed, but almost immediately the tone took on a completely different nature. Miss Green attempted to solicit *me* for sexual favors, offering as well as coming around to my side of the desk saying she could 'scratch my back if I scratched hers.' I assumed she was referring to giving her the clinic position and when I rebuked her, she immediately got upset and ended up storming out."

"Bullshit," Ramsey seethes behind me.

Continuing and ignoring his outburst, Miller adds, "Like Miss Wilson stated, I came to the door, not sure if I should go and comfort her, but deciding to just let her cool off and reach out again about the inappropriate nature of the interview at a later date."

The main faculty member narrows her eyes. "Why didn't you immediately report this to a colleague?"

"Maisie," he says with a head tilt. "I didn't want to embarrass Miss Green. She's an above average student and I was giving her a fair shot at the clinic position. I don't know why she chose to resort to these methods to get there, but after doing some digging around, I think I have some evidence that this is not the first time she has gone down this route to get ahead academically."

My forehead crinkles in confusion.

Miller stands up, pulling a thumb drive out of his pocket and passing it over to the student who said he could plug it in. Miller sits back down, shuffling his hands in his lap and waiting as the student starts up the projector and plugs in the flash drive.

I stare over at Miller utterly confused how he can so blatantly lie. Is this how he's gotten away with things in the past? Poppy said I wasn't the first girl he made uncomfortable. Does he really think he's that charismatic that he can just spin whatever tale he wants, and anyone will believe it?

You believed it last semester.

My stomach drops and I face forward.

The student turns around, nodding to Miller and he continues. "I believe Miss Green has been sleeping with my TA for good marks throughout the majority of this semester."

My eyes bug out of my head. *What the fuck?* I look back at Ramsey, but he's glaring so hard at Miller that Royal has to put a hand on his arm to help hold him back.

"When Miss Green's false accusations came to my attention, I realized there would be a simple way to prove my innocence. I have a camera installed in my office, for this exact purpose to be honest."

I look at the panel, all their attention completely on Miller right now. The main faculty member seems to be the only one who picked up on what he just admitted, eyes narrowing further as she stares at him.

"When I went to pull up the footage from April eleventh, though, I found that my cameras had been tampered with. Unfortunately, I do not have any footage from the date of the interview."

"Real convenient," Ramsey growls.

"I thought so too, Mr. Adams," Miller says, turning to look at Ramsey. "Since I suspect you are the one who tampered with them." He faces forward again. "When I looked through the archived footage, I found that it was only a couple days after the incident I have brought in for you to review that they were mysteriously disconnected and no longer actively recording." He nods to the student who brings up the only video on the thumb drive and presses play.

I'm surprised my stomach can drop any further, not having just spilled out my ass at this point.

There on the projector screen in fast forwarded grainy black and white is me showing up to Ramsey's office hours and the two of us against Miller's door before I open my coat and Ramsey picks me up and fucks me against Miller's desk.

A collective gasp goes through the room and this time I do sink down in my seat. I can only imagine who is holding Ramsey back this time.

"You motherfucker!" he yells, chair scraping back.

"Stop the video!" the main faculty member yells, the male student somewhat stupefied before jolting at her words and turning to press pause. The shot gets frozen on a clear shot of me, completely naked and writhing underneath a fully clothed Ramsey. The boy scrambles to close out of the media player window before just unplugging the flash drive altogether.

I can tell that I'm shaking but everything just feels cold and far away. A sex tape of me completely naked was just played in front of all my friends and family as well as at least a dozen random strangers. I feel bile rise in the back of my throat as my vision seems to tunnel in on one spot on the floor.

"As you can see, I have reason to believe that Miss Green has been soliciting my TA for grades and decided to use the same tactic on me for a position at my clinic. However," he says and takes a second to frown as if he's sorry for me or sorry for this outcome.

I suddenly want to let Ramsey kill him.

"When it didn't work with me, unfortunately I believe she decided to spin things around and placed a false report with the school, hoping to utilize her connection with Mr. Adams in her favor."

The panel murmurs amongst each other, some a little more adamant than others.

"Dr. Miller, with your awareness of what was on that drive, we feel that it was extremely inappropriate for you to allow that to be shown in the manner that it was and there will be consequences." The main faculty member says, knuckles white where she grips her pen. She shuffles her shoulders before continuing. "That being said, we will take this new evidence into consideration. Is there anything else you would like to add?"

"Not at this time, Maisie."

The main faculty member openly glares at him. The group murmurs again before turning toward me.

"Mr. Adams, would you please stand again?"

I feel Ramsey get to his feet, his anger practically vibrating the air around me. My vision continues to pulse in and out of focus as I hear her address him.

"Would you care to elaborate on your involvement with Miss Green?"

Ramsey takes a second to collect himself before answering. "Yes," he says through his teeth. "Miss Green and I *are* involved, but it developed organically over the semester and was never utilized for anything Dr. Miller is suggesting. In fact, I brought the personal nature of my relationship with Autumn up to Dr. Miller on the first day of classes when I realized it could potentially be a grading issue. I offered to switch TA positions or simply not grade for that one, but Dr. Miller was the one who insisted it would be fine. We agreed to split the class alphabetically for grading, with him taking the half that Autumn was in so that I never had the ability to grade *anything* she turned in. While the location may have been inappropriate, Autumn had nothing to gain from our relationship, and we merely fell into it due to proximity and feelings we had for each other beforehand."

Something cold runs through me, somehow icier than my current numb state.

"Was anyone else aware of this grading arrangement?"

Ramsey breathes out through his nose. "Just me, Dr. Miller, and Miss Green."

The girl is writing on her notepad again and I feel the need to scream build up in me. Tamping it down, I continue to stare ahead, feeling everything continue to crash around me.

"Dr. Miller, what do you have to say about this arrangement?"

"Unfortunately, no conversation ever took place. Mr. Adams and I graded whatever we each had time to, and he often took Miss Green's work to grade for himself. I believe that's why she was doing so well in my course."

"You fucking li—

Royal must pull Ramsey down because he slams back into his chair with a grunt.

I feel a couple tears silently leak out and pinch my thigh to stop myself from letting anymore get through.

The panel discusses things more before turning back to face the room.

"Thank you to everyone who participated in today's hearing. Given the amount of evidence and level of severity of the situation, we will be taking some time to discuss and deliberate on what actions should be taken and if this matter should be escalated or not. Dr. Miller, you will continue to be suspended from teaching until a decision is made and Miss Green, we advise that you do not speak about this with anyone else while you continue to attend your classes. We will send each of you an email with a follow up date when a decision is made."

"Can I just add?" Miller says, and the main faculty member sighs before nodding to him. "Please be lenient on Miss Green. I believe she is a troubled girl, and I don't think disciplinary action alone would be the right course of action. I'm sure there's something the school can do to help her rather than simply punishing her."

"Fucking bastard." This time the words are uttered with a cruel finality from Royal himself.

The main faculty woman nods. "We will take that into consideration. You're free to go."

And with that, Miller stands up and leaves the room.

45

AUTUMN

The panel each pick up their materials, huddled together and already discussing things as they head out of the room. I sit there for another minute waiting for my limbs to feel like they're actually attached so that I can simply crawl out of this room and into the ditch I currently feel like curling up in.

That went so much fucking worse than I expected.

"Fall?" Ramsey whispers, hand touching the back of my neck.

"Get away from her," Mom's voice breaks me out of my frozen stupor. I look up, finding her, Sage, and Aaron standing in front of me.

Ramsey scoffs. "That's rich coming from you."

Mom reels back like he's slapped her. "What exactly is that supposed to mean?"

I swiftly stand, not caring if I collapse, just needing to stop this catastrophe before it adds to the previous one. "Ramsey, can you give me a minute with my family?"

I can feel him hesitate behind me, before he takes a deep

breath. "Okay. I'll be with Mira and Marshall when you're done."

I hear him walk away, the rest of my friends still in the room and quietly talking a few rows back.

"What are you guys doing here?" I say once it's just the four of us in earshot.

Mom glares. "The school informed us that you had a disciplinary hearing. Sexual misconduct, really Autumn?" she hisses. "Can you imagine how bad this is going to be when it gets out? I'll be surprised if your grandmother doesn't write you out of the will for this one."

I jolt back. "I didn't do anything. I was the one who was sexually harassed."

Mom rolls her eyes and Aaron glances around, seeming more concerned with who might be listening in than the actual conversation. Sage is biting her lip looking between me and Mom.

"Autumn, please, the hearing is over, there's no reason to continue with these frankly *weak* lies."

"Excuse me?" I can feel an anger growing inside me, the warmth of it actually chasing away the numb coldness the last hour of humiliation set off inside me.

"We were all in the room just now, Autumn. We saw what your professor showed everyone, or did you forget you just had a sex tape entered as evidence in a disciplinary hearing?" Mom's face is turning red, and she reaches up to slide her fingers back and forth over the diamond necklace around her neck. "You came up with a good plan, I'll give you that. Accusing him before he could accuse you, but he had actual evidence against you. You had your little boyfriend and one of his little friends to simply say they agreed with you. Next time, pay someone off to lie a little better instead of spreading your legs." She narrows her eyes and shakes her head before adding, "And maybe consider who you're accusing before you start all of this. Dr. Miller is married with children. Did you really think that panel would believe he'd risk all of that to proposition *you*?"

"Mom," Sage gasps, eyes wide and fists clenched.

Mom ignores her and Aaron just puts his hands in his pockets, looking behind them.

I know I'm standing still, but the anger washing through me makes me feel like I'm vibrating. It chases all remnants of numbness from my limbs. I look at the floor, shaking my head and then hear myself laughing.

"Autumn, get yourself together!"

I laugh some more, looking up at my mother. "I don't understand why you even came here, Mom. Why you dragged Aaron and Sage with you. Clearly you think so little of me that I cannot fathom what modicum of interest got you to drive hours here just to sit through this ridiculous hearing." I shake my head again. "I get that you had to raise me, that I'm the giant disappointment of the Green Dynasty, which technically I'm not even a fucking part of."

"Watch your mouth," Aaron says, speaking to me for maybe the third time in my life and glancing around to see who might be listening.

He only spurs me on. "But I genuinely don't understand how you two can consider *me* the perpetrator of everything evil in your world. *You*," I say, turning toward my mother, "had an affair and schemed your way into the Green fortune." Mom opens her mouth, but I continue without stopping. "And *you*," I say, turning to Aaron, "decided to stay with her for whatever fucking reason."

Aaron narrows his eyes at me.

"I honestly wish you had just put me up for adoption or thrown me into a fucking river at this point because either of those fates would have been better than this miserable fucking family full of secrets and judgement and bullshit!" I'm panting when I finish my tirade, Sage smiling a little as she stares at me.

Aaron and Tina are both glaring at me, faces red and completely still. "You do not speak to us like this, you ungrateful bastard," Aaron says, eyes on me for the first time ever.

I laugh. "Go fuck yourself, Aaron."

He reels back, nostrils flaring.

"Don't contact me, don't speak about me. From now on, you have one perfect daughter, just like you always wanted." Sage's smile falls and I feel a slight pang roll through me.

Tina takes a step toward me, rage vibrating her slim frame. "You are the worst thing that ever happened to me," she hisses before turning and taking Aaron's hand as they start to walk out together.

"And you were the worst thing to happen to me!" I scream after her, tears blurring their departure. Hysteria bubbles through my blood as her words crack through my chest and rip open the parts of me I thought were finally closed.

I feel a hand on my arm, but it disappears when Tina yells, "Sage, let's go," from the hallway.

"I'm sorry," Sage whispers before scurrying out of the room after her parents.

I stand there, feeling the silence of the not empty room press in on me.

My knees buckle and I almost collapse. My chest gapes open, everything I've ever tried to hold inside seeping out and rushing away from me. I'm going to be expelled. I have nowhere to go. I'm alone.

The weight of everything hovers over me and just as I'm

about to let it drop, to let it crush me entirely, a voice behind me snaps my body to attention.

"I'm proud of you, Fall," Ramsey says.

I turn around, finding him in the row behind me again. He's looking down at me and the look in his eyes twists something inside me and sharpens every blade I carry buried beneath my skin. The anger we share flares through me, filling all the open parts and burning white hot at all my ragged edges. And like I always do with him, I lean into the fire.

When he reaches out for me and I step back, out of range.

"We're done, Ramsey."

His face morphs, disbelief taking over. "What? What the fuck are you talking about?"

"This." I gesture between us. "It's over. Go take pity on someone else." I spit the words out, swallowing the rising tide of lava threatening to erupt inside of me.

"Pity? Fall, you just—

"I just lost everything, Ramsey!" I fold my arms over my chest, holding myself together more than anything. "A video of us having sex was just shown to everyone I know and more than a handful that I didn't." I shake my head once, withering under my own words. "I'm about to be kicked out of school, and even if by some miracle I am allowed to stay, I can't afford another week let alone three more years now that I'm done with the Greens." My breath hitches, knees shaking so bad I'm sure I look like I'm vibrating in front of him. "My academic career is toast. I have no money, nowhere to go, and no real last name." I look up at him, slicing my nails into my skin as our gazes meet. "You want me to believe that changes nothing for you?"

Ramsey tries to take a step forward, the first row of

chairs stopping him. "None of that changes a fucking thing!" he hisses, anger slamming into me.

Good. He should be angry with me. I'm not the only one who's life was just imploded with that fucking hearing.

I shove my shoulders back, a pit of resolve forming inside me. "It changes things for me." I swallow fire. "We're done, Ramsey."

Ramsey steps back, eyes roving over every inch of my face as I set my jaw, refusing to look away. He clenches his fists, stepping back up and leaning even further toward me. "You're lying."

"No, Ramsey. For once, I am making a decision about the two of us with complete clarity."

"Bullshit! Everything you just mentioned is happening and you want me to believe you currently have complete clarity?" When I don't say anything, he looks to the side. Shaking his head once, he lets out a mirthless chuckle. "You know what?" He kicks the chair in front of him a little to the side, shoving his way closer to me. I stand my ground, refusing to back down. His hand comes up, and he grabs my jaw, making me gasp. My resolve wavers.

His face lowers as his manic eyes bore into mine. "I'm not letting you blow this up right now. We can be over in your mind if you need some time to figure things out. But when the dust settles, you fucking call me, Autumn. Because I'm in love with you and I'm going to be there to help you figure things out on the other side."

My eyes widen as his words hit me, burrowing into the part of my heart that is decidedly dedicated to him. Pain cracks through my bones, almost making me bow, but I hold it all in.

"You're not in love with me, Ramsey. You hate me," I whisper.

His jaw ticks. "Tell yourself whatever the fuck you need to, Fall." He leans even closer, lips brushing mine as he whispers, "But you know I'm not very patient."

And with that, he releases me, leaning back and letting cool air fill the space between us. The burn of where his fingers held my face lingers.

He stares down at me for a beat before turning and heading out, following the same route the Greens just took. Royal nods to me before following Ramsey out, the silent guy following them both.

All that remains are my friends, the group of them all looking at me with varying expressions of sympathy.

"Oh, Autumn," Mira says, tears in her eyes.

I take a step back, shaking my head and feeling my usual flight response creeping up.

"Blossom," Aria calls, but I've already turned and bolted from the room, needing to find someplace where I can finally break down in complete darkness.

46

RAMSEY

"I need you to intervene for her," I say once Royal, Lev, and I make it out of the building.

"I was going to anyways," Royal responds, walking beside me to the car. His long dark peacoat has a tall collar which he flips up against the wind. "That hearing was bullshit. This type of thing shouldn't be handled by a *panel* of faculty and students. And he shouldn't be allowed to just openly fucking lie like that." He shakes his head. "I'm already planning to call my dad."

Lev opens the back door to Royal's car, and we both slide in.

"No, let's say calling him is plan B. I have an idea for how she can win this thing."

Royal glances over at me. "Let's hear it."

"Well, I know I didn't tamper with any cameras considering I had no idea they were even in there or I never would have fucked Fall in there or let the video evidence of it exist once I found out."

"Naturally." Royal nods.

"So, how much you want to bet the footage from the interview isn't lost at all?"

Royal's creepy cut up smile slowly slides into place. "You want Lev to hack in and see if he has them? It's possible he tried to delete the footage." He turns toward Lev who is currently driving us back to the house. "Think you could still retrieve it if he did?"

"Is probably sitting in his trash folder, waiting to get routinely wiped after sixty or ninety days," Lev says in his heavily accented voice. He nods once, keeping his eyes on the road the whole time. "I can find it."

"Thanks, Lev," I say toward the front.

"Miss Autumn doesn't deserve this," Lev adds with another nod.

I clench my fist, remembering her little speech to me about us being over. The solid thing ripped in fucking two hearing her take out her frustration on us. But I knew she would. She works in patterns, having set routines, even if no one else sees them.

I'll give her space this time. As much as I want to go hunt her down, throw her in my Jeep and drive us out to the middle of nowhere until she loses this notion that we don't belong together, I know that won't work with her. She'll just fight me tooth and nail and end up hurting herself more when she tries to hurt me.

I saw the devastation in her eyes. She thinks she just lost her academic career, the shitty fucking excuse for a family that she unfortunately had, and therefore all financial protections she had in place, even if she didn't think she was using much of them. Everything crumbled out of her control, so she tried to tear down the only other thing she saw standing.

If she needs to tear me down to feel in control, I'll let her do it for now. I completely understand going to crazy lengths to try to stay in control of literally anything. But I wasn't lying when I said she only got so much time. And then I'm coming for her.

"She'll calm down and realize," Royal says, as Lev pulls into the driveway.

"Let's just deal with getting the footage right now." I push open the door, not even waiting for the car to completely stop let alone Lev to come around and open it for me.

Storming into the house, Harley looks up from his spot at the kitchen island. "Take it, things did not go well?"

"Understatement," I murmur. I shed my jacket and shoes, Royal and Lev catching up as I stand there and seethe.

"Follow me," Lev says, taking us past the kitchen and into the hallway where he and the other guards stay on the left side of the house. We head into the first room on the right, and he sits down at a desk equipped with three connected monitors. Several more are mounted to the wall, showing rotating security footage of different angles around and inside the house interspersed with footage from different spots on campus that Royal tends to frequent. Dimitri sits in another chair at another desk, monitoring things while tossing a ball into the air and catching it.

Lev wakes up the sleeping triple monitors, logging in quickly and pulling up some program that looks completely foreign to me. Give me a cadaver and ask me to dissect and label each organ and I could probably do it at this point, but computers are merely vessels for virtual therapy, submitting essays, and watching porn in my opinion.

I grab a vacant wheely chair and sit down in it backwards, folding my arms along the back and placing my chin on them. Royal leans against the door frame, coat still in place and hands in his pocket. We all stare at the monitors for another two hours while Lev works.

"Okay, I'm into his work computer. I don't think he is on it." He clicks around, typing something quickly. "I'll start looking around." Lev drags a window over onto another monitor and it looks like a mirror image of another computer home screen. "If it's not here, footage probably uploads directly to a personal computer, in which case, I'll need to figure out where he lives. Wait for him to get on it so that I can access remotely. Might take some time, but most people use their computers at least once a day. Most likely, I can get on it before panel makes decision."

I nod, continuing to watch him search around on Miller's pseudo computer screen. I feel like I need to be here, like if I let myself leave this up to Lev or Royal on their own, all I'll have to do is sit around and think about how I just want to go find Fall and throttle her for ending things. Then hold her while she deals with the aftermath of everything else.

"It's not here," Lev announces after some time. "He must have the footage sent to his personal laptop." He sits back. "His address should be on file at Imperium Coast. I can hack around and figure out what network he has for Wi-Fi." He starts typing again, eyes flying around the screens. "If we get lucky, he will be online, and I can try to access remotely and wait until he leaves." Lev starts typing again, not waiting for anyone to answer him. "If not, waiting game begins."

We are not lucky. Lev sets something up that will ping when Miller accesses his laptop on his network and then sits back, checking in with the other guards on his phone.

My phone buzzes in my pocket another hour later and I pull it out.

TANNER

your girl is here.

I click his name and instantly call him, getting up and walking out of the room.

"Hey," he says when he picks up. The noise behind him is boisterous and dread flies through me.

"Where are you? Autumn's there?" I ask, heading for the front door.

"Yeah," Tanner says. "I'm at Sullivan's. She was here when I arrived with the team. Seems to be pretty deep at this point."

I exhale sharply, remembering the last time I was at Sullivan's bar last semester when Harley told me my underage sister was there drinking with all her friends. Those friends including Autumn.

I grab my coat, already slipping into my shoes again. "I'm on my way. Watch her while I drive, Tan?"

"Will do," he says before hanging up. I grab my keys and head out to the Jeep. Climbing in and starting the car, I pause, taking a second to slam my hands against the steering wheel several times. If she would have just let me help her, she wouldn't be wasted at a bar downtown drowning her sorrows. God fucking damn it, I shouldn't have left her alone.

I pull out of the driveway, pushing the speed limit as I race toward Sullivan's. The streets are packed, and I realize it's a Friday night, the day having not even registered when I got in the car to come down here. I finally find a place to park, having to walk a couple blocks over to get back to the light of the main strip of downtown. I head straight for Sullivan's, the bell over the door barely announcing my entrance over the rambunctious din of the Friday night crowd.

I spot Fall immediately, her red hair a dead giveaway in a slightly sagging high ponytail, swishing back and forth as she sways on one of the bar stools and waves her glass toward the overworked bartender currently trying to keep up with the college kids shouting orders at him.

I sigh, walking up behind her and nodding to Tanner from where he sits a few tables over, eyes glued to her. "What are you doing here, Autumn?"

Her glassy eyes meet mine as her head whips around, hand holding the glass out slamming against the bar top when she forgets to keep it up. "R-r-ramsey? What are yoooooouuuuu doing here?" She tries to furrow her brows but just ends up crossing her eyes at me.

"Heard you were drunk at a bar." I reach forward and take the empty glass out of her hand, sliding it down the bar a little ways away from her. "Figured you hadn't planned a ride home."

She huffs, pouting and turning back around to face away from me. "Go away. We're nothing anymore remember."

I clench my fist to stop myself from grabbing her. She's drunk and upset. I need to stay levelheaded.

"Come on, I'm taking you home." I gently wrap my hand around her wrist, tugging slightly.

She rips her arm free, shaking her head too much. "I don't want to go back to your house."

The solid thing in me resurrects a little bit at the idea that she considers my house home. "Your dorm, Fall. I'm taking you back to your dorm."

"Don't wanna," she huffs. She's staring forward a little too intently, tucking her chin and swallowing.

"Are you going to throw up?" I ask, leaning in closer.

She nods, looking up at me and I gently pull her off the stool, placing my hands on her shoulders and walking her through the crowd toward the bathrooms. They're single stall non-gendered rooms and I jiggle the locked handle on the first one before turning her toward the second and finding it unlocked.

She rushes over to the toilet, falling to her knees and starting to throw up.

I run my hands through my hair, not sure what to do with them now. "You okay?"

Her head snaps to the side, watery eyes finding mine. "Why are you in here?"

"I came to hold back your hair."

"It's in a ponytail," she says incredulously.

Pulling my hair a bit, I huff. "Yeah, I realize that now."

She starts to say something else, but then her stomach rolls and she pitches back over the toilet, puking again. I stand against the door, not sure if she'd let me rub her back.

When she's finally done, she sits back, flushing. "I think I want to go back to West Tower now," she cries, voice hitching a bit.

My body aches at the tone of her voice. "Okay, Autumn. I'll take you."

She nods, getting up and coming over to the sink. She washes her hands twice before cupping some water and rinsing out her mouth three times. I grab some paper towels and pass them over to her when she gets caught staring at her reflection for a couple beats.

Walking out with her, I take her hand, pulling her into the alleyway behind the building so we don't have to press through the crowd again and she can sober up a bit in the cold night air.

"I'm pathetic," Autumn mumbles, leaning against the

wall of the building across the alleyway and tipping her head back to stare up at the sky.

I step up to her, placing my hands in my pockets to stop myself from touching her. "You are not pathetic."

She rolls her eyes down to look at me without tipping her head forward. "I am drunk, having dipped into the funds my not-so-stepfather was forced to provide by the biological mother who thinks I'm the worst thing that happened to her. Funds which will probably be moved tomorrow, and I will be absolutely destitute." She starts laughing. "I should have probably tried to pull as much as I could, so I'd at least have something to buy food with or get started wherever the fuck I'm going to go."

I take my hands out, no longer caring about this stupid ban she's put on our contact. I grab the sides of her face, pulling it down so she looks at me levelly and bringing my own face closer so we're sharing air. "You are not pathetic, do you hear me? Those people are a waste of fucking organ donations, and you not thinking to use their money until you are wasted and reflecting shows how much of a good fucking person you are. You're a college freshman who got drunk on a Friday night." I shrug, grinning. "That's nothing out of the norm. You are perfectly normal, if not above average in my opinion."

She laughs, sniffling at the end. "I tried to make you hate me."

"I know, Fall." I sigh, touching my forehead to hers before stepping back and letting go of her. "Let's go. You're going to get cold even if you don't feel like it."

Fall laughs, starting to turn off the wall and take a step with a mischievous grin, but I catch her around the middle, pulling her in against me. "Do not run away from me," I growl.

"Do you need help?"

We turn and there's a petite brunette cautiously stepping toward us. A man stands behind her, hand gripped in hers as he assesses the two of us.

"Noooo," Fall slurs. "He's my...um." She hesitates.

"I'm her boyfriend," I say, glaring at the couple.

The girl looks to Autumn, and her head just falls back to look up at me before she starts laughing. "I'm fine," she says, suddenly sounding a lot more lucid and looking back at the couple.

The girl looks her over before nodding. "Have a good night," she says, heading into the bar with the guy.

"Let go of me," Fall says in a low tone.

I release her but keep my hands hovering nearby in case she stumbles.

Instead, she pivots around, swaying for a second before glaring up at me. "You shouldn't say shit like that."

I step closer to her. "Like what?"

"Boyfriend." She hiccups. "You lied to them."

I shake my head. "No, I didn't, Fall."

"Yes, you did!" She laughs, the sound high pitched and off kilter. "We're not even dating, Ramsey! We're in a fucking 'arrangement.'" She tries to use finger quotes, getting a little distracted by her own fingers.

I step forward, scooping her up and making her yelp. "We've been dating since the beginning of the semester, Fall. Stop squirming."

"Put me down! I'm too heavy." She tries to launch herself out of my arms, forcing me to grip her tighter than I usually would.

"You're my daily starter rep, sweetness. This is nothing." I jostle her to prove the point, then regret it when she looks a little green.

"You bench press my weight?" she screeches.

"Bench press. Dead lift." I look down at her with a smile. "Hip thrust." I wink.

She goes still in my arms, and I walk in silence for a few beats. "Why would you do that?"

I look down, seeing tears in her eyes and wishing she could walk right now so I could clear them from her lashes. "Because I like being able to throw you around. And you like being thrown around. Why wouldn't I do that?"

"Because I'm not worth making changes to your fucking workouts, Ramsey!"

I stop, shifting her in my arms so that she's standing, but pressed against me with my arm around her waist. Grabbing her jaw, I tilt her head up to look me in the eye. "You are worth so much more than a simple change to my workouts, Autumn. Don't you dare think you are worth less than that. I would change *anything* in my life if it made yours more comfortable." My tone is deadly, and I keep her trapped facing me when she tries to pull away. "Listen to me, Autumn. You are worth everything. Do you understand me?"

"Fall," she says in a mushed tone since I'm still holding her jaw.

"What?" I release her face, letting my hand drift down to lightly circle the side of her neck.

"You call me Fall. Not Autumn. Fall."

She sways a little, knees buckling and I hunch down, picking her back up. This time she wraps her arms around my neck and rests her head on my shoulder.

"That's right, sweetness. You're my Fall," I whisper the words into her hair, kissing the top of her head and walk the rest of the way to my car.

47

AUTUMN

I wake up Monday morning to an email about the hearing. They want to reconvene.

They've reached a decision.

My nerves skyrocket, Aria having to talk me down several times as I pick out an outfit and get ready. I have to stop myself from calling Ramsey more than once, knowing he'd be here in an instant if I did. The way he was Friday night at Sullivans. The way I know he always would be if I let him take care of everything.

But I need to stop relying on him. Even if by some miracle I don't get disciplinary action, I can't afford the Coast on my own. This is my last few weeks here and then there's no way the two of us can work since I don't even know what I'm going to do next. How I'm going to live after this.

I take a deep breath, pushing the mounting panic back down. One step at a time. I'm going to figure this out. On my own. Like I always do.

That's the mantra I silently chant on my way to the same classroom from Friday.

I can do this. I have to do this.

Walking into the room, I startle to find Mira and Bentley already sat in the back of the classroom. All of them give me reassuring smiles and the panic shrinks a little as I stare at my group of friends. Aria squeezes my arm before going to join them.

I take a seat in the same spot where my life imploded when the doors open again and my grandmother walks in, cane echoing against the floor as she elegantly glides through the entrance. Sage follows behind her and for a second, I almost think Tina and Aaron are going to follow, but the doors simply close.

Melissa Green walks to the second row behind me and takes a seat on the end, both hands atop the crystal adorning her cane. My sister slides in beside her, giving me a quick smile and...a thumbs up?

Dumbfounded, I turn back around. What are *they* doing here?

Miller is already seated, legs outspread and hands comfortably resting against his stomach as we all wait for things to start. The panel is mostly here as well, minus the main faculty member whose chair is currently empty in the center.

The time ticks on, her lateness growing past ten minutes when the door finally opens again.

Ramsey walks in first, looking at me quickly and making my heart squelch.

I'm in love with you.

My eyes sting when he looks away and heads to the row behind my grandmother and Sage. Royal and the guy from Friday follow close behind him, taking their seats in the same row.

The main faculty member walks in after them, smiling

from ear to ear. She takes her seat, settling down and addressing the room.

"Thank you everyone for joining us again. The panel has discussed what was brought forth last week and we had made a decision."

Miller rubs his hands together, sitting forward.

"However, new evidence was just presented to me that I think the panel should take a look at before we deliver our decision."

My eyebrows rise and I glance back at Ramsey. He stares straight at Miller, arms crossed and a faint smirk ghosting his lips. I turn back around, eyes catching on Mimi and Sage for a beat.

"New evidence?" Miller says. "That's not how this works. We submitted everything last week."

The main faculty member sets her eyes on him and smiles sweetly. "Well, as you stated last week, you haven't had to attend one of these before. We are not a court of law, Dr. Miller. Until a decision is made *and recorded*, new evidence can be presented to the panel as it arises."

"What new evidence is there?" the female student who took a lot of notes last time asks.

The main faculty member holds up a thumb drive and my skin crawls. Please tell me there isn't *another* fucking sex tape to play.

She hands the thumb drive off to the same student who set it up last week and he hesitates, glancing over at me.

"It's okay, Roger. I've viewed this one ahead of time and it's not porn."

The student nods, getting up and plugging it into the projector again. Clicking on the first video in the file, grainy black and white footage of Ramsey and Miller sitting in his office begins to play. Their lips move but we can't hear what they're saying.

"Please turn the volume up, Roger."

Roger taps something on the projector a few times and their voices filter into the room.

"Autumn," Miller's voice says over the speakers. *"Yeah, she can be a bit disordered, but she's very driven. Seems determined to leave here with a 4.0, but she's still only in her second semester."* He pauses on screen, playing around on his laptop before adding, *"Not too bad on the eyes either. First time she came to an advising meeting."* He shakes his head, smirking. Then he looks up and winks at Ramsey. *"If I were in my twenties again, am I right?"*

Ramsey immediately responds with, *"And not married, right?"* in a cold tone.

I whip around, looking back at the actual Ramsey. He finally looks over at me, giving me a small smile and nodding at me to face forward. I do as he commands, tuning back into what's happening on screen.

"It might not be a good idea for me to TA the class she's in. We have a...personal relationship," on-screen Ramsey says.

Miller glares at him in the video.

"Not like that. She's my little sister's best friend. I probably shouldn't be involved in the class she's taking since it might be considered a conflict of interest."

My stomach falls as I watch, realizing this must have been after our first class together, after he cornered me and gave me a panic attack, threatening to ruin my GPA.

He offered to drop his TA spot that early on? For me?

Miller waves his hand on-screen. *"No big deal. We'll just make sure you don't grade anything she completes. I was going to have us split up the class for grading anyway so you can just take the second half of the list."*

The video cuts off and the main faculty woman nods to Roger. "The next one please."

Another grainy black and white video pops up. This time of Dr. Miller alone in his office. I watch as I appear on screen, coming into his office in the clothes I wore the day of the interview. My throat tightens and I stare blankly forward as the events of that day play out on the screen, my own voice echoing in the room along with Miller's.

When the video cuts off, the main faculty member levels Miller with a glare. "Seems that footage was not lost after all."

Miller's face is almost purple, his hands clenched into tight fists atop the desk in front of him. "That footage is only accessible on my personal computer. Whatever those fucking criminals just submitted, it was obtained illegally!" He points back at Ramsey and Royal without breaking eye contact with the panel. Most of them are sneering or openly looking at him with disgust.

"Mr. Reznikov has guaranteed that this footage was obtained by purely legal means."

Mr. Reznikov fucking lied then. I have no doubt Royal used illegal means to obtain this footage for Ramsey.

"And once again, we are not a court of law, Dr. Miller. How evidence is obtained for submission to the panel is neither here nor there. Given the new evidence presented, please allow us to reconvene momentarily."

The panel leans back, talking amongst themselves for all of two minutes with a lot of head nods and angry glances over at Miller.

"We have come to a new decision," the speaker says once they all sit forward again. She looks over at me, another kind smile touching her eyes. "Miss Green, I apologize if playing that footage led to opening any freshly healing wounds. It was unfortunately necessary in order for us to reach our decision. You are completely absolved of any accusation levied against you last week and no negative marks will be placed on your academic transcript." She looks back over at Miller. "Dr. Miller, the most *we* can do is continue your current suspension, tacking on a 'without pay' to the end of it. We will also be recommending termination in our write up to the Dean and she will be the one to give you your ultimate disciplinary action." Looking out at the room, she adds, "Thank you everyone for attending. This hearing is adjourned."

I feel like there should be a gavel bang or something marking the end of all of this, but everyone on the panel just gets up and starts heading out.

"Fucking outrageous," Miller says, standing up and letting his chair fall to the ground in his wake. He turns around and faces the guys three rows back. "You stole that footage off my computer somehow and I'm going to prove it and take you lot to a *real* fucking court."

"Good luck with that, *Mr.* Miller," Royal says, blinking calmly. The guy next to him glares with a single dark expression, feeling like a very potent threat as he stares at Miller who walks out of the room without even looking at me.

I sit back, letting myself take a breath of relief. I'm not expelled. I'm not academically shamed.

I'm just too poor to keep attending college or house myself.

I knit my fingers together, trying to focus on the win as tears come to my eyes, this time somewhat happy ones mixed in for the first time in days.

Ramsey did this, a voice in the back of my brain softly reminds me.

I startle, turning around to look back at him, but he's already gone, the entire row he was sitting in unoccupied. I glance around, but the only people left are my group of friends, all smiling and holding thumbs up at me, and the two family members who randomly decided to come today.

I glance over and realize they've gotten up and are heading toward me. Standing, I squeeze my fingers, bowing my head a bit as Mimi stops in front of me.

"I need to make some calls. Stay with your sister until I return." Without another look back, she walks out of the room, long skirt trailing on the ground behind her.

I furrow my brow, glancing over at Sage before sitting back down. Sage takes the seat next to me, sitting with her hands underneath her thighs.

"I'm really happy things turned out this way," Sage says, swinging her legs underneath her and smiling over at me.

I nod. "How'd you guys know to come today?"

She sighs, laughing a little as she exhales deeply. "Well after the shitshow on Friday, I called Mimi."

I tilt my head, wondering why my sister thought to reach out to our grandmother after everything I said last week.

"I told her everything, how Mom keeps us apart, treats you like you're not part of the family, talks down to you at every turn. And I told her I hate ballet."

"What? You do?" My shock must look funny because Sage starts to laugh.

"Oh yeah. That shit is Mom's dream, and she's made me parrot her ever since she could lace a pair of pointe shoes onto my feet." She laughs again and I study her, realizing I don't think I've ever seen Sage so carefree. She always seemed small and meek in my memories, hiding behind Mom, or following her barked orders.

Guilt gnaws at my insides. "I should have paid attention more."

Sage snorts. "I don't blame *you*, Autumn. I know you were suffering just as much at home, trust me." She rolls her eyes. "Anyways, I told Mimi about your hearing and everything that happened after, how Mom and Dad didn't believe you, but I did."

My heart soars at that.

"And I told her about what you said, about Mom's affair and wanting to be put up for adoption." Her shoulders fall a little as she whispers that last bit.

And just as my heart hits its peak, it nose dives.

"You told Mimi about that?"

She looks over at me, nodding. "Yeah. Turns out she already knew about the whole affair thing."

Holy shit.

Sage shrugs. "She came over this weekend and absolutely reamed Mom and Dad out. Well, in Mimi style." Which means she sat on a chair and chastised them with a very austere tone that felt like being sliced through with razors. If our mother can be trusted to recount it that is. Mimi has never turned her ire on me, so I don't actually know what it's like firsthand. "She had them transfer your guardianship over to her. The paperwork was just filled out, I don't know if it's been submitted or what all goes into that since you're not a minor anymore, but Mom had all the emails from the school forwarded to Mimi's personal assistant."

Holy shit. My head spins with this onslaught of information. Apparently while I was wallowing and agonizing over what to do next, my family was reshaping itself.

"She asked me if I wanted to come stay with her and

Mom tried to object, but Dad..." Sage looks a little forlorn as she stares into space a bit. "Dad said it would probably be better if I went with her."

"Oh Sage, I'm so sorry." I reach out, placing my hand on her shoulder. "I know what it's like to be rejected by them and I never wanted that for you. Ever."

Sage looks over at me, eyes coming back into focus. "I know. I know they seemed to dote on me compared to you, but they never really talked to me, just about me or at me. I don't think either of them know how to actually be a parent and although it hurt, I think Dad letting me go with Mimi was the best thing he's ever actually done *for* me." She smiles weakly and I squeeze her shoulder.

"So, I've been staying with her while she figures everything out. It's actually not so bad. She pretty much leaves me alone and her house is huge."

I smile remembering my idyllic summer at her house. "Oh, I know. I love Mimi's house."

"Well, that's good to hear, since you'll probably be staying there over your summers throughout medical school."

My brow furrows just as Mimi walks back in, stopping in front of the desks Sage and I sit at. We both stand, smoothing out our clothes and attempting to look presentable in front of her.

"Autumn dear, I'm sorry you had to go through something like this. You did the right thing reporting it and I am very proud of the young lady you have become. I could not ask for a better direct heir to the Green name."

"Ma'am? I'm not...well, Sage said...you know about—

"Your conception? Yes, I am aware of *Christina's* indiscretions. But I do not believe that should fall on the head of the child." She stamps her cane with her proclamation. "You have been my granddaughter since the moment I met you, despite what your parents might have told you. Your last name is Green. Is that understood?"

I nod my head, feeling a bit dizzy. "Yes, ma'am." Mimi has been the only member of my family that I actually liked being around *because* she didn't treat me as different.

Mimi nods. "And I will not hold it against you that you no longer wish to be associated with the poisoned branch of our family tree. Sage informed me on the events at the first part of this hearing, and I am taking actions to remedy the situation. You will come stay with me at the end of the semester and I will see to it you have funding for the rest of your education and anything else that you may want or need beyond that."

My eyes widen. "Oh, that's too much. I don't need..."

"Child, I will not allow you to reject the means we have to help you achieve your goals simply because my arrogant son does not wish to take on the responsibility. I know you do not have another option. As the matriarch of this family, I should have stepped in sooner, but I cannot remedy the past." She shuffles her shoulders and stands a little taller. "Going forward you will be treated as a member of this family. I am already in the works of having the trusts I set up for you and your sister modified so that you can access them prior to your twenty-fifth birthdays. I will also provide a place for you to come to when you cannot stay at school. A home, if you would like to think of it as such. And I will rewrite my will as soon as we return to ensure that you both are taken care of when I am no longer around to do so. Is that understood?"

I stare at her for a moment, gaping. The uncertain future I pictured just an hour ago suddenly clears as everything slowly stitches itself back together around me. I nod when she clears her throat, feeling so overwhelmed and grateful. "Thank you, Mimi. Thank you so much." Tears start leaking out of my eyes again, fully one hundred percent happy this time.

Mimi nods once. "Your sister will also be staying with me," she says as she nods over at Sage who smiles and nods to me. "So, you may see her on your breaks and of course stay in contact by whatever means necessary."

"I think she means texting," Sage whispers behind her hand, giggling. "Mom never let me text you, monitoring my phone time at home and barely letting me communicate with the girls I actually liked at ballet." She rolls her eyes and again I start to see the gilded cage my sister was actually existing in while I was left outside.

"Now, we must return home so that I can get all the paperwork settled. I called my bank and had an account created in your name with a small amount of provisionary funds added. The card should be in the mail in the next week or so, but if you need to use it beforehand, you should be getting an email about setting up some sort of mobile option or how to call them and set it all up or something." Mimi waves her hand. "Lisa, my assistant, usually handles all my online stuff, so if you need any help, feel free to call her at any time. When you come home for the summer we will sit down and flesh out how much you think you'll need for spending money each semester and work out how to get that transferred regularly from your trust so that you can start funding your own expenditures."

I nod, ears ringing from how much overwhelming information I'm getting in this room yet again. "Um, I would like to work too, if that's okay? I've never had a job and if I can't get one that will look good on my medical school apps,

I still want to get something where I am earning my own money too."

Mimi smiles, eyes crinkling at the corners. "I don't see why not." She nods her head once more.

Sage bounces on the balls of her feet, clapping. "This is the best fucking day."

"Language, Sage," Mimi admonishes, smile only dimming a little. "Good luck with the rest of your semester, Autumn. I will see you in a few weeks." With that she heads out, not even looking back to see if Sage is following her.

Sage looks between her retreating form and me, pouting a little.

I reach forward, wrapping her up in our first ever hug. "If she gives you a new phone, get my number from her and text me. I think we're going to have a lot to talk about."

Sage nods against my shoulder, wiping a tear from her eye when we pull apart. "I will. Plus," she laughs wetly, "we'll have all summer!" She leans in and hugs me again, squeezing harder than I expect.

She flits off after Mimi, waving at the doorway with a big smile. I wave back, watching her leave and taking a second to breathe once they're gone.

"Holy shit, Autumn, you're fucking rich," Aria laughs, coming over with Mira and Bentley.

I laugh wetly and Mira wraps an arm around my waist. "I guess I can tell my mom to stop setting up the guest room for you. She was ready to move you in the second I told her what happened last week."

"Wait, what?" I startle, but her arm stays wrapped around me.

"Yeah, if things didn't go well today, I also called my grandfather to pull some strings if needed. I already texted to call him off, but we weren't going to let you get expelled."

Bentley rubs the back of his neck sheepishly. His grandfather, Judge Tyson Marshall, is a Coast legacy and the reason Bentley basically had guaranteed admission here.

Aria shrugs. "I was going to offer up our lumpy couch for the summer, but figured you'd have better offers. It's always available though, Blossom." She reaches out and squeezes my forearm.

Tears continue to pour out of me as I look around at my best friends and realize I was never actually alone in this. None of them would have abandoned me or let me sink. Warmth envelops me as they all smile back.

"Everything's all worked out now though, isn't it?" Bentley says, leaning down to hug me.

I nod against his shoulder, but my eyes stray over to the empty third row, heart aching to see the man who occupies the entirety of it still sitting there.

48

AUTUMN

I don't hear anything more from the student hearing, but a permanent substitute is made for Miller's position, and we only miss one class. Still Ramsey doesn't show up and the rumors of what happened start flying.

"I heard he got a student pregnant then tried to blame it on the TA."

"No way, he was dealing drugs. Molly Perkins said she used to buy from him all the time."

"Yeah right, he probably just got sick of working for this place. I heard the professors have to swear a blood oath to the fucking mafia to work here."

I doodle on my notebook, waiting for the last class before our final to start. The door opens and my heart leaps, instantly crashing and burning again when it's just the new prof and no one else. I haven't even seen Ramsey on campus, constantly looking out for his black Jeep whenever I hear a car drive by.

Every time I've thought to call him or send a text over

the last two weeks, I imagined how angry he must be with me and even trying to figure out how to apologize and grovel after the things I said feels impossible.

I'm a chicken shit.

I shake my head, continuing to doodle and only half paying attention to the final review questions the prof is answering.

My grandmother's magical door to financial security has made me realize that I have so many more options than I originally thought. I had a whole spiral session with Mira and Bentley about it the other day, realizing I picked pre-med because it would be financially secure in the long run and I wasn't sure if I even liked it.

But they talked me off the ledge as per usual.

"Autumn, *why* did you pick pre-med?" Mira asked, sprawled out on her couch while I pace the living room floor across from her.

"I just answered that. Because eventually I would be making good money." I ran a hand through the ends of my curls, pulling them a little and continuing to pace.

"Yeah," Mira said, sitting up. "But why *pre-med*? I mean there's law school and psychiatry and hell you could have gone toward dental school if all you wanted was a stable job that makes good money. Why did you pick pre-med?"

I stopped pacing, turning to face her and Bentley. He sat on the floor, long legs out in front of him as he ate all the popcorn we made for the currently paused movie on the TV behind me.

"Because I wanted to help people. I wanted to help make them feel better."

Mira smiled. "And now that you don't have to worry about the money aspect anymore, has that really changed?"

My eyes flicked down to Bentley, and he shook his head slightly.

"No, it hasn't," I said with determination. "I still want to help people. I want to learn about medicines and injuries and learn how to fix them." I sighed, smiling at my best friends. "I want to be a doctor."

"Hell yeah, you do," Bentley shouted, holding a hand up. Mira high fived him from behind and they both cheered for me. I took a dramatic bow, laughing as I stood up.

"Now sit back down so we can finish this god-awful movie," Bentley added, shoving another fistful of popcorn into his mouth.

We watched the movie, and I fought the urge to ask Mira how Ramsey was doing or if he'd asked about me. That wouldn't be fair to her.

Ramsey's her brother and I'm sure some part of her is mad at me for treating him how I did. Especially after everything he's done for me these last few months.

As the class continues to drone on in the background, I flip to a new page in my notebook, writing *Dear Ramsey,* at the top and pouring everything out that I'm too scared to send in a text.

After the final a week later, I climb the stairs up to the fifth-floor biology professors' department. I'm not sure if he'll have cleaned out his TA cubicle yet, but I figured if he hasn't, I can leave the letter on his desk like the coward I am. And if he has, I'll have to buck up the courage to walk over to his house and give it to him directly.

Or maybe just leave it in his mailbox.

The floor is fairly deserted, most profs no longer having office hours with the semester pretty much at a close. The cube farm is completely empty, none of the cubes you can see into at the entrance having anything in them.

I start to walk around, already figuring Ramsey's will be cleared out as well, but I pull up short when I find a mop of messy curls and silver circular glasses sitting at his cube typing away on his laptop.

Fuck.

My heart attempts to gallop out of my chest. He's here. I didn't make a contingency plan for in case he's here.

He hasn't seen me yet, so I start to back away, attempting to get away cleanly, but of course he turns and his eyes hone in on me with that same predatory look he gave me almost four years ago.

"Fall," he sighs, the word seeming to float out of him and carry all the weight he's been holding off him.

I just stare, transfixed by the magnetism that's always existed between us. Shaking myself out of this stupor, I hold out the letter dumbly. "I wanted to give you this."

He glances down at the letter, then at the six feet of space separating us before looking back up and waiting.

I sigh, closing the gap and holding the letter out to him.

"What is it?"

I shake the letter, trying to get him to take it. "It's a thank you letter."

He looks up at me. "A thank you letter? Like something our parents made us write for all our birthday presents in third grade?"

"Well maybe *your* parents," I grumble.

He smirks, reaching out and taking the letter out of my hand finally. His fingertips brush the back of my hand, and I shiver, ripping it away and shoving it into the back pocket of my jeans.

He watches me, just holding the letter as he sits here. "What does it say?"

I sigh, shoulders dropping with the motion. "It's a letter Ramsey. You're supposed to *read* it."

He stands up slowly, toes touching mine when he reaches his full height. "Humor me," he says, looking down at me. His glasses slide down the bridge of his nose, and I have the errant thought to reach up and push them back up for him.

I bite my lip, looking away and fidgeting under his stare.

"Hey," he says, calling my eyes back up to his. "Whatever it is, I can take it. And I won't retaliate. I promise." He reaches up and crosses over his heart with the hand still clutching the unopened letter.

I take a deep breath, squaring my shoulders. "It says thank you."

"Yeah, I figured that much, Fall. Thank you for what?"

I close my eyes, taking a breath and then start. "Thank you for wanting me. For making me feel wanted. And for always reinforcing that point." I swallow, tipping my head down and fixating on the center of his chest. "I'm sorry if I ever made that hard for you. I never really understood what you saw when you looked at me and I think I took some of that insecurity out on you sometimes because I always assumed we would end once you saw more of me." My palms start to sweat, and I rub them on the outside of my thighs. "Thank you for keeping me safe. Even in the really little ways. You didn't have to go out of your way to do that, but you always did and I'm sorry it took me this long to see it. And thank you for compromising with me. Our arrangement didn't call for that, but you did it anyways, checking in and accommodating me all the time." I start to talk faster, the words I already expelled onto paper fighting their way out as quickly as possible. "Thank you for helping me fill myself up with all this light. For a really long time I felt like I had a crack right through the center of my chest that my mom and the world kept prying open more and more. But being with you made me feel like it was filling up and I don't even think you realized when you were doing it half the time. And thank you for saying you love me. I'm not sure if you meant it or not, but no one has ever said that to me, let alone made me feel it." I pause, looking up at him as I add. "Thank you for loving me. I will cherish what that felt like forever."

As I speak, I can see Ramsey going stock still, his features freezing into place except for that one forehead vein that always pops out when he gets particularly pissed off.

"I ended the letter by just saying that I will forever be grateful for everything you did for me this semester, including saving me with that footage. Which you very clearly stole somehow. I didn't put that in the letter because I didn't want to incriminate you. But you definitely did commit a crime for me. So, thank you for that as well. Oh, and thank you for the—Ramsey?" I stop, noticing that his teeth are bared and he seems to be growling or groaning in the back of his throat.

He stands there, glaring down at me for another minute before reaching forward and snagging my jaw in his oh so familiar hold. My body melts underneath it at this point, eyes practically rolling back in my head as he brings me closer to speak right in my face.

"Don't you dare thank me for *any* of that. I didn't do any of those fucking things for your *gratitude*. All of that is the bare fucking minimum you deserve, do you understand me?" He's seething mad, the words coming out harsh, but floating into my skin and setting me on fire nonetheless.

I try to talk but his grip is too tight, words coming out mushed.

"No, you're done speaking right now."

This time my eyes actually do roll back in my head. Fuck, I really love this side of Ramsey.

He takes a deep breath, looking away for a second to collect himself. When he looks back, his voice is tired and soft. "Can we be done now?"

I quirk an eyebrow, getting lost in the turn in conversation.

"With this stupid fucking break *you* wanted to take. Can we be done with it?"

My organs all seem to pulsate inside me, feet feeling like their levitating as I lose all sensation. I reach up, tapping his hand so that he'll release me.

He considers it for a second and I narrow my eyes. His fingers loosen, cupping my face still, but allowing me to move.

"You want to continue our arrangement?" I ask in a confused tone.

"Fuck, no, Fall." He leans down farther to speak against my lips. "I don't want an *arrangement*. I want to be your boyfriend, your person, your fucking *everything*."

My breath catches in my throat.

"I love you, Fall. I want to fight with you, and fuck you, at the same time, at different times, whenever I can. I want to take you out on dates and bring you home to my mom and just walk around with you being *mine*. And I'm so tired of not talking, not seeing you, not touching you. I sleep terribly when you're not with me, you know?"

I bleat a laugh, somewhat hysterical and wondering if I've snapped and hallucinated this whole thing.

His eyes narrow. "Something funny, Fall?"

I nod emphatically. "Uh, yeah. I thought I was coming up here to leave you my thanks for setting my bar way too fucking high letter and here you are, grabbing me, and professing your love."

"Yeah, well, Harley told me to wait and slow down and that lead to me almost losing you, so I'm not fucking around this time." He shrugs one shoulder, a hopeful smile splitting his face. "Does that mean you're agreeing to the new terms?"

I laugh, whole heartedly this time. "Yes," I breathe, feeling a million pieces come together and land in just the right spot. "Yes, I agree to all of it. I'm in love with you, too, Ramsey."

He sighs, eyes closing slightly as he lets my words wash over him. "Thank fuck," he says before descending once more and capturing my mouth.

I thought I cracked myself wide open again when I tried to tear us apart. But I think I just pulled everything he gave me out and pretended it was never there.

He just keeps throwing it at me though. I don't think he ever stopped, not even aware how much his steadfast love has slowly filled up the part of me that I thought would always be a gaping abyss right in the middle of who I am.

Ramsey pulls back after a minute. "Mira told me you're like filthy stinking rich rich now? What's that about?"

I laugh, wrapping my arms around his torso and leaning into him. "It's a somewhat long story."

Ramsey smiles. "Well, start from the beginning. We have plenty of time now, Fall."

He sits down, pulling me to sit on his lap and settling me into him. I bring my hands up, wrapping them around his neck and starting to explain Mimi and everything that happened three weeks ago. As I talk, I realize this is my happy place, the place where I'm most comfortable, right here in his arms with all his focus pointed directly at me.

I would have scoffed at the idea less than a year ago. *Me* in love with *Ramsey Adams?* Yeah, right.

But here we are. And I don't think either of us could have expected it.

EPILOGUE I

RAMSEY

Six weeks later

Fall has been naked all day, and everything is right in my world.

It started with me waking up to her sucking my cock, something I discovered she had never done before a couple weeks ago and something we've had quite a fun time exploring together. Especially when the first time, she merely sucked for longer than three seconds and I immediately blew, without much warning. I instantly checked on her, worried that the whole ordeal would put her off blowjobs entirely, but she just laughed, my cum running down her chin and distracting me a bit.

When she finally calmed down enough to speak, she giggled and batted her eyelashes at me mockingly. "Was I *that* good?"

"Shut up," I retorted, kissing her and groaning when I tasted myself in her mouth.

Since then, we've tried it a few more times, but this morning she decided to wake me up that way, something we had discussed a few times before. Somnophilia is definitely something I'd always wanted to try with Fall, but I refused to do it without talking it through, making sure she understood what it meant and had thought the idea through before consenting. Even then, I only started with some light licking until she was fully awake and I could dive in.

But after this morning, I'm thinking I might kick it up a notch. Maybe put one of her new toys inside her before she is fully lucid. We've been playing with some vibrators and plugs too, having the whole summer to ourselves to just lay around and fuck.

Or we would, if Fall didn't insist on getting dressed at some point every day and going out to do mundane things like eat and socialize.

She's been talking with her sister a lot lately, the two of them catching up on nearly two decades worth of missed sisterhood. It means I get kicked out of their conversations a lot, sent to go get something or even told to "go play with your friends" once. I'm allowing it for the summer because it's the first time the two of them have been able to do this. But once we get back to school, I'm putting my foot down and demanding more of Fall's time. I'm already going to have to contend with her classes and this new endeavor to get a job that she has.

I'm supportive I swear.

I just don't like anything that takes her away from me more.

And sure, I'm taking a gap year, under Diane's advisement. She made me realize I need to slow down and *take some time* to refocus and process some stuff before I set into another rigorous courseload. But I'll be busy working at the gym and helping Harley set up a new physical therapy partnership with the hospital. And then there's med school apps and interviews and decisions.

Ones that I don't think I want to make alone anymore.

The Coast doesn't have a med school, offering the pre-med track in undergrad but that's as far as it goes. Which means next year, we'll be at different schools. And I'm not sure how well I'm going to cope with that.

"Have you thought about where you want to go to med school?" I ask, running my lips up the center of Fall's chest.

She giggles, the sound heaven in my ears. "I'm starting my sophomore year, Ramsey. I haven't even thought much about the MCATs yet."

I nod, nuzzling in against her throat. "I could defer another year or two."

She pulls back, staring up at me. "No, you cannot. Ramsey, med school is four years and then there's at least four or five years of residency. You can't put that off longer just because you want to hang around and fuck me any chance you can."

I shrug, snuggling back in against her. "It sounds like a good enough reason to me."

She rolls her eyes. "Be so fucking for real, Ramsey." She runs a hand through my curls, tangling her fingers with them and petting in a way that I'm sure would make me purr if I were a cat. "You're going to go to whatever med school *you* want to go to, and we're going to visit each other on weekends and breaks and summers and facetime and text 24/7, and you'll be so busy you won't even notice the time we're not together."

I scoff. "Impossible," I mumble against her skin. I rub my hard cock against her thigh, moaning a little with the friction. "I want to decide on a med school together," I say more clearly.

Her hand stops moving in my hair and I sit up to look down at her when I say this. "If I have to go for the first two years on my own, then fine, but I want to discuss it and plan for you to eventually join me."

She studies me. "I might not get into the same one you do."

I roll my eyes. "Sure, you won't, miss 4.0 GPA I-wanna-get-an-internship-sophomore-year. You be so fucking for real."

She pouts. "I didn't get that internship, remember?"

"No, but you got one with the bone and joint center for next summer already. Trust me, you'll have the pick of med schools. So, I want to plan this out together."

"We've barely been dating a month," she hedges, a tiny smirk appearing at the corner of her mouth.

I reach down, smacking her ass somewhat tamely considering I have to push her up and swat before she falls back down. "We've been together for at least four months. And I don't give a shit about time, Fall. We've been at each other's throats for nearly four years in one way or another."

She smiles, cheeks pink and eyes bright. "Okay," she whispers.

"Yeah?" I double check. Always a good practice with her.

"Yeah, bar any freak accidents or mental spirals where one of us attempts to implode everything, I will plan my future with you, Ramsey Adams."

I lean down, swiping my tongue into her open mouth and holding her tight against me as we kiss.

"One more thing," I say pulling away again.

She groans, rubbing herself against me and I take a second to fall into that before leaning down and biting her lip in admonishment.

"What?" she says impatiently.

"Move in with me?"

She's quiet, looking up at me without changing her expression.

"And Harley, and Royal, and Tanner, and Smith, and a bunch of Russian dudes?" I add to try and sweeten the deal.

At this, she quirks an eyebrow. "You want me to move into the Ravens' mansion?"

"You were practically living there half of last semes—Ravens' mansion? Is that what you guys call it?"

"I voted for 'Murder Mansion,' but Bentley pointed out that it's a murder of crows not ravens."

I shake my head, glancing out the window over her bed and into the sunny afternoon happening in her grandmother's backyard. "The guys are going to love that one."

She puts her hands on my cheeks, lightly pulling me down to look at her. "I can't move in with you next year, Ramsey." She delivers the blow with a soft tone, leaning up and quickly kissing me to take away some of the sting. "I can't leave Aria all on her own. She's family now, Ramsey."

I sigh. She told me all about what the little goth one said to her to convince her that I was in fact falling in love with her when I was. It makes it harder to hate her for needing Fall when I do too.

"We can have plenty of sleepovers though," Fall adds, wiggling against me again and smiling coyly.

I shake my head, a smile unable to leave my face. "I guess that will have to suffice. But I want you to use some of that trust fund money to upgrade to a suite. With your own bedroom and more specifically your own door." I lean down and nip her collarbone. "That way I can sleepover on the nights you want to stay there."

She giggles, squirming against me again and slowly

shutting down all ancillary thoughts. "Okay, but if I keep spending trust fund money like this, you're going to end up supporting us eventually," she mocks.

I roll my eyes. "Yeah, sure." Then I kiss up the side of her neck, sucking her ear lobe into my mouth at the end of my trail. "I will gladly support you...and whoever else happens to come along..." I bite down a little harder and she squeaks, slapping my chest.

"Don't even joke about that!"

EPILOGUE II

AUTUMN

Two and a half years later

My stomach is once again leaking out my ass because of Ramsey Adams.

Okay, and I guess this time it's pretty much fifty-fifty my fault too, but if even one of these strips turn pink I'm definitely going to blame him at first.

"Breathe, sweetness. Either way, we'll be okay." Ramsey runs his hands up and down my bare arms, either trying to generate warmth or just fidget while we wait. I bite my thumbnail, staring at the row of pregnancy tests currently littering the sink in the green bathroom at the Coast house.

It's Christmas break and we decided to spend the two weeks Ramsey has off alone in this house where everything started. Except every morning like clockwork, I have woken up nauseous, and Ramsey commented that my tits were falling out of my bathing suit when we decided to go for a dip yesterday, and I just felt like something was off. Ramsey drives to the Coast almost every weekend he can and I go down to the city to see him when he can't leave for that long and we still fuck like rabbits. I didn't want to stick with the pill after hearing some of the side effects Sage had from being on since she was twelve to help time her periods for ballet. And my doctors suggested the shot, but I forgot to get it re-upped one too many times for it to be a solution for us.

So, condoms have been our main safety net and it's probably the one thing anyone could call Ramsey a boy scout about having on him. Always prepared this one.

But accidents happen. And they're not a 100% guarantee.

"Hey, Fall," Ramsey calls, turning me around in his arms and wrapping them around my waist to keep me tethered against him. "We're okay. Either way, you hear me?" He waits, staring down at me and giving my ass a light squeeze. "If you are, then we figure it out. And if you're not, then *we figure it out*. Together. Like everything else, got it?"

I nod, letting him take the reins on this one.

The image of a little curly haired boy with Ramsey's eyes and my freckles pops into my head. It feels like my ovaries shudder at the idea, and I take a deep breath.

I'm about to enter my second semester of my senior year in undergrad. My med school apps have been sent and while this next semester might be considered the easiest of all of them, a baby would definitely rock the fucking boat.

And Ramsey is wrapping up his sophomore year in med school. No way we'd be able to juggle everything with him entering residency and a fucking toddler while I'm just hitting my stride at med school.

Oh my god. What if I don't get into DWSU and Ramsey and I are at different schools next year? Would we have to come up with some convoluted custody schedule, passing the baby back and forth on weekends and getting absolutely no time to ourselves?

"Fall, I can see your brain spiraling." Ramsey grabs my

jaw, the gesture grounding me like it always has. "Talk to me."

"Ramsey," I utter, voice breaking and tears welling in my eyes. "What if I'm pregnant?"

He reaches up, swiping at the tears as they fall. Then he leans down and kisses the tip of my nose. "Will you hit me if I say, I'll be excited?" He looks at my shocked face and chuckles. "I mean, I completely get that a baby right now would not be ideal and it's going to change a lot of our plans." He considers it for a second. "Okay like all of them. But a little mini human that's a mix of the two of us? They're going to be so fucking amazing."

I giggle through my tears, some snot joining the mix as I try to sniffle it back.

"If you are, then we discuss it. It would be fully up to you what our next move is, sweetness. I would never ask you to change things that much if you don't want to." He shrugs. "If now doesn't feel like the time for you, we wait."

I realize what he's saying and let the pendulum of that decision swing back and forth, waiting for it to settle one way or the other. "Thank you," I tell him. "For letting me take the lead on that choice."

"Always. If you are pregnant, I've done everything I can do for the next however many months. The decision of if you physically want to go through all that will always be your choice. Now and every time, for the record."

I nod, sighing. We should have set a timer. The instructions just said wait three to ten minutes, which was such a large gap of time, I kind of started panicking about what to even set the timer for and that lead to Ramsey having to calm me down over a fucking timer which lead me to spiral about how the fuck I could possibly be a mother when I can't decide what to set a timer for and—

Deep breath.

"Should we check?" I place my hands on the outside of his covering both sides of my face.

"One second," Ramsey says, holding me in place. "I also want to say, that if you are, and we do have to figure it all out, I'll quit medical school."

My eyes bug out of my head. "What? No! Absolutely not, Ramsey! You are not quitting med school. You've worked so hard to get this far."

"And so have you. A baby is going to affect one if not both of our careers in the long run. You want to help people, Fall. I don't have that same drive for it."

I raise an eyebrow, and he shakes his head.

"I mean, I do want to help people, but it's not a need for me the way it is for you. I would be just as satisfied being a stay-at-home dad and learning to cook and doing our laundry and taking care of you. And anyone else who comes along. Got it?"

I swallow, knowing he means it but feeling like I'm taking something from him if we make that compromise. "We'll figure it out. Right? If I am pregnant, then we'll figure it out. Together." I point a finger in his face. "No rash decisions. We'll have more to figure out than just that so hold on a second, let's confirm one way or the other before we start making grand declarations, okay?"

"Okay, Fall." He leans down, kissing me and making my toes curl. "I love you. No matter what."

"I love you, too. No matter what."

He releases my face and I turn around, his hands landing on my hips. We walk forward together, coming up to the sink and looking down at the strips.

All of them have a deep red control line. And right next to every single one is another, slightly less vibrant pink line.

"That means pregnant, right?" Ramsey asks, picking one of them up and looking closer.

I swallow, the news settling as it slides down my throat and into my apparently not so vacant stomach. "Yes. Ramsey, I'm pregnant."

Ramsey drops the strip and grabs me by the waist, picking me up and spinning me around the room with a loud whoop. Putting me back down in front of him, he tries to contain the effervescent joy bubbling out of him. "How do we feel about this?"

"Well, I think one of us is very excited," I say, laughing.

He squints down at me. "Just one of us?"

I take a deep breath, feeling my nerves prickle but not spike as I let the idea settle a little more over me. "I'm not panicking as much as I thought I would be." I place a hand on my stomach, wondering how long I've been carrying a little hidden passenger without knowing. "Ramsey," I say with a small smile. "I'm pregnant."

"Fuck yeah, you are, sweetness." He beams, stepping up so his toes are touching mine and grabbing my hips. I've never understood his obsession with squeezing me, but I've also never complained about it either.

"We're going to have a baby," I whisper.

I think Ramsey nearly jumps out his own skin with how excited he is. And looking up at him, smiling at each other like idiots, I can see it. This is something he would find total contentment in. He'd be just as patient with our kids as he is with me, if not tenfold more. And he's learned so much about communicating and helped me work through my emotions alongside him figuring out his own. He's going to be an amazing dad. I think I could be a mom if he's there next to me the whole time.

As I'm standing there, marveling at him, he suddenly freezes. "Wait here," he says all the sudden, letting go of me and rushing out of the bathroom.

I stand there, feet sunk into the plush forest green bathmat and wait as my boyfriend leaves me alone in the bathroom with a bunch of positive pregnancy tests.

He comes rushing back in a minute later, something in his hands hidden behind his back.

"I planned to do this much more romantically on a weekend getaway with snow all around us and everything, but I can't wait another second now that we know about the baby."

I lock up, watching him sink down to one knee and pull a ring box forward and present it to me.

Tears blur my vision again and I quickly swipe them away. Well at least I can blame them on the baby hormones now.

"Autumn Dahlia Green, love of my life and now mother of my child, more pending." I scoff and Ramsey winks at me. "We can't have just one, Fall. They'd be a menace. Imagine me without Mira to level me out growing up."

"Mira leveled you out growing up?"

"Oh, definitely—hey you're distracting me." He shuffles his shoulders, getting back into position. "Fall, sweetness, my little witch, I want to spend fucking forever with you. And at this point, I'm really hoping you want to spend forever with me too. Will you promise to fight with me and fuck me every day for the rest of our lives? Will you marry me?" He opens the ring box, presenting a gorgeous gem that looks like green smoke captured in a crystal-clear polished stone. It's surrounded by sparkling diamonds and the most beautiful fucking ring I've ever seen.

I start blubbering and almost miss the last word of his proposal.

"Please?" he says in the most heartbreakingly soft way.

I'm nodding, and crying, and I just barely push the word, "Yes," past my clogged throat, emotions fully choking me at this point.

Ramsey launches up, capturing my face and kissing me long and hard. I try to kiss him back, but I'm crying and also trying to wipe my own tears off his face, and we just end up laughing in each other's faces.

He grabs my left hand, taking the ring out and sliding it onto my third finger while I watch with more choked sobs.

"We're going to be a family," Ramsey whispers, pulling me into his arms and kissing the top of my head as I hold on to him.

I don't know how long we stay in the bathroom, me trying to stop crying and Ramsey being ever so fucking patient with me, but when we finally make it out and into another room, I realize we not only have a lot of life decisions to make, but now a whole ass wedding to plan.

"Don't panic, we'll figure it all out," Ramsey assures.

I laugh, looking over at him happily. "I'm actually not panicked at all. I know exactly who will be perfect to help execute the perfect little quickie spring wedding."

Ramsey raises an eyebrow, still rubbing a hand over my back cautiously.

I smile up at him. "How do you feel about Vegas for spring break?"

THE END
(FOR NOW)

Next up is the following standalone story in the Imperium Coast series, YELLOW CARD.

THANK YOU FOR READING

Thank you so much for reading GREEN LIGHT! This easily became one of my favorite stories to write and I really hope you enjoyed Autumn and Ramsey's story!

If you liked it, please leave a review! Even just star ranking really helps out indie authors like me. Your support means everything to me!

WANT MORE IMPERIUM COAST?

Check out Bentley, Janette, and Axel's story TRUE BLUE to see how one group project leads to a whole lot more.

Want to see how Mira and Harley began? Check out the first half of their story SEEING RED!

WHAT'S NEXT?

Next up is Tanner's book YELLOW CARD! What happens when the star hockey goalie needs help finding someone and the one person who can help is the only girl he hates to see coming? Find out in this grumpy x sunshine romance coming June 2026!

ACKNOWLEDGMENTS

There are so many people involved in my writing/publishing process and every time I sit down to write these I always worry that I'm going to leave someone off. So let's see if I can get this right.

Firstly, Kristin, thank you for getting me to actually sit down and write this one. And for hyping the shit out of it. Honestly that's the main reason this book exists.

Grace, thank you for letting me come in and bother you everyday when I get stir crazy in my room. And thanks for making sure I eat something every now and then.

Cat, Mitch, Alex, Peter, Dan, and Zach, thank you for all of your support and the best friendships. I may cringe every time you tell someone about my books in front of me, but I'm also so so so grateful for it. Every time.

Bianca, thank you for all of your feedback on this one. Your comments on the first chapter helped me reshape the rest of the story months later and it made everything so much stronger.

Therapist Rachel, (sorry for the title, but this is how I differentiate in conversation), thank you so much for helping me get to a point where I could actually do this whole publishing thing. Four years ago, I would have never thought I could do some of the things I've done (solo travel???? me????) but now I have 3 books published and a life I really love. Thank you for helping me get to this place.

And lastly thank you to YOU, the reader, for spending time in this weird little world I created in my head. It's one of my favorite places to be and I'm really glad you came along this time. I hope you stick around because I have so much more I want to do at the Coast!

ABOUT THE AUTHOR

Alacia (pronounced uh-lace-ee-uh) Hale is a contemporary romance writer with a penchant for messy and angst-ridden chaos characters. She loves writing stories filled with devotion, banter, and spice, a mixture that often leads down some intense and twisty paths. When she is not writing, you can find her drawing, travelling, or trying to keep another doomed plant alive. She currently lives in Upstate NY with her best friend, grumpy black cat, crazy orange kitten, and a head full of fictional people.

Want to keep up with everything Lacy and her future releases? Sign up for her newsletter to get regular updates.

ALSO BY ALACIA HALE

<u>The Imperium Coast Series</u>

True Blue: A Why Choose University Romance

Seeing Red: A First Chance University Romance

Green Light: An Academic Bully Romance

Yellow Card: A College Hockey Romance

White Knuckled

Grey Area

Red Duet Part II